A COLD PARADISE

GEORGE ZELL HEUSTON

ISBN:978-1-990830-77-8

Prominence Publishing UPDATED 12/18/2024

To all my FBI colleagues who fought
in the heat of the Cold War

CONTENTS

1

Mid-July 1968: Paradise, Mount Rainier, Near the Nisqually Glacier

The shot came soundlessly out of the consuming whiteness of fog and wind and grazed his neck. Bradford Lehman spun, and in one motion slipped out of the shoulder strap of his Kelty frame pack, drew the Walther pistol from his waistband, and sprawled askew on the snow. The pack lay against his body partially screening him from the direction of the shot. He lay on his left side, both arms extended. But in his right hand was the Walther, and he was looking over its sights. Bradford felt the adrenalin well up. It was not born of fear, but of anticipation. He did not fear. He focused. The fog was blowing through in patches driven by a hard southwest wind. Whoever shot him had caught but a brief sight of him and pulled the trigger. The wind must have drifted the bullet just a touch. Still, Bradford thought ruefully, it was a hard touch. His neck bled into the snow. At least the cold killed the pain. Staring into the fog he saw the faintest flicker of darkness low against the snow. He shifted his sights toward the spot. A bulky figure shrouded all in white, except for a dark pair of gaiters, was edging toward him. It was fifteen yards away and closing with slow predatory precision. Evidently the figure was banking on the assumption that his shot had been fatal, for Bradford hadn't moved so much as a muscle in what seemed like an eternity.

Slowly Bradford eased the front sight of his pistol onto the figure's center of mass. Then a reminder, a still small voice, spun through his head: *The caliber of this gun is too small to penetrate thick clothing.* He let the pistol ease back down the body toward the dark gaiters covering the figure's white climbing boots. *Yes, a good viewable and vulnerable target. But damn it's small.* Bradford chose the lower left leg. The leg shuffled and stopped as it moved forward. He lined up the pistol's front sight and let his breath out slowly. The leg stopped. Lehman squeezed the trigger. He felt the gun's smooth recoil. The figure dropped straight down with a scream and balled up, clutching the leg. Then a hand holding a large black pistol extended itself toward him. Bradford smoothly shifted his sights to the mask of skin and eyes under the figure's white balaclava, and again squeezed the trigger. The figure uncoiled, lurching in writhing spasms. Blood blossomed the snow behind the head. *No rush now, Bradford.*

Lehman half-rolled away from his Kelty, reached into the pocket of his shirt, pulled out a fresh magazine, and replaced the partially empty one in his Walther PPK. The figure now lay silent, contorted. Bradford got up into a kneeling position. He felt a trickle of blood running down his neck onto his shoulder. A metallic taste of iron reached his tongue. It came from freshly spilled blood steaming in the air – either his own, or the corpse's – or both. Suddenly Bradford felt nauseous. He braced his hands on his thighs and breathed deeply to keep from retching.

Get your wound covered. Now. Lehman reached into the cargo pocket of his wool climbing knickers, pulled out a red cotton scarf, and scooped a handful of snow into its folds. Then he rolled up the scarf and tied it snugly around his neck. Lehman's nausea abated. It was supplanted with a sharp, searing pain from the wound. The cold from the snow tucked into the scarf helped deaden the throbbing into a tolerable burning ache. *Red scarf over blood --the colors will match.* He forced a half smile.

Satisfied that he had staunched his bleeding, Lehman stood, and walked the few steps over to the object in the snow that had so recently tried to kill him. He gazed down. "All white except green gaiters," Lehman muttered, shaking his head. "Dumb bastard." The hearing of his own words startled him. Was he turning to stone inside, like the FBI and Agency men who had trained him? "No, Lehman," he said aloud, "you were always stone inside. Those boys just polished it up for you."

Tough talk, Bradford, but you're not John Wayne. This shit is real. Stop the tough talk. You're not stone. Lehman's mind ran wildly in all directions at once. *There is love, compassion, and respect in you too. What an odd combination, Lehman -- you're weird.* He took a deep breath, and put his head down. His hands began shaking. *Move!* He knew this was his only solace.

Lehman laid the body out spread-eagled in the snow and bared its head. He pulled out his camera and methodically shot top-to-bottom pictures of the corpse, turned all pockets inside out, and repeated the process. Slowly his hands steadied. He bagged the contents and stuffed them into his Kelty pack. They included six full pistol magazines taken from the breast pockets of the corpse's white parka. *This son-of-a-bitch came loaded for a fight, Bradford.*

Lehman looked to pry the pistol from the dead man's right hand. But the trigger finger of the corpse's stiffened hand was still inside the trigger guard. Prying it out would be dangerous. He knelt down, clasped the dead man's hand in his, and pushed. There was a muffled "pop" as the gun went off, taking a divot out of the snow. He repeated the process six more times until the slide on the dead man's pistol locked back, empty. Then Bradford carefully pried it out of the hand. It was heavy and had a silencer attached. An inscription on the frame read: "MDL. TTC CAL. 7.62X25, C.A.I. GEORGIA, VT, CUGIR, ROMANIA, 1952."

Bradford removed the magazine and slipped the pistol into his Kelty. The assailant had carried no pack – not even a water bottle. Lehman checked his watch. It was 0600. Time was becoming a factor. Hikers and climbers would soon be along, and though Lehman was not on the regular climbing path toward Camp Muir on Mount Rainier, he knew that people wandered everywhere on the mountain in late July.

Bradford pulled out a length of one-inch nylon web sling normally used to tie clients into climbing ropes. He cinched the corpse's feet together with one end, grabbed the other end, and started dragging the body. It slid limply, easily. The nearest convenient crevasse was a hundred yards to the left on the Nisqually Glacier. There he dumped it. The sound of the corpse's falling began with a hollow *thump,* as it bounced off of a snow ledge fifteen feet down, then quickly became muffled, distant.

Bradford retraced his steps, and carefully kicked snow over the slide tracks and the thin globular line of blood that pointed like a jagged red arrow toward the crevasse. He carefully covered over all the blood at the scene of the shooting, including his own. He picked up all of the expended brass cartridges from the Russian's Tokarev and the two from his own Walther PPK.

It began to snow again and the wind picked up. In minutes all trace of Lehman's deadly fight with his attempted killer would be erased. The majesty of the mountain and its high white world would be regained. All would be mute -- forgotten. On the big mountain, all traces of mortality were evanescent.

Lehman shouldered his Kelty and trudged slowly back to his quarters at Paradise. His wound had stopped bleeding, but he needed to get a look at it and clean up. Suddenly he felt tired. Very tired.

2

SUMMER, 1966: TWO YEARS EARLIER

A mere two years -- in the days of The Cold War, free love, Rock and Roll, and the Vietnam War -- were enough to propel a healthy young man into grave danger. Two years was all it took for a draftee in the war to graduate high school, be called up, serve out his commitment in the steaming jungles of Southeast Asia, and to come home again, wounded, scarred, or in a box.

Meanwhile the world turned. Lives went on at home, and as often as not, the fortunate returning young veteran would be greeted more out of hatred and yawning curiosity than respect. He met hatred when he got off the airplane, walked the gauntlet of anti-war protesters, and was spat on and called a "Baby Killer." He met complacency when he arrived back home: "Where have you been?" townspeople would say. Some veterans found it easier to accept the hatred. Bradford Lehman's time to be a veteran was inexorably approaching.

*   *   *

Bradford Washburn Lehman was born in the small logging town of Shelton, Washington, on the Olympic Peninsula, at the beginning of the Cold War. His father, Benjamin Franklin Lehman, practiced law there. He had two life passions, the mountains and the law, in that order. Bradford thus grew up following his father into the mountains of the Olympics and Cascades.

Bradford's ethnic roots were German and Bulgarian. He stood five feet ten inches tall, and weighed one hundred and fifty pounds. Though not strikingly handsome, he was good looking in a wholesome way. His cropped brown hair, quickly bleaching blond in the high summer sunlight of the mountains, formed to a small widow's peak above a high forehead. Tanning easily, his skin bronzed deeply, thus adding to a perception that he spent his time outdoors. His clear grey-blue eyes, normally mischievous and warm, flashed instantly into steely resolution when they perceived a threat. His nose was straight and well proportioned. But it was Bradford's mouth, with its even white teeth and broad smile, set above a firm lower jaw, which mirrored his personality. It was home to a teasing wit that occasionally got him into trouble with his teachers. He expected them to teach. When they didn't, he discerned no reason to learn from them. Thus a middling achiever in school, Bradford followed graduation from high school in the mid-1960s by enrolling at the University of Puget Sound in Tacoma. There he majored in History. But in that summer of 1966, between high school graduation and the commencement of his studies at the University, Lehman began working and walking in his father's footsteps as a guide for the Rainier Guide Service. The RGS was headquartered at Paradise on the south, or Nisqually Entrance, to Rainier National Park. At seventeen, Lehman was already a well-seasoned mountaineer -- broad-shouldered and "lean and mean," as his father proudly observed.

Lehman's self-perception was that of a man of clinical pragmatism. Indeed, he was a man, and had long been one. He never cried at a death or funeral, even those of his grandparents. He loved them, and they him – at times tenderly. But he understood, as he always had, that life ends. They had good lives. By his lights their deaths could not be lamented, except in a selfish sense. He was not a fatalist -- just unselfish.

The imprint upon Bradford Lehman's social identity sprang from early perspectives on life and death. He climbed Mount Rainier for the first time when he was eleven. On that climb a party member was struck and injured by rock-fall that narrowly missed Bradford. When he was twelve years old Bradford was nearly killed in an avalanche. When he was fourteen he witnessed the near-death of his sister in a fall into a crevasse. When he was sixteen he was knocked unconscious by falling ice on a glacier, and suffered a cracked vertebra in his neck. Bradford Lehman intimately knew the danger of mountaineering. Yet he loved it. He considered being in the mountains a privilege and comfort.

* * *

In the summer of 1966, RGS guide Bradford Lehman accompanied a special client to the mountain's summit -- Robert McNamara. Robert S. McNamara was the United States Secretary of Defense. He was the scion of the war against communism and the brains behind U.S. Strategy in the Vietnam War. He was also an avid outdoorsman, and climbing Mount Rainier was on his checklist. Jim and Lou Whittaker led him on the climb up the "Dog Route," as the guides referred to it. From the South side of Mount Rainier, starting at Paradise, the route proceeded up a broad ascending ridge to Camp Muir at ten thousand feet. This was high camp. Lehman had no particular interaction with McNamara on the hike to Muir, other than to observe him. All guides observed. It went with the trade. It was immediately evident that

McNamara was tough. Lean and wiry, he had the cut of an athlete, though he limped slightly from an ankle injury he had sustained playing tennis a few weeks before. It did not slow him.

The guided party left Camp Muir for the summit at one thirty in the morning the next day. This was standard protocol, since the object was to climb the remaining four thousand five hundred vertical feet to the top, and to return to Muir, before the heat melted and weakened the snow bridges on the path. The route spanned two big glaciers: the Cowlitz, and the Ingraham. Being a junior guide, Bradford was not on McNamara's rope. But as it turned out, he led the rope team following McNamara. Jim Whittaker was leading Robert's rope team and Robert was on the tail end of it in the client's rightful place. Lehman thus climbed a step or two behind McNamara. To Bradford's surprise, the Defense Secretary, on this starlit night with a half-moon silvering the snow, was ebullient.

Lehman had only one client on his rope. His name was Rubayat Castellano, a barrel-chested man, whom he assumed was a member of McNamara's security detail. Others around him, including McNamara, called him "Rube." Jovial, with a graveyard sense of humor, Rube was beginning to complain of a headache.

"Rube, you're doing splendidly," Lehman shouted back. "At the next rest stop we will get you some aspirin and a salt pill. It'll knock that headache you've got. Take deep breaths at the top of each step. You are also fighting the altitude a little."

"Jeez, I thought this would be easier," Rube quipped. "The air is so rare back in Washington D.C. that I assumed I'd be acclimatized," he said with a forced toothy grin.

"Ha!" McNamara exclaimed, on overhearing the conversation. Then he turned to Lehman. "How old are you son?"

"Seventeen, Mister Secretary."

"You look a lot younger than you act."

"You don't, Mister Secretary," Lehman said, in a flat bold tone.

McNamara threw his head back and laughed. Rube coughed to stifle his own. "Call me Bob."

"It doesn't seem right," Bradford responded. "But if you direct me to call you Bob I will. But I won't when we're back down in the parking lot with all the press and dignitaries hanging around. I'll call you Robert." McNamara laughed again, followed by another choked laugh by Rube on the other end of Lehman's rope.

From that moment forward an invisible wall came down -- the obligatory social barrier that greatness, in any society, imposes between high leaders and low followers. Yet the mountain they climbed tended to have such an effect. It broke down barriers in many ways: the body, the will, and petty pretenses. And it built up others: fear, resolve, respect, and the brotherhood evoked in the sharing of it all. They slogged on.

By the time the party reached the top of Disappointment Cleaver and witnessed the crimson dawn of a clear summer's day, young guide Bradford Lehman had undergone a relentless barrage of questions from the Defense Secretary.

"Where are you from?" McNamara asked.

"Shelton, over on the Olympic Peninsula."

"What does your father do?"

"He is a lawyer; a good one. But back in the 1920s and 30s he guided up here. His parents kicked him out of the family home in Tacoma during the Great Depression when he was sixteen. They couldn't feed him anymore. So he spent nine summers and two winters up at Paradise."

McNamara fell silent. There were only the chunking sounds of ice axes and crampons on glacial ice. "So you are a legatee in this business?"

"Yes. I've been hiking and climbing around this hill all my life."

"Quite a hill here. It's kicking my butt," McNamara said.

"You're doing exceptionally well — for a Democrat. Democrats usually want to be carried up."

"Ha!" the Secretary let out another wheezing laugh, reached back, and slapped Lehman's shoulder. The party had progressed past thirteen thousand feet, and was cresting the final bergschrund. Bradford looked back to check on Rube, who had gone quiet.

"How are you doing Rube?" Lehman asked.

"Okay," came a breathless reply.

"You're doing fine. Just three or four more rope lengths and you'll be at the crater rim. You can see the dark rocks of the rim already." Bradford pointed upward with his ice axe.

"So, Lehman," the Secretary asked, "Have you pondered what you're going to do about the military?"

"You have your draft going. So, in a few short years I'll be following you on your rope!"

McNamara chuckled.

"But actually, I am enrolling in Air Force ROTC at the University of Puget Sound and will be commissioned as one of your myriad minions upon graduation."

"Are you against the war?" McNamara asked.

"Not at all. My father hates the communists, and so do I, from the history I've read. I would rather fight them in Vietnam than here."

"What have you read?" A tone of interest peaked in the Secretary's question.

"I love history. I particularly enjoyed Churchill's series on *The Second World War*, and his *History of the English-Speaking Peoples*."

"Yes. That covers many of the issues," the Secretary mused.

"Come on up Bob, we're at the crater rim!" Jim Whittaker's voice carried back from the summit rocks. He coiled the rope in while McNamara huffed up to him. Lehman turned and coiled in Castellano, and the two walked side-by-side the last rope length.

"He likes you," Rube observed. "I don't know whether it's your tender age or what, but the Secretary would never put up with being spoken to that way."

"Maybe it is because Bob is relaxed and focused on the climb," Bradford said. "There are few places a big wig in his shoes can doff his official face and relax. Rainier is one of those places."

"Damn, I guess it is, because I have never seen him this way. He is as tough a fellow as I have ever worked under, and that includes my boss J. Edgar Hoover.

"Well, get Hoover up here and loosen him up."

"He could never relinquish control, especially to a kid like you. God, what a sight that would be!" Rube guffawed. "Besides, this isn't the Director's venue. He's a city boy and does not like to get his hands dirty – *his*, that is."

The Whittakers, the Secretary, Lehman, and other party members un-roped in Mount Rainier's crater and walked the quarter mile over the flat snow to the summit register. It was 0830. The trek up had taken six hours and forty-five minutes – a respectable RGS climbing time from Camp Muir to the summit. The Secretary signed in, had photos taken with the Whittakers on the true summit, and sat down to eat a sandwich. The day was clear and the temperature above fourteen thousand feet was a windless thirty-eight degrees.

"Bob, we have plenty of time," Jim Whittaker said. "You look to have lots of energy left for the trip down. What say we get up and take a stroll around the crater rim? Few climbers actually do this, but it gives you a complete three hundred and sixty-degree view of all the landmarks around the Northwest."

"Sure, Jim!" McNamara stood up excitedly. He grabbed his ice axe and started to follow Jim and Lou. Then he turned. "Lehman, come with us. Rube, it's okay, you stay here and finish your lunch." Rubayat Castellano looked relieved and nestled back down, his back against a big rock, and took another bite of his baloney sandwich.

The small group started at Columbia Crest, the true summit of Rainier, at 14,411 feet, and walked the crater rim counter-clockwise, skirting big rocks, and clanking along in cramponed boots over the pumice.

"That is Liberty Cap over there," Jim said, pointing to a large peak to the west. "It is one of the three main summit peaks of this mountain. Before Rainier blew up last time, about five thousand six hundred years ago, you can see where the angles of the outer lines of Liberty Cap's ridges, along with those of the Ingraham Glacier we climbed today, would converge about three thousand feet above us. That was the pre-eruption summit of the mountain."

"So Rainier is still active?" McNamara asked.

"Yes. See the geothermal steam rising up out of the pumice here in patches as we walk along? The yellowish spots seem to be the hottest."

"The yellow is sulfur," McNamara interposed.

"Yes," Jim nodded. "And looking around the crater rim you can see steam coming out of caves formed by the snow. There is an extensive cave system under the snow filling the crater here."

"Have you explored them? What are they like?" McNamara asked.

"Briefly in 1954, Lou and I checked them out. They run all around the rim and continue down several hundred feet into the crater's center. There's a large chamber there, maybe thirty feet high and more than a hundred feet long, and a pool of water."

"Fascinating, don't you think Lehman?" McNamara gave Bradford a fatherly nudge.

"Yes it is," Lehman responded. "It would be fun someday to have the time to explore them more."

"Early mountaineers would summit the mountain and stay overnight in the caves to keep warm," Jim continued. "Also, climbers trapped up here by storms have comfortably survived in them until the weather broke, and they could safely descend the mountain."

The conversation shifted to surrounding views. Morning sun had burned off most of the haze, and as the group walked McNamara exercised his famous memory. He named off all the surrounding peaks and their elevations that Jim had pointed out to him at Camp Muir, and on the climb to the summit: "Mount Rainier's third summit, Point Success at fourteen thousand one hundred and fifty-eight feet; Mount Saint Helens, nine thousand fifty-six feet; Mount Hood, way down there in Oregon, eleven thousand two hundred and fifteen feet; Mount Adams at twelve thousand two hundred and eighty feet; Glacier Peak, ten thousand five hundred and forty-eight feet; and finally up north, Mount Baker at ten thousand seven hundred and eighty-one feet."

"Outstanding, Bob!" Jim said. "You are now a full-fledged Cascade climber. Most North Westerners don't know the elevations of these mountains."

"Details are my passion -- and my business," McNamara said.

An hour completed the walk of the crater rim, and Robert, far from being tired, seemed the more energized.

"Okay folks, time to saddle up and get off this hill," Lou Whittaker announced.

The party re-crossed the crater and roped up. Castellano and Lehman's rope was tucked in between Lou and Jim's teams, which meant that on the descent McNamara was again next to Lehman, but this time immediately behind him. Jim anchored the Secretary's rope. Heat was building on the glacier. Snow softened and built up under crampons. Several times Lehman heard a quiet grunt as McNamara rolled his injured ankle, but the Secretary never slowed his pace, and continued his conversation.

"So, young Lehman, what is your goal in life?"

"To get my rear end, and yours and Rube's, down off this hill."

"No, wise-ass, for the long term." McNamara was bantering, but always probing.

"My old man wants me to practice law with him. But as you know, there's a war on. I plan to get my commission in the Air Force, do my required time, get out, and go to law school on the G.I. Bill."

"Good plan. You going to fly in the Air Force?"

"That is my intent. But I'm afraid my eyes will keep me out of it. They are not 20-20 uncorrected, so I have to have a 'Plan B.' Since I will major in history, I figure I will fit into an intelligence slot or something like that if I can't fly. That is what the Air Force has told me a history degree equates to on its Ouija Board, or whatever it uses to come to such conclusions."

"It is a Ouija Board that they use," McNamara said, smiling, "-- and little else."

"But it's a sophisticated one, right?"

"Not sophisticated. Just big and expensive. It has its own room in the Pentagon."

3

June 1967: "Sign Here"

Bradford Lehman completed what was for him a stellar freshman year at the University of Puget Sound. As he had related to his former client, Robert S. McNamara, Lehman majored in history and signed on as a cadet in Detachment 900 of the U.S. Air Force's Reserve Officer Training Corps at UPS. He lived off-campus in a house owned by the University, and found, to his and his father's delight, that he took to academic life and ROTC. If there was a major impetus to Lehman's spurt of growth and maturity besides working in the professional world as a mountain guide, it was a gesture by Robert S. McNamara.

Two weeks after Lehman came down from Mount Rainier and began studies at the University, a package arrived at his off-campus address. Inside was Churchill's series, *A History of the English-Speaking Peoples,* hardbound in gilded leather. Each of the four volumes carried a gold printed notation: *"With warmest regard, and in remembrance of a wonderful climb of Mount Rainier. Best Wishes Bradford!"* They were signed in the bold sweeping hand of a confident man – *"Bob McNamara."* Under the signatures appeared more gilded script: *"Robert S. McNamara, United States Secretary of Defense, September 18th, 1966."* Lehman was astonished. September 18th was Bradford's birthday.

*   *   *

The Rainier Guide Service's climbing season began the first week of June. Lehman had just enough time to take final exams and move into the guide quarters in the basement of the Henry M. Jackson Visitors Center. The following few days were spent by Lehman and other guides in carrying supplies to Camp Muir and in scouting a route to the summit. Jim Whittaker, the first American to conquer Mount Everest four years before, was not at the RGS. He had other business interests, and spent much of his time on the lecture circuit. His twin brother Lou guided intermittently. He had a ski and mountaineering store in Tacoma that he was struggling to keep afloat.

Herb McGill operated the Rainier Guide Service. Herb, thin and wiry, was in his mid-thirties. He was a longtime climber, guide, and former Park Ranger. He ran a tight ship at Paradise. The RGS, along with offering the standard two-day summit climbs, ran five-day mountaineering and expedition seminars, trips to the Paradise Ice Caves, and glacier and ice climbing schools.

Bradford Lehman enjoyed the change that living up at Paradise brought. He owned a 1962 Triumph Herald 1200 convertible, which he found to be nimble on the tight corners of the Park's roads. Paradise itself was aptly named. It was perched up among spectacular mountain meadows at five thousand four hundred feet on the southern flank of Rainier. Though still covered in snow in June, it quickly melted, and alpine flowers of all colors sprang forth in profusion. To Lehman the old Paradise Inn also felt like home, with its rustic charm, huge stone fireplace, and hand-hewn timber interior.

By contrast, the Henry M. Jackson Visitor's Center was newly constructed in a "modern" design. It was several stories high, constructed of poured concrete, round like a flying saucer, and squatted incongruously amid the stately alpine firs, like a wrong button on a formal shirt. Park employees and guides quickly came up with their own moniker: "The DUB" (Day Use Building). The RGS facility and guide quarters resided at the DUB, a few hundred yards down the road from the Inn.

It was the third week in June, and Bradford Lehman was enjoying his first day off from guiding. Already he had summited the mountain four times, taught several day climbing schools, and co-instructed one five-day seminar. He was tired.

Bradford bought a cup of coffee at the Inn's malt shop, and stepped through the twelve-foot-high double doors onto the outside entrance deck. He sat down on a log bench and let his aching muscles relax. It was ten in the morning, and the parking lot was packed with private cars and the Rainier National Park Company's bright red tourist busses. Bradford took a deep breath of the thick clean air, flush with sounds and fragrance. Alpine Lupine and Indian Paint Brush were pushing through remnants of the winter snows. He closed his eyes from the bright sunshine and let the sounds of Paradise wash over him: laughter; car doors opening and slamming; happy chatter of human voices from many lands and languages; and exclamations of how big and beautiful the mountain was. The aroma of the coffee from his cup wafted up. There was something rich and magical about the smell of coffee outdoors.

Amid the hubbub, Lehman's ear caught the voice of Ranger John Ring answering a lady's question: "No ma'am, you cannot drive to the top of Mount Rainier. No, not even with chains on your car's tires. You have to climb it. It is very big, and much more remote and farther away than what it looks like from here. In fact, it was used as the training ground for the 1963 American Everest Expedition. Sure. You're welcome ma'am. Postcards? Yes. Go right in that door there, and turn right at the Gift Shop. Have a wonderful visit."

"Hey, Brad, finally enjoying a day off?" Ring asked.

"Yes, John." Lehman squinted one eye open. "Did anyone ever tell you that you have a melodious 'Ring' to your voice? You can sure schmooze the tourists."

Ring smiled and sat down. A rangy six feet tall, weighing one hundred and eighty pounds, with a thin inquisitive face, hazel eyes, and black short-cropped hair, he was as tough as a leaf spring on a truck. John Ring was a Climbing Ranger – one of two so designated at Rainier by the National Park Service to enforce regulations, assist with the routes, coordinate rescues, and provide an official presence on the upper mountain.

"The standard route up Disappointment Cleaver is going to be a bitch this summer," Ring observed.

"For sure."

"We had a near-record snow pack last year, but this year there are twice as many crevasses and it's kicking our butts trying to maintain a route."

"Tell me about it. Yesterday it took my clients over nine hours to summit. Two snow bridges, that were solid for parties the day before, were gone. We had to route-find and re-wand as we went."

"If it keeps up we may have to close the mountain."

Lehman looked surprised. "Close the mountain – really, John?"

"Yup. To all private parties, that is. The RGS will be the only group allowed to operate on the hill. And if that happens, you will be forced to use the Gibraltar route."

"Jeez, I hope not," Bradford winced. "Moving clients over the rappel point on the ledges up there would be a nightmare."

"Well," John said cheerily, slapping Lehman on the leg, "I thought I'd come by and brighten up your first day off." Ring stood and started to walk away. Then he stopped and came back. "Oh, I almost forgot. You have a friend coming to meet you."

"Who?"

"Dunno. Not your dad, though. I overheard a phone call over at the Ranger Station. I was told to go find you and let you know."

Bradford nodded, waved Ring off, and took another sip of coffee. He again closed his eyes to the music of the sparkling day. He was too tired to ponder who the visitor might be.

Lehman did not know how long he had nodded off. Maybe it was only a few minutes. But something gently drifted him back into consciousness. Someone was sitting right next to him.

"Hey, kid." The words came in a deep, resonant voice. It was familiar. Bradford looked over into the broad ruddy face of Rubayat Castellano.

"Rube! What in the name of all that's good and holy are you doing up here?" Lehman exclaimed, jumping up and clapping Castellano on the back. "How are you, old man?"

Rube was in his early forties. He had the look of a boxer, with a broad chest, powerful arms, and a bulbous nose that angled slightly askew. Lehman wondered in the instant if it came from fighting or drinking. *Probably both*, he thought. Yet, in the penetrating dark brown eyes, and beyond the gritty demeanor of the man, Lehman discerned a depth of wit and intelligence, and a glimmer of kindness.

"Great kid," Rube said, with a wide toothy grin. "But it took me three weeks to get the aches out of my legs and knees after our climb last summer."

"You up here to do it again? For a mere fifty-dollar fee, and thirty more for the rental gear, you can buy a summit climb and another two days of misery."

"God, I hope not! Come on," Rube grabbed Bradford's arm and turned him toward the malt shop in the Inn, "I'll buy us another cup of coffee and we'll take a walk. We've got some catching up to do."

*　　*　　*

"Here, sign this." Rube pulled out a sheaf of typed papers from inside his shirt, a pen from his pocket, and held them out to Lehman.

"You know, Rube, my old man is an attorney, and he has always told me never to sign anything I haven't read and completely understand."

"Yeah, I have been through that drill with him already. He is a very interesting fellow, your dad. Damned good man."

Bradford looked shocked. "When and where did you meet him?

"At his law office on the third floor of the Reed Building in Shelton a couple of days ago." Rubayat rattled off the words, then said, "Look inside the papers."

Paper-clipped to the first page was a small note in the distinctive chopped handwriting of his father: *"Brad, sign these. BFL."*

"What is it?" Lehman asked.

"The document is what is known in the business as a Non-Disclosure Agreement. You are eighteen now, Brad, and are no longer a minor. You are legally bound by your signature."

"That sounds serious. Am I in trouble of some kind?"

"It is very serious." Rube smiled. "But no, Brad, you are not in any trouble -- quite to the contrary. If you will kindly sign the document, I can tell you more."

Lehman glanced again at his father's cryptic note, and signed the last page.

"And if you will please initial the bottom of each of the first three pages… Great!" Rube broke into a broad smile, tucked the papers back into his shirt, and shook Bradford's hand. The grip was strong. Lehman matched it. "Congratulations, kid. You're on board, and we can now chat further. You have been investigated and are assigned a clearance of Top Secret. Information that you and I share, and share with others with the same clearance, may not be shared with anyone else under any circumstances. Period. Got that?"

"Yes," Lehman said.

"That includes your peers, fellow guides, supervisors, other officials, family, girl friends, priests, or anyone else, is that clear?"

"Yes."

"And if you run into *any* resistance or prying, or questions, on the part of *anyone,* I want you to immediately call the number I'll give you, okay?"

"Yes." Bradford was becoming increasingly baffled.

Without breaking stride, Rubayat Castellano began: "Lehman, I am a Special Agent of the FBI. I can show you my credentials if you wish, but I work for J. Edgar Hoover's Foreign Counterintelligence Division. I have been in the FBI since completing my service in World War II, in the Office of Strategic Services, AKA, the OSS -- the forerunner to the CIA.

"So, you worked with Wild Bill Donovan?" Bradford asked excitedly. It was Rube's turn to be surprised.

"Yes, how did you know that?"

"I'm a history major, and I have an avid interest in the history of warfare."

Castellano whistled. "I'm impressed, kid. Maybe he was right to select you."

"Who is 'he'?"

"Bob McNamara."

4

Later The Same Day

Bradford Lehman and Special Agent Rubayat Castellano continued their stroll along the east side of the Alta Vista trail above the Inn, and on upward toward Panorama Point and the Nisqually Glacier. It would be a full two hours, past noon, before they returned to the Inn. There was much to be discussed in Castellano's briefing of Lehman. It took place in the intervals between passing hikers and tourists, and at an isolated boulder overlooking the Nisqually Glacier, near Glacier Vista.

"We are obtaining information from diverse intelligence sources," Rube explained, "that indicates the Russians have a particular interest in this location, meaning Mount Rainier. It is common for the KGB's agents in the United States to favor such locations, such as our national parks, for contact with their assets."

"What are assets?" Lehman asked.

"Spies. The Russians use dead drops to communicate. Say I am a KGB agent, and you are my asset. I set up a pre-arranged place where information and money can be exchanged – like beneath this big boulder we're sitting on. At the bottom of it I will conceal a rusty old pop can. In it will be money and instructions for the next meet. Now, Lehman, it won't do in the spy business for me as your handler, 'Sergei Kutisnutsoff,' to meet you directly on this boulder, right?"

Lehman nodded.

"That puts both of us together at the same time and place. That is called a 'live drop,' by the way. In most instances it is bad form. Always risky. So instead, I arrange a signal down near the Paradise parking lot, indicating that I have filled the dead drop located at the base of this boulder. This signal may be a small piece of surveyor's tape tied to a tree limb or a stack of orange peels next to the trail. On second thought, I wouldn't use orange peels because the damned birds and squirrels around here would steal them -- but you know what I mean."

"Yes," Lehman said.

"You, Mister Asset and Spy, drive up to the parking lot. I, Sergei, am not even in the area. I left some hours, or even days before, to drive back to wherever the hell I came from, and am now busy writing up reports and filling out paperwork. The Russians are at least as bad as we are on that score, you know." Rube shook his head. It was evident he disdained paperwork. He continued: "You, Mister Asset, dressed all 'touristy,' take out your binoculars and act like you are viewing the mountain. But ha! There, on that tree a hundred yards up the trail is the surveyor's tape, fluttering ever so gaily." Rube made waves with one hand to simulate a fluttering tape.

Lehman nodded.

"Now Mister Asset, you grab your little day pack, saunter along the trail up here to the boulder, dig around a little at its base, and find the rusty old pop can that we've agreed to use as a drop container. You open it, take out the money owed to you as a faithful friend of Mother Russia, and insert your next batch of stolen classified U.S.

information. You then carefully put the can back in its hiding place, and walk casually back to the parking lot. But there is one more task that awaits, Brad. Do you know what that is?"

"It must have something to do with the signal. The tape?"

"Yes kid, precisely," Rube said, grabbing Lehman's shoulder. "You first take the tape down off the tree. This in turn signals Mister Kutisnutsoff that you have cleared and refilled the drop. A day or two later Sergei saunters back to the boulder, puts the pop can and its contents in his pack, and departs the area. And that's how a dead drop works. Clean and low risk."

"So that's what is going on up here?" Lehman asked.

"Well, that's where this situation gets murky, and also where we need your help. Our independent intelligence sources point to a significant increase in interest up at Mount Rainier. We have seen dead drops here before, but they have gone dormant. There has been no activity for the past two years. It is as though something operationally intense is focused here – something that it is of a high enough importance that the Russians do not want to risk compromising it by running dead drops."

There was a long silence. Five miles away, up high on the mountain in the Nisqually Icefall, a large serac collapsed with a distant booming roar. Large chunks of snow and ice avalanched, crashed down two thousand vertical feet, and finally careened to a stop where the glacier flattened into a broad shelf at ten thousand feet.

"Damn that is impressive," Rube said. "I can't believe you dragged my ass up that monster last year. Bob made me do it. But now I'm glad I did."

"So Rube, tell me how The U.S. Secretary of Defense fits into all of this. Why me?"

Rubayat chuckled, and thought for a moment, as though sorting out the right words to use. "First, understand that though Bob runs the Defense Department and the Vietnam War, he is not the head of the FBI and CIA. But he does get his hand into intelligence operations and he is briefed on them. When the CIA and I briefed him on the elevated Russian intelligence interest in Mount Rainier, he was fascinated. Of course, more discussions escalated into more meetings, and more meetings brought in bigger guns. My boss J. Edgar Hoover was now directly involved, along with the Director of Central Intelligence, Richard Helms. What our collective analysis concluded was that the GRU, Soviet Military Intelligence, has somehow supplanted the KGB as the primary operators here at Mount Rainier. That may explain why the local dead drops, traditionally run by the KGB, have dried up. GRU agents are real hard-asses – straight out of the Soviet Army's elite military academies. They are far more wedded to communist ideologies than the KGB. The United States to those GRU boys, is a dire overarching enemy. And their philosophy for combatting us is down and dirty. They are aggressive, and because they are true Cold War hardliners, their organizations are difficult to compromise and penetrate." A few moments of silence followed. Rube noticed that Bradford's head was down, concentrating.

A flood had washed over Bradford Lehman. His mind raced, trying to process Castellano's information and give it context. He had read of the GRU, and knew that it was an intelligence organization in the Soviet Union. He vaguely knew that it was run by the military, and that -- "Wasn't the GRU created and overseen by Leon Trotsky in 1918?" Lehman spoke the words aloud as he thought.

"Yes!" Castellano replied excitedly. "Excellent, kid! You *do* know your history."

"No, I don't yet know history. I am studying -- but apparently not fast enough for what is happening here. Wasn't Trotsky also a member of the first Politburo formed in 1918 right after the revolution? He later fell into disagreement with Stalin, was exiled, and fled to Mexico."

"Yes!" Rube echoed again, this time louder. "I'm amazed, kid. I've got agents back at the office who don't know that."

"And wasn't he ultimately assassinated?"

"Yes, Stalin's boys hunted him down and killed him in 1940."

"And do you know how they killed him?"

"Yeah, *dead*, that's how they killed him," Rube said.

"They slammed the pick of an ice axe through his head as he slept," Lehman said.

Rube let out a low whistle. "I didn't know that myself, kid. That's interesting."

"Also ironic, don't you think? The ice axe is our main piece of mountaineering gear up here on Rainier."

"It sure as hell is."

"And look at this --" Bradford swept his hand across the view of the glacier and the mountain -- "it is a national treasure. And now you are telling me that the Cold War even comes here."

"Yes, it even comes here, Brad, like it does everywhere else."

There was a long pause as Castellano let his words sink in. Happy chatter of hikers on the trails carried over on a crisp, light breeze. The glittering white cliffs of the Nisqually icefall hung far above, quietly waiting to unleash another crashing cascade of ice and snow. For any climber venturing near, it would be deadly.

Maybe this place is not as pristine as it seems. Bradford let the thought muse his mind: *Everything in nature strives to balance. It is that relentless, and sometimes deadly movement toward repose in nature, and historically in man, that must play itself out -- even up here. Especially up here. On the mountain its character is crumbling rock and ice that falls somewhere to a quiet place. That is called Nature. In man it is expressed in rivalry, conflict, and bloodshed. That's called History. Lehman, you love reading history. But this is your chance to actually be a part of it.*

"I'm in Rube," Bradford Lehman announced.

* * *

"We've got to get some weight back on you," Rube said, as he finished ordering them both twenty-ounce Porterhouse steaks. Castellano and Lehman were seated at a corner dining table in the Paradise Inn's large open dining room.

"You don't need any extra weight Rube," Bradford needled.

"Yeah, I know, that's what my wife keeps telling me. 'Keep it up and you'll be in the Fat Boy Program,' she says."

"What's the Fat Boy Program?"

"A forced weight reduction agenda dreamed up by Hoover. Every agent must keep his weight under control, you know, meet the chart requirements for weight versus height and all that crap." Rube picked up a large fresh roll, slathered it with butter, and ate it in two bites. "Gotta have that lean G-Man look. But anyway, screw it, there are ways around that." Rube waved his hand dismissively.

"How so?" Lehman asked.

"In the FBI there all these Hoover-driven administrative rules: no coffee or newspapers in the squad room; no wrecking a Bureau car for *any* reason; no haircuts on FBI time; no illicit pregnancies in the office female staff; no accidental discharge of weapons. That last one's sort of reasonable, but what the hell..." Castellano looked incredulously at Lehman, "shit happens."

Bradford burst out laughing. "Is that really true?"

"'Fraid so, kid," Rube mumbled through the salad he was wolfing down.

"But there are Hoover's rules, and ways around Hoover's rules. Agents are very creative."

"How so?"

"Well, they stow the newspapers in the office bathrooms in the stalls, and read them there as they take their morning constitutionals. That's why agents call bathrooms 'libraries.' As for coffee, the first lead of the day for squad members is to go to some coffee joint that the front office doesn't know about. Of course the empty suits in the front office are always trying to find out where agents drink their coffee. One day, down in the Seattle Office, some disgruntled clerk tipped off the Special Agent in Charge, 'S-A-C' as we call him, J. Earl Mills, and he actually walked into the coffee shop."

"What happened then?" Lehman asked.

"Well, we looked up, took one look at the SAC, and stampeded out the back door. All but one guy, that is."

"So the SAC nailed him?"

"He tried. He walked up to the agent and said, 'You're in big trouble now. Get back, and meet me in my office in fifteen minutes.' The agent didn't move. He just sat still, quietly sipping his coffee. This enraged Mills. 'Didn't you hear what you were ordered to do?' Mills shouted. 'Oh yes, Mister Mills, I heard you,' the agent said, smiling. 'Then why the hell aren't you complying? That's insubordination.' 'No, Mister Mills,' the agent said, 'I am not complying, and I am not insubordinate. You see, I retired from the FBI yesterday."

Lehman and Castellano were still laughing when the steaks came.

"Thanks young lady!" Rube said, favorably eying the pretty brunette waitress.

"You're most welcome, sir," she said. "Can I get you two anything else?" Rube noted that as she spoke, her sparkling dark eyes were looking at Lehman.

"You two don't know each other?" Rube said, nodding in Bradford's direction.

"Perhaps," the waitress replied softly.

"I don't believe so," Lehman said, eyeing her intently.

Rube looked at her nametag. "Teo, is that right?"

"Yes. It's like pronouncing the letters, *'Tee Oh.'*"

"Well Miss Teo, meet my friend's son, Bradford Lehman. I've been like a godfather to this young man. He guides up here, you know."

"Nice to meet you Teo." The words came out firmly, but Lehman felt himself blushing.

"You too," she said, her voice warming. "I have met most of the other guides, so why not you until now?"

"I've been up on the hill."

"Staying at Camp Muir?"

"Yes."

"I'm hiking to Muir on my next day off. I can't wait. Maybe I'll see you up there. Or maybe I'll see you around a little later this evening after the dining room closes?"

"Sure. Thanks, Teo. Again, it's good to meet you." Lehman was regaining his composure. Teo nodded, smiled, filled up Lehman's water glass, and left.

Castellano gave Lehman a Cheshire smile. "She is a beautiful girl."

"I can't differ with you there…"

Castellano paid for the dinner and the two men wandered up to the second floor balcony. They pulled up chairs to a small reading table.

"Look," Rube said. "You are only partially briefed into this situation. Here's what we are going to have to do. A week from now we will fly in here with a U.S. Air Force helicopter out of Fairchild Air Force Base, over in Spokane. You will be gone from this job for three to five days, and then we will fly you back. You will return in time to work the Fourth of July weekend, which Herb McGill tells me is the busiest time of your guiding season. It is imperative though, that we further brief and train you. You are now on our payroll too, and are earning a thousand dollars a month -- on top of the thousand you get up here at the RGS. That okay with you?"

"Yes Rube, that's fantastic!" Lehman said. "Why?"

"Because you are going to earn every last penny of it." Rube's words were emphatic. There was coldness in his voice that sent a chill up Bradford's spine.

I am out of my league in the spy business. Lehman shook off the thought. "How are you going to break me away from my climbing schedule?"

"That has all been handled," Rube said, his voice warming. "We rented your exclusive services from the RGS. McGill is well compensated for it, and is happy. He will adjust the work schedules. But of course tomorrow you will be up on another summit climb. While on it, keep your eyes open for *any* anomalies, on the mountain, on the route, with clients, and other climbers. Got it?"

"Yes, Rube." Lehman felt his stomach tightening with excitement.

"Great, kid! Again it's a pleasure having you on board. We will pick you up a week from today at 0500 hours."

"Where?"

"Up on the Paradise Glacier next to the Ice Caves. The chopper can get in there without being heard from Paradise. That's two and a half miles away with a ridgeline in between, so allow enough time to be there, okay?" Rube stood up, and Bradford stood up with him.

"What should I bring? Any gear?"

"Nothing. Just yourself." Stow your climbing gear in McGill's office. There's a padlocked locker there for you to use. We don't want the other guides to wonder why you have been hired for a special climb, and then left your gear behind. McGill knows you are not going on a climb, but he doesn't know where – and he doesn't care. We paid him very well. He will maintain that cover story."

"What is the cover story?" Lehman asked.

"That you are taking clients over to climb the Sherpa Glacier route on Mount Stuart."

"That's a great trip. How did you land on that one?"

"Your dad told me about it when we were shooting the bull over coffee at Nita's Café, down in Shelton. Man, he sure loves climbing."

"That he does," Lehman replied. "That he does."

Special Agent Rubayat Castellano walked with Lehman out of the Paradise Inn into the late afternoon sunshine. The parking lot was emptying out and the big red tourist busses were gone. Rube handed Bradford a slip of paper with a phone number on it. "If anything comes up call this number from the pay phone booth by the Inn's front desk. If it's urgent and you need to see me, or any of my esteemed colleagues, simply say 'Tallyho' to the person answering, and hang up. Then go sit by the fireplace. If it is less urgent, say 'The flowers are beautiful up here.' Hang up, and wait for a call back. The phone will ring within a minute. Got it?"

"Got it," Lehman said.

Castellano opened the door of his car, started to get in, and stopped. He turned back. "If you are in a jam you have backup. John Ring is one of us." Rubayat again started to get in and stopped. He looked back with a smile. "And kid, take care of yourself with the girls. Damn, she is pretty. Teo was it? Damn! Let me give you some old agent's advice – don't let the wrong head do your thinking."

5

June 1967: Training, First Evolution, Mica Peak

After he met with FBI Special Agent Rubayat Castellano, Bradford Lehman spent the rest of his day off organizing his gear for the next day's summit climb. The task completed, Lehman walked up to the Paradise Inn to watch the nightly park employee talent show. The place was packed with guests and visitors. Bradford lost himself amid the singing and skits. He wasn't listening to them. He was pondering, trying to cope with the day's events and conversations with Special Agent Castellano. He stood over by the big stone fireplace. The heat of the fire felt good against his aching calves. Lehman was edging into top shape. One or two more summit trips, and his legs and the rest of his body, would recover in half the time. Lehman felt a hand placed softly on his shoulder. He turned and looked into the face of Teo.

"Hi Brad." The voice was silken and spoken with a smile.

"Hi Teo, good to see you!" Lehman looked squarely at her now, and marveled. Teo's hair was worn pinned up when she was waiting tables. But now, her long dark hair wrapped around an exquisite smiling face. She stood relaxed, in jeans and a pale red sweater. Her hand remained on his shoulder. It was her limpid dark eyes that immediately attracted Bradford. They were bright, intelligent, understanding -- and they were happily taking stock of him. He allowed himself do the same with her. He focused on her full lips. They were covered with a hint of red lipstick. The lips, and the bright white teeth behind them, formed a smile, innocent and sensuous. He felt his heart beginning to pound. He took a half step backward -- just far enough that her hand remained on his shoulder – and looked her over. *Five feet five inches tall, athletic, strong straight shoulders, gorgeous full breasts, alabaster skin, round hips giving her a 'hourglass' figure, and long legs. Damn, Brad, she's right out of your dreams.* He took a deep breath and heard himself speak: "There are a couple of seats open by the fire. Would you like to sit down?"

"Yes, I'd love to, Mister Lehman," the lips said. "I have been running all day waiting tables." They sat facing the fire, with their backs to the festivities of the talent show. "Wow, it feels good to get off my feet."

"Tell me about yourself," Bradford said. "What brings you up to Paradise?"

"The Mountain, the Park, and the need for some college spending money. My dad pays the rest."

"I saw under your name on your name tag that you are attending Pacific Lutheran University."

"Yes," Teo nodded and smiled. "I will be a sophomore there. History is my major."

"What? That's my major as well, and I'm across town from you at the University of Puget Sound!"

"No kidding? Wow, that's amazing!" Teo's eyes were alight. "What are the odds of that?" There was a pause as the two stared into the fire. "Speaking of odds, Brad, I was thinking about you after I served you in the Dining Room. You looked familiar. And then it donned on me about an hour ago. You were that guide on a summit climb of Mount Rainier that I did with my dad last year in June. I was not on your rope, but I definitely remember you." Teo scanned Bradford's face intently as if verifying.

"Oh -- I remember you now too -- I think," Lehman said. "Was your dad an official of some kind for Standard Oil? He had this quiet young girl with him who I didn't see much, because you were farther back in the party, and it was cold, and you always had your parka hood up."

"Yes! That was me!" Teo laughed. "And my dad was on your rope, and yes, he works for Standard Oil."

"Indeed he was, now that I recall. He was a great client, and a good strong climber. So were you. Well it *is* a small world." Lehman touched Teo's knee, and she nodded and leaned a little closer. Bradford thought for a moment, watching the firelight dance across Teo's face. "Was it Mulaney, or Milarkey? The last name—"

"Maloney," Teo broke into a laugh, tossing her head back. "My last name is Maloney. But that's good, you almost got it!"

It was midnight before Maloney and Lehman parted company by the big fireplace. The crowd had dwindled to pockets of Park employees sitting around chatting. Teo stood up, and again put her hand on Lehman's shoulder.

"You are heading up for a climb tomorrow?"

"Yes. Then I will be gone for a week on a special climb. But after that I'll be back, and perhaps we can see each other again?" As Bradford spoke the words, he gently took her hand off of his shoulder and held it in his.

"I would love that," Teo said, smiling softly, and looking into his eyes. "Gray-blue. Just what I remembered."

Lehman felt the urge at that moment to take her face in his hands and kiss her -- but he didn't.

"Be safe," Teo said.

*   *   *

A week later, after two more ascents of Mount Rainier, Bradford Lehman rendezvoused with the U.S. Air Force HH-43 Huskie helicopter near the Paradise Ice Caves. He enjoyed the hike out to the landing zone. Lehman left his quarters at 0400, at the first pale hint of light, and took his time covering the two and a half miles of trail over to the Ice Caves. He ambled slowly, letting the burn in his legs dissipate as he stretched them. He crossed Edith Creek Basin, hiked up to the top of Mazama Ridge, and over toward the Ice Caves. He was surprised how much snow had melted since he had been there the week before. Herb McGill had sent Lehman and another RGS guide over there to see if the Caves were open yet. They weren't. Tons of snow still covered their entrances.

Several fat, furry marmots whistled shrilly in the cold quiet air, warning each other that Bradford was coming. They dived into their dens among the rocks as he passed.

Bradford carried no pack, as instructed -- only a water bottle in the cargo pocket of his wool knickers. He reached the pickup site on the Paradise Glacier twenty minutes early, sat down on a large flat rock, took a long drink of water, and promptly dozed off.

Lehman awoke to the distant sound of a helicopter approaching from the east. The HH-43 hugged the landscape, flew directly over Lehman, circled, and landed 50 feet away. Bradford walked around to the back of the chopper, avoiding the whirling canted blades. He was familiar with these helicopters on rescue and body retrieval missions. Huskies had deployed out of McChord Air Force Base in Tacoma. With their long, intermeshed counter-rotating blades, they were excellent for high altitude work, with a service ceiling exceeding twenty-five thousand feet. The crew chief buckled Lehman in, closed the back clamshell doors, and gave a thumbs-up. The HH-43 lifted off, banked into a hard right turn, hopped the ridges over Indian Bar, and skipped out of Mount Rainier National Park at one hundred miles per hour, headed east. The crew chief motioned Lehman to put on the headset hanging on the bulkhead.

"Hey, kid, how do you like the ride?" It was the voice of Rubayat Castellano. Surprised, Bradford looked up toward the cockpit. Rube's helmeted head was leaning around the right seat looking back. He gave Lehman a "A-OK" signal, and Bradford returned it.

"This is a fantastic ride!" Lehman exclaimed.

"Sure is. Hell of an invention, the helicopter."

"When did you learn to fly one?"

"That's a story we'll have to address over a beer sometime. Some say I never did learn to fly one." The helmet of the command pilot in the left seat nodded emphatically. Rube smiled and turned his attention back to the cockpit.

The Kaman Huskie refueled at Moses Lake Airfield, then flew on to Fairchild Air Force Base, where the crew chief got out and another man got on. The bird lifted off, flew a few minutes more, and flared to a landing at the Mica Peak Air Force Station. Mica Peak was a radar installation perched at five thousand feet in the mountains east of Spokane. It was 0830 hours.

"Let's get some breakfast." Rube pulled off his flight helmet, grabbed Lehman by the arm, and led him over to the mess hall. Steak and eggs were waiting.

*   *   *

Rube introduced Lehman to the man who had boarded the helicopter at Fairchild. "Brad, meet Otto Palmrich. He's a CIA man. We've worked together on numerous operations. He is also a climber."

Lehman shook Palmrich's hand. Otto looked to be about thirty years old, with a thin face and steel gray eyes. He was tall – over six feet – and lean and wiry. He walked with a slight limp.

"You have the cut of a rock climber, Otto," Lehman said. Palmrich smiled and nodded.

"And you have the look of a big-mountain man," Palmrich said, adding, "I have heard a lot of good things about you." His voice was even and clear, but with a touch of a German accent.

Lehman was ushered into a small recreation room. The pool and foosball tables had been shoved over to a corner. "This has been commandeered as our classroom," Rube said, as he turned on the lights. All the window shades were pulled down and Rube and Otto slipped thick red files out of their briefcases and placed them on a long table. They were marked "TOP SECRET."

Rube offered a chair. "Have a seat, Brad, and we'll get started. Do you want some coffee?"

"Please, Rube. I'm running on a sleep deficit since coming off the hill yesterday afternoon."

Palmrich nodded and picked up the phone on the table. He ordered several large carafes… "And throw in some donuts and other goodies. Knock First. Okay." He set the phone down and opened one of the files. Castellano opened his.

"Comfortable?" Otto asked looking up.

"Yes," Lehman said. The chair he was offered was stuffed red leather, and it reclined. Otto's and Rube's were the same. They were out of place in the sparse room.

"Okay," Otto began. "We don't have much time to train you, and we may be able to skip a couple of instruction blocks here, if I may prevail on you with a few questions."

"Fire away," Lehman said.

"Tell us what you observed today from the time we picked you up," Castellano said.

"For starters," Lehman began, "You were seven minutes late arriving at the pickup location on the Paradise Glacier this morning. Since you chose to hug the ground and fly the canyons, you hadn't considered the southwest winds down low around that side of Rainier. I figure you ran into about a fifteen knot headwind on the last leg of your trip." Otto and Rube glanced at each other. "Next, the HH-43 has a relatively short range, which I figure to be about 200 miles. You had to refuel on the way back at Moses Lake, and the chopper was already stripped almost bare inside – no rescue gear or extra seats – all taken out to save weight and extend range. Next, you landed at Fairchild and the crew chief got off and Otto got on. The crew chief is the only fellow in the mix I have seen so far who may not actually be part of your operational group, but merely a local crewmember, picked up to make sure you knew the way to the landing zone up at Rainier. He may even be stationed out at McChord, where normal HH-43 rescue operations take place. Next, Rube, you landed the chopper up here at Mica Peak, because it was a bit sloppy. We bounced."

Castellano's face flushed with a trace of indignance.

"That's about it for the flight," Bradford said. "But why did you land me up here at five thousand feet on Mica Peak instead of remaining at Fairchild? I figure it was because you do not want me to lose my high-altitude acclimatization. Whatever you have up your sleeves, it seems to bear an aspect of urgency. I have a feeling you have immediate work in store for me high on the mountain. Next, Otto, I see that at one time you broke your left ankle. You have a slight limp, are pigeon-toed in that foot, and have had it for a while. My guess is that your accident occurred from a leader fall on high angle rock. Likely you yanked out a couple of pitons before your partner's belay stopped you, and you slammed into the cliff, breaking your ankle. You also look vaguely familiar. I think you might have been written up in Summit Magazine a few years ago -- for a first ascent somewhere in the Rockies. But Otto Palmrich wasn't your name then. I'm sure of it." It was Otto's turn to blush. A long moment of silence followed.

There was a loud knock at the door. Rube and Otto quickly closed their files. The coffee and donuts had arrived.

Otto and Rube were convinced that Bradford Lehman had formidable powers of observation, and excellent recall of details. They skipped that block of instruction, along with report writing. They had already perused Lehman's answers to his recent history essay exams at the University of Puget Sound. They knew his grades before he did.

Over the next two days, Lehman was briefed extensively on the operational workings and tradecraft of the KGB and GRU, and on their respective missions. Otto echoed what Rube had told Lehman about the KGB drop sites drying up around Mount Rainier, and that "The little we are able to discern seems to point to an elevated GRU interest in the mountain – not so much the Park per se, but in Rainier itself."

Castellano then spoke extensively of world affairs, as they pertained to relations between the Soviet Union and the United States, and the Cold War in particular: "As you know Lehman, being a potential draftee in Bob McNamara's war in Vietnam, things are escalating. U. S. troop commitment is growing, and that effort is being matched by escalation of Russian support and activity in Southeast Asia. The Cold War that we have been fighting with the Soviets since before 1950, with development and deployment of the nuclear arsenals and delivery systems of both countries, is now expressing itself in a 'hot' proxy war between the two super powers in Vietnam. The 'Domino Theory,' propounded by McNamara, John F. Kennedy, and now Lyndon Johnson, dictates that communism is a cancer. The Commies are no good at feeding their own people, but they are damned good at expanding their global influence through incitement, revolution, and force. And once a country falls under the aegis of the Soviets or Chinese Communists, unless the U.S. steps in and resists, contiguous countries to the fallen country will, in turn, fall."

"That is exactly what my father has been saying since I can remember," Lehman said. "I grew up with all those 'duck and cover' exercises at school, and the threat of nuclear attack, especially since the 1962 Cuban Missile Crisis. And that hasn't gone away either – at least where I live."

"No Brad, it hasn't," Otto said. "Keep in mind that the Soviets, as represented by the various departments of the KGB back in Moscow Center, which control global operations, are a solid political organ of the Soviet state, both internally and externally. A hell of a lot of money and effort goes into what we term 'perception management,' or propaganda, both to keep their own people in line, and to undermine our own political, democratic, and social institutions. Hence we see the rise of the anti-war movement in this country. It is not a spontaneous grass-roots phenomenon, but a focused, purposeful policy of subversion that forms the core of the philosophy, or cancer, as it is preached and spread through communist doctrine, as practiced Soviet-style."

"The moral is to the physical as three to one," Bradford said.

"Yes! Where did you get that?" Rube asked.

"It is one of Napoleon's maxims. The Soviet Union is run by an oligarchy of tyrants then…"

"Precisely," Rube said. "Kid, you're a fast study. Understand that KGB Agents are largely recruited from the equivalent of our American Ivy League schools, like Harvard, Princeton, or Yale. Military GRU agents, on the other hand, are gleaned from top Soviet academies roughly equivalent to America's West Point and Annapolis, or Britain's Sandhurst. They are trained from the beginning to view the U.S. as their archenemy. So, Lehman, how would you expect them to see the world?"

"*'For now we see, through a glass darkly'* – Paul's New Testament letter to the Corinthians," Bradford said soberly. His head was in his hands and he was staring into the floor. He looked up: "They view themselves as relentlessly hunted, and threatened by the United States. Therefore, they must hunt and attack relentlessly. They know nothing else, nor wish to."

Otto and Rube smiled at each other.

"Well Otto, I think we can cut another day off of Lehman's training. He's ahead of the schedule. Let's get dinner and have a beer."

* * *

The next day at Mica Peak, Castellano and Palmrich focused specifically on Mount Rainier as a possible Russian target.

Agent Castellano spoke first: "For purposes of simplifying things for my benefit -- not for yours Lehman, or you Palmrich -- I am GRU agent Sergei Kutisnutsov." Rube slipped into a deep thick Russian accent to play his character. "What is my mission? Is it passive or active? By passive, I understand that nothing is to be destroyed or blown up. I do not like that, because that is not for which I was best trained. But, for Mother Russia, I do it. I am directed to place special sensor on big mountain Rainier, to listen or record." Rube, fully in character now, slid his thumbs across the fingers of his cupped hands searching for the right English words. "Em, what is it? Communication intercepts maybe? Or radio repeater device perhaps?

"Sergei," Palmrich said, "if that is your mission, you will have to have a steady, long-term power source. It would have to be a portable nuclear generator. But even that would be heavy to carry up the mountain."

Rube looked incensed. *"Too Heavy?* What you think, I am pussy KGB agent? He leaned menacingly toward Palmrich. *"Nothing too heavy to carry for Mother Russia!* I am son of general who fought in Great Patriotic War, and am grandson of officer who fought in Russian Revolution." Castellano's face was flushed, and he thumped his chest for emphasis.

"Young man, sitting there in nice soft leather chair, so quiet. What do *you* say?"

Bradford pondered the question.

"You, Bradford, what wrong? Has cat got your tongue?"

Lehman smiled. "Mount Rainier is unique in the United States, and indeed the world, because it is a large glacier-covered active volcano, situated close to major West Coast urban, shipping, and industrial centers. Boeing, as you know Sergei, builds the B-52 heavy strategic bomber, which can carry nuclear bombs and devastate your country. Close to Mount Rainier is also a massive power grid pulling electricity on above-ground transmission lines from hydroelectric dams on the Columbia River."

Rube held up his hand: "You are wrong, young Bradford, Mount Rainier is not active."

"Yes it is Sergei." Lehman felt his face turning red. "I took the National Park Service's head geologist to the summit of Mount Rainier late last summer. I got an earful about Rainier's volcanic potential. The mountain is what is termed 'intermittently active.' It sleeps for periods, and erupts. And when it blows next, *all hell* will break loose for populations and cities in the Northwest. Massive lahars will combine with the exploded volcanic materials. The lahars, or mudflows, made up of melted glaciers and rock, will cascade through surrounding valleys. The whole Puyallup Valley, as an example, was filled in and made fertile, by an ancient lahar from Rainier. The debris from that event is over five hundred feet deep." Lehman paused to reason further.   Castellano and Palmrich did not interrupt.

"Furthermore, Sergei," Bradford continued, "the eruption itself would carry radioactive debris and ash over surrounding cities, and over all of the electric transmission lines that serve them. Since Northwest dams furnish the bulk of the power to the entire West Coast, disruption of that grid would be catastrophic, and long-term. Speaking of dams – and reservoirs -- all water behind them would now be radioactive and poisoned. There would be no drinking water." Bradford paused again, deep in thought. "Fascinating concept," Lehman muttered, almost to himself. "If the Russians placed a nuclear bomb on or near the top of Mount Rainier, the explosive effect of the device could be greatly magnified – no, exponentially magnified." Lehman took a deep breath. "The question is, Sergei, do you have such a device?"

Otto stood up excitedly. "Yes, Bradford you are on the same page as we! What you have described is what we call a 'force multiplier.' This is what Rube and I, and a few others, including McNamara, and FBI Director Hoover, are asserting – that the Russians are targeting Rainier to place a portable nuke up there as a 'failsafe' option, in case the Cold War goes hot all at once. If the Russian bombers and missiles cannot get through our conventional defenses, they will have this as a backup."

"Or, they will set it off anyway," Lehman said. He sat quietly for a moment with his head in his hands. Then he looked up, shook his head, and pointed to it. "I feel like *this* is going to explode."

Castellano walked over and gave Lehman a slap on the back. "C'mon kid, it's almost lunch time. Let's go get another steak."

Bradford looked up and smiled. "I could use a steak. But who says I want to eat with you, Sergei? You are an asshole."

* * *

Lunch that day on Mica Peak was a turning point for Bradford Washburn Lehman. Before that day, he had been a climber, RGS guide, and college student. Now he was something else that he had yet to define. It would take contemplation and time. Rube and Otto sensed the change. And now Lehman was their colleague, albeit still a "kid," in Rubayat's eyes.

Bradford felt as though he had been yanked from one orbit of his life into another that was new and strange -- riskier and deadlier -- than shepherding clients up Mount Rainier. *Damn, I'm too young for this,* he thought. And yet, one to see perspectives, Bradford knew that at his tender age of eighteen, he could just as easily be dodging enemy bullets in Vietnam. So many of his high school friends from Shelton were already over there, or were headed that way. *Yes, Bradford, on balance you are lucky. You will be fighting on your turf -- not theirs. That is a huge advantage. You have grown up on this mountain and have summited it from all sides. Few Americans -- and no Russians -- know the hill like you do.*

Lehman wished then that he could seek his father's counsel. But he already knew what his father would say: *"Do it. And be vigilant."* Benjamin Franklin Lehman, former RGS guide, naval officer in World War II, and Mason county Prosecutor, was direct, pithy, and vehemently anti-communist.

* * *

The next morning after breakfast, Castellano and Palmrich briefed Lehman on the gadgets he would use on the mountain. He was handed a compact Rollei 35mm camera with a bag of fifty rolls of film.

"Shoot as much as you want with this," Palmrich said. "You will need to become proficient."

"Speaking of shooting," Rube said. He slid a small silver-colored pistol, its slide locked open, across the table. "And kid, today you'll be shooting a lot with this. It is a German Walther PPK .32 caliber pistol, serviced for use in cold weather, and sweat-proofed. It'll never rust."

Lehman picked up the weapon. It folded into his hand like a natural extension.

"Special pouches have been sewn into the beltline inside the front of your wool climbing knickers," Rube said, "and also on a couple of pairs of jeans we've had modified for you. The pouches will function as holsters for the Walther. We have also reconfigured the padded shoulder straps on your Kelty frame pack with custom pouches so you can holster and draw from your chest, and from either side of your body if you wish."

Otto then handed Lehman a six-volt Eveready dry cell battery.

"I've got plenty of these for my headlamp."

"This is not for your headlamp, Brad." Otto said. "Well, in a pinch it is. The top terminals will work for that. It is a radiation detector." Palmrich gave a twist, and the top screwed off to reveal a calibrated meter and a length of thin wire that led up to the negative terminal. Otto popped off the terminal with his thumb and pulled out a small earpiece at the end of a wire. "You put this earpiece in, and if radiation is present you will hear crackling. The more crackling, and the faster it goes, the closer you are to the radiation source and the more intense it is. The meter inside also records the readings, which are displayed as thousandths of a roentgen per hour. That is known as the 'radiation count.' You have four feet of hairline cord for the earpiece. It auto-retracts. To use the device, you do not need to unscrew the body all the way. Place the earpiece in and give the battery a quarter turn and then back again. This will activate the unit. To confirm it's on you will hear a soft 'beep'. With that, you are ready."

"Man, it looks just like a regular Eveready battery," Lehman said, turning it in his hand. "Same weight, too. How can I tell it apart from my regular headlamp battery?"

"The regular six-volt dry cell will have silver-colored terminals," Palmrich said. "The detector's wire terminals are gold. And here," Palmrich pointed to two dime-sized metal discs on one side of the device, "the device is designed so that when this side of the unit is taped side-by side, against the metal casing of a regular six-volt Eveready dry cell, it will recharge itself from the dry cell. Taping the batteries together won't attract attention – it will show that you're organized, with a spare battery readily available."

"What do I do if I hear crackling?" Lehman asked.

"Take an altimeter and compass reading. Try to Fix the spot as best you can," Rube said. "If you keep climbing and it gets stronger, take another position fix. That may give us a vector to its location."

"Man, you guys know that with the wind we get up on the hill, the unit could be crackling in my ear, and I may not even hear it," Lehman said.

"We know," Palmrich said. "Just do the best you can with it. Remember, the unit is also recording the hits."

"Okay, Otto," Lehman shrugged.

Rubayat, Otto, and Bradford broke for a lunch of filet mignon, Idaho baked potatoes, fresh green beans, salad, pie, and ice cream. In the afternoon they went out to the pistol range and Lehman put five hundred rounds through his newly issued Walther PPK .32 caliber pistol. He practiced drawing and firing from the special holster pouches on his pack and from his new clothes.

"Keep your finger out of the trigger when you're reaching for that thing," Rube boomed, over his ear protectors. "You don't want to lose your chance to have kids."

Bradford Lehman shot near-perfect scores with both hands. "I'm ambidextrous," he informed his surprised trainers. The only handgun he had shot before was his father's Smith & Wesson Model 15, Combat Masterpiece. It was a .38 caliber revolver. Compared to the smooth, sleek handling of the Walther semi-automatic pistol, the Model 15 was like holding a stick of wood. Lehman loved the Walther PPK.

"So Rube, you ever shot someone?" Bradford asked the question sitting at a picnic table at the shooting range. He was taking a break with Castellano and Palmrich.

"Yeah, kid."

"Can you tell me about it?"

"Sure. I was a first office agent stationed down in Little Rock, Arkansas, in the late 1940s: The call comes in over the speakers in the bullpen – that's the moniker for an agents' open work area. So we all pile into our Bu-cars and motor down to the bank. By the time we roll up, the local police have the bank robber cornered on a sidewalk. He's shooting, the cops are shooting, and of course, being red-blooded young FBI agents, we join the fray. The robber has a butt-load of ammo on him, along with four revolvers. He shoots from behind a blue U.S. Postal Service mail box, then runs fifteen feet, crouches down behind a yellow fire hydrant, shoots, and runs back to the mail box. He keeps doing that, and the damned gunfight seems to be going on forever. I fire all six round from my 'Roscoe --'"

"What's a Roscoe?"

"—My Bureau-issued Smith and Wesson .38 Special revolver. 'Roscoe' is Bu-speak for 'revolver.' So I am kneeling down behind the front wheel of my Bu-car reloading, when I look up and there's a redneck with a .22 rifle parked next to me with his beat up pickup truck. He's behind it, plinking away at this suspect. I show him my credentials and shout: 'Who the hell are you?' He gives me a toothless grin, digs around in his pocket, holds up a badge, and says: 'Arkansas Police Benevolent Society, Little Rock Chapter.' I say: 'Great, cover me while I reload!' He nods and keeps on plinking. I reload, and all the while I can hear the Bu-car getting hit with rounds. I am not going to stick my head up over the hood again, so I go prone next to the car and look under it. I can see the suspect's feet under the mail box, so I take a good squint with the sights and shoot at his right foot. He squeals like a stuck pig and gives up. 'Get me a doctor!' he screams. An Arkansas State Patrolman, staying behind the cover of his cruiser, slides a pair of shiny silver handcuffs over to the suspect and says in a deep, slow, southern drawl: 'Put these handcuffs on, son, behind your back. And get 'em on real tight now, or we'll gut-shoot you.' He does what he's told, and we drag him off to the hospital under guard. And that's my big gunfight story." Rube chuckled and opened another can of beer from the cooler on the table.

"So what about your redneck witness – the guy who backed you up?" Bradford asked.

"Never did identify him. After the fight was over he put his .22 rifle back into the gun rack in his truck and drove away."

"Great story, Rube!"

"Yeah, thanks, kid. That was my full-immersion baptism into FBI gunfights. Southern-style."

"So you think the Arkansas State Patrolman would have gut-shot the robber if he didn't comply?"

"Yup…." Rube took a long swig of beer and wiped his lips with his sleeve.

6

WANING DAYS OF JUNE 1967: BACK ON THE HILL

The HH-43 Huskie flared for a landing on the Paradise Glacier at 0430.

"The Ice Caves are open!" Lehman exclaimed through the intercom.

Rubayat Castellano's voice came back from the cockpit: "Yeah, kid. Mister DuPont spoke, and the caves opened."

"So one of your guys blew the Caves open with TNT?"

"No idea how that could have happened. But it looks like that cave now has dollar signs written all over it for the Rainier Guide Service."

"Thanks, Rube. Okay, I'm out the door." Lehman pulled off his headset, unbuckled his seatbelt, jumped off the back deck, and scrambled clear. Rube and the command pilot gave a thumbs-up, and the Huskie lifted off, flying west through Stevens Canyon. Castellano was headed back to McChord AFB, and then on to the Seattle Office of the FBI, where he was temporarily assigned for the current operation.

Bradford Lehman walked back along the trail he had hiked three days earlier. He felt as though he had gone through a time warp. *Listen, Lehman, don't get too tightly wrapped. Don't worry about anything you cannot control. Enjoy yourself up here in Paradise and on the hill. Just be professional, and as your old man says, 'be vigilant.' You always have been. Beyond that, relax.* He tapped the Walther PPK holstered inside his waistband. *Maybe when the chicks see the bulge there they'll dig me.* He laughed out loud. It felt good.

Lehman stopped to have breakfast at the Paradise Inn Dining Room. It opened at 0600. The quiet bustle of sleepy tourists being seated, and reading their papers over coffee and orange juice, was a reassuring scene.

"Hi stranger!" Teo Maloney, dressed in her crisp lemon-colored waitress uniform, with collar and cuffs trimmed in white, slipped up beside Bradford. As she leaned over to pour his coffee, her face came close to his. "I missed you."

"I missed you too, girl," Lehman said. "And I'm glad to be back."

"I have a day off tomorrow," she said. "It starts after my dinner shift is over tonight. Want to get together?"

Bradford looked into Teo's soft dark eyes. "For sure. I'll see you by the front desk or at the fireplace at eight-fifteen." She gently squeezed his shoulder.

Lehman finished his breakfast and walked down to the Henry M. Jackson Visitor Center. "Hi Herb, how've things been since I left?"

Herb McGill looked up from the RGS equipment rental counter and smiled. Other guides in the room greeted Lehman with "Good to see you Brad," or "How'd the climb go?"

"Good to be back guys. The climb went well."

"What climb did you do?" Gary Olin asked. Gary, at twenty-seven years old, was one of the senior guides on the staff of the RGS. At five feet eleven inches, his lean wiry build made him look taller. He had blond hair of medium length. It was perennially askew, and topped a fair-skinned face, set with kind, pale blue eyes.

"We did the Sherpa Glacier route on Mount Stuart," Lehman replied.

"Damn, I've always wanted to do that climb," Olin said, and turned to Herb McGill. "Why didn't these rich clients ask me to take them? I'm senior to Lehman!" The words were spoken with a semi-serious smile.

"Simple, Gary," McGill said, "because Lehman has climbed it before and you haven't. We put our best boot forward here at the RGS, you know." Olin grumbled and turned back to the clients he was gearing up for a summit climb. Herb waved Lehman back into his office and closed the door.

"It really is good to have you back, Brad. We have been slammed with clients signing up for climbs."

"That's good news Herb. But I've got more good news for you. I just returned from an early morning walk out to the Ice Caves to get the kinks out from the 'climb.' The Caves are now open."

McGill's jaw dropped. "How in the hell did that happen? They were blocked solid with snow and ice only a couple of days ago!"

"Don't know, Herb, but now you're in business for running that trip."

"Damn, that is great news!"

"So what's my schedule? When do I go up the hill?"

McGill smiled, looked down at the climbing schedule on his cluttered desk and back up at Lehman. "I'm not sending you up again for two days. I have hired another temporary guide, so we are good on the manpower. By the way, we have moved you down the hall to a two-man room from the four-man one you were in. You will be bunking with our beloved climbing ranger, John Ring. Your stuff is already moved in there."

"Why?" Lehman asked.

"Well, John is the 'cop' on our floor, and the other guides want to pop a beer or two in their rooms, and you know, alcohol is not allowed -- Park rules and all. So when the need to move someone in with John came up, you weren't here. You got the short straw."

"That's fine with me. John Ring is a hell of a good guy."

*   *   *

Bradford Lehman loved the Paradise Inn. He was beginning to love it more because of who was nestled against him by the big fire. Teo had a ready wit and laugh, tempered with quiet sincerity. She loved mountains. She had grown up hiking and climbing in them, and her body, though womanly full and soft, was trim. She was in excellent physical shape.

"What a grand trip today Brad," Teo said, squeezing his arm.

"Wasn't it though?"

They left early that morning, and drove down to the parking lot at Reflection Lake. They shouldered their packs, hiked up the Pinnacle Peak Trail, turned right at the high notch at the top of the Tatoosh Range's ridgeline, and scrambled to the top of Plummer Peak. Then they hiked back down to the notch, roped up, and climbed the steep crumbling cliff on the south side of Pinnacle.

Bradford and Teo reached Pinnacle Peak's summit in time to witness the sunrise. He watched Teo as she signed the register. The light sheened her long black hair, and turned her face gold. He put his arm around her, pulled her to him, and kissed her. It started feather-soft, but as their lips lingered in the long moment, the kiss became firm and full. Bradford gently cupped his hand behind Teo's head. He felt her breath start, and her body relaxing against his. Her hair smelled like lavender. Lehman closed his eyes and let his lips slowly part from hers. He took a deep breath and turned back to look at Mount Rainier. Its majestic immensity dominated the northern view.

Teo reached up, gently turned his head toward hers, and softly kissed him again. Neither spoke.

Lehman got up and shouldered a few coils of the goldline climbing rope they were tied into. "Let's go do Castle Peak, girl," he said. "It's next on today's itinerary."

As he turned to descend Pinnacle, anchoring Teo on the rope, Bradford's eye caught a flash of light from high up on Rainier. He called for Teo to stop. She was already down-climbing the summit chimney. A few seconds later he saw another flash; and this time his eye placed it near Rainier's crater rim. Someone was signaling with a mirror. He saw two more flashes, spaced five seconds apart, and then they stopped. It was not an SOS call for help. Lehman relaxed. It was common for summit climbers to use mirrors to signal friends down at Paradise.

"What's wrong, Brad?" Teo's voice wafted up from the rocks of the chimney sixty feet below.

"Nothing, Teo. I'm getting organized. Go ahead, girl. I'm right behind you."

Lehman and Maloney climbed Castle Peak, and then moved east along the Tatoosh Range, climbed Unicorn Sister, and finally Unicorn Peak, where they ate the lunch that Teo packed for them. They rappelled off the top, scrambled down rocks and talus slopes to Snow Lake, and hiked out to the trailhead at the Stevens Canyon Road. They then turned and walked west, two miles up the road to the Reflection Lake parking lot, where the car was parked. Lehman put the top down on his Triumph, and they drove back up to Paradise. It was four o'clock.

After an early dinner, the two collapsed by the Inn's fire, reflecting upon a joyous day of climbing, and being in each other's company.

"You know, Teo, you're a damned good climber." Bradford spoke softly near her ear. "And you are tough, too."

Teo blushed. "Thanks Brad, but with you leading the way for me it was easy. You are wonderful to watch when you climb. It seemed that every step, and every move you made on the rock, was effortless."

"You're sweet, girl, but I'm not comfortable on the rock as I am on snow and ice. Other guides up here, like Don McPherson and Fred Stanley, are far better on rock."

"I don't believe it!" Teo teased, hugging Lehman's arm.

"Most of my time has been spent on Rainier and other glaciated peaks around here. As far as rocks go, I've dodged more falling rock than any I ever climbed. But Teo, I want to compliment you on your toughness."

"How so?" she said, her voice inquisitive.

"You did the whole series of peaks today in new boots. After Castle, you were limping with blisters. But you never complained, and you never quit. You, young lady, are tough. Very impressive!" Bradford reached over and tweaked Teo's nose, then brushed the thick black hair away from her eyes. Teo blushed again and let her weary head fall on his shoulder.

*   *   *

Over the final week of June, 1967, the Rainier Guide Service's route to the summit of Rainier continued to deteriorate. Lehman and Gary Olin carried up and installed two twenty-four-foot aluminum ladders on the Ingraham Glacier, to span large crevasses that had opened wide in the summer heat. Bradford also completed two more summit climbs.

Each time he climbed above Camp Muir, Lehman carried his Eveready headlamp batteries, gave the "Gold Eveready" a turn, as he'd named the device given to him by Castellano and Palmrich, inserted its earpiece, and listened for any feedback from the sensor. Once, climbing above the bergschrund at thirteen thousand three hundred feet, Lehman thought he had heard faint crackling, but it only lasted a few seconds. The wind was gusting. Bradford wrote it off to the rattling of his parka hood.

Strange too, were the sounds of three cracking *booms* he'd heard each time he was up near the summit. He knew they were sonic shock waves, generated from aircraft breaking the sound barrier. Lehman was accustomed to hearing them on the mountain, but they normally came one at a time, spaced many seconds or minutes apart. There were many U.S. fighter planes deploying to Vietnam, or on aerial maneuvers high in the stratosphere. The airspace over Mount Rainier was busy. But the three quick successive shock waves were baffling.

The clientele on the RGS summit trips were the "normal crop" of outdoorsmen and women attracted to climbing Mount Rainier. They came from all walks of life, and some from different countries. Bradford had his other ear tuned for any client with a Russian accent. *Why should I overlook the obvious?* he figured. Like the other guides, Lehman routinely had to manage seven to nine clients on his rope. The mountain brought out either the best or worst in people. Lately the clients had been of the latter kind. They were coming up to climb the hill out of shape and out of sorts. Trips with people of this ilk tried the tempers of the guides, and made climbs, coupled with a deteriorating route, more tiring.

Lehman could never get enough rest. On every break he lay down on the snow and slept. He found himself nodding off while climbing. All during this time the tiny earpiece in his right ear was silent. It had only been a week and a half since he had arrived back from his training at Mica Peak. Already it felt as though months had passed. Bradford was beginning to have notions that he had just dreamed the whole crazy experience: The Russians, a nuclear threat, the FBI, the CIA. *Actually, Lehman, it can't be a dream. It's too bizarre.* The thought surfaced a wry smile. But up on the great glaciers of the mountain, Lehman had to admit, he was home. Up here -- and down at Camp Muir and Paradise -- was home. It was the world. It was reality.

Bradford cast a glance to his left down into the morning haze, at the tiny parking lot and buildings of the Paradise Inn and the DUB. He saw the razor thin ribbon of road that wound in and out of the park, along the valleys, and switch-backed down steep alpine ridges. It connected somewhere in the broad blue horizon, to the outside -- to another universe. Occasionally his eye caught the flash of a car's windshield in the morning sun. He thought about his joyful climb along the peaks of the Tatoosh Range with Teo. He thought of Teo.

"Falling!" The faint, disembodied shout, emanating from a client somewhere far below on his rope, put Lehman instantly into a self-arrest. The pick of his Grivel ice axe was levered into the hard glacial crust and was held in a triangular vice formed by Bradford's legs, arms, and chest, pressed down against the shaft of the axe. The crampons on his boots were toed into the snow at shoulder-width. The rope was tight. He looked back over his shoulder.

"Joe, what's the matter?" Joe, and two of the clients behind him were in self-arrests. He couldn't see beyond them.

"I think Dave fell into a crevasse back there," Joe wheezed.

"Joe and the rest of you, stay down in your self-arrests," Lehman shouted. "You all did a super job of stopping Dave. I am going to get up. Don't be afraid. No one will slip."

"But the rope is so tight!" came a client's voice.

"That is normal. Stay down and in your arrest position. I'll anchor you." Bradford slowly released the pick of his ice axe, stood up, and looked back. Dave, the fourth client behind him on the rope, had stepped into a hidden crevasse and had fallen in up to his hips. Bradford knew exactly what the client was experiencing – the body wedged in the snow over a hidden crevasse – the feet swinging free, feeling for a foothold that wasn't there, dangling over hundreds of feet of dark yawning space. It had happened to Lehman countless times on glaciers.

Bradford unclipped the carabiner from the nylon web sling around his waist, planted an ice screw in the hard snow, and clipped it into the tie-in loop of his rope. His team was now anchored, and he was free to move down the line toward Dave.

"How're you doing Dave?"

"Not good. I can't get out! My legs are dangling in thin air!" There was a hint of panic in David's voice.

"No sweat my good man. We will have you out in a jiffy." Lehman called to the clients below Dave to get up and take a few steps uphill to provide slack in the rope. He took another carabiner off of his waist loop and clipped into the rope a few feet above Dave.

"Wow, you're doing great, Dave." Bradford's voice was calm, encouraging. "The solution here is simple. All you need to do is slowly lean forward as far as you can, Dave, and grab the end of this prusik sling I toss to you. Once you've got it firmly in hand, say 'go', and I'll pull you out. Got it?" Dave nodded, his mouth grimly set, and his tongue out. *I hope he doesn't bite his tongue off.* Lehman turned and leaned hard into the hill.

"Go!" Dave said.

Bradford heaved himself uphill. Dave slithered up and out of the hole in the crevasse, crawled several feet on all fours, and then stood up. His face was white.

Lehman gave him a slap on the back. "Great job my man!" Then he turned to the other clients and told them to get up. The rescue was over. It went routinely with the job of a RGS guide.

Another few rope lengths put Lehman and his team at the crater rim. As they un-roped, Bradford gathered his clients near and told them, over tearing gusts of wind, how proud he was of them. "You all did superbly, just like you were trained," he said. "You are real mountaineers now, and together you have proven we are a team." The clients' confidence soared. Their grumbling and complaining stopped. It became a good climb. *"The moral is to the physical as three to one."* Attitude rules.

7

EARLY JULY 1967: FIRST SIGNS

"We got a hit." FBI Special Agent Rubayat Castellano rolled the words out fast and flat, like dice on a crap table. Bradford Lehman was sitting in the corner of the Glacier Room Bar in the Paradise Inn, with Special Agent Castellano and John Ring. Ring and Lehman were bantering about who had the fastest summit times and the most climbs for the season. They fell silent and looked at Rube.

"What do you mean?" Lehman asked.

"First, Brad, let me tell you that John, here, is one of ours. He has been on the periphery of our investigation into the Russian activities up here, and has now been briefed deeper into them. He has a 'need to know,' as we say in our business, and is on board. You and Ring will work together from here on out. Now let me explain what I mean about the 'hit.' That little gold Eveready dry cell you've lugged up and down the mountain has given us some data."

"How can that be?" Lehman asked, perplexed. "I haven't handed it over to you guys to check out yet. It is still in my pack."

"I know, and you have been most diligent in activating it on your trips," Rube said. "What we didn't tell you at Mica Peak is that the device puts out quick burst transmissions when it is electronically interrogated on a special frequency by our reconnaissance aircraft."

"You mean spy planes?" Lehman asked.

"Yes," Rube said. He had a satisfied smile on his face. "The first squadron of SR-71 Blackbirds was recently activated down at Beale Air Force Base in Northern California. The SR-71 flies at three times the speed of sound. The bird's actual speed and altitude capabilities are classified, but it is god-awful fast." As if to offer a toast to it, Rube lifted up his glass and took a large swallow of beer. "It's a marvel, and the Russians, those sons-of-bitches, don't have anything that comes close to matching its performance." He belched. "Damn, kid, I'm still eating the chili I had six hours ago at that round building down the road here."

"The Visitor's Center."

Rube nodded. "In any event, we have flown the SR-71 over Rainier as part of its north-south mission profile, and bingo -- the Eveready worked like a charm. The SR-71 captured the data."

"Wait, Rube, does the Blackbird have a triple sonic boom?" Ring asked.

"Yes, and it is a sound to behold."

"Well," Lehman said, "I have beheld it. It sounds like part of the glacier is breaking loose. It scares the hell out of me."

"Scares the hell out of me too," Ring said.

"The point," Rube said, "is that we have an active radiation source somewhere near where you were climbing. It is weak but definitely registering as an anomaly. It has peaked a lot of interest at the SOG -- enough that we are having one made for Ranger Ring here to carry as well."

"What's the SOG?" Lehman asked.

"Sorry, kid, the acronyms slip out. It stands for 'Seat of Government' -- you know, FBI Headquarters, 'Hooverville'. And it has grabbed the attention at the CIA, the DOD, and every other three-letter outfit back in D.C. Jeez, what a cluster." Castellano looked down and shook his head. The beer and altitude at Paradise appeared to be encouraging his diatribe. He took a deep breath and continued: "I'm four expense vouchers behind, and the supervisors and clerks keep riding my ass about all the petty bullshit." He sighed. "Five more years before I'm 'KMA.'"

"What's KMA?" Ring asked.

"'Kiss My Ass....' It's Bu-speak for successfully reaching the age of retirement. It's a hell of a lot harder for the Bureau to screw with you once you are KMA. Because if they do, you can always leave, with full retirement pay. You can tell the empty-suits to go pound sand if they demand something stupid – which is what empty-suits do. That's their job. It's what defines them."

"But wouldn't that just get you in trouble?" Bradford asked.

"Naw," Rube said. "Getting an agent in 'trouble,' as you say kid, requires a lot of paperwork and effort. The supervisors know that if they do go to all that effort, the KMA agent will just retire before they can make anything stick. So being KMA is nirvana for a street agent." Castellano took a deep breath and sat back in his chair, staring at the wood plank ceiling, his eyes wishful. Then he shook his head and leaned forward. But," -- Rube raised his glass to a toast -- "screw them. Right now, I'm up here at Paradise, and in good company with you and John, and all this grand scenery. And those bastards aren't." Rube downed the last of his beer. "When does the dining room open?"

*　　*　　*

Climbing Ranger John Ring, a seasonal ranger at Mount Rainier National Park, was working summers, while finishing up his Masters Degree in Business Administration at the University of Washington. At times playful, but normally reserved, Ring was tough -- both inside and out. In 1963 he served a year in Vietnam in the 5th Special Forces Group in Kontum Province in the Central Highlands. There he had trained, organized, and led Montagnard tribesmen to fight the Viet Cong and the NVA (North Vietnamese Army). He worked closely with a cadre of CIA officers, and helped them gather intelligence on movements along the Ho Chi Minh Trail, the main supply route of the NVA into South Vietnam. He had been wounded in action. Back in the United States, with his service commitment completed, he attended college on the G.I. Bill. He kept in loose touch with some of his CIA buddies. An avid outdoorsman and climber, John Ring had summited all the major peaks in Washington State.

"So John, what did you think of the 'hit' Rube said we got from the Gold Eveready?" Bradford asked in low tones. He and Ring were sitting in corner chairs by the big fireplace in the Inn. Castellano earlier announced that he was going to bed, but had returned to the Glacier Room. Few guests or tourists were around yet, as the Dining Room was still open for dinner, and it was mid-week.

"Man, Brad, this is weird," Ring said, speaking just above a whisper. "I thought I left all that crap back in the jungle. But one thing is certain – if Castellano, and Palmrich, and Jack Rose are on this operation, it is deadly serious."

"Who is Jack Rose?" Lehman asked.

"CIA man. Rube told me that Jack may be joining the operation. I worked with him for a few weeks in Vietnam – thin build, thick glasses, erudite. Smart man, that Rose. Hell of an intellect with a rapier-like analytical mind. The shit can hit the fan and Jack remains his same imperturbable self. He and Rube only work cases coming straight from the top. Rube told me that Jack was being brought into the loop on this. Right now I guess he's somewhere in Southeast Asia – likely in Laos, up near the Plain of Jars.

"From the top -- like from McNamara?"

"Yeah, like from anywhere up there, from the President on down."

An old man shuffled over to a chair next to Lehman and Ring and sat down. Bradford stared into the fire for a moment. "Remember, John, when I used to be a guide and you used to be a ranger?"

Ring laughed. He stood up and slapped Lehman on the shoulder. "I'm heading back down to the DUB. See you later."

Teo was off-shift, dressed in a shapely tan cashmere sweater and jeans, and sitting next to Brad. He had held John's chair for her, even though it was against the rules for employees to sit in them at busy times. The big comfortable chairs were for the guests of the Inn. And it was busy, as the crowd was building to watch the talent show at nine o'clock. Lehman looked at Teo and brushed her hair back over her ear.

"How did your shift go, girl? You look radiant."

"Wow, we were short-handed tonight," Teo said, blowing her bangs up as she let her breath out through pouting lips. "Ellen didn't show up for her shift, so the rest of us had to pick up her tables."

"It doesn't matter. You still look radiant – no, beautiful!" Teo smiled and playfully squeezed Brad's knee. "Careful, girl, that's PDA, and you know PDA is against the rules."

"Rules!" She said, getting up. "Let's go for a walk."

Dusk was settling into nightfall as the couple walked out of the Inn and along the trail behind it toward Myrtle Falls. They held hands. As they passed the back of the Inn they heard a metallic crash. Lehman instinctively tapped the Walther at his waist. *It's there.*

"Look, it's a mother bear with two cubs!" Teo exclaimed. A big black bear had knocked over a garbage can and was casually rummaging through it, while the cubs rolled playfully nearby. The Inn's kitchen door flew open and Harry Pappajohn, the head chef of the Paradise Inn, came running out the door yelling in Greek and banging two large pan lids together. The sow, acting more nonchalant than scared, looked around for her cubs and herded them off around the far corner of the Inn. The door slammed, and all again was quiet. Bradford and Teo laughed, and sat down in the meadow next to the trail. A yellow gibbous moon was rising above the dark outline of the Tatoosh Range, bathing their meadow in soft silver light.

Teo leaned over and kissed Bradford long on the lips. There was passion in it -- but a controlled passion – a sensuous reserve. Lehman liked that. It spoke of character, along with affection. Clearly they had affection for each other. It was deepening.

The next day, Maloney and Lehman were off work, so Bradford took Teo on a hike over to the Paradise Ice Caves. She had never seen them, and Lehman wanted to get some practice taking pictures with his newly issued Rollei camera. The morning fog was burning off in the Paradise Valley when they left the Inn after enjoying a leisurely breakfast. They meandered along the trail through Edith Creek Basin. Lehman had his Rollei out taking pictures of the flowers and the landscape, which frequently included Teo. He loved the smooth workings of the little compact camera, with its pop-out Carl Zeiss lens, and built-in match-needle exposure meter on the top of its body. The Rollei was no bigger than a deck of cards.

As they cleared Edith Creek Basin and switch-backed up to the top of Mazama Ridge, a long line of RGS clients came streaming past, herded along by Gary Olin.

"Hi Gary, how's it going?"

"Good, Brad." Olin stopped next to Lehman. "I'll tell you what though, it sure didn't take long for McGill to ramp this trip up to the public. Strange how the entrance to the Caves was completely buried one day, and open the next."

"You're right. Herb doesn't miss an opportunity when it comes to earning a dime."

"For sure. But this Ice Caves trip is one of his most lucrative."

"Must be. Look at all the clients you have in tow," Bradford said. One man in the group caught Lehman's eye. He was bigger than the rest of the clients, well muscled, with short blond hair and a chiseled round face. "Where did you get the big boxer?" Lehman asked quietly.

"Dunno. He just showed up at the last minute. He came fully equipped, didn't need any rental boots. Paid cash, and that was it."

"Have you talked to him?"

"No, and he hasn't said a word to anyone. He'll get his camera out and take a picture once in awhile, like all the rest of the clients."

"Gary, can you do me a favor? Can you bunch all of the clients together and I'll get a group picture. You know how McGill likes his RGS marketing pictures."

"Sure." He called his clients into a group along the trail. Lehman took a few steps up the hill.

"Okay everyone, say cheese!" Bradford shot three quick pictures. "Thanks Gary. Thanks folks!" Bradford and Teo waved, turned, and headed up the trail.

The Paradise Ice Caves were formed by wind following cascading water, as it fell from an upper ridgeline into a huge snow basin. They were the largest mapped ice cave system in the world -- a complex that splayed out over ten miles long.

Lehman and Teo stopped at the entrance of the main cave and put on parkas. Bradford took Teo by the hand and stepped inside. They walked along a bubbling creek, turned left along a side chamber, and were enveloped in darkness.

"This is amazing!" Teo said. "Oh, now my eyes are adjusting to the dark. Look at that patch of purple there, and above us, green light!"

"Yes girl, near the entrance here, some light filters through the ice in spots. The colors you see are caused by the minerals in it." Lehman took off his Kelty pack, pulled out a Coleman lantern, and ignited its mantel. The hiss of the gas lantern was the only sound to be heard in this part of the cave, and as the light gained its full brightness, indentations and cupping in the ceiling and walls reflected back like mirrors. As Teo and Lehman walked, the lantern in Bradford's hand swayed, causing the walls to dance.

"This is a fairyland!" Teo said, flinging her arms around Lehman's neck and kissing him.

"Careful girl, we don't want to break the light. Then I'd have to feel my way out of here with you. That would be a long, slow, exhilarating process."

Teo slapped Bradford playfully on the shoulder. "You're bad, young man!"

"Yes, girl, but when it comes to such possibilities, red-blooded young men are." She gave him another hug and kiss.

A half hour later, Bradford and Teo re-entered the bright sunlight on the snowfield. They walked over to a big flat rock and sat down for lunch. Hikers were trickling in along the trail, and readying themselves to explore the Caves.

"Brad," Teo said softly. She looked into his eyes over her sunglasses as she handed him a sandwich: "Why am I so happy with you?"

"Who wouldn't be?"

Teo laughed and snorted, choking on her bite of sandwich. She continued to chuckle as she took a long drink of water.

"Look, girl, we have something together between us," Bradford said, his voice more reflective. "I'm new at this part of life -- meeting you, and wishing to be with you whenever I'm not. But it is natural, so I've read, when a young man and a girl..." Lehman stopped and looked Teo over, "No, not a girl -- a beautiful woman – meet, and love the same things, and take to the magic of this mountain, and Paradise and... and coalesce."

Teo moved her face close to his and placed her finger on his lips. "'Coalesce.' What an exquisitely chosen word. Well, I'm truly flattered, Brad, that you call me a beautiful woman, and even more so that the words come from an amazing man. You are, you know. I've never met anyone like you."

"Teo, we are both very young. There could be others out there we haven't met yet," Lehman smiled. "But you're right, there probably aren't, and never will be, anyone else like me." He looked at Teo over his sunglasses, and bobbed his eyebrows at her in mock flirtation. Teo threw her head back and laughed, scooped up a clump of snow below the rock they were sitting on, and plopped it on Bradford's head.

* * *

"So, John, what do you think about what's going on up here? On top of being a hell of a climber, you are a combat vet. I have no perspective on any of this." Both John Ring and Bradford Lehman were reclining on their beds in their quarters in the DUB.

"Well Brad, I may have combat experience but I have no more perspective on this than you do. Nukes on Rainier – and in our backyard, not in some obscure jungle overseas. They've got some real balls playing in our yard."

John's response surprised Lehman. *Ring was a Green Beret. He could kill people with his little finger, and he has no better insight here than I do?*

"Do you know anything about the Russian GRU?" Lehman asked.

"Only that they are the elite of the Soviet Military. It was rumored that some of the Russian voices we intercepted from the North Vietnamese Army's tactical radio communications may have been Spetsnaz, or GRU. We also had sightings on patrol, of big blond Caucasians embedded in some forward NVA fighting units.

"Big blond Caucasians," Bradford mused. "Yeah, guys like that would stick out like a sore thumb in that environment."

"Oh yes. Like a sore thumb." John spoke emphatically, as though he had witnessed it.

"But John, what would you say if you saw a big blond guy hiking along as an RGS client on a trip to the Ice Caves?"

Ring scoffed. "Wouldn't give it another thought. Big blond guys probably take that trip all the time."

"Strangely, it is a bit rare."

"How so?"

"The Ice Caves trip is the shortest and easiest the RGS offers up here. Consistently we run thirty or more clients over there on each trip. And most of them are little old men and little old ladies."

"What are you saying, Lehman?"

"I'm saying, that on a walk out to the Caves today, I passed Gary Olin with his clients. They were all over fifty years old, except one. The one exception was a big blond-haired guy who didn't speak, and didn't want to make eye contact."

"That still doesn't add up to anything, Brad."

"I agree, John. But how about this? When I got back I went into the RGS office and checked the names on the roster for the 0830 Ice Caves Trip, run by Gary Olin. One of the names was a 'G. Roskovsky.'"

Ring perked up. "That's interesting. But how would you ever hope to connect a 'Roskovsky' on the roster with the big blond guy? The name might belong to a little old Jewish lady from New Jersey."

"You're right Ring, it would be difficult. But there is one more item that may make a difference. I shot a group picture of them. Got 'em all with my new Rollei."

8

July 1967: Moving the Route, and First Love

On the way out the front door of the Henry M. Jackson Visitors Center, AKA the DUB, John Ring tossed a small plastic tube to Bradford.

"Here Lehman, your face has been taking a beating. Try this stuff instead of the Sea & Ski sunburn lotion you've been basting yourself with. It was provided by one of our good friends. Put it on a couple of times a day and you'll never get sunburned again. It's called 'sun screen.'"

"I'll give it a try John, thanks. See you on the hill."

Lehman and senior guide Gary Olin, turned to the large clump of clients in the Paradise lower parking lot. Olin led them in a long line up the Alta Vista Trail, through the flowering meadows toward the big mountain, where no flowers grew. Bradford brought up the rear. Olin set out on a "rest-step" – a slow, short, plodding walk, customary for a RGS climb. The key was to let the legs rest a fraction of a second at the top of each step. Lehman kept an eye out for clients who were scrambling with their feet, and using up energy. Nerves and anticipation led to scrambling for a new climber, and wore them out.

It was the July Fourth weekend, and McGill had stuffed the RGS summit climb roster to the maximum. Olin and Lehman were guiding a party of thirty clients. Other guides, including Lou Whittaker, were already on the hill completing their climbs, and heading back down. No one in the RGS carried radios. Only Ranger John Ring carried a heavy handheld Motorola -- "The Brick," as he called it, to communicate periodically with the Park's radio dispatch office down in Longmire. Ring was on the hill with Bill Butler, an old climbing warhorse, and a legend in the National Park Service. William Butler had worked up at Rainier with Lehman's father, back in the 1930s. He saved a score of lives in rescues on the mountain in his long career, and retrieved the bodies of a score more of those less fortunate. Though in excellent shape, Bill was in his mid-fifties and nearing retirement. He built a cabin down on Hood Canal on the Olympic Peninsula on his vacation time, and couldn't wait to get off the hill for good, and "kick my feet up by the water," as he was frequently heard to say. The slopes of Mount Rainier were a young man's venue.

Lehman's party crested Panorama Point and took a break at Pebble Creek. It was hot and sunny. Bradford squeezed the thick clear liquid out of the bottle of the sunscreen John Ring had tossed to him, and slathered it all over his face, ears, neck, and arms. He was skeptical, but if Ring swore by it, it was worth a try. Climbers and hikers swarmed all over the trails below, and on the Muir Snowfield above.

Olin looked at the crowds and back at Lehman. "Happy Fourth of July, Brad! This weekend is going to be a zoo, like always."

"Yeah, Gary, except this year the route is a real bitch, even on the Cleaver."

"Disappointment Cleaver is always a bitch," Gary shrugged.

Olin and Lehman's RGS party reached Camp Muir at three o'clock. The place was a madhouse.

"Is it always this crowded here?" one of the clients asked.

"No, it's usually worse," Lehman lied.

Higher up the hill that afternoon on Disappointment Cleaver, Lou Whittaker's party was descending off of its lower end when a client kicked a rock loose and broke the ankle of a teammate below him. Lou and RGS guide Fred Stanley were able to slowly maneuver their party and the victim down onto a flat area on the Ingraham Glacier. There they met up with rangers Butler and Ring. Ring called Longmire Dispatch, and a rescue helicopter was launched from McChord Air Force Base. At Camp Muir, around the corner on the Cowlitz Glacier, and a thousand feet lower in altitude, Lehman and Olin heard the sound of the approaching helicopter. They knew some kind of rescue was underway. Three hours later Whittaker and Stanley arrived at Muir with their bedraggled clients.

"We had a client break his leg on the Cleaver," Lou commented, in his usual thick voice. "An Air Force helicopter rescue unit came in and did the extraction, so it turned out okay. Long damned day, though."

"How is the route holding up Lou?" Olin asked.

Whittaker shook his head and smiled. "What route? We repositioned the ladders. That should work long enough for you two to get your clients through, but it's not going to hold more than a day or two. You may be the last ones up the route." Lou grabbed a cup of coffee from the Guide Hut, and then he and Fred rounded up their clients and slogged off toward Paradise.

Lehman and Olin slipped out of their bunks at midnight, dressed, ate breakfast, and rousted the clients out of their sleeping bags. They were leaving an hour ahead of schedule.

Up beyond Cathedral Gap on the Ingraham Glacier, the party encountered the fixed aluminum ladders. Weeks of use and glacier movement had warped their twenty-four foot spans, and spooked many of the clients. Lehman talked and goaded them over the gigantic crevasses, as they sat straddling the ladders' sides and scooted across. The beams of headlamps never reached the bottoms of these yawning dark holes – they faded out in the blackness. *Probably just as well they can't see,* Bradford thought.

Finally, past the ladders, the party swung northeast onto the lower nose of Disappointment Cleaver. The clients' rope teams were coiled tightly together to avoid kicking rocks onto each other. They followed a fixed rope for three hundred feet, before zigzagging up the steep scree and snow of the Cleaver, to its crest at twelve thousand three hundred feet. The party took its first long break there, as a hint of dawn colored the eastern sky. Other private parties were also on the route and their headlamps made up a string of tiny winking lights that draped the mountain for more than three thousand vertical feet -- from Cathedral Gap, extending all the way to the bergschrund above Lehman's party at over thirteen thousand feet. Bradford curled up on the hard snow and slept.

A man was coming at him. He was huge, smiling, taunting, relentless. Lehman swung wildly with his ice axe but it merely glanced off the hulking figure. No matter how hard Lehman fought, the man kept coming -- smiling, taunting, relentless. Bradford started awake, gasping for breath.

"You must have been dreaming," Olin said, sitting next to him. "You kicked your leg and your crampons barely missed me."

"Sorry, Gary," Lehman said groggily. He checked his watch. He had only been asleep five minutes.

"Saddle up! Let's go, the summit awaits!" Olin announced to the clients. Lehman got up slowly, shouldered his Kelty, and spoke to his rope team. "Let the ropes uncoil, now that we are back on the glacier. Watch your teammates, and keep the slack out of the rope like you were trained."

The next thousand feet brought steep ice and large crevasses. They topped out of that pitch, traversed left above a huge serac, and followed the rutted climbing trail to two crossed wands marking an "X" at the snow bridge over the bergschrund. The bridge, spanning fifteen feet and steeply angled where it connected to the uphill lip of the crevasse, was clearly on its last legs. A large blue supporting plug of ice, and combed with icicles, was now gone, swallowed by the huge maw of the bergschrund. The party tiptoed over the remnants of the bridge, and slogged on toward the crater rim. All the while, private climbers of all shapes and abilities stumbled around and through the RGS rope teams, headed both up and down the mountain. An hour later put Lehman and Olin, and their RGS charges, on Rainier's summit.

Lehman ate his lunch and scanned the crater rim, watching for anything out of the ordinary. The problem was, there was very little that could be considered "ordinary" about a Fourth of July weekend climb of Rainier. *Be vigilant, Lehman.* He dozed off with the sandwich in his hand, half-eaten. An hour later he was back across the crater with Olin, corralling the clients and roping them up for the trip down.

"Gary, did you see anything interesting while you were lounging around and I was sleeping?"

"Not really. There was a mirror flash on one side of the crater about a half hour ago that was answered by one on the other side. You know, 'I flash you, you flash me,' dopey stuff. Celebrating the Fourth, no doubt." Three loud sonic booms sounded from high up in the stratosphere. Lehman looked up, shielding his eyes from the sun, trying to locate the SR-71. There was nothing. *It is probably already up by the Canadian Border by now*, Bradford thought. The party headed down the hill, and dragged itself into Camp Muir at two o'clock that hot afternoon.

John Ring stepped out of his ranger tent and greeted the party. "Hi Gary and Brad, glad to have your group back without mishap. Brad, I got a call on the radio from your boss McGill. He requested that you stay with me tonight and help me scout the Gibraltar route tomorrow. Effective today, the Park Service is closing the mountain to all private parties. Bill Butler dropped the hammer on the Dog Route. It's too dangerous. I concur."

Olin looked at Lehman and back at Ring. "We do too," Gary intoned,

his voice revealing fatigue. "Brad, I'll herd the clients back to Paradise. Good luck up there on the ledges. The Gib Route is going to be a bitch as well." He turned and began organizing the clients to leave.

John Ring moved into the Guide Hut, and started cooking dinner. He wanted to let Lehman rest.

"Damn, Ring, you're using up a whole box of matches there," Bradford said wearily. You're a Ranger. You should only need one match."

"Why is it that only one careless match can start a forest fire, and it takes a whole freaking box to start a stove or a campfire?" Ring asked, frustrated.

"I don't know, Smokey the Bear, that's an interesting philosophical question. Let me ponder it…." Bradford collapsed on a bunk, his boots and crampons still on, and fell instantly asleep. He awoke at eight the next morning to the smell of coffee, sausage, and powdered eggs. Lehman looked down at his feet. Crampons were sticking out of the end of his sleeping bag. "Why the hell are my boots and crampons still on?"

John looked at him with a wry grin. "Because you were dead out when you got back to the hut and I didn't want to wake you. I unzipped a sleeping bag and put it over you, like a blanket. You must have kicked a little during the night. The crampons poked through the bag. I got a picture of it!" Ring said, still smiling.

"Jeez, I can't believe I didn't take my boots off. McGill is going to crap if he sees his bag all torn up like this," Bradford complained, as he reached down and yanked the end of it off of his crampon spikes.

"Naw, he rarely comes up here, and he buys cheap bags for the RGS clients anyway. He can buy another cheap one. That aside, it is a great morning for scouting the Gib route, partner. Let's eat."

Lehman had slept seventeen hours straight. Now he was ravenously hungry.

"Man, I haven't seen anyone eat that much in a long time," Ring said, as he and Lehman roped up.

"I'm carrying an extra ten pounds in my gut -- but it feels good," Bradford said.

The two men roped up and departed Camp Muir moving quickly, and climbed straight up the Cowlitz Glacier. Lehman led.

"Sorry I wasn't much for conversation last night," Lehman said.

"That's okay Brad, you needed sleep. But it did make me blue that we couldn't talk."

"Whenever I'm blue, I just make sure I start breathing again."

"Wise-ass."

"Hey, John, that sunscreen you gave me is a miracle. I didn't have any sunburn at all after putting it on. Who gave it to you?"

"Rube handed me a couple of tubes of the stuff. He said it wasn't cleared yet by the FDA. He got it from some contact he had in Canada. You're right, it is amazing. No peeling, no blisters anymore."

"Damn that felt good to get a good night's sleep. My legs are on fire, but the walk today will do me good. Say, how did the rescue go a couple of days ago?" Lehman had now walked himself fully awake.

"Good. You know Butler is a class act. He and Whittaker had the whole process wired. Lou shouldered the victim and carried him over the ladders by himself. He's incredibly strong."

"I saw the orange dye patch in the snow up on Ingraham Flats, where the landing zone was. How did the chopper perform?"

"The pilot was amazing. He brought that bird in on the first pass, set it down, we loaded the victim, and the chopper took off. The whole pickup took no more than five minutes. You know they use those double-bladed helicopters out of McChord. The one that did the pickup this time was not painted the usual gray, but in jungle green camouflage. Looks as though the unit is getting ready to deploy to Vietnam."

"Things are definitely heating up there," Lehman said.

"Isn't it great to be climbing again for a change instead of guiding?" Ring asked.

"Sure is. Two totally different endeavors. Climbing is about mountains in people. Guiding is about people in mountains."

"Well stated, young Lehman. You are quite the philosopher."

"What a bull-shitter you are, Ring. It's bound to get you promoted."

Lehman and Ring zigzagged around several crevasses on the steepening upper end of the Cowlitz Glacier, climbed the talus slope beyond, and reached Camp Misery at eleven thousand six hundred feet.

Camp Misery was aptly named. Perched on a high notch separating Cowlitz Cleaver from Gibraltar Rock, the camp was little more than a flat bivouac spot that was routinely raked by high winds. On this day the wind was mild. Bradford and John sat down and checked the equipment cache that Ring and Butler had packed up there the week before, in anticipation of closing the Disappointment Cleaver route: ice pickets, a five-pound sledge hammer, rock helmets, a fifteen-foot aluminum ladder, six hundred feet of seven-sixteenth-inch goldline climbing rope, one thousand feet of quarter-inch nylon line, rock pitons, ice screws, a bundle of five hundred marker wands, and a medical kit.

"You cached a medical kit up here. Nice touch, Ring,"

"Thanks. And there are some extra Eveready six-volt dry cell batteries in there too."

"Any special gold ones?"

"No Brad, you and I have the only two around here that I know of," Ring chuckled. "Rube gave me mine three days ago, as I was walking out of the parking lot to do this gig."

As they had a bite to eat and took a short break, Lehman and Ring pulled out their "Gold Eveready" radiation sensors. Bradford familiarized Ring on their functions.

"Man, I had no idea the government was putting this amount of money and resources into this operation," Ring said. "They're playing some serious hardball here, using custom sensors like these, and a SR-71."

"It sure seems like the big leagues to me. But isn't it ironic?"

"How so, Brad?"

"To put so much money and sophisticated technology into this project -- and to turn around, and rest the whole damned thing on two clowns like us?"

Ring, who was taking a drink from his water bottle, choked, and fell on his side.

"Let's go check the rappel point," Lehman said.

They scrambled a few hundred feet above Camp Misery to a broad rock ledge leading around the western face of Gibraltar. This ledge had been the crux to the Gibraltar route on Rainier since the 1890s. In 1938, however, a thirty-foot section of the ledge collapsed, and a fixed rope was placed in the void to allow climbers to drop twenty feet down to the next lower ledge.

Bradford whistled. "This rappel point is an accident or a death waiting to happen, John. Look up, there's a thousand feet of crumbling rock above us, and this is a perfect funnel for it."

Ring looked up, and nodded thoughtfully. "I agree. You've been up this route more than I, Brad. What should we do?"

"The day is young," Lehman said, glancing at his watch. "We should explore a little, and see if we can access that lower ledge from a less exposed location."

Lehman and Ring walked back to Camp Misery and began searching west along the Cowlitz Cleaver where it bordered the

Gibraltar Chute. Three hundred feet over, and fifty feet down, they picked up the contour line of the ledge.

"Here is a short drop-off down to the ledge, and it isn't exposed to rock-fall," Ring said.

"John, that looks perfect." Lehman said, as he walked up and inspected it. He slapped Ring on the back. "Let's go grab the ladder and gear, and get this route in."

Over the next three hours, Lehman and Ring fixed the aluminum ladder into the rock face with pitons and nylon line. They then scrambled north along the lower ledge for three hundred yards, until it merged with the Gibraltar Chute. There they placed a fixed rope at the access point. Working together, but un-roped to speed their progress, Lehman and Ring fixed another three hundred vertical feet of rope into the fifty-degree ice pitch of the Chute's upper neck. This section was anchored with aluminum pickets, pounded in behind a snow bollard they chopped out with ice axes. It was now three o'clock. There came a sudden *Boom-Boom-Boom*, heralding a passing SR-71.

"Shit, that scared me!" Ring exclaimed. "That sonic boom sounds like the rock-fall we have dodged all day long."

"Well, Ring, you and I have apparently made our most recent contributions to the safety of the free world. The Blackbird just sucked the data up from our little Gold Geiger Counters. I feel safer already. Don't you?"

"Oh yeah, I feel so much safer," John said, rolling his eyes. "Hey, Brad, we've got the main part of this route nailed in. Let's get the hell off this thing and back to Camp Muir.

"I'm game. Give me some of the wands in your pack, John. We'll mark the route real good on the way down to help out the RGS party headed up here day after tomorrow."

Lehman and Ring were back down at Camp Muir in an hour and a half. This time, Bradford took off his boots and crampons. John pulled out the large portable Motorola radio, stored in the RGS Guide Hut, and called down to Longmire Dispatch.

"Longmire, this is CR2 (Climbing Ranger 2), come in."

"CR2, this is Longmire, go ahead."

"Be advised that the Gibraltar Route has been fixed, and is now marked, and passable. We did not wand from the top of Gibraltar to the summit, but that section looks straightforward, and should pose no problems. Copy?"

"Copy, CR2, good job. CR1 (Bill Butler) advises you come down tonight and take your day off tomorrow. You are due for a rest."

"Copy, Longmire. I'll be on my way, over."

"CR2, advise Lehman to stay the night at Muir and come back tomorrow, when the next RGS summit party arrives there, so he can brief them on the new route, copy?" Lehman nodded.

"Lehman acknowledges. CR2 out."

"Longmire out."

Ring switched off the Breadbox and put it away. "Sorry Brad, I had hoped we might grab a couple of beers tonight in the Glacier Room. We'll tip a couple tomorrow night okay?"

"Okay, John, thanks for the break today. It's the first time in weeks I have climbed with a colleague. I really enjoyed it."

"Me too, Brad." Ring put his pack on, waved, and swung off in long plunging strides, down the Muir Snowfield toward Paradise.

Lucky bastard, Bradford thought. *I could be down there in no time too -- and enjoying the company of a beautiful woman.* He felt himself longing for Teo. It was the first time he had experienced that emotion. Bradford, like other young men his age, dated and had occasional girlfriends. But Teo was different. He closed his eyes and the details of her face were instantly and vividly in his mind. It made him feel hollow inside, and he forced himself to move to overcome the feeling.

Lehman turned back into the hut, opened a can of beef stew, and began heating it on the propane stove. The contrast of this day with the July Fourth weekend, could not have been more striking. Then, Camp Muir was crawling with people. Today, only Lehman was here. He looked over at Muir Peak, standing one hundred feet higher, and marking the southwest edge of the saddle where the huts were situated. The big black raven that had made Muir his summer residence for as long as Lehman remembered, was perched proudly on the top, as was his habit during good weather. The raven was a harbinger of bad weather. Even before his Thommen altimeter's sensitive needle registered the slightest drop in barometric pressure, the stately black bird sensed the coming of bad weather. Spreading his broad wings, he would leap off his rock perch, and gracefully ride the wind currents to lower ground near Paradise. Rarely, there were times when the raven would depart Camp Muir, sensing something other in the air than bad weather. Otherwise he was a loyal tenant at camp.

Just you and me, big guy. Bradford whistled and tossed a piece of bread, swathed in peanut butter, out onto the rocks. The big bird spread his graceful wings, swooped down, and accepted the offering. He did not pick up the bread and fly away, but stood a mere ten feet away, and casually ate it. Lehman smiled. *He's thinking the same thing – 'Just you and me, big guy.'*

Bradford went back into the hut, stirred the beef stew, filled a big jug with water, and walked outside with a bar of soap and a towel. It was time to clean off some of the sweat and grit he had accumulated over the past few days.

Lehman sat on the front steps of the Guide Hut, coffee in hand. It felt good to get clean, and the cold melted snow water used in the process left him invigorated. The waning western sun burnished the rocks and the Public Hut. He turned and looked down the Muir snowfield. Down past Anvil Rock, at Moon Rocks, a solitary figure was climbing toward Muir. The pace of the hiker was quick and steady. Lehman stepped inside, grabbed the binoculars, and looked. *It's Teo!* He ducked back inside the hut, slipped on his boots, and jogged down the snowfield in long bounding strides. He met her below Anvil Rock and gave her a bear hug.

"Teo! What are you doing here?"

"I came to see you," she said, breathlessly. He picked her up off her feet, spun her around, and slipped. They both fell down in the snow, laughing.

"Come on girl!" Bradford lifted Teo to her feet, took her pack, slung it over one shoulder, and grabbed her hand. Side-by-side they trudged on to Muir. Tomorrow was Teo's day off.

Lehman stopped with her at the entrance to the Guide Hut. Dusk descended over the vastness of the mountain, lustering its color into a deep alpenglow rose. It played around the delicate features of the soft oval face and dark silken hair of the woman standing in front of him. He pulled her gently to his chest and held her. Then he took her head in his hands and kissed her on the lips. It was a long, longing, caressing kiss that blended tenderly into the stillness of the air, the earth, and the fading light.

Teo sat next to Bradford on the steps of the hut, her fingers folded around a steaming mug of coffee. They gazed south toward Paradise.

"Look at all the stars," she said. "Even with no moon yet tonight, I can easily see our tracks on the snow. It's amazing how much light the stars put out."

Lehman nodded. "I often turn my headlamp off on a climb and let the moon or stars light the way, if the track is well defined -- like it is by this time of the season -- it's easy to see. It takes some getting used to. Depth perception changes under star or moonlight. Sometimes you look at a shadow on the snow, and think it is hollow like a sun cup. But when you place your foot there, it's actually a lump. Strange." There was a long pause.

"I have been worried about you Brad." Teo spoke softly, placing her hand on his back. "You've been working so hard putting these climbs in, and I know you must be exhausted – and I miss you!" She leaned over and kissed him.

"I've missed you too, girl. The normal route was falling apart, so we've had to put more time in up here resetting the trail and the ladders. Now the Park closed Disappointment Cleaver, so John Ring and I spent today up on Gibraltar, opening up that route.

"I know, John told me about it. I met him near the top of Panorama Point and we chatted. He's a great guy."

"Yes, John Ring is a great guy, and a damned good climbing ranger."

"He said it was a joy to climb with you today."

"Likewise, for sure." Lehman stood up and stretched. "Let's go in, pretty lady. Look girl, you and I have known each other only for a few weeks, and most of that time we've spent away from each other. I want you to sleep here with me tonight. I am not going to put any moves on you…" Bradford paused, looked into Teo's eyes, and smiled. "You can take any bunk you want, and I will take another. You can't know how happy I am that you are here." Teo   smiled back. "I think I can," she said, with a faint smile. Lehman laughed, reached out, and messed up Teo's hair.

"I want that lower bunk there, and I want you in it with me," Teo said. Her voice was firm and emphatic.

Bradford zipped two RGS sleeping bags together, and laid them on the bunk.

"Turn off the lantern please," Teo asked.

Lehman turned the nob on the Coleman lantern, and the light went out with a little "pop." It was pitch dark. He pulled off his climbing pants, slid the Walther pistol out of the waistband holster, and carefully placed it high on the top of a cabinet by the door. He left his long underwear on. He turned to get into the bunk and stubbed his toe on its metal leg. He swore. They both laughed, and he crawled in next to Teo. She was in her long underwear top and bottoms, the same as he. They kissed. The warmth of her soft body next to Bradford flowed into him. It magically washed away all apprehensions that bedeviled his mind: the clients, the disintegrating routes on the mountain, the FBI operation, the fatigue. Simultaneously, the wisdom of the words spoken by Castellano was full on his mind -- to be careful. So too was the sorrowful example of his father and mother, whose lives, and those of his and his sisters, were unceasingly darkened by a one-night stand at Paradise long ago. *I am too young and inexperienced to judge what is right in love, and what isn't. Be careful.*

"Teo, thank you so much for coming," Bradford repeated himself, awkwardly.

"The pleasure is mine," she said.

They lay still next to each other. Lehman turned on a flashlight and let its light shine off of the rough plank ceiling of the hut. "I am afraid," Bradford finally said.

"I am too -- a little," Teo replied.

"Why, girl?"

"Because of where we are: together, here, now. It is scary. I have never been to bed with a man before. I have never even been alone with a man for a whole night."

"I have. Believe me, it is *way* over-rated."

Teo laughed, and let out a little snort. She put her hands to her face and kicked her legs out of embarrassment.

"So why did you make the decision to come up and see me?" Lehman said softly.

"Just to see you. I miss you. I didn't know for sure that we would be alone. But it did cross my mind as a possibility. When I met John down at Pebble Creek… Then I knew we would be alone. I could have turned around, but my feet wouldn't let me. They demanded that I continue. John must have sensed what I was thinking, because he said 'I know Brad will be thrilled to see you.'" She smiled, and looked into Lehman's eyes. "Why are you here in bed with me now, Brad?"

"Because I miss you. I miss being with you. I see your face whenever I close my eyes. I miss your touch, your looks, your wit, your happy spirit, your companionship." His voice trailed off as he looked at her. *Kiss her, Bradford.*

Lehman stroked Teo's hair, ran his finger down her forehead along the bridge of her nose, and touched her lips. They were soft, open. He let his lips close on hers, first tentatively, then more firmly. Teo's breath quickened. He kissed her neck and moved her top aside to kiss her shoulder. Bradford switched off the flashlight. The darkness of the hut was textured now with a gloss of moonlight shining through the small glass window. He let his hands slide onto her ample breasts, which rose gently with her breathing and pressed around his fingers. Her mouth opened now as she kissed. She let her tongue rest against his. She felt the power of his broad shoulders, and ran her hands down the outsides of his lean muscular arms. She smelled the freshness of the Nivea Cream on his wind-burned face, and felt his passion in the measured rising of his breath.

"Teo, I don't, I've never..." Lehman pulled away.

Teo placed her finger on his lips. "Hush," she said softly. "I haven't either. But I have started on the pill. There is a time Bradford. You took my dad and me up Mount Rainier last summer. I dreamed of you when I went back home. But of course, you were far away in another state and on the mountain. I had a boyfriend back in California, but I broke up with him. He pushed too hard to make love. He didn't care about me, only himself. I'm not like that. Neither are you. My old boyfriend wasn't worth it. But *you*, my handsome man -- *are*." Teo's hair fell back around her on the pillow. Her dark eyes shined in the moon's embracing silver light. "You are the guide," she whispered. "Lead me."

Bradford Lehman and Teo Maloney, both eighteen years old, began their loving experience in an old stone hut, high on a big mountain. Their youthful hands and bodies moved, touched, and reveled, bringing to reality what each had imagined making love should be like -- somewhere they loved to be, with someone they respected, and with the alluring promise that living in a magnificent moment may lead to others more lasting -- to love itself perhaps.

Teo was overcome with the power of Bradford's control, and of his consummate concentration on fulfilling her. He listened to her building delight and danced to it. It was evident by his lovemaking that Bradford cared for Teo with a deep perceptive intensity, and shared with her who he was in the same measure.

The fleeting hours of the night bore witness, until, as the new day carried its brightening light through the small window, the two spent lovers slept happily in each other's arms.

Lehman got up at nine o'clock, and made coffee and breakfast as quietly as possible, thinking Teo was asleep. But she lay quietly, watching his mannerisms and movements.

"Bradford?"

"Yes girl?" He poured her a mug of coffee and brought it to her. She raised herself up on one elbow to take the cup, and the sleeping bag slipped off her shoulders. She made no effort to cover up.

"That was the most wonderful, incredible, fantastic experience I have ever had. You sure know how to lead! That couldn't have been your first time!" Teo smiled coquettishly.

"One may easily make the same observation of you, young lady," Lehman kidded, as he sat down on the bunk next to her, pulled the sleeping bag back up around her shoulders, and kissed her on the forehead. Then he looked into her large dark eyes. "It was my first time. I waited, like you, and I can only echo your words and add to them. You are beautiful, Teo. It springs from the inside, from your kindness, warmth, and wit. But I'll tell you what, girl. You are a marvel to behold." He reached into the warm sleeping bag, cupped her breast in his hand and kissed her. Teo took a deep happy breath, fell back onto the bunk, and opened up the bag.

"I'm ready again," she said, "Come, my amazing, handsome guide. It's cold here in my birthday suit. Let's warm up!"

An hour later, Lehman and Teo sat together in the sunshine, watching the next party of RGS clients cross Pebble Creek and plod their way toward Muir. Bradford put the binoculars on them.

"Looks like McPherson has a sizeable group in tow for a mid-week climb. I count twelve all together."

"What can we do to get the place ready for them?" Teo asked, her arm around Lehman's shoulder.

"You clean up the hut, and I'll get the climbing ropes out and set them up for tomorrow."

Bradford retrieved four one-hundred-fifty-foot goldline ropes from the storage alcove in the back of the hut. He strung them out full length and parallel to each other on the adjacent Cowlitz Glacier. Then he walked the length of each one, passing the rope through his hands, carefully inspecting it for cuts or fraying, and tied the knots and loops that each of McPherson's clients would clip into.

"I made a new pot of coffee for you, Brad." Teo's voice called him back.

RGS Guides Don McPherson, and Jay Olin -- Gary's younger brother -- plodded up the last few feet to Camp Muir with their clients. Don's primary expertise was on rock. Six feet tall and rail-thin, with unruly thick black hair, McPherson was in his mid-thirties. He had achieved several big-wall first ascents, the most notable of which was a highly technical climb of Liberty Crack, on Liberty Bell, in the North Cascades. Jay Olin, at five feet ten, was a little shorter than his older brother Gary. He had rugged good looks, dark blond hair, and a fair complexion. His face and lips were perpetually sunburned. Like Gary, he was a highly experienced climber and guide.

Lehman briefed Don and Jay on the new route, and on the changed location of the ladder farther down below Camp Misery.

"Good job Brad," Jay said. "And thanks for laying out the ropes for our teams. We'll get the clients up and out of here early."

"We are going to have to allow a lot more time to summit this hill on the Gib route," Don said.

"Speaking of getting out of here," Jay added, looking over at Teo in the Guide Hut doorway, and giving Lehman a smile, "you need to. McGill has scheduled you for the next two days off."

Bradford and Teo descended the Muir Snowfield in fast happy strides. They kidded, laughed, and also talked seriously about school, friends, and families, and ended up in discussions about history, and the courses they intended to take. Other hikers and climbers were headed up to Muir, and Lehman observed all the men intently as he passed them. *Like trying to find a Russian in a haystack,* he chuckled to himself. He felt the holster inside the waistband of his wool knickers to confirm that his Walther pistol was there. *"Is that your gun in there, or are you just happy to see me?"* he imagined Teo asking. And she would ask, because their friendship -- and now intimacy -- would inevitably take her there. He pondered shifting the weapon to the shoulder-strap holsters on his Kelty, but he liked it in the waistband because he could feel it there, and it gave him a better sense of security and control over it. *Insecure bastard.* Lehman smiled. He knew that one of two things must happen if the FBI operation heated up: either he would have to push Teo away, and not tell her why; or she must be briefed into the operation.

I have to bring Teo in. Rube won't be happy. But that's life. I need her. I can't afford to miss her. Lehman knew this was purely selfish on his part – to bring someone, innocent and unwitting, into a dangerous operation. But Lehman also sensed that Teo was up to taking the step. *Hell, Bradford, the devastation of a nuke going off up here will take us all anyway – in a bright, flashing, blink of an eye. And if we are close enough to our enemies and fail, we will be converted directly from matter into pure nuclear energy in a millionth of a second.* Lehman made up his mind. He felt himself relaxing.

Bradford pulled Teo into the trees on Alta Vista, perched above the Paradise Inn, and kissed her. She looked at him with happy surprise.

"Teo," Lehman said, stroking her jet-black hair, "I'll go back to the DUB and get organized and cleaned up. You do the same here at the Inn. Then I'll be up to see you. I will meet you next to the Malt Shop in a couple hours – say, twelve-thirty, okay?"

Teo smiled, took Lehman's sunglasses off, and looked into his eyes. "Gray-blue. Beautiful. Twelve-thirty." She kissed him.

9

An Hour Later: A Bear in the Park

"We have more interesting information," Special Agent Rubayat Castellano remarked casually. "My counterparts are indisposed for this meeting, and could not make it." Castellano, Lehman, and Ring were sitting in the corner of the bar. Castellano faced the door, keeping an eye on it, even though the door was locked. It was 1130 hours. No one else but Bruce the bar tender was in the room. Rube saw Ring and Lehman glancing at Bruce.

Castellano asked Bruce to take a break. Bruce left the room.

"Good call, guys, I forgot about Bruce. You are both becoming security-conscious. That's a good sign. Bruce is an asset of mine, checked out, vetted, all that crap, but he's not allowed to overhear our conversations." Rube smiled. "Ruskies like to drink, so the first person we want in our pocket is the bar tender. The next nearest bar from this place is outside the Park entrance at the Gateway Inn, eighteen long miles away."

"Did you say Longmire?" Lehman chided.

"No, wise ass, *long miles.*"

"How do you like your new Chevy Caprice?" Ring asked. "Looks good in the parking lot up here. Completely unofficial-looking."

Rube eyed John warily, unsure if Ring was serious. Deciding that he was, Rube answered. "The beast drives like a charm. Had it up to one hundred and fifteen miles an hour on a straight stretch coming out of Tacoma."

"What's up Rube?" Bradford asked. "It must be something important, if you're driving like that with the Caprice."

"We got the film processed that you sent us, along with a copy of the RGS Ice Caves Roster with the name 'G. Roskovsky' on it. And guess what?" Rube lowered his voice, and leaned forward over his beer with a toothy grin. "He is Genady Roskovsky, a GRU Major working as a Soviet Military Attaché, a 'SMAT,' as we call them. He is stationed at the Russian embassy in Washington D.C. 'State'-- that's the United States State Department for short," Rube nodded to Lehman -- "State approved his official request to travel to Seattle to visit the Boeing plant there, or some bullshit. But guess what? Just as the CIA gets your film developed, State calls saying that the Boeing liaison representative there reported that Roskovsky never showed up."

"Doesn't the FBI routinely tail SMAT men?" Ring asked.

"Hell yes!" Castellano said, his face flushed. "But we didn't receive the damned Teletype lead until yesterday. Typical bullshit. State takes its sweet time notifying the FBI. Bunch of empty-suits over there."

"What's an empty-suit Rube?" Lehman asked.

"An empty-suit is some supervisor or muckety-muck, regardless of the agency, who is totally incompetent to work the street. So he gets promoted, and keeps getting promoted, because he's a suck up, until he eventually gets to the top. That's why street agents use the expression 'Empty-suits float to the top'." Rube punctuated his rant by taking a long swig of beer. "Anyway, if you are ever showering up after a workout at the gym, and a State Department guy walks in, don't drop the soap." He took another drink, let out a long sigh, and continued. "So, young Bradford, you covered our lead. Great work out there. I can't show you the pictures you took of the Ice Caves group here, but in the first two Mister Roskovsky hunkered down in the back row. But in your last shot he stood up, and you nailed him."

"So now what?" Lehman asked. Ring looked at Rube, seconding the question.

Castellano lowered his voice again. "First, we need to ask ourselves 'what does this indicate'? The 'now what' follows that. Major Roskovsky took a big risk in coming up to Mount Rainier. Empty-suits don't like taking big risks, especially by themselves, because it could jeopardize their careers. How big a risk was it for Genady? The FBI would have arrested him and 'PNG'd' him back to Moscow on the spot. Sorry, kid. PNG in our business stands for Persona Non Grata, meaning 'unwelcome person' in Latin. All the Diplomats love Latin and French terms for what they do. Lipstick on a pig, you know. I wonder if there's a Latin phrase for 'Screw the Pooch'? You can be damned sure the French have one." Agent Castellano took another swig of his beer. "Anyway, it is now clear that whatever the GRU is up to on this mountain is of extremely high priority. And this gives credence to Bob's theory that the Russians are planting a nuke up there -- or are attempting to. By the way Lehman, McNamara sends his regards. And he told me to tell you and Ring that you're doing great work."

"So he likes me, and will keep me safe up here and out of the Vietnam War?" Lehman joked. Rube, taking a drink, spit out part of his beer and cleaned it up with a napkin.

"Ha! That's a good one kid!" He slapped the table with a big meaty hand. "Bradford, he likes you, but not enough to keep you out of the war. He likes the fact that you and Ring are proving his theory – winning his arguments for him, with all the bureaucrats and politicians back in D.C. Your identification of a SMAT GRU agent up here bolsters his theory, and Hoover's, that the Russians are targeting the mountain. So, I will pose the question to you two gentlemen: what does this mean?" Rube went quiet, letting the question sink in.

"That someone in their outfit screwed up," Ring said. "That's the only reason they would risk sending a supervisor up here."

"Excellent point, John, my thought precisely," Rube said. "What about you, kid?"

Lehman was staring down at the table. He looked up. "Yes, it may mean that -- but it could be more. John, you know first-hand that the routes on Rainier this summer are shot to hell. The Park Service has just closed the mountain to private parties. Now, think of this thing from the Russian's perspective. No matter how good they are as killers or climbers, they don't have a clue compared to the RGS guides about Mount Rainier -- its routes, its history, its weather. I believe that if they are targeting a location somewhere high on the mountain, the route and the shitty climbing conditions we are experiencing this summer has them fit to be tied. If, like Rube says, the Russians are even more bureaucratic than we, I'll bet that some 'empty-suit' back in -- Moscow Center, is it?"

Rube nodded approvingly.

"-- That some clown in Moscow Center is sitting back there with a schedule to get things done. And whoever they have sent over here to get it done is failing to meet the schedule."

Castellano reached over and shook Lehman's hand. "Brilliant, kid! There may be no limit to what you could accomplish as a FBI

Special Agent someday, as long as you are not concerned with all the others who will claim the credit for your work… So let me finish the scenario for you. The empty-suits at Moscow Center don't know or give a shit about the conditions on Mount Rainier. If Genady's boys won't do the job, Genady's career is in the crapper. He'll be overseeing an outpost somewhere in Outer Mongolia, counting goat turds. And what does that mean?"

"It means that Genady is getting desperate," Ring replied.

"And because of that," Lehman added, "he will be putting more pressure on his agents up here. And that means the Russians will be taking more chances, and making more mistakes on the hill."

"Exactly!" Rube said. "So keep your eyes peeled. And remember, Russians who are desperate are doubly dangerous." Now finish your beers, or I will. I have to get out of here and write all this crap up, along with my damned expense vouchers."

"Hang on a minute, Rube," Lehman said, as Ring got up and left the bar. Castellano sat back down. "I have an issue to bring up."

"What's the matter kid, been letting the wrong head do your thinking?" Rube smiled.

"Not really. But I now have a girl up here who I really like, and…"

"And you had sex with her. Protected, right?"

"Yes, but –"

"But what, kid? You can't tell her anything, remember that."

"Yes, but I carry that Walther PPK in my front waistband. It's only a matter of time before she finds it."

Castellano smiled. Then he turned serious, thinking. "It's Teo Maloney, isn't it?"

"Yes."

"She's a beauty. And a nice kid too. If I were twenty years younger, and in your shape… Let me think on this. I'll plead your case to the empty-suits. Maybe we can brief her in, and sign her to a nondisclosure. I will be back in a week, same time, same place. Maybe I'll have a CIA weenie with me. He can buy the beer for a change." Rube gave Lehman's shoulder a squeeze. "I understand your situation, Brad. I was young once. Hang in there. I know you will."

Bradford checked in with McGill at the RGS to confirm that he had the next two days off, and was happy to learn that he was not scheduled for a summit climb for the next week. He threw his dirty clothes into the wash, and walked back up to the Inn. It was twelve-thirty.

10

LATER THE SAME DAY: SETTING THE BEAR TRAP

"Hi, splendid woman!" Lehman said.

"Hi my wonderful guide!" Teo beamed.

Bradford bought them both milkshakes from the malt shop and they drank them out on the benches at the Inn's main entrance. The stable weather was holding. Tourists exited the bright red Mount Rainier tour busses parked in front of the Inn, and filed past, chattering excitedly.

"Good to be back?" Lehman asked.

"No, I have to go back to work tomorrow," Teo pouted.

"Well, we've got a few hours left before that," Bradford said, leaning over and nudging Teo off balance. "What say we hop in my car and drive somewhere?"

Lehman put the convertible top down on his little Triumph Herald, and drove several winding miles down from Paradise. He turned left onto the Stevens Canyon Road, and stopped at Reflection Lake. For a time, they both sat on the hood of the car, quietly taking in the image of Mount Rainier. The big mountain was majestically framed, both in its reflection on the still water, and by the alpine firs that folded in around it on either side.

"Perfect for a picture. Teo, stand over there." He pulled the Rollei out of his pocket and clicked the shutter. "Want to walk around the lake?"

"Sure!" Teo strode over and grabbed Bradford's arm, hugging it against her. "I can't get over last night. It happened way up there." She pointed toward Camp Muir, whose stone huts were swallowed up in the dark smudge of rock lining the saddle at the top of the Muir Snowfield, six thousand vertical feet above them. "You are very good as a guide, Brad, but you temper that with a great sense of humor. You are the same as a lover!" Teo closed her eyes, smiling. It was a dreamy, fulfilled smile.

"You are a very beautiful young lady, and you temper that with humor too," Bradford said, covering a tinge of embarrassment.

Teo turned and looked at him. "But you are actually a very shy person aren't you, Bradford?"

"Yes, Teo. You would not have given me a second look if we were in High School together."

"Oh, sure I would have!"

"No, because you are reserved as well, even though you were the prettiest girl in the school. So you wouldn't have approached me -- and I certainly wouldn't have approached you -- because I am shy, and you are beautiful." Bradford pressed her nose with his index finger.

Teo blushed. "But you are so strong, and wise for your age, Bradford, and *really* handsome too. And that makes you the most incredible lover!" She kissed him softly, sensuously.

Lehman held her face, framing it in his cupped hands. "We must remember, girl. We do not yet have the perspective of age or experience in these things."

"I know, Brad," Teo said, and then added with an impish smile, "but we sure have the hots for each other. There's perspective in that!"

*   *   *

Late that same afternoon Lehman sat down for a beer with John Ring to consider Castellano's latest intelligence information.

"It looks as though we're going to have to think like Russian agents now," Ring said. "What do you envision their next steps will be, Brad?"

"For starters, they might place an agent on a RGS summit climb. Odds are, the GRU has no clue about the Gib Route. That means they only have two options: The agents can pay their dues, and climb with the RGS to familiarize themselves with the route; or, they can try to explore their way through the maze of ledges on Gibraltar by themselves. Both carry risks. Fortunately, both options play to our strong sides."

"How do you figure?" Ring asked.

"Climbing with the RGS risks being watched very closely. They know that it's the guide's job to do so, and that is a real downside. They can't wander off on their own, and anything they do, out of the absolute ordinary, will be scrutinized. Plus, they never want to relinquish control. It is not in their nature. My guess is that they will be extremely uncomfortable in that situation. They are familiar with being tailed in circumstances where they have the ability to lose the surveillance. Rube has regaled us with stories about that. Being roped together with a guide forecloses any such opportunities. If they climb with the RGS, they will likely photograph the hell out of the route.

So we'll have to see who has his camera out all the time, including at night, when we negotiate the ledges going up."

"Great points, Lehman," Ring said. "It looks like you've thought out their alternative from the RGS side, but what about from mine?"

"Yours is the most interesting John, and I'll wager, the most likely -- especially once I screw with them."

"How are you going to do that?"

"Remember how we wanded, and marked the hell out of the route?"

"Yeah, marking the trail is crucial, particularly on a new route, and up the Gib."

"Precisely, John. But say we wait a few days. All the RGS guides now know where the new ladder is placed. It is nowhere near the old rappel point we checked out. It is actually *down below* the southwest side of Camp Misery, and cannot be seen from the camp. The old worn trail from Misery leads *up* from the camp. The Russians will be prone to follow that old trail. If..." Lehman's voice trailed off.

"If what?" Ring asked.

"...If I pulled the wands leading over to the new ladder. The guides wouldn't care. They've got the route memorized. They would think the wind blew them away. But the Russians..."

"Great idea!" Ring interjected. "The Russians will almost certainly get lost. They will either stumble around and eventually retreat back to Muir, or they will signal for help, and Butler and I will have to go get them. And once we do, we've got them in hand, and can ID them."

"Exactly, John. And that is why you are pivotal to this plan. Make sure you take your camera and ticket book. Cite them for something. The more information you can squeeze out of them in your 'official policing' role as a ranger, the better. But don't screw with them too much. Just cite, and let them go. Put some sticky tape on the back of your ticket book so you can get their prints for Rube when they sign for the ticket. Make them all sign it."

"Damn, Lehman," Ring shook his head. "You are beginning to scare the shit out of me. You're too fast a learner in this spy business."

"It's only because you are able to compare, John."

"What do you mean?"

"I'm only a fast learner because you aren't."

Ring gave Lehman a shove. "Castellano is right. You are a smart ass."

11

First days of August 1967: Springing the Trap

"Teo, take care, I'll see you in a few days," Lehman said, kissing her goodbye.

She grabbed his arms and whispered: "I want *you* to take care, my wonderful guide. Be safe." Teo had taken a quick break from her work to see Lehman off on his summit climb.

"You're a doll." Bradford hugged Teo again, pulling her strongly into him. Then he turned quickly away. He longed for her already.

Lehman and Don McPherson ambled up the trail toward Camp Muir, clients in tow. The weather was hot and clear, without a breeze. It was typical for this time of the summer. Lehman could hear his father's words: *The best times to climb Rainier are the last five days of July, and the first five days of August.*

The hike to Muir was trying in the heat. The Snowfield was like a reflector oven. Lehman and McPherson took extra care to ensure that the clients stayed hydrated. At Muir they laid out the ropes, and put the clients to bed early.

"We'll have to leave at eleven-thirty tonight, Brad," McPherson said. The ladder up on the route slows clients down, and adds at least a half hour each way to the climb."

"I agree," Lehman said softly. He was deep in thought, formulating how he was going to set the trap for the Russian Bear.

The RGS party was on its way up the Cowlitz Glacier by 2330 hours. It was a strong group, and Camp Misery was reached by 0300. As the clients took a break and ate a snack, McPherson walked west down to check the piton anchors to the ladder. Bradford switched off his headlamp, and quickly hiked the hundred yards north, up to the old rappel point. He knelt down and unsheathed the knife from his belt. It was a razor-sharp Gerber Shorty, forged out of a single piece of high-grade stainless steel. Its slick sleek handle was wrapped with black friction tape to prevent it from sliding in his hands. Fumbling in the darkness, Lehman reached out to the thick rappel rope hanging by a piton pounded into the rock face where the old "1938 ledge" had collapsed. He pulled the rope back toward him and cut it in one motion. The rope fell away. A few small rocks kicked loose and rattled with it into the blackness below.

That should take care of the sons-of-bitches. Damn, now I'm even thinking like Rube talks. Lehman chuckled to himself, sheathed his Gerber, and walked back to the group.

"Where'd you go?" McPherson asked. He was sitting with the clients, with his water bottle out.

"Murphy's law my friend," Lehman spoke loudly so the clients could hear, "No one cares where you are, until you try to sneak off and take a leak." They nodded in knowing affirmation. McPherson smiled. "Okay Don, I have a very strong team on my rope. Why don't I lead here?"

"After you, Brad. Be my guest. You put in the route."

Lehman's crampons clanked and scraped against the aluminum ladder. Looking down past the rungs and between his feet, his light caught faint images of crumbling rock ledges plunging precipitously to the bottom of the Gibraltar Chute. He descended the ladder quickly, moved a few feet over on the ledge, and yelled up for his next client to follow. As his client moved, he coiled in the goldline. The teams would climb bunched together along the Gibraltar ledges to keep the ropes from hanging up on rocks. He cinched up the strap on his Bell TopTex rock helmet. His four clients down-climbed the ladder with a minimum of fuss. Bradford talked them down with reassuring chatter: "Rob, you're doing magnificently! Dan, don't look down between your feet. Just look at your hands and reach down with your boot to the next rung. I know it feels weird with crampons on, but keep moving. You're doing great."

With all his rope team off the ladder and coiled next to him, Lehman then moved north along the ledge, which varied from two to four feet wide, with an overhang six feet above. This shielded climbers from rock-fall that rattled down frequently from high up on Gibraltar's western face.

Bradford turned the first corner on the ledge, and his headlamp spotted the rappel rope he had cut away from the old route. It was lying in a heap a few feet in front of him. He took his pack off, stuffed the rope into it, and turned to the client immediately behind: "Rob, we are crossing an open area here on the ledge that is extremely exposed to rock-fall. Let's move quickly across this to minimize our risk here. Pass the word back that they will be moving faster until we all get through it. Then we'll slow down again." Lehman heard the word passed. "Okay, let's move," he said.

Bradford climbed steadily along the rubbled ledge as it meandered several hundred yards to its apex at the Gibraltar Chute. Periodically, rocks crashed down from somewhere out of the blackness far above, smashed themselves against the overhang, and spun wildly past the party, to impact the Nisqually Glacier hundreds of feet below. It was unnerving; but Lehman's team was moving well. Behind him, however, he heard McPherson's shouts goading his clients along. Dawn was coming, and Lehman switched off his headlamp. *I need to leave as much power available for the little Gold Geiger Counter as I can.* Lehman did not bother to insert the earpiece. He needed all his hearing to listen to his clients and to be on guard to dodge rock fall.

The RGS party finally came together at the bottom end of the fixed ropes that Lehman and Ring had installed in the Chute.

"Look folks," McPherson's voice was stern as he briefed the clients, "this next pitch up the ice chute is steep, but nothing you haven't been trained to handle. Trust your crampon points. They will hold you. Grab hold of the fixed rope with your left hand and climb up using it as a handhold. You can use the shafts or pick of your ice axes to balance yourselves with your right hands. Keep the slack out of the rope to your teammates. We go straight up here three hundred feet, and then it eases off a lot. Beyond that, we zigzag around some big crevasses, and then we will be looking at the crater rim." He glanced at his watch. "As good as you all are, I figure we can summit from here in four hours. Any questions?" There were none. He turned to Bradford and pointed with his ice axe. "Okay, Lehman, press on."

The relentless fifty-degree angle of the ice slope in the upper throat of the Gibraltar Chute strained the nerves and calf muscles of the clients. The fixed rope was a blessing -- for guides and clients alike. Lehman made good time to the top of it, and checked to confirm that the aluminum pickets, and the ice bollard anchor point for the fixed rope, remained secure. Looking back along the RGS rope teams strung out below, and satisfied that none were straggling, he turned and followed the guided trail, marked with bamboo wands with short pieces of red surveyor's tape flapping at their tops. The wind had picked up, and Bradford heard them rattling before he saw them.

The RGS summit climb finally reached Rainier's top at eleven-thirty -- twelve hours after leaving Camp Muir the night before.

"Good job in setting the route above Gibraltar. At least that part of the climb is straightforward."

"Thanks Brad." Don took off his wool watch cap, and ran his hands through a thick tousled shock of black hair.

"You need a haircut Don," Lehman remarked, as he slowly clicked overlapping panoramic shots of the crater rim with his Rollei.

"Damned good camera you've got there," McPherson said, ignoring Lehman's suggestion. "They're expensive. Your dad buy it for you?"

"A good friend did. He's kind of like my dad."

"Good friend indeed, if he bought that for you. He must be rich."

"He is, but you wouldn't know it in talking to him. He bitches about money all the time."

"I sure wouldn't if I were rich." McPherson let out a deep sigh.

"Don, a grizzled old rock climber like you was ordained by God to be poor."

"Guess so," Don said, smiling wearily. "Let's get these clients off the hill. I'll lead down, you bring up the rear." McPherson cut the rest on top short to allow more time for the descent.

Three loud sonic booms cracked. Lehman looked up into the clear blue sky. The SR-71 Blackbird was on the job.

Except for a few slips in the Gibraltar Chute by the clients, who were promptly stopped by the fixed rope, and sharp tugs on their climbing ropes from Lehman and McPherson behind them, the climb ended well for clients and RGS guides. They arrived back at Camp Muir dead tired, but safe.

Two hours before, as the party passed back through Camp Misery, it was easy for Lehman, bringing up the rear, to pull out the several wands marking the new detour over to the ladder. Bradford also kicked away as many footprints as he could. As he walked by the equipment cache, he hid the wands under a big rock. He knew Ring was hiking up to Muir that afternoon. There he would set up his dutiful watch over all who purposed to be on the big mountain – nefarious, or otherwise.

"Hi Brad," John Ring's rugged narrow face appeared over the top of the Guide Hut's open Dutch Door. Lehman jerked awake and felt for the Walther at his waist.

"Careful buddy, friendlies coming in," Ring smiled.

"You carrying yours?"

"Yup," Ring said, "I wouldn't leave the DUB without it. Compared to what I used to carry, I can't even tell I've got it on."

"Well, Ring, you needed something there to show people that *something is there*," Lehman needled.

Ring guffawed.

"But seriously John, I pulled out the wands marking the trail from Camp Misery to the new ladder. And I also cut away the rappel rope hanging off the old upper ledge, just in case they try to exercise the great training Mother Russia gave them, to drop down to the route that way."

"Dastardly of you. I can't decide if you're more like the FBI or the CIA."

"Neither one, John," Lehman said in a tired voice. "I am merely a common dastard."

"Thanks for staying up here. I saw McPherson coming down a little bit ago and he said you were staying to 'rest up and come down tomorrow.' I appreciate that, since Butler couldn't make it. He had to drive some visiting empty-suit, from headquarters in D.C., around the Park."

"Timing is everything with empty-suits. Jeez, John, we are starting to talk like Rubayat Castellano."

Ring laughed. "Did you happen to peek into the Public Hut, across the way?"

"No."

"Well I did. And two gorillas are stuffed back in the shadows in the corner bunks. And they were talking softly – *in Russian.* I hate to say it, but it looks like you called it Brad."

Lehman jumped out of his bunk. "Man, they didn't waste any time."

"They sure didn't. That GRU Major you photographed near the Ice Caves a couple of weeks ago must have given them a royal ass chewing.

"Did you spook them?"

"No, I don't think so. I simply poked my head in with my Smokey the Bear Hat on, and gave them a wave."

"You didn't!"

"Naw, I popped my head in, looked around, and left."

Lehman smiled and poured Ring a cup of coffee. "Did you bring the brick?"

"Yes. I brought the Motorola, and of course we've got the big portable radio here in the hut. Your call sign is RGS1 by the way."

"We'd better stay off the radios unless there's an emergency," Lehman said. "They may be monitoring. Let's hang tight and see what happens. If they are going to take a run at the route they will probably leave right after dark. If they do, you and I can pull out the lawn chairs, sip our coffee, and watch their headlamps from down here. It is going to be a clear night."

Lehman went back to sleep while Ring cooked dinner. At 2200 hours John gave Bradford a nudge. "Your dinner has been ready for three hours and our Russian-speaking climbers over in the Public Hut just left. They were really quiet about it."

Lehman got up and ate, and at 2245 he and Ring walked out of the Guide Hut with their folding lawn chairs, cups, and a thermos of hot coffee. They sat in the dark shadow of the hut so as not to be seen. Midway up toward Camp Hazard, two headlamps winked as the climbers turned the corner on a large crevasse.

"They're following our wands," Ring said.

"Dead-bang on the route," Lehman agreed. "And they are making good time. They should arrive at Camp Misery in under two and a half hours."

"This is cool, Lehman. It's like watching a movie at the drive in, don't you think?"

"Kiss me John, and I'll tell you." Ring tipped Lehman out of his chair.

The broad sweep of the Cowlitz Glacier, and the black brooding hulk of Gibraltar looming above it, dwarfed the tiny winking lights of the climbers. Bradford and John watched as the lights gained the scree slope below Camp Misery, ascended it, and drifted into the dark notch between Cowlitz Ridge and Gibraltar. The lights bunched together for a few minutes. Then they began moving up the worn trail toward the 1938 ledge and the old rappel point.

"This is going to get interesting," Ring said. His voice was low and tense. The lights went out as the climbers disappeared around a rock outcrop.

"They are at the old rappel point," Bradford said, almost to himself. Minutes -- then nearly a half-hour ticked by.

"Shit, maybe they have set up their own rappel and are on their way across the ledges," Ring said. As he finished his words the two lights reappeared, and began descending back to Camp Misery. John gave a sigh of relief.

"They're screwed now," Lehman said.

An infinitesimally small Cold War drama was unfolding on the mountain. The coffee in their aluminum cups grew cold as Ring and Lehman sat watching, mesmerized. The lights came together for some long minutes, then spread out in separate directions around the camp, then came back together. More long minutes elapsed. Then, abruptly, the headlamps began moving swiftly down the scree below Camp Misery.

"Man, it looks like they're running," Ring said.

"It's now 0200, and they want to get down and clear out of Muir before we wake up," Lehman said.

Ring and Lehman poured out the cold coffee in their mugs, and replaced it with hot coffee from the thermos.

Bradford looked around at the stars. There was only the paltry sliver of a moon. "Waning Crescent," he said. "Not much to climb on." He yawned, and took a sip of coffee.

"Falling!" Ring shouted. The word, stabbing into the stillness, came out as though John himself had fallen. Lehman jerked his head back and saw the two lights sliding, one below the other. "They're above a big crevasse. Stop!" Ring's voice raised an octave. Then the lower light disappeared and the light on top stopped. "Shit. Dumb bastards. One is in the crevasse and the anchoring climber finally stopped him. Now what do we do, Brad?" Silence followed, as Ring and Lehman fully grasped the gravity of what they were witnessing.

"We wait and watch, John," Bradford finally said. His words came out flat, smooth, and clinical.

"But this is now a rescue, and I'm obligated –"

"It may or may not be, John," Lehman cut him off. "These clowns chose to disregard your Park's rule that the mountain has been closed to all private parties. Furthermore, if we race up there now we will blow the operation, because they would know we have been watching them out here when we should have been asleep in there." Bradford jabbed a finger toward the Guide Hut. "We watch and we wait. Let's see how well Mother Russia trained these tough GRU agents in crevasse rescue."

Both men went quiet, focusing on the one small headlamp, now fixed in place a few feet from the black maw of the big crevasse.

"I sure wish we had a way to get a better look at them," Lehman said.

"Damn -- we do!" Ring said. He sprang up from his lawn chair and walked over to his tent on the snow adjacent to the Guide Hut. He emerged with a set of binoculars. "Rube gave these to me. They are low-light night lenses."

As the minutes ticked by, John and Bradford took turns holding the heavy binoculars. Lehman was amazed how clearly he could see the image of the climber struggling so far up on the Cowlitz Glacier -- he was spread-eagled in a self-arrest position, clinging to his ice axe.

Very sloppy self-arrest technique. He's lucky he stopped. Bradford sensed the desperation in the man. He had a fleeting feeling of empathy. But it was only fleeting. Lehman had been in such situations before. But he knew how to conduct a "self rescue" on a glacier, and he always carried the equipment with which to accomplish it. He ticked through the steps in his mind. *Hell, I went through this drill a few days ago with the clients. If the man in the crevasse is a climber, and not injured, he can prusik out of it on his own.* But that was not happening on this chilly morning, high on the Cowlitz Glacier.

"I don't see any progress with the man in the crevasse," Lehman said. "He should be prusiking his way out by now." Lehman checked his watch. "It's been over a half hour and the guy on top is still in a self-arrest." He handed the binoculars back to John.

"Holy Shit!"

"What happened, John?"

"The guy in the self arrest stood up. He is now moving down the trail! The guy has turned below of the crevasse and is headed down. He's not even hesitating, or looking back. He's not walking that fast either. Shit, he must have cut the rope on his buddy!"

12

August 1967: Paradise, The Next Day

"Thanks for calling the number I gave you kid," Special Agent Rubayat Castellano lifted his frosted mug of beer to toast Lehman. "You got me out of the office, and this time I brought a money bag." He tossed his head sideways to acknowledge CIA Agent Otto Palmrich.

"Great to see you Brad," Palmrich said. He shook hands with Lehman, and then extended his hand to John Ring. "Good to see you again, John! Quite a contrast to our last meeting in Vietnam."

"Good to see you Otto!" Ring said, shaking Palmrich's hand. "And yes, the contrast is surreal."

Palmrich raised his beer mug. "This is a very interesting operation you have going here. We will all see much more of each other in the future. Cheers!"

The four men in the Glacier Room clicked their glasses together and drank. They were there two hours before the bar opened.

"Okay kids, let the meeting come to order," Rube said. He pulled out a notebook and pen from the knapsack lying next to his leg.

"Pritzl's paying the bills, but I have to do the paper. Tell us what happened. Ring, you go first."

"A couple of days ago I observed two climbers huddled in the back of the Public Hut at Camp Muir."

"Describe them."

"Not much to describe," Ring said. "Both were large males. They wore dark clothing, and sat on bunks way back in the darkest corner of the hut."

"Did they speak to you or to each other?"

"They spoke quietly, and only to each other – in Russian."

Rube looked over at Palmrich, then continued. "Anyone else there?"

"No," Ring said. "Actually I was surprised because it was on a Monday afternoon and Camp Muir is normally completely cleared out by then. The RGS climb had headed down to Paradise. I thought the Public Hut was empty."

"Did you see if they had any equipment?"

"If they did, it was well-stowed. I didn't see any. I took a quick look inside, scanned the place, and left."

"After this incident, we checked the Public Hut end-to-end, and nothing was left behind then, either," Lehman added.

"What happened next?"

"The two large males left the Public Hut at ten o'clock -- 2200 hours," Ring continued. "I was in the Guide Hut with Lehman, and heard them leave precisely at 2200. Then I woke up Brad. We waited until 2245 hours, and then walked out to watch them."

"From where?" Rube asked.

"We sat out in front of the Guide Hut -- in its shadow -- on lawn chairs, and watched them climb. They ascended the new RGS route toward Gibraltar and reached Camp Misery. From there they climbed up to the old 1938 ledge, to its rappel point. We couldn't see their lights during this time, because they were behind a rock buttress."

"How long were they out of your sight?"

"A half hour or so."

"Then what, John?"

"And then the lights re-appeared, came back down to Camp Misery, and stayed together for fifteen minutes or so. Then the lights split up, moving all around the area of the camp." Ring paused, watching Castellano scribble away on his notepad.

"Go ahead." Rube motioned for John to continue.

"Then they quickly descended, retracing their steps back down the trail on the Cowlitz Glacier. Now it was about 0200 hours. Suddenly I saw the bottom climber on the rope team peal off."

"What do you mean 'peal off'?"

"He fell. His headlamp bounced as he slid. He pulled the tail-end climber off of his feet, and then they were both falling. They slid possibly seventy-five feet and then the lower climber disappeared into a big crevasse. His light went out and we never saw him again. The uphill climber finally arrested the fall, and stopped about twenty feet above the crevasse."

Rube flipped to a new page in his notebook. "Okay, then what?"

"Lehman and I took turns watching this guy through your special binoculars," Ring said. "But he didn't do anything for upwards of a half hour. He just laid there looking back toward the crevasse. Then all of a sudden the climber stood up, walked back over to the climbing route, skirted around the bottom end of the crevasse, and kept walking. He never stopped to look into the crevasse for his buddy or anything. He simply kept going."

"What happened after that?"

"Well, since the climber was headed back our way, Lehman and I folded up our chairs and went back inside the Guide Hut. We thought about going back out to check on his progress. But now he was really hauling ass downhill, so we decided not to risk being seen, and stayed inside."

"Good decision," Rube said. "When did you make contact with him?"

"At 0445, we heard crampons clanking on the rocks below the Guide Hut. I opened the door and asked him what he was doing alone out on the Cowlitz Glacier. He didn't answer, but kept on walking. He did not stop at the Public Hut, where he had been holed up with his missing buddy a few hours before. He kept walking with his crampons on, right out onto the Muir Snowfield, heading south toward Paradise."

"So that's when you ID'd him, John?" Rube asked, his eyes still on his notebook.

"Yes. Lehman and I left the hut, and walked toward him. I told him to stop. He looked back, and for a second I thought he might actually take off running. He quickened his pace for a few feet and then stopped."

Rube looked up at Lehman, who nodded in confirmation.

"So, I pulled my flashlight out and shined the guy," Ring said. "He didn't want to look into the light. Avoided it. He kept turning partially away. I asked him his name. He mumbled that it was 'George Coleman.' I badged him, and said: 'George, you know it is against Park regulations to climb on Mount Rainier's glaciers solo. *You are climbing by yourself,* right?' He nodded, and mumbled that he was alone. I asked him to produce a driver's license. He dug around in the top flap of his pack and pulled out a wallet with a Virginia driver's license. I have already given you a copy of that information."

"Yeah, skip that part, John," Rube said. "Then what?"

"Then I tried to chat this George Coleman up, but he was clearly unhappy about being stopped, and wouldn't talk, so I jacked him a little."

"How so?"

"I said, 'Mister Coleman you seem to be a bit unhappy about being stopped by me. I don't ordinarily get up this early, but nature called, and who do I happen to see walking off the Cowlitz Glacier so early in the morning, and right past my camp? It's Mister George Coleman -- who apparently likes to climb big mountains by himself, and doesn't care a whit about Park rules or regulations. So, I am going to write you a citation, Mister Coleman. It is for climbing solo and un-roped on the glacier up here. Please note that this is a federal violation carrying a fine of three hundred dollars. Also note that the citation is also a summons. You are directed to appear before a Federal Magistrate in Seattle, Washington, no later than two weeks after the date shown on this citation.' I then passed the ticket book over to Coleman, and told him to sign at the bottom. He had to take his gloves off to do it. Boy, he looked pissed. But he didn't say anything. Just glared at me. Then I said, 'Have a nice day Mister Coleman.' And he turned and beat feet down the Muir Snowfield toward Paradise."

"Did you see or talk with Coleman again?"

"No."

"Lehman, is that the way you saw the whole thing? Do you have anything else to add?

"No, but John has something to show you."

Ring nodded, and pulled a plastic sack out of his knapsack by the table, and handed it to Rube.

"What is this?" Palmrich asked.

"It's my citation book with the carbon copy of the ticket, and George Coleman's signature on the top."

"Damn, nice job, Ring!" Rube said.

"Careful with it though, Rube," Ring said.

"Why?"

"Because on the back of the citation book is sticky tape. Coleman's fingerprints are on it. I bagged the whole thing up for you right after he walked off. Honestly, Rube, *I'd* like to take credit for all this -- but our young 'Super Spook,' Bradford Lehman here, set this all up."

*　*　*

"Hey Nancy, can you slip me into one of Teo's empty tables for dinner?" Nancy Olszewski turned from her podium at the entrance to the Inn's Dining Room. Lehman, cleaned up from his summit climb, and fresh from his debriefing by Castellano and Palmrich in the Glacier Room, was dressed in faded jeans and a blue flannel shirt. He smiled at Nancy. A buxom brunette from Chicago, studying hotel management, Nancy stood five feet three inches tall, and sported a shapely trim figure and sparkling brown eyes. Olszewski had decided to break out of the city for the summer, and travel west to work at the Paradise Inn. She had never seen Mount Rainier, or the Northwest for that matter. She marveled at the splendor of the landscape, and reveled in the change from big city life.

"Hi stranger! Great to see you! Hey, I've got an idea. Why don't we surprise Teo?"

"Love to!"

Olszewski looked back into the room, checked to see that Teo had gone into the kitchen, and motioned Lehman over to a small corner table. She sat him down facing the wall.

"I know the route has been tough this summer," Nancy said, patting Bradford on the back. "You've put in more time up there than any of the other guides." Nancy bent down and spoke softly in Bradford's ear. "And your server here tonight has been pining for you -- big time."

Lehman smiled. "And I for her."

"Dinner tonight is on the house."

"Wow, Nancy, thanks. But I can pay."

"No, I insist. I run the place!" She smiled and walked away.

Lehman stared down at the table. It truly had been a difficult summer. *If Nancy only knew the real story of what was going on up here.* His mind wandered. He dozed.

"Good evening sir, may I help -- Brad!" Lehman started awake. Instinctively his hand went to his waistband, and the concealed Walther pistol. Remembering where he was, he stood up. Teo set her water carafe down and gave Lehman a long hug. He felt her arms around his back and her warm soft breasts against his chest. No hesitation. No formality. Just joy. He felt a blush of passion. It felt good.

"I've missed you so," she whispered.

"Hi beautiful." Bradford spoke the words softly, directly. "I've missed you too. But you know what? We both have days off tomorrow. And John has gone down the hill for a couple of days on business. We have my room at the DUB all to ourselves."

Teo looked into his tired eyes. "I have really been worried about you, Brad. But now you are back, and I am thrilled. I'm off at eight." She squeezed his shoulder, then stood up, took out her pencil and pad, and said firmly in her most professional voice: "Now, sir, may I take your order?"

"You already have," Bradford said, giving Teo a wide exhausted smile.

* * *

Earlier that day, at the debriefing in the Glacier Room with Agents Castellano and Palmrich, a plan had been formulated. There would be an attempt to recover the body of George Coleman's phantom climbing partner. It would need to be done quickly. The next week's weather on Rainier was due to deteriorate.

"At least his sorry ass is refrigerated up there," Castellano mused, tapping his pen on the table. "Okay, here is what we're going to do. Palmrich and I will take Ring down to McChord Air Force Base and arrange for a helicopter to fly you boys as high up on the Cowlitz, and as near to the big crevasse, as it can get you. Three days from now is the sweet spot for this operation, I figure. That will be next Monday. Ranger Bill Butler, and Palmrich here, will first climb to Camp Muir, give the "All Clear" that no one is up there, and secure the area. Then the bird will come in, and insert Ring and Lehman at or near the big crevasse." Rube pointed to them. "You two will yank Mister 'FNU LNU' (First Name Unknown, Last Name Unknown) out of the crevasse, bag him up, and call the bird back in for extraction. That will be by mechanical hoist. That is 'Plan A.' If Plan A goes sideways, 'Plan B' will entail Lehman and Ring, supported by Palmrich and Butler, bag-dragging FNU LNU down to Muir, to be picked up by the helicopter there. Any questions?"

"Any helicopter operations on the mountain will inevitably bring press scrutiny," Ring said.

"We have a cover story for that," Palmrich replied. "This operation will be characterized as 'an Air Force high altitude rescue exercise, conducted by Detachment 5, of the USAF's Western Air Rescue Center, out of McChord Air Force Base."

"If Ring is going with you, where do I meet the helicopter on Monday?" Lehman asked.

"Good question, kid." Rube said. "Does that Triumph Herald of yours work?"

"Works great."

"Do you know the air strip down off the east side of the Nisqually River? It is about ten miles outside the Park near a blink in the road called Mineral."

"Yes, sure do."

"Be there at 0945 on Monday. In the meantime, get some rest. It has all been cleared with your boss McGill. You are off through Monday."

"Thanks, Rube."

"Oh, and another thing. Teo is off until Monday too. She has been partly briefed into this operation. She does not yet know about the possibility of a nuke up there, though, so keep that quiet. But she does know we are working against the Russians."

Lehman nodded, and put his head down, deep in thought. There were a few seconds of quiet in the room. Bradford expected some ribald teasing about his burgeoning relationship with Teo, but there was none. It was quiet. He looked up.

"Brad," Castellano said, his voice, normally booming, was mannered and soft. "Teo Maloney is a real sweet kid – an all-American girl. Her dad is an executive for Standard Oil down in San Ramon, California. He's a great guy, too. Turns out he has assisted us previously on some matters overseas."

"Did you brief him in as well?" Lehman asked.

"Teo is eighteen like you, so technically we wouldn't need to, but we did. Mister Maloney is rock-solid reliable, and is familiar with the intelligence business, at least from the industrial side. He readily remembered you, Brad, from his RGS climb with Teo last summer. He was mightily impressed with what you are doing for us. He supports Teo's decision one hundred percent."

"And what is her decision?" Bradford asked.

"She's in, kid. Didn't hesitate a second. Damn, she is pretty. If I were twenty years younger, I'd –" Rube was cut off by John Ring.

"Congratulations! Let's have a toast." Four mugs of beer clanked together. "To a successful operation on Monday!"

*   *   *

Only a nightlight lit the room. Teo and Bradford nestled together on Lehman's bed in his living quarters in the DUB.

"Brad, I've been so worried about you. I just knew something else was going on." She kissed him. Her lips were warm and soft, like melting butter. "I want you to know that I am so proud of you, and that I am here for you. I know you cannot discuss much of what you do up there, and that is a huge burden. I've seen it in you, Brad, and I can't believe how you have been able to handle it all."

"Well, beautiful woman, I am handling it so far, I guess. But this whole business with the Russians is so incredibly unreal, now that I'm up close in an actual operation. I'm finding out that it's one thing to sit back and study the history of our conflict with the Soviets. That's "ivory tower" stuff – conceptual abstractions about economics, war, politics, democracy, and communism. All neat and tidy. And it's a hell of another thing to actually be involved in the conflict, toe to toe, with people who will kill us -- and even their own -- to win. I've been thinking about Professor Prins back at UPS, and his fight with the Dutch Resistance against the Nazis during World War II. I have a newfound respect for him – and for Rube, and the other agents who've been on the front lines in the Cold War. It blows my mind that Castellano has actually been in combat in that endeavor since before I was born."

Teo listened quietly, with her arm around Bradford's shoulders. "I see what you are saying, Bradford. Rube and the others are professionals, like you said. They have been trained and have many years of experience. You have been brought into this situation right out of the blue. Normally that would never happen. But I know why it did happen to you -- here. It is because you are steady and smart, and because you know the mountain so well. That is why I'm proud of you."

"Teo, I'm only a cog in a huge grinding wheel that turns incessantly, even up here in Paradise. Jeez, that sounded banal!" Lehman shook his head and chuckled.

"Oh, Brad, but you are such a *fantastic cog!*" Teo whispered in his ear. Bradford and Teo laughed, and he hit her playfully with his pillow. Then he rolled on top of her. They kissed long and passionately.

"Turn out the light Bradford," she said. "We are both off work until Monday."

13

August 1967: Recovery
Operation, Cowlitz Glacier

Lehman Switched off the engine on his Triumph Herald next to the small airstrip near Elbe. It was 0915, on Monday. He had enjoyed the drive down from Paradise, past the lodge and Park headquarters buildings at Longmire, and through the primeval timbered forests at the lower elevations of Rainier National Park. Some of the moss-draped firs were three hundred foot giants, twenty feet in diameter, and over five hundred years old. Driving and walking among these silent, seemingly immutable living patriarchs, always calmed Lehman. Saved from the saw by the boundary of the Rainier National Park, they simply sat, caressed by the mountain air, and lived. *I am ready to simply sit, and live – and love.*

The colors were beginning to turn toward fall, and the deep sheens of green and brown were a welcome relief that contrasted with Lehman's long summer spent high on the mountain, where his views were saturated with glaring variants of white, brown, and black – of rock, snow, and glacial ice. He also enjoyed the Park's narrow winding roads, the quick responsiveness of his little Triumph on the many hairpin turns, and the smooth shifting of the car's gears. Lehman was not one to race. That was not his nature. He was deliberative. But he was also only eighteen. He drove with aggressive confidence.

Bradford stepped out onto the grass of the airstrip, stretched, and pulled his green Kelty frame pack out of the back seat. He rechecked his gear one last time: ice axe, strapped to the Kelty's side frame post; ten carabiners; nylon web slings; four pulleys; a snow fluke; eight ice screws, two Jumar ascenders; two full water jugs; trail mix; extra clothing and gloves; sunscreen; crampons; headlamp and the ever-present Eveready batteries, Gold Eveready included; a dozen bamboo wands; a compass; an altimeter; and his little Rollei camera. Lehman already had his climbing boots on, with gaiters zipped on over them, extending up his blue wool knicker socks to keep snow out of his boots. His Walther was tucked snuggly into the waistband holster of his heavy broadcloth climbing knickers. Bradford leaned the pack up against the car, slipped into the front seat, and slept.

Lehman awoke to the sound of a HH-43 Kaman Huskie heading his way. It was 0945. It settled down softly next to the airstrip, fifty feet from Lehman's Triumph. The pilot shut down the helicopter's big turbine engine.

Rube, helmet off, walked over to the car. "Ready to go kid?"

"Yes Rube, all ready."

"Put your crampons on here. They won't hurt the floor of the chopper. We have a rubber mat in there so you won't slide around." Castellano picked up Lehman's pack and carried it to the helicopter, complaining all the way how heavy it was. Bradford donned his crampons, locked his car, pocketed his keys, and followed. The points of his crampons stuck in the soft turf, making walking awkward. The team gathered around the big drooping blades of the Huskie. When they were stopped, Lehman thought, the machine had the appearance of a resting dragonfly. He was introduced to USAF Command Pilot, Rick Champion.

"Captain Champion here, is the most experienced rescue pilot in the CONUS," Special Agent Castellano said.

"What is the CONUS?" Lehman asked.

"Sorry kid, you're the only non-military team member here. CONUS stands for 'Continental United States.' Champion returned to the States last April, after a tour in Vietnam. He pulled off some remarkable rescues over there. But over the past three years, Rick has also logged the most hours on Rainier and on other mountain rescues here in the Cascades." Castellano looked down at a large note card in his hand.

"I'm glad he'll be at the controls of this machine, and not you," Lehman said.

"Me too," Rube said, with a toothy grin. "We all want to walk away from this gig." Castellano glanced back at his card and continued. "So, Lehman, here's the drill for this operation: You and Ring will fast-rope off the back of the bird here…" He pointed to the back clamshell doors.

"You mean rappel?"

"No, fast-rope," Rube said. He showed Bradford the rope. It looked like the ones Lehman had climbed in the gym -- much thicker and coarser than climbing rope. "You will practice this a few times before we lift off. Then Champion will fly us up there and try to attain a stable hover over the lower lip of the target crevasse up on the Cowlitz. Then you and Ring slide down the fast-rope and begin extraction of the body. Meanwhile, Champion will back the bird off and land down at Camp Muir. When you two and the body are ready to be lifted out, Champion will spool up, fly back up to the crevasse, and I will winch you guys, and the body, up into the bird. The body goes up first. Got it?"

"Yes," Lehman said. Ring nodded.

"Oh, and another thing," Rube added. "Champion and I will be on oxygen. It is required for aircrew members in unpressurised aircraft above ten thousand feet. You two do not need oxygen, since you are not aircrew, and are both acclimatized. So we are foregoing that equipment for you guys. The masks and cylinders will just be two more items to get in your way, and the masks will impair your vision." Ring and Lehman nodded.

Under John Ring's instruction, Lehman practiced grabbing the thick rope hanging off the tail boom beyond the back ramp, and sliding the five feet to the grass.

Ring handed Bradford a new set of thick black leather gloves. "These thick gloves are essential, Brad. Because we have crampons on, we can't clamp onto the fast-rope with our feet. If our boots get too close, the crampons will catch, and we could be flipped off of the rope. That means we will have to do all the braking on this descent with our hands." Lehman nodded.

They fast-roped the few feet from the Huskie's rear ramp to the grass, first without packs, and then with them on. They also practiced clipping into the onboard winch, and being pulled up to the ramp. Rube operated the winch.

Finally, Ring turned to Castellano and Champion and gave a thumbs up. "We are good to go."

"Hey, Rube, who's that guy in the suit sitting in the big Chevy over there under the tree?" Bradford asked.

"Shit, that's Anderson, the ASAC. He's spying on us."

"What's an 'ASAC,' and what do you mean by spying?"

"He is the Assistant Special Agent in Charge in Seattle. He has been directed by the SOG to stay out of this operation, but he's watching and reporting on this to J. Earl Mills, the SAC in Seattle. I'll fix his ass. Help me detach these back doors." Rube flipped some latches, and John and Bradford unhinged the Huskie's Plexiglas clamshell doors, walked them forty feet away, and stacked them in the grass next to the airstrip. Meanwhile, Castellano sauntered over to the ASAC's car, chatted for a minute, and then walked back to the bird.

"What did you tell him Rube?" Ring asked.

"I told Charlie to watch the doors until we get back. I told him they cost ten thousand dollars each, and must be watched, and I thanked him for coming out all this way to help," Rube said, with a grin. It was an evil grin.

*   *   *

The Huskie lifted off of the airstrip and climbed in a wide circle through broken clouds, staying to the south of the Tatoosh Range and well away from Paradise. Rube, normally chatty on the intercom, was quiet. They were all quiet. Lehman sat belted into his web seat with his Kelty pack on his back. It pushed him uncomfortably forward, so he and Ring sat facing each other bent over, gloved hands on knees.

"You look alluring in goggles Bradford."

"Jeez, get a girlfriend, Ring. We live together. Now I'm afraid to 'drop the soap,' as Rube puts it." They laughed. So did Champion and Castellano, who were listening on the aircraft intercom.

Bradford Lehman should have been tense, but he wasn't. The higher the Huskie climbed, the more relaxed Lehman became. He felt the air thinning with the altitude, and growing cold. It was like meeting an old friend. He breathed in deeply. *Now I'm on my turf.*

The Huskie, its engine whining, reached the elevation of the big crevasse. Command Pilot Champion surveyed it by flying tight circles above the steep slope of the upper Cowlitz Glacier, below the crumbling basalt cliffs of Gibraltar Rock.

"That's it, at ten o'clock low." Ring spoke into the Intercom. That is where FNU LNU went in."

Champion banked slightly, and looked down past his left flying boot through the Plexiglas bubble below his pedals. "Got it."

"Yup, that's the one," Lehman confirmed. "You can barely make out the slide marks where he went in."

"Copy," Champion said.

"Eleven, dead on the nose." Rube called out the altitude.

"Going into a hover," Champion said. He held the bird directly over the crevasse, then drifted it gently to the downhill side.

"Okay, Ring, dump the fast-rope," Rube said. John kicked its coils out the back and watched as it straightened itself sixty feet below.

"Ten feet off the snow," Ring said.

Champion, catching gusts of wind, deftly lowered the HH-43 in its hover, until the end of the rope lay on the snow with ten feet of slack. "Great, Rick, hold right there, Ring said." Lehman felt the pilot making swift subtle control movements as he hovered, adjusting his machine to the high unstable air. *Damn, he's good.*

"Lehman, unbuckle, stand up, and hang onto the center ceiling bar here with me," Ring said. "I will go first. When you see me standing clear of the rope, you go, just like we practiced."

"Copy." Bradford stood, grabbed the bar, and nodded to Ring.

"I'm out in five," Ring said. He took his headphones off, reached out, grabbed the rope, and quickly disappeared below the floor of the flight deck.

"I'm out in five," Bradford said, as he took his headphones off. He glanced up to the cockpit to see Rube in the right seat, helmeted and wearing his oxygen mask. His head was turned toward Lehman and he was giving a thumbs-up. Lehman returned it, turned, and focused all of his concentration on the rope swaying in the furious downwash of the Huskie's rotor blades. He reached out, felt the large weave of the rope solidly in his gloved hands and looked down. Ring was off the rope and standing clear.

Lehman let his feet lift off the deck of the chopper and swung out into the cacophony of wind and noise. He kept his boots wide, as he slid down the rope with his hands. He hit the surface of the glacier, and let go. The heat from the friction of the descent warmed his fingers. He stepped away from the rope.

Ring was on his radio: "CR2 and RGS1 are clear." Without acknowledging, the Huskie rotated ninety degrees, then nosed forward down the broad steep glacier, as John and Bradford bent over, protecting themselves from the violent rotor wash. The scene rapidly became quiet as the sound of the rotors died away.

"This is a big bastard," Ring whistled, looking down into the crevasse. "It must be four hundred feet deep."

"Let's hope our ghost climber didn't fall that far, Lehman said. "We didn't bring that much rope for our pulley system."

"Okay, Bradford, who goes, who stays?"

"Flip a coin. I call tails."

John pulled a quarter from his pocket and flipped it in the air. "Heads, I win. I'll stay up here."

Ring grabbed his ice axe and quickly carved out a small platform beyond the lower lip of the crevasse, opposite the faint slide marks on the uphill side. He then dug a snow bollard behind the platform, tied a nylon web sling around the bollard, and buried a snow fluke behind it. He clipped the cable ring of the fluke into the web sling. "We are bombproof now brother," Ring said.

Meanwhile, Lehman pulled out his goldline climbing rope, tied a figure eight loop on the end, and clipped it into the anchor's web sling with a locking carabiner. He attached two Jumar ascenders onto his waist harness, hung two carabiners with pulleys on the other side, and clipped six more assorted carabiners, with ice screws, into places in between.

"You look geared up pretty good there buddy," Ring said, smiling, as he clipped his own seat harness into the anchor point with a twenty-foot length of web sling. He then reached into his pack and handed Lehman another radio. "Here, Brad, take this with you." He fitted the strap around Bradford's shoulders, turned the unit on, and handed Lehman an earpiece. "The cord to the earpiece on this thing has a microphone built in, Brad. It activates automatically when you speak. That way you can be hands-free." Lehman nodded.

"Radio check," Ring keyed his radio.

"Copy, loud and clear CR2," Bradford acknowledged. "Let's go."

Lehman gathered the heavy goldline and lobbed it over the lower edge of the crevasse. "Fastest way to get the kinks out of it." He glanced over the edge to confirm that the rope was hanging straight. Then he clipped his seat harness into the anchored goldline with a carabiner-wrap, took tension on the rope, and eased out over the lip. He switched on his headlamp, nodded to a 'thumbs up' sign by Ring, and rappelled down into the blackness of the big crevasse. On his way over the edge, Lehman unslung his ice axe and slipped its shaft under the rappel rope, leaving it there on the lip to keep the goldline from sawing its way too far into the snow.

"Thirty feet."

"Copy, RGS1."

"Sixty feet, still no sign. Damn, it's dark down here."

"Copy."

"Seventy-five feet, no sign."

"Copy, RGS1."

"Whoa! What do we have here?"

"Say again, RGS1."

"CR2, are my transmissions being heard outside of this crevasse?"

"Let me check, RGS1. CR2 to CR1."

"CR1," Ranger Bill Butler's voice came back from Camp Muir.

"Can you copy RGS1's transmissions?"

"Negative, CR2."

"RGS1, your transmissions are blocked by your location. Only I can copy you."

"Good CR2, because I found him. The body is crumpled up on a small ledge at about a hundred feet. It is bent in half."

"Copy RGS1."

"Drop me down the long goldline from your pack, CR2. You've got three hundred feet of it, right?"

"Roger, RGS1. It is the same length as the one you're on…"

"Okay, CR2, uncoil that rope, keep both ends up where you are, anchor them, and toss me the bight of it with a carabiner-pulley combination."

"Roger, RGS1, will do. Give me a couple."

While John Ring prepared the extraction rope above, Lehman carefully looked the body over. It was a large Caucasian male dressed in thick navy blue wool pants and a military-style white down-filled parka. It was unnaturally contorted, and lying precariously on a small snow ledge. The right leg was bent at a sharp angle. *Broken*. The face was hooded and buried into the snow. Lehman tied himself off on his rope to free up both hands. He sat comfortably in the big hole, almost hanging free, his toes barely touching the side of the crevasse. He had rappelled three feet below the body on its precarious perch, and was careful not to disturb it. *If this small ledge breaks loose I will lose him.*

Looking down with his headlamp, Lehman could not discern a bottom to the huge crevasse. Looking up, he saw distant daylight slivering its opening. He pulled the Rollei 35T out of his breast pocket, clipped on a hot shoe flash attachment, and started shooting pictures of the corpse and the surrounding areas. He took one photo looking up one hundred feet to the opening of the crevasse, and one looking down between his cramponed boots into the icy darkness. Lehman thought back.

There was a time -- not many years before -- when Lehman was terrified of falling into a crevasse. Climbing on glaciers as a young boy, he feared their depth and darkness. Then one stormy spring day on Mount Saint Helens, he stepped through a hidden crevasse. He was stopped first by his hips. He shouted to his father, and saw him slogging toward him, leading the next rope. Then, as Bradford leaned forward struggling to pull himself out, the rest of the snow bridge broke away with a dull "crump," and he found himself swinging in thin air, twenty feet down in the dark hole. The snow bridge disappeared below without a sound. The fear back then had welled up and grabbed him by the throat. So much so, that Bradford could not even scream. It was just as well, because doing so would not have gone over well with Frank Lehman. Presently his father's head appeared overhead at the lip of the crevasse. There was a smile on his face. It was a smile that said *'Congratulations, you are now baptized in the sport.'* His father told Bradford to relax and breathe – and enjoy the beauty of the place down there. "We'll have you out of there in a jiffy," he said. "But you're fortunate, son. You are protected down there. It is windy and cold as hell out here." Frank Lehman was a man who always saw the upside of any predicament. *It's all about attitude, Lehman. And now look how far you've come – a hundred feet down here in a big beautiful crevasse -- hanging around with a frozen dead Russian. Frank Lehman would be proud.*

"CR2 to RGS1, goldline coming your way."

"Copy, thanks." Bradford looked up to see a doubled line slithering his way with a carabiner-pulley clipped into the bight.

"Got it CR2. Both ends secure up there?"

"Copy RGS1. Both ends are secure and anchored."

Lehman reached over and carefully clipped the carabiner into the rope on the body's waist. "The body is now secured on the doubled rope and on the pulley."

"Copy RGS1, that's great."

"Now we have to get this bastard out," Lehman said. He paused… "Okay, CR2, I am going to break the body loose from this ledge, and then I'll Jumar up my rope."

"Copy RGS1."

Lehman reached out, grabbed the back of the corpse's parka, and pulled. It didn't budge. He pulled again. Nothing. Finally, he jammed his boots into the underside of the snow ledge, grabbed Ring's doubled goldline clipped into the corpse's waist, held his breath, and heaved. There was a loud crash, as the snow ledge broke loose and cascaded into the darkness. The body, still in its same folded, contorted shape, spun lazily from its attachment pulley on Ring's goldline. Lehman, also spinning in his harness, let his breath out. The steam from it drifted across the beam of his headlamp like a light fog.

"RGS1, are you okay?" Ring's voice -- loud in Bradford's earpiece -- broke the enveloping stillness, where Lehman now swung lazily next to the corpse of the dead GRU agent, Mister FNU LNU.

"Roger, CR2. I broke the body loose, and the ledge fell away. Hang tight, I am coming up."

"Copy, RGS1, good work. See you in a few."

Bradford keyed his radio once to acknowledge Ring, and then turned it off. He snapped his Jumar ascenders onto his rope, fed their rope stirrups down through the front of his seat harness, and fitted his boots into them. Holding onto the right Jumar's handles, he lifted his right leg, pushed the right Jumar up the rope to take in slack, and stepped up. The Jumar was designed with a built-in cam that slid up the rope, but not back. His weight was now transferred from his seat harness to his right foot. He mirrored the movement with the left Jumar, sliding and stepping up in it with his left foot. In this way, alternating feet, he rapidly ascended his rappel rope. In a few minutes Bradford was out of the big crevasse and standing by John Ring.

"Next time, Ring, I win the toss and you go in the hole," Lehman said, panting for breath. John smiled. "Ready to pull, Ring?" John nodded, gloved hands on the doubled extraction line. Lehman clipped a Jumar onto one side of it, and snapped the end of the Jumar into the anchoring web sling with a carabiner. Ring and Lehman could now pull on that strand of the goldline, and the corpse would be hoisted up without sliding backward after each pull. With the pulley attached to the dead man's waist, they enjoyed twice the mechanical advantage.

"Ready, pull!" Ring said. Bradford and John put their backs into the work, grabbing the rope, and pulling it back through the Jumar with the rhythmic resemblance of sailors raising anchor on an old sailing ship.

"Do you want to sing a shanty, Brad?"

"No, John. The last time I sang one it was out the other end when I had the runs."

"I said *shanty,* not *shitty...*"

Despite the levity, their combined strength, coupled with the pulley system, moved the crevasse recovery along smoothly. The Russian's broken and doubled-up body popped over the lip of the crevasse, with chunks of the snow ledge it rested on still attached.

"Damn, Lehman, with the strength and brains we have, this thing could not have gone better!"

"Those are my attributes, John. What are yours?"

"Wise-ass!" Ring said.

Bradford retrieved his ice axe from the lip of the crevasse. Ring pulled a body bag out of his pack, and keyed his radio:

"CR2 to CR1."

"This is CR1, go ahead CR2," Bill Butler's voice came in smooth and clear, with its pleasant southern drawl.

"Advise the bird that this phase of the practice exercise is completed."

"Copy CR2, the bird will be there in 20."

"Roger CR1, CR2, out and monitoring."

"CR1, out and monitoring."

While they waited for the helicopter, Lehman photographed the outside of the crevasse and the surrounding area, while Ring carefully chipped snow away from the body with his ice axe, and then worked to straighten the corpse so he could fit it into the body bag.

"Damn, Ring, I hear all that crunching. Take it easy with that thing."

"Well, it's all frozen an doubled up, and... Shit!"

Bradford looked over. "What's the matter John?"

"Come and see this."

Lehman squatted down next to Ring. "Damn, Ring -- that's a bullet hole."

*   *   *

The Huskie, with FBI agent Rubayat Castellano standing on the open back deck next to the hoisting winch, slid carefully into position over Lehman and Ring as they slipped the body bag into a climbing hammock and positioned it for the hoist. Rube lowered the hoist's cable. Ring snapped the secured body bag and hammock onto it's hook and gave a thumb's up. Rube lifted it into the helicopter. It was now 1330 hours, and the wind was picking up. The cacophony of sound and downwash of the rotor blades beat on Ring and Lehman and they covered their heads. The hoist cable returned.

"After you my good man." Ring nudged Bradford, who clipped in and was lifted up. Then Rube dropped the hook back down to Ring. With John finally on board the Huskie and buckled in, Champion deftly nosed the bird out of its hover, and flew low, down the Cowlitz Glacier behind Anvil Rock. Then he made a wide, shallow turn to the west, and headed for Paradise. Captain Champion flared the bird, and touched down in the lower parking lot, by the Visitors Center.

"Why are we landing up here?" Lehman asked.

"Slight change of plans kid," Rube said. "We are letting you and Ring out here, and whisking our FNU LNU -- with his hole-in-the-head gunshot wound that he sustained from falling into a crevasse -- off to an autopsy at Madigan Hospital, Fort Lewis."

"But my car is down in Elbe. How am I going to get it?"

"No, Brad, its right there in the parking lot," Rube pointed. "And we filled it up for you – with premium. Triumphs of that year run better on premium."

"But I had the only set of keys…"

Rube smiled and nodded his helmet. "True, kid. Blame it on Palmrich. He went to locksmith's school. He had to practice. See you in a couple."

"But Rube, didn't you also leave that FBI ASAC down in Elbe, watching the doors? What about him?"

"What about him? I can't think of a better use of an ASAC than watching those doors. He's out there, all alone, with no phone, and no radio coverage. Don't worry kid, we'll be back with the chopper tomorrow morning at the latest, to pick up the doors and spell him."

Jeez, Lehman, there certainly seems to be no love lost between FBI agents and their superiors. Lehman shook his head, took off his headset, and jumped off the back deck of the helicopter. Champion and Castellano waved, the Huskie lifted off, and the noise faded away.

"Hi Brad!" Lehman turned to see Teo's beaming face. She was standing next to John in her lemon-colored waitress uniform, with her raven hair gathered up. She and Lehman hugged. *Damn, it feels good.*

Teo stepped back, hands on her hips. "You two come on up to the Inn with me. I have an open table and I know you are both very hungry."

Ring and Lehman sat in the Dining Room of the Inn. They had just made it there before it closed to prepare for the dinner customers. Only two other tables were occupied on the opposite side of the big room. Nancy Olszewski, all smiles as usual, seated them at Teo's assigned table and filled their water glasses.

"Our esteemed Head Chef, Mister Harry Pappajohn, tells me that you fellows can disregard the lunch menu," Nancy said. "He'll serve you anything you want. He personally recommends that you both order his twenty-four-ounce Porterhouse steaks. He received a new shipment of them this morning. Your server's name is Teo Maloney. She will take your orders." Nancy winked at Bradford.

"Hey, Miss Manager," Bradford said, "may John and I trouble you for some coffee? We are in dire need of it to keep our eyes open. We missed our usual naps today."

Nancy laughed. "Coming right up -- and it's fresh!" She walked away. Suddenly both men felt dead tired.

"Why did you have to go and mention naps, Lehman? Now I can't keep my eyes open."

"Relax, John. You're getting sleepy... very sleepy," Bradford said, mimicking a hypnotist's soft voice. Ring gave him a shove.

"The coffee will bring you back, John. You can take a nap later. It should do wonders for your disposition."

Ring smiled wearily. "I don't know why I'm the spent one here. You are the one who did all the work today, Brad."

"Nonsense, Ring, you worked your ass off up there. I witnessed it. You flipped a quarter and actually caught it. At that altitude it takes a phenomenal amount of energy, athleticism, and concentration to do that." John laughed.

"Well, Lehman, I have a tiny tidbit of information for you on that," Ring said, sporting a tired Cheshire grin.

"What's the tidbit?"

"It came up tails. You actually won the toss."

"Ring, you son-of-a bitch!" It was Lehman's turn to give Ring a shove.

"Careful, man, you're spilling my coffee. But seriously, Brad, you teach crevasse rescue routinely at the RGS. I get training on it twice a summer, if I'm lucky. And this season, since the route on the hill has been such a bitch, I have only had time to practice once with Butler out on the Nisqually."

"I suppose," Lehman said, smiling. "But you sure know your helicopter operations, John. And you taught me enough about fast roping out of the damned thing, that I didn't kill myself. Actually, it was a thrill."

"Hi gentlemen, may I take your order?" Teo stood next to Bradford. She smelled like fresh roses.

"Love your perfume, Miss"– Bradford glanced at her name tag – "Teo, from Pacific Lutheran University."

"Well thank you, sir. I get so many compliments on that. It is called *Essence of Bear Grass.* It is standard issue to all waitressing staff here in the Park."

"Damn! Is that what that flower is called? On my trips past them in the meadows toward the Ice Caves, I've been telling the clients it's *Elephant's Breast.*"

Teo laughed, and put her hand over her mouth. Regaining her professional composure, she placed her hand on Bradford's arm and looked at John. "Mister Ring, what would you like to order today?"

"A twenty-four-ounce Porterhouse steak, medium rare, with a baked potato and all the trimmings."

"Very good sir." Teo sheathed her pad and pencil in her apron, and walked away.

"But Brad, she didn't take your order," Ring said.

"She already knows it."

14

AUGUST 1967: EXTRACTION DEBRIEFING TWO DAYS LATER

Special Agent Rubayat Castellano sat in his usual chair, facing the entrance door to the Glacier Room. The door was locked. The bar was not due to open for another two hours. Lehman, Ring, and Palmrich surrounded Rube at the table.

"Where is Bruce the bartender, Rube?" Lehman asked, looking up at a clean-cut young man with short black hair and bulging biceps.

"Bruce will open and work the bar today in a couple hours for the normal customers. That bartender there is Special Agent Pete Schapp. He recently got back from bar-tending school. Said it was the best FBI training he ever had. Lucky bastard. Some guys get all the best training. He is now known among his cohorts as 'Pete Schnapps.' Anyway, cheers!" The beer mugs clanked, formally bringing the meeting to order.

"We got the autopsy results back on FNU LNU," Rube said. "You two busted him up pretty good getting him into the body bag. I understand. He was frozen. He was still frozen when we got him to the pathologist at Madigan. You must have frozen your ass off getting him out of there, Lehman."

"RGS guides are inured to such conditions." Lehman enjoyed needling Castellano, and sensed that Rube enjoyed it too.

"Let's proceed before the bullshit gets too deep," Rube said shaking his head. He pointed to Lehman, opened his notebook, and pulled a pen from behind his ear. "Tell me what happened."

Over the next forty-five minutes, Bradford recounted the entire recovery operation. CIA Agent Otto Palmrich listened, quietly nodded on occasion, and smiled -- especially on the parts Bradford related about the pulley system he had rigged up to extract the body. Rube wrote quickly, flipping to new pages often, as he filled them. He asked Lehman no questions. At the end he closed his notebook and shook his writing hand. "Damned thing was beginning to cramp up," Castellano said, waving over another round of beers. "Is that the way you saw the operation, Ring? Anything to add?"

"No, nothing to add," Ring replied. "Brad thoroughly covered it."

Rube and Otto sat quietly for a few moments.

"That was an excellent extraction," Otto finally said. "If I were to try that it would have taken half the day instead of under two hours, and I would have had six other guys there helping me. I was skeptical that only the two of you could do this, and lobbied against it. But he --" Palmrich nodded his head over at Castellano -- "overruled me. You know, when the FBI is on the case no one else is in charge. At least that is what we encourage them to think."

Rube grunted. He was deep in thought. "Okay, Ring and Lehman, what do you think the autopsy results revealed?" Rube asked.

"That FNU LNU died of a gunshot wound falling into a crevasse on the Cowlitz Glacier, like you said," Ring answered, taking another swig of cold beer.

"Lehman?" Rube looked at Bradford.

"He was a Caucasian man in his early thirties, six feet tall, weighing one hundred eighty, to two hundred pounds. He had short-cropped black hair, a light moustache and beard, likely grown since he was on the mountain. He had a scar on his upper lip, so he may have talked with a slight lisp. He had a open fracture of his lower right leg, with the broken section displaced at right angles from its normal position. It might actually have been a compound fracture, but I couldn't tell. The pants covered it. The gunshot wound to the left temple had gray-looking powder residue around it, so it was taken very close, perhaps even in contact with the skull. There was no exit wound. So the force of the shot was only strong enough to penetrate the skull and rattle around inside. There was a lot of dried blood around the wound. This indicates that FNU LNU was alive when shot, and his heart continued beating for some unknown time after it was taken. Since we saw him slide into the crevasse, and did not see any attempt by George Coleman to rescue him, my guess is that FNU LNU committed suicide down there, thus freeing Coleman to stand up and walk away."

"Damn, Lehman, anything else to add?" Castellano asked. There was a trace of pride on his face.

Bradford thought for a few seconds. "Yes. He was left-handed, because the shot was to the left temple. And he was wearing an old clunky 'military-style' pair of heavy ten-point crampons, issued by Mother Russia, I'd wager."

"You wagered well, young man, and so did I. I have just won a five-dollar bet with an empty-suit back in Seattle, that you could glean more out of what occurred than he. But of course, my victory is pyrrhic. He's a cheap bastard, and will be transferred, or retire, before he ever pays up."

"I know who that is," Otto said.

Rube continued: "The autopsy findings were exactly as you described, Lehman, but with more medical terms thrown in. You know, long Latin terms for doctors and lawyers -- good 'billable' words. The Pathologist also found evidence that the corpse had been operated on in its youth to close a cleft pallet. Now, about the bullet wound: the powder residue around area of the entrance wound is called 'stippling'. Do you know what that means?"

"I believe so," Bradford said, "Stippling describes a pattern, shading, or picture created by small dots. Artists use the ends, or points, of their brushes to paint using this technique. The method was developed in the 1880s by French artists Georges Seurat, and Paul Signac, and was initially mocked by art critics of the time as 'Pointillism.' However, stippling actually gave rise to a whole new genre called Neo-Impressionism. And the 'Pointillists,' some experts argue, formed the avant-garde movement in painting. This movement was closely connected to the rise of anarchist political philosophy in the nineteenth century. From the historical side, Pointillism ultimately buttressed Marxism, and the communist revolution in Russia, in 1917. And the rest, as we are now painfully aware, is history." Lehman looked around the table.

"Why is everyone staring at me? Didn't I answer your question, Rube?"

"Shit, kid, did you ever. Where in the hell did you get that?"

"Art Appreciation 101, taught by Professor Francis Chubb, at the University of Puget Sound," Lehman said. "It was a required course. I finished it this spring semester, and it's fresh on my mind. So Rube, the stippling you describe from the autopsy must be created by small dots of gunpowder that escape the barrel of the gun along with the bullet?"

"Precisely." Rube said, clearing his throat and shaking his head. Palmrich and Ring were both sitting back in their chairs smiling, with their hands clasped behind their heads.

"What are you two mopes grinning at?" Rube asked.

"I would love to see Hoover and McNamara, or Helms, here with us now," Palmrich said. "McNamara would send Lehman another engraved book, this time on Pointillism. Helms would promote him, and Hoover would fire him for being a smart-ass know-it-all." Ring burst out laughing. Castellano's scowl turned to a toothy grin. He took a long swig of beer and raised his hand for another mug.

"So kid, what we believe our dead GRU man here utilized to do this great deed for Mother Russia, and us, was a pen-gun like this." Rube pulled a small metal cylinder out of his backpack and placed it on the table.

"Has it been made safe? May I pick it up?" Lehman asked.

"Yes, it is unloaded. Go ahead."

The gun was roughly the size and shape of a pen. Bradford noted that it even had a pocket clip like a pen. He unscrewed the barrel.

"So," Rube said, "you simply insert one round into the barrel here, screw the two ends back together, slide this little knob along its track on the outside there, and rotate it into the notch. That's the trigger."

Lehman used his thumb to slide the knob, which compressed a spring in the tube behind the bullet chamber and slid it into the notch.

"The pen gun is now cocked," Rube said. "Reach your thumb up, flip the trigger out of the notch, and the inner spring drives a firing pin against the primer in the round. And the rest -- as you say kid -- is history."

Bradford looked at Rube.

"Go ahead Brad, there is no round in it, like you observed."

Lehman flicked the trigger and the spring drove the firing pin home with a loud *snap*. "Simple," Lehman reflected. "No, elegant."

"Yes!" Palmrich exclaimed. "*Elegant*! The Bureau says 'simple,' and the CIA says 'elegant.' Good for you, Mister Lehman!" He waved for another beer.

"Are you done?" Rube said.

"I am *finished*." Otto replied

"Wise-ass," Castellano rolled his eyes.

"You know Brad, the real reason why it would have taken Palmrich and his mopes six hours to get the goon out of that crevasse?"

"No, Rube, why?"

"Because it was very dark down there, and those pussies are afraid of the dark, especially if there's a dead body in it." Everyone, including Otto, burst out laughing. Rube reached into his pack, pulled out a sheaf of eight-by-ten-inch glossy photographs, and handed them around.

"Damn, that Rollei you gave Brad takes spectacular pictures," Ring whistled. "You think you could spare another one for me?"

"Absolutely, John," Palmrich said. He pulled a new Rollei camera from his knapsack and handed it to Ring, and then slid ten rolls of film over to him.

"Thanks Otto!"

"My pleasure, John, fire away."

Lehman too, was stunned at the richness of the colors in the photos, and at their clarity. He was immediately transported back, hanging in his seat harness in the big crevasse, next to the crumpled body on the ledge. The flash on the camera caught the essence of an unwelcome, uncompromising scene: the body bent in half with a leg askew, the faceless head buried in the snow, the long dagger-like spikes of the corpse's old crampons -- even a small tear in the fabric on the inner left leg near the top of the boot. Lehman took a deep breath and looked up. "I know how the fall occurred."

"Tell us, kid." Rube opened his notebook and grabbed his pen.

"See that small rip along the inner seam of the left leg there, above the boot?" Lehman handed the photograph around the table. "It was right there in front of me and I missed it," Lehman began, his words sounding apologetic. His eyes were closed, and he now spoke as though he was in the scene -- living it:

"FNU LNU is descending in front. That means he has less climbing experience than George Coleman. FNU LNU is walking down the hard crust of the Cowlitz, and he is not walking wide enough with his crampons. In other words, he lets his feet drift too close together. As he steps down, he catches the inseam of his left pant leg with the points of his right crampon. It immediately flips him into a fall. Coleman, who is the anchoring climber, is also careless. He lets slack build up in the rope. So LNU falls free for ten feet or more with his right crampon caught in his left pant-leg. The rope snaps tight, and slams LNU down on the ice breaking his right leg. Now he is completely out of it. He doesn't even try to self-arrest with his ice axe because of the pain."

Castellano looked up. He had a grim, '*Serves that Commie bastard right,*' look on his face.

Lehman continued: "The slack comes tight and sling-shots Coleman off of his feet. It is a true '*Oh shit*' moment for him, and he immediately puts himself into a self-arrest and prays – no, communists are atheists – he *hopes* that he can stop the fall, before they both plunge into the big crevasse below them. Unfortunately, Coleman's hopes are not completely answered. His buddy LNU, disappears into the crevasse. Coleman desperately drives his toes and ice axe into the snow. That action, coupled with the friction caused by the climbing rope between them cutting into the uphill lip of the crevasse, finally brings Coleman to a stop, less than twenty feet from its edge.

"But now he's up shit creek without a paddle," Rube exclaimed.

"Precisely. He is alive and finally stopped, but now he has a crevasse rescue on his hands. And since there is only a two-man party, he has no clue how to extract his buddy. So he lies there in the snow. The rope feels like it is cutting his waist in half. He can't talk to LNU who is down in the hole." Bradford pointed to the pictures of the crumpled body. "No way can they communicate with each other. The crevasse deadens LNU's shouts. So being 'up shit creek without a paddle,' as you say Rube, Coleman now tries to think of a way out. Minutes tick by. Coleman, his body prone against the snow, is getting colder. He is becoming hypothermic. Then his ear picks up a faint *'pop.'* He understands now, that LNU has made the supreme sacrifice for the Motherland. LNU has committed suicide with the pen-gun."

Lehman took a deep breath. Sweat beaded up on his forehead as he continued, almost in a trance: "Now, Coleman has a chance. He cuts the rope with his knife, but the body does not fall with its full force, because the climbing rope has frozen into the lip of the crevasse for nearly half an hour now." Bradford extended his arms shoulder-high and lowered them slowly. His watchers were mesmerized. "It sort of *slithers* LNU down like an elevator, until his body catches, and comes to rest on the small snow outcrop a hundred feet down. That explains why the ledge here in the pictures sustained the weight of the body -- and yet I was able to break it loose." Lehman opened his eyes and nodded. "Yup, that's what happened."

The men at the table remained silent, visualizing the scene, looking at the photos. There were two pictures on the roll of developed film that particularly struck Castellano. One, illuminated by the flash and Bradford's headlamp, looked down between Lehman's feet. It showed his boots and crampons in thin air, and below them was a dark, infinite void. The other was shot straight up, showing a jagged window of distant sky and light – the maw of the big crevasse.

Bradford broke the silence. "The rope recovered with the body was not commercial climbing goldline, but three-strand, soft-laid, seven sixteenth-inch diameter white nylon rope. In other words, it was yachting line. It may be purchased at any hardware store, and has a static load rating of about three thousand pounds -- very close, in practical performance, to goldline. My dad roped me in with it all the time when I was little."

"Your dad was cheap?" Ring asked.

"No, practical," Lehman said. "He bought it right off the spool at Ferguson's Hardware Store in Shelton, after carefully inspecting every foot of it. He liked the soft feel of it – easier to tie knots, and easier to break open the weave, to inspect for damage. But yes, John, it so happened that it was a lot cheaper." Lehman smiled. "He would only use those ropes for one season and then retire them from climbing. The yachting line was more susceptible than goldline to being weakened by the ultraviolet in sunlight. So Rube, before I forget, can you check the autopsy photographs in your file again? Look for any small fragments of cloth stuck in the points of the corpse's right crampon."

Castellano opened the autopsy report and flipped to the attached section of photographs. "Shit, kid, you nailed it again!" He slid the file over to Lehman, and Ring and Palmrich crowded close to look. Caught on an inside middle spike of the GRU agent's crampon was a tiny fragment of cloth. It matched his pants.

"Rube, with your presumed permission," Lehman said, "I did a little checking to see if I could place a name on our FNU LNU corpse, or trace any activity of George Coleman. I asked my colleagues at the RGS if they recalled any clients named George Coleman. None could. Then I asked Doug Gandy, our RGS Equipment Manager, if he recalled talking with anyone recently who had a lisp. He vaguely recalled that a man, generally matching FNU LNU's description, came into the RGS and rented an ice axe. It was a three-day rental, normal for a summit trip. But the axe was never checked back in. Gandy indicated that it was a bit strange – not that the axe didn't come back, that happens fairly regularly -- but that the man just rented an axe and no other equipment, no clothing, pack, or crampons. Nothing, other than an ice axe."

"Is that unusual?" Rube asked.

"Yes. Normally equipment goes out in packages to outfit clients for climbs. It is rare for anyone to only rent an ice axe." Castellano flipped his notebook open again, and made a note of it.

"When Doug gets some free time he will try to find the record and pull it for me," Lehman said.

"And in the meantime," Rube added, "our Identification Division will try to match the finger prints to any known GRU agents. By the way, the Chief of the Identification Division back at FBIHQ sends his regards, Ring and Lehman. He said the sticky tape caught clear prints of the index, middle, and ring fingers of Coleman's left hand. It also caught some hairs and fibers. That section at the Laboratory Division is looking at those."

"So he's right-handed," Bradford concluded.

"You got it kid," Castellano replied…. "As usual."

"This event will definitely set them back," Palmrich said. He was leaning back in his chair hands clasped behind his head, looking at the ceiling. "And it will give us a little breathing room."

"Yeah, and it's going to give the empty-suits back at Moscow Center fits," Castellano concurred. "But only temporarily. The bastards never give up easy. They are done for this evolution, but the GRU will be back next summer – and with a vengeance, I'll wager."

"Jeez, Rube," Lehman said, "you sure are rough on supervisors, no matter where they're from."

"True, kid. But it's my philosophy that if you're going to be a supervisor – especially in the FBI -- you'd better be a leader. And you'd better back up your street agents. I've had a few like that. Damned few. They are gems. But really, street agents are as hard on each other as on their superiors."

"How so?" Bradford asked.

"I'll give you an example. I was stationed in Las Vegas. One of the street agents was water skiing one weekend out at Lake Mead, and had the end of his index finger ripped off. Got the damned thing caught in a loop of the tow rope when he was being pulled out of the water. So he went to the hospital, got what was left of the finger sewn up, and took a couple days of sick leave to recover. The day before he came back to work, the SAC called an all-agents conference. He said: 'Look, this guy has gone through a lot. It's been traumatic for him, and he's sensitive about it. I don't want any of you mopes jacking him up, or giving him a hard time about this when he comes back to work tomorrow. Got it?' The SAC took out his cigar and looked sternly around the room. His eyes settled on our resident wag, Special Agent Jerry "Fluffy" Daugherty. 'And that especially means *you*, Daugherty.' Without missing a beat, Fluffy raised his hand. 'Honest, Boss, I'd never do such an unkind thing to one of my fellow agents. I swear. Scouts Honor!' He gave the SAC the Boy Scout salute – with one finger missing."

"What did the SAC do?" Bradford asked.

"He just shook his head, put his cigar back in his mouth, and left the room. The victim agent was forever known after that as 'Fingers,' or 'The Finger.' Whenever another supervisor asked for additional manpower, for a raid or surveillance, the agent's supervisor would say: 'Sure, I'll give you The Finger.'"

15

LOVE AND LAST CLIMBS

Bradford Lehman sat again in the bright sunshine, steaming coffee in hand, on his favorite bench, in front of the entrance to the Paradise Inn. Excited tourists streamed past. Lehman closed his eyes, lightly dozing, listening to many languages mixing together into the music of happy people. Lehman cherished happy people, perhaps because he came from a household containing two relentlessly unhappy parents.

Teo was a happy person, and smart, and kind, and by anyone's measure, beautiful. It was the former qualities in Teo that sealed his deep attraction to her. She was due to meet him and to share a day off with him tomorrow. Did he love her? Lehman didn't fear the word so much as he was terrified by it. Was it the lure of Paradise and the mountain, and the woman dedicating her energy to him? Was it because he was under the double pressure of guiding at the RGS and working as an "Operator" in a deadly Cold War conflict? Deadly was an understatement. But it was not that pressure on young Bradford's shoulders that addled him. It was the living, breathing, and deeply intimate question of love. And Teo was his first. This reality alone, compounded his confusion on the question. He had no perspective. Bradford was wise in one respect. He never let his ego, or confidence in his craft, degrade into smugness. Correspondingly, he would not allow any sexual relationship with a woman to dissolve into superficiality. He did not celebrate, or live that way. It was not his nature. This he knew, made him vulnerable. That was the answer: *I am terrified of being vulnerable.*

"Hi Brad!" Teo sat down next to Lehman, with her coffee in one hand. She rubbed her other hand along his back.

"Hi girl! Would you like to go for a hike?"

"I'd love to." Teo smiled. She was wearing a close-fitting royal blue sweater over a white turtleneck blouse, and tight blue jeans. Every soft inch of her young body reflected a joyful womanhood.

"God you're gorgeous, girl," Bradford said, looking her carefully over. There was genuine awe in his voice.

Teo blushed. "Sometimes you talk to me like you're looking at the mountain."

"I *am* looking at the mountains!"

Teo threw her head back, laughed, and nudged him. "Come on, Brad, it's four in the afternoon, and all the RGS Ice Caves trips are done for the day. Let's go back there. They are so lovely, and the Indian paint brush is turning."

"Shall I grab the Coleman Lantern?" Bradford asked.

"No, my guide, she said softly, her eyes looking closely into his, "just take my hand and lead me." They walked.

"Tell me about your day," Bradford said, as he reached up and swept Teo's hair over her ear, so he could better see her. He could close his eyes at any time and see Teo's beautiful face: the straight nose, perfectly-proportioned, her full lips, the limpid pools of her large dark eyes, her straight white teeth, and above all, the loving smile. That instant clarity and vision had never happened to him before. Lehman asked Teo the question because he wanted to listen, and to think about the words her lips effortlessly formed, and about the lips themselves, lightly covered with pale red lipstick. They were happy lips. Teo slipped her hand out of his, and rested it on his broad shoulder as they continued their stroll.

"I had a good day," she said. "Wonderful people at my tables -- a family from New York, another large group from Arizona, and a couple from Colorado. Their kids were all very well mannered, which always makes me thankful, and they all loved the mountain. They were energized and excited to be up here at Paradise. That makes the job worth it -- the people I meet who love the mountain. Some love it at first sight. Others don't. But I try to coax them to look beyond themselves, and appreciate what they see."

"Did you love the mountain at first sight?"

"Yes! Like I've told you, my family and I have been coming up to Mount Rainier almost every summer, for ten years. We stayed at the Inn sometimes. On other vacations we stayed in Ashford, at Pappajohns Hotel. We hiked much of the Wonderland Trail around this side of the mountain. Only day hikes, though. My mom and sisters didn't like to camp. But my dad and I vowed that someday we would climb Rainier -- and last summer we *did* climb it, with the RGS -- and with you, my amazing man." Teo punctuated her words by kissing Lehman softly on the lips. They walked on.

"Did you ever love anything else at first sight?" Lehman asked.

Teo's face blushed crimson. She turned her face slightly and looked down. There was a long pause. A light puff of wind swirled strands of her hair as she looked down at her feet. Teo lifted her head and stared straight at Bradford, focusing her dark shining eyes on the man walking next to her.

"Yes," she said softly.

Lehman knew in that moment that Teo Maloney was struggling with the same questions as he. She hadn't spoken the word *love*. She had said one word – 'yes' -- and remained quiet.

The two lovers crested the top of Mazama Ridge, found a big flat rock away from the trail, and sat down, looking west toward Paradise. A grizzled old alpine fir stood behind them, its dense needled branches serving as a break from the cooling breeze. Somewhere high on the Nisqually Icefall, a serac the size of a building collapsed with a thunderous boom. They looked over at the mountain. A huge avalanche of ice and snow tumbled a thousand feet to the lower glacier, where it came to rest. A large white cloud of ice crystals drifted slowly away from the debris. The sound died away and the big mountain regained its serenity.

"No one is around here this late in the afternoon but us," Lehman said softly.

"Yes, they're all getting ready for the dinner bell. The Dining Room will open in half an hour." Teo glanced at her watch. Bradford was not looking at the Inn. He was savoring the profile of her face as she spoke. Gently he reached up to her chin, turned her lips to his, and kissed her tenderly. But as the two lovers touched lips and embraced, Teo's kiss became stronger, her breathing deeper, as the passion in her vied with restraint. Correspondingly, Bradford's passion rose. He pushed back her raven hair and kissed her neck. He wanted to make love to Teo right there. He placed his hand on her breasts over her sweater, kneading gently, remembering how the soft skin felt as his fingers played over them, when they had made love for the first time. *Yes, Bradford, this sweet woman loves you, and you love her. But you cannot say it to each other yet. Funny how words unspoken are some of the most powerful.*

As they kissed, Teo's hands slipped down Bradford's chest and touched him gently along the zipper of his jeans, all the while her lips full on his. Suddenly she caught her breath. "Brad! what's this?"

Lehman reached down and drew out the Walther pistol.

"My god, Bradford, why do you carry that?"

"Because, Teo, the Russians carry them. Rube put me through extensive firearms training at Mica Peak over spring break, and issued me this pistol."

"And you've been carrying it with you up here ever since?"

"Yes, girl. John Ring must carry up here as well – everywhere. Rube made it an absolute requirement. He says we're in a 'combat zone,' with the GRU targeting the mountain. He said the GRU plays only one game – for keeps – and firearms are a hallmark of it." Bradford looked into Teo's eyes. "I never actually asked Rube if he briefed you on the firearms requirement. Did he talk to you about the risks?"

"Yes," Teo said, her eyes wide and fixed on the weapon. "But I didn't…I had no idea…" her words failed her, and trailed off.

Lehman re-holstered the pistol, and put his arm around her. "And all this time you thought I was just happy to see you, right?"

Teo's shocked face froze for a moment. Then she threw her head back and laughed, letting out a snort. She clasped her hands embarrassingly to her mouth. She kept them there, looking alternately at Lehman's face, his pants, and the silver Walther pistol he was holding.

"Your eyes are even more beautiful when they're surprised," Lehman said. He kissed her forehead and stroked her hair. Then he got up, and pulled Teo to her feet. "Come on girl, let's walk back and get some dinner. I was going to tell you about this tonight in my room. John is down the hill tonight and tomorrow, so we again have it to ourselves…" Lehman hesitated. "That is, unless you need to rethink your relationship with me. If so, I completely understand, though not on the level of longing for you. I long for you to be with me, Teo."

"Oh, Bradford, and I long to be with you." For the first time Lehman detected fear -- and a touch of sadness -- in Teo's dark eyes. *Is there doubt in them too? Is this too much for her? Is this the end of our short time together? If, so, you really can't blame her, Bradford.*

"I feel so sad that you are in this, my man," Teo said softly. "You are too young to be involved in these things." She squeezed Lehman's hand as they walked. The sun was turning red on the western horizon and late afternoon shadows purpled the meadows.

"Men of my age, by the thousands, are involved right now in Vietnam. Some are my old high school classmates. Some won't come back. It is dangerous here, yes, Teo. But less so than if I were in a steaming jungle, in a completely foreign environment, and --"

"And what, Brad?" Teo asked.

"-- And without you." Lehman felt his throat tightening up with those last words. They strode on for another minute. Teo was quiet. "So you see girl, on balance I am indeed fortunate." He kissed her cheek.

Teo stopped, faced Bradford, and pulled him toward her. She kissed him long on the lips, and hugged him. It was a strong hug, stronger than she had ever given him. Then she pushed him out to arm's length, and looked long at Lehman.

"Brad, I have been so afraid to tell you this…" Tears were in her eyes.

"Tell me what?"

"That I love you, dear man. I have loved you from the moment I first saw you on the summit climb with my dad last summer. I have been so afraid, because it isn't time to tell you, even after we made wonderful, unbelievable love together for the first time. And I know I'm taking a big risk in telling you this now, Bradford. Love is a special word – I have never used it lightly and never will. It represents to me something intimate and ultimate, and my saying it makes me very vulnerable. But I am saying it to you now, Brad. I am saying it because whatever happens from now on -- whether we stay together or part ways someday -- I want you to know that I love you now, at this moment, with all my heart and soul, and that I have always loved you, and that I always will love you. Your face and your personality have been in my mind's eye as the man of my life since I was a little girl. You are so wonderful and special to me."

Lehman felt tears well up in his eyes. He looked into Teo's. They sparkled with joy, and with the direct, disarmed vulnerability that the words *'I love you'* inevitably bring, when they spring from the lips and the heart.

"I love you Teo," Bradford said. "I have been wrestling with when, and how, to tell you. You too deserve to know how I feel, and I am telling you now, because you have given me the courage to face my own vulnerability. I don't know what the future holds. I would love that it holds us together forever. But we cannot know that – not yet – not as young as we are, and under the circumstances we are in up here. If we stick it out together, we still have so much growing to do. So often, simply growing up and maturing splits people. My parents suffered that fate. The only problem with them is that they are still together."

Teo detected stress in Bradford as he spoke of his parents' marriage. It was the stress of abiding sadness. It took her slightly aback. But when she replied, her voice carried a mixture of joy, relief, and understanding. Despite his reservations, he had overcome them, and spoken the words, *"I love you Teo."* Tears began streaming down her face. "Bradford, I am so relieved I finally told you. Bradford, I am so proud of you. I pray for you all the time, and now that I know you have to carry a gun --" Teo paused. Then she spoke firmly: "I should have better understood the danger involved. I should have known that you might have to carry one. I am so sorry I was shocked. It brought all my concerns for you right before my eyes. Please don't worry about that. I have fired guns a lot on my uncle's ranch, rifles and handguns. I am not afraid of them." Her words raced out.

"Teo, it's okay." Bradford wiped the tears from her eyes and embraced her. "We are both learning that this pristine place is not so pristine when it comes to the outside world. For me, and now for you, we are in a war – even here. I always saw this place as a sanctuary from the rest of the world. Not anymore."

That night Teo Maloney and Bradford Lehman made passionate love together, in the warm pleasant darkness of Lehman's room, and spent themselves in each other's arms.

Such are the celebrations that follow declarations of love, the survival of a dangerous climbing season on a big mountain, and the emerging threats that were inexorably unfolding into another deadly chapter of the Cold War.

* * *

Lehman summited Mount Rainier twice more before Labor Day brought an end to the 1967 RGS guiding season. The "Gib" route took its inevitable toll. Though there were no fatalities, Lehman cracked his Bell Toptex rock helmet, bent the frame on his Kelty pack, and badly dented the Gold Eveready radiation sensor in the pack's outside pocket. This occurred on the Gibraltar ledge. He had crossed under the old exposed rappel point, when the client behind him dropped the coils he was holding, and became tangled in the climbing rope. Bradford hustled back across to free the client and push him out of the exposed gap, when a rock struck Lehman and knocked him out. There was little sound that he could recall – only an impact that brought stars to his eyes and then darkness. He woke up sprawled on the floor of the ledge a few minutes later, with Gary Olin's headlamp glaring in his eyes.

"You okay, Lehman?"

"Yeah, Gary. I'm okay, I think. What about the client?"

"You shoved him out of the way. He's fine. Do you want to turn this party around?"

"No, let's move on a bit and I will see if I can walk it off." He did.

The RGS party safely summited, and returned to Camp Muir, and Paradise. Lehman did not tell Teo what happened, but she heard about it almost immediately from Gary Olin. Teo scolded Lehman for not telling her. She did it in the manner that only a loving, concerned, woman can – by grabbing Bradford's hands and looking him sternly in his eyes. He promised to confide such things to her from then on… "I will if you give me a neck rub, girl. It still hurts."

Teo efficiently attended to her waitressing work at the Inn. But she constantly worried about Bradford, and he in turn, worried about her worrying. In that ancient man-and-woman process of fussing, passion, and compassion, friendship and love grew.

16

THE DAY AFTER LABOR DAY 1967: RUN THE BEAR OUT OF THE PARK

"Well John, Brad, and Otto, we have come to an apparent respite in the operation to keep the Russian Bear out of the Park. Congratulations!" Special Agent Castellano said.

"A toast!" Palmrich stood up with his mug of beer. They all stood. "Here is to 'Running the Bear out of the Park'!"

"To running the Bear out of the Park!" Mugs clanked. Rubayat Castellano emptied his, and waved for another one.

The stately old Paradise Inn was nearly empty. It officially closed on Labor Day. The tourists and summer Park employees were all gone, except for workmen boarding up the large glass windows, and preparing the place for winter. Teo had stayed up at Paradise. Lehman would drive them both off the hill to Tacoma, and to school, after Castellano's debriefing. But now, during the meeting, she was happily enjoying driving Bradford's Triumph Herald on the Park roads. It was the first time Teo had driven a car, since she reported into Rainier National Park to start work, back in June.

"Brad, while you have your meeting with Rube, I'll warm your car up for you!" she said.

He tossed her the keys. "Have fun, girl! Do you remember how to drive a manual-shift car?"

Teo rolled her eyes and waved goodbye, tossing her long black hair away from her face.

"Is the Glacier Room secure?" Rube glanced at Special Agent Pete Schepp, AKA "Agent Schnapps," tending the bar, who gave a thumbs-up.

"Well, gentlemen," Rube said, "we have some interesting information to share from our end." Castellano motioned to include Palmrich, who nodded. "Mister Genady Roskovsky, our GRU Officer, and Soviet Military Attaché out of Washington D.C., who risked his career to hike to the Ice Caves and got photographed by young Lehman here, has been recalled to Moscow," Rube said. "Moscow Center cut short his assignment -- by over two years. So kiss his sorry Commie ass goodbye!" The men hooted and clapped.

"That's a 'Hoover Stat,'" Palmrich proclaimed.

"You're right Palmrich, not one, but several. And I am claiming every goddamned one of them!" Rube gave a Cheshire grin to Lehman and Ring. "Just to clue you two neophytes in: a 'stat' in the Bureau is short for 'Statistic.' The FBI runs on stats, and so does the CIA. They are real big with the Directors and Congress. It's how they measure work performance, and 'earn' their next year's budget allocations. Lifeblood of bureaucracy -- smoke and mirrors shit." Rube grinned again. "Roskovsky's 'career enhancing' early recall to Moscow Center is Hoover Stat One. Hoover Stat Two: we got a positive identification back on FNU LNU. Brad, to your credit," Castellano continued, "you tried to run that lead down on LNU by checking the RGS paperwork on the rental of the ice axe, but it couldn't be found. Not surprising. These shifty bastards routinely steal paperwork to cover their tracks. It would have been easy to do by simple distraction over at the RGS rental counter, with all the clients milling around in that small lobby, being outfitted and all. But not to lament -- the Ident Division came back with a hit on the prints. Mister LNU turns out to be Boris Velantin, a known GRU agent. Kiss his ass goodbye."

"How so, Rube? This Velantin guy died on the mountain in a crevasse with a bullet through his head," Lehman said. "How is that a 'stat?'"

"It's called a 'neutralization,' Brad. It doesn't matter whether Boris did it to himself, or if the mountain did it to him. It's a stat – Hoover Stat Three. And it's a rather important one in our business -- icing on the cake, as it were. Our FBI counterintelligence mission is a three-step process: identify, penetrate, and neutralize. We've accomplished all three steps with old Boris here. Castellano took a swallow of beer, wiped his lips, and continued. "By the way, Brad, I reimbursed McGill and the Rainier Guide Service for the ice axe Velantin stole. It doesn't show up that way on my voucher to Mister Hoover, but it's in there." Rube finished his mug of beer, and waved over another.

"Nice touch, Rube," Lehman said.

"Oh, I almost forgot," Rube said. "Boris Velantin talked with a slight lisp. His English was good, but the lisp made him stand out in the business, and he was thus more of a minion for the GRU than a mainstream operator."

Castellano cleared his throat. "Hoover Stat Four: the fingerprints Mister Ring here so craftily culled from the man who called himself George Coleman, came back with a hit as well. The person you cited that night, John, was Georgi Kulikov. He is a Ukrainian, also in the GRU, with the rank of Captain. He is well connected politically in the Communist Party, and we anticipate he will survive this 'setback.' We will see more of him later. He is now officially known to the FBI as Georgi Kulikov, AKA, George Coleman. Because of his fluency in English, he is viewed as a valued 'American' operative. He has connections with Spetsnaz. I suggest, Lehman and Ring, that the next time you run into Kulikov, you carefully watch his hands."

"Why, Rube?" Lehman asked.

"Because, kid, he is snake-dangerous. He is a suspected assassin. Currently he is out of the United States. FBI checks at Seattle-Tacoma Airport, revealed that Kulikov boarded a flight to Vienna, Austria, three days ago. From there he will travel back to Moscow Center. But we expect him to return for the completion of the GRU's mission here."

"We are more convinced than ever, thanks to your efforts," Otto Palmrich said, nodding to Lehman and Ring, "that it is the GRU's intention to place a portable nuclear weapon on the summit of Mount Rainier as a 'failsafe' solution, in case of thermonuclear war. If their bombers and missiles cannot get through, we believe they will trigger these devices in order to cause -- or create the impression that they can cause -- Mutually Assured Destruction, or 'MAD' as we term it, in the event of a war. This MAD theory, propounded by Robert McNamara, Director Hoover, and others, is gaining traction by what is observed right here on Mount Rainier."

"Let me add some recent background and perspective to what Otto told you," Rube said. "Only two months ago the Israelis fought the Six-Day War with the Arabs in the Middle East. The Arabs attacked Israel, but got their butts kicked. We backed Israel, and the Russians backed the Arab states. This is another example of a 'hot,' or 'proxy' war breaking out as a subset of overall Cold War tensions, and the overarching mission of the Soviets to spread communism, and by extension their control, throughout the world."

"But the Russians didn't directly commit their own forces to that conflict," Ring said.

"True, they didn't, thank God," Rube said, "because that would have brought the U.S. into it, and we easily could have seen a World War III. This brings me to what we suspect up here on Mount Rainier: that the GRU's die-hard militant faction is driving this operation. We believe that a Backpack portable nuke is in the mix. GRU political officers working in North Vietnam actively militate against America; and they do the same working with the Arabs in the Middle East against Israel and America. I am confident we will neutralize these bastards here on the hill. But it will take time and patience."

The group was silent as it digested the information provided by Palmrich and Castellano.

Rube broke the silence. "Okay folks, let's get to the next, and more enjoyable, order of business. He waved for another round of beers.

Special Agent Rubayat Castellano stood up, holding his cold mug of beer. "All of us here in this room, at one time or another, and multiple times, have put their lives on the line during this long Cold War."

Lehman was surprised to see Rubayat's eyes misting up, and his tone turning emotional.

"Some in this room have sacrificed more recently than others." Rube nodded again to Ring and Lehman. "And in recognition of their efforts and sacrifice, I am directed by Mister Robert S. McNamara, the Secretary of Defense, the Director of the Federal Bureau of Investigation, Mister J. Edgar Hoover, and the Director of the Central

Intelligence Agency, Mister Richard Helms, to state the following --"
Rube picked up a piece of paper and began reading:

"'We wish to express our sincere collective appreciation to Jonathan M. Ring, and Bradford W. Lehman, for their assistance and expertise in the performance of the operation herein. It is through their assistance and expertise that intelligence of significant value to the United States has been, and continues to be, developed. It is ultimately upon such sacrifices and contributions, by Jonathan Ring, and Bradford Lehman, that success in these vital matters of national security may be attained.'"

Castellano looked at Lehman and Ring, and handed the letter to them. Then he and Palmrich, and the other agents guarding the room, applauded.

"What does this mean, Rube? Lehman asked.

"You can see that all three of these rather high officials signed this letter. It means, Brad, that you and John have received a special written letter of commendation. Letters on this order, co-signed by the Secretary of Defense, and the Directors of the FBI and CIA, are damned rare. It is roughly akin to the British military's tradition of being 'Mentioned in Dispatches,' but only a hell of a lot rarer than that."

Lehman nodded his understanding. "This is a great honor Rube, but I..."

"You and Ring earned it kid," Rube said, raising his hand, cutting Bradford off. His voice turned deeper and more serious. "You two can also see that the letter is marked 'TOP SECRET.' It is not to be divulged in any way, under any circumstances. Separate copies of this letter will be placed in special classified files marked for each of you. These special files will follow you around for the rest of your careers in federal service, regardless of what armed service or agency you may be in. Again, my hearty congratulations."

FBI Special Agent Rubayat Castellano pulled himself up ramrod straight. He and CIA Agent Otto Palmrich shook Ring and Lehman's hands. They all had a couple more rounds of beers, and then Castellano and Palmrich concluded the meeting.

"We have barely cracked the nut on this GRU operation," Rube said. "Our people have a lot of work to do. There is a ton of intelligence data, some from reconnaissance, and SigInt, Signals Intelligence, and HumInt, Human Intelligence, that remain to be analyzed."

"Any luck with the SR-71 and our Gold Eveready's?" Ring asked.

"Yes, John, we are seeing some tantalizing results," Palmrich said, choosing his words carefully. "The SR-71 is a spectacular platform, especially in its photo-recon capabilities. We are still working to tweak the other sensors on board, including those supporting the special Gold Eveready Batteries you two carried so religiously up the hill."

"John and Bradford," Rube said, "we will be contacting you both periodically before next summer's RGS season. It will include further briefings and training for both of you."

*   *   *

As the men left the Paradise Inn for the last time in 1967, Rube looked over at the blue Triumph Herald in the parking lot, and noticed Teo inside. He walked over to the car with Lehman. "Get in, Brad," Castellano said.

Lehman sat in the driver's seat, and Rube motioned Teo to roll down her passenger window.

"Hi Mister Castellano!"

"Hi pretty young lady! So you and Bradford here are an item?" Rube's voice was soft, concerned, and fatherly.

Teo blushed. "Yes we are."

"You know, when I first saw you in the Dining Room alone, and Lehman on the mountain alone, I said to myself '*Why don't these two get together?*' And here you are! Teo, I know you are proud of this man here. And Bradford, I know you are proud of this girl – no, woman. I have spent many years observing people, and I have never seen any couple more compatible. Both of you are good looking, but you, Teo, much more than Lehman here."

"That's an understatement, Rube!" Bradford said.

"Both of you love the outdoors and climbing," Rube continued. "Teo, when I interviewed your dad during your background investigation, he said that you and he climbed Rainier last year."

"Yes! And with this man as one of our guides," Teo said, grabbing Bradford's arm.

"And both of you are very intelligent, and both of you are wise beyond your youth," Rube said. "Actually, when I look back on my miss-spent youth -- hell, at eighteen I didn't have half the clue that each of you has about life, and the way to live it. You two amaze me. I climbed the mountain with this guy here last year, too. I bitched the whole way. Lehman got my ass up there and back. I want you to know, Brad, that I count that climb of Mount Rainier as one of the most rewarding efforts of my life. You two can have a hell of a lot worse things driving you together than that big beautiful mountain behind me." Rube shot a thumb back over his shoulder.

"Now, you are probably asking yourselves." Castellano continued, speaking his words with deliberation, "'*Is it love that I have for Bradford?*' '*Is it love that I have for Teo?*' Let me say this, again drawing on many years of experience – yes, you both love each other – yes, it is real, and yes, it is the type that is lasting. You then are saying to each other, *'But we are both so young, only eighteen. How can we know it is love? We have no perspective yet; we haven't lived long enough yet.'* Ah, I see you both nodding," Rube smiled knowingly. "Let me tell you unequivocally, from what I judge of you, you are both a good ten years ahead of your ages in maturity. So don't let that trouble you. Will you grow? Of course, look at me!" Rube patted his stomach, "But the crux of it is: *"Will you grow together?'* I predict, based on your solid steady characters that you will. It is going to take patience -- and believe me a hell of a lot of humor -- for you two to make it in life. I'm not trying to marry you off now or tell you to go do it. Indeed, under the circumstances, with both of your ongoing commitments to the present operation, I counsel against it. This operational matter will take time to resolve. All I am saying to the two of you is -- *live.* Let life take you to where friendship and love is. There are enough dangers and pressures in this adventure of ours up here at Paradise to drive normal relationships off the cliff. Yours has just gotten stronger. My hat is off, especially to you Teo, because you have to worry and wait. There is nothing more difficult than to have to be on the outside, in the dark, waiting. *Nothing tougher.* And you, young lady, handle it with class. As for Lehman there, you know he is quite special. That is what drew you to him. We honored him in our meeting. You are proud of him. So am I. I wish I was at liberty to tell you all that he has done here for his country. But I can't." Abruptly, Special Agent Rubayat Castellano straightened up. "That's enough bullshit for now," he said in his usual sonorous voice. He waved and walked away.

17

Spring 1968: Second Training Evolution, Mica Peak

Bradford Lehman enjoyed his studies at the University of Puget Sound, but for one overarching fact: Teo Maloney was not there with him. The same could be said for Teo. They saw each other on weekends, and during the week after classes. Lehman, a "late bloomer," had grown, and now stood a full six feet tall. He stayed in shape by working out in the gym at the University's Field House, and by running the stairs at Baker Stadium.

Teo and Bradford concluded their sophomore years with excellent grades. Lehman continued to distinguish himself in ROTC, and was awarded a "full ride" scholarship by the U.S. Air Force, to cover his junior and senior years. He failed the eyesight requirement for flying school, as he had anticipated. But Professor Walt Hunter generously allowed Bradford to take the aviation ground school with the cadet pilot-trainees of his ROTC class. And with the extra money Lehman earned working for the FBI and CIA, he obtained his private pilot's license. Bradford often rented a Cessna 150 out at Tacoma Industrial Airport, and on clear weekends, flew Teo around Mount Rainier, over the Cascades and Olympics, or out to Ocean Shores, on the Pacific Ocean side of the Olympic Peninsula.

It was on one such outing that Lehman flew Teo over to Sanderson Field, near Shelton, to meet his parents. Though Ruth, his mother, welcomed Teo, Frank Lehman remained distant. He was preparing to divorce Ruth, and the timing for meeting Bradford's steady girlfriend was unfavorable. Teo did not let the coolness of Bradford's father affect her natural upbeat temperament however, though conversations remained largely limited to Frank's discussing prospects and conditions on Rainier for the upcoming climbing season. He did not bring up any subjects relating to Bradford's work with the FBI. He was a man of professional discretion, and well knew when not to ask questions.

Lehman also flew Teo down to San Ramon, California, to visit her parents. Bradford enjoyed them more than his own. They were warm, welcoming, and convivial.

* * *

Captain Walter Dean Hunter, Professor of Aerospace Science, Air Force ROTC Detachment 900, University of Puget Sound, asked Cadet Master Sergeant Bradford Lehman to stop by his office for a few minutes after class. Lehman knocked, and was told to come in. He walked in, came to attention, and saluted:

"Cadet Master Sergeant Bradford Lehman reporting, Sir."

"At ease, Lehman," Hunter said. Hunter, a highly decorated Captain in the U.S. Air Force, with a Silver Star and a Distinguished Flying Cross among them, was an affable man as long as things went well. When they didn't, he was swift to set students straight -- but always in a way that a cadet learned from the experience. Six feet tall, with a football player's build, Hunter had lost all his hair from the stress of being a U.S. Marine in combat during the Korean War. When he arrived at the university of Puget Sound, he was in his thirties. He sported a fighter pilot's persona and bearing, but without the swagger. Lehman wondered why Hunter had called him in.

"Lehman, have a seat."

"Yes Sir."

Hunter pulled two cigars out of his drawer, lit them both, and handed one to Lehman with a smile. "Take one Brad. I don't like smoking these alone." Captain Hunter then reached into his top drawer, pulled out an envelope and slid it across the desk to Bradford.

"Here's a set of orders for you." Hunter sat back and unbuttoned his Class-A uniform blouse to get comfortable. He crossed his legs and Lehman noticed Hunter's polished half-boots, popular with Air Force fighter pilots. The boots were technically "out of uniform," but the regulation was overlooked for fighter pilots who had served tours in Vietnam. Walter Dean Hunter had flown two tours there: the first in 1963, and the second in 1966, immediately prior to his current assignment to Detachment 900. Both were as an Air Commando in the 1st Special Operations Squadron, based out of Bien Hoa Air Base.

"Brad, you are requested by a friend of mine, Otto Palmrich, to report to Mica Peak during your spring break, coming up here in two weeks." Hunter glanced over at the calendar on his wall, then looked back at Lehman and smiled. "Please, Brad, relax and enjoy the cigar. This is completely informal."

Lehman relaxed, and began smoking. It was a good brand. "Yes Sir, I was told of that possibility early last fall."

"I am aware of that," Hunter nodded, still smiling, "and I am now at least partially informed on your mission and accomplishments." Hunter rocked his head back, let out a smoke ring, and watched it float to the ceiling. He glanced back down.

"How old are you, Lehman?"

"Nineteen, Sir."

"Well, Brad, my hat is off to you. Unfortunately, none of the rest of the staff here, including Colonel Delaney, will be taking them off to you. But that's the way the spook business works." Hunter splayed his arms and shrugged.

"That's fine with me, Sir. I haven't yet earned my way here, so it doesn't matter if they know."

"Well, Brad, in fact you already have earned your way here. You, and the rest of the staff here just don't know it yet. But I do." Hunter smiled and let another smoke ring float to the ceiling. "I also heard of your commendation by several three-letter agencies, as well as by the Secretary of Defense. You have no idea how rare that is -- let alone at your age." Hunter stabbed his cigar into the air for emphasis.

Lehman did not know how to respond to Hunter's observation, so he remained quiet. Hunter sensed his unease.

"I am proud of what you have volunteered to do, Lehman, and of your service. I know you are uncomfortable in this setting, but we are now colleagues. And whenever I see you in more informal surroundings, that is how it will be from now on, okay?"

"Yes Sir."

"And when I'm not around here, call me Walt."

"Yes Sir, Walt."

Hunter laughed, then became serious. He leaned forward. "I have been on several operations with Otto Palmrich. He is absolutely outstanding at what he does. Anyway, I am flying you over to Fairchild Air Force Base in the T-33 jet trainer assigned to the brass here at McChord. And I will fly you back at the end. In the envelope you will find a pass to get you and your vehicle through the Main Gate. Park it at the Officers Club. Put the pass on the driver's side dashboard.

A blue flight-line truck will pick you up at the time noted." Hunter stood up and shook Lehman's hand.

* * *

"Hey babe, great to see you!" Lehman sat in the parking lot in front of Teo's dorm at Pacific Lutheran University. Teo had blossomed as well. She now stood five feet six inches, and her figure, perfect before in Bradford's eyes, was even more stunning.

"Hi, handsome guide!" She threw a night bag into the back seat of the Triumph Herald, and slid into the passenger seat. She leaned over and gave him a strong, longing kiss. It was the weekend before spring break.

"Guess where we're going, girl."

"Aren't we heading back to your place?"

"No. I have a surprise for you. Would you like to take a drive out to Quinault Lodge?" Teo's eyes widened.

"Yes! That would be fantastic, Bradford!" She kissed him again as Lehman started the Triumph and headed south toward Interstate 5, Highway 101, and the rain forest of the Olympic Peninsula.

Teo knew that Bradford would be spending most of his spring break over near Spokane. Agent Rubayat Castellano had given Lehman a heads up about it a couple of months before. While Lehman was training with Rube and others, Teo was due to fly commercially to the Bay Area the next weekend, to visit her parents in San Ramon.

"Girl, you look ravishing, you know that?" Lehman said, as he steered the little Herald down the onramp to I-5, and merged into traffic.

"Yes, I know," Teo said, in a low sultry voice. They both burst out laughing.

* * *

On the first morning of spring break, Lehman was waved through the main gate at McChord Air Force Base. He parked his Triumph at the Officer's Club, and was transported to the flight facility, where Captain Hunter fitted Lehman with a helmet and flight suit, and briefed him on the ejection procedures for the T-33. Then they were driven out to the bird. The crew chief buckled Lehman into the rear seat, checked his parachute harness, flipped the switches that armed the ejection seat, and plugged in Bradford's oxygen mask and radio/intercom connectors. Those preparations completed, the chief gave Lehman a 'Thumbs Up' signal. Lehman returned it and the chief climbed down and pulled his ladder away. Captain Hunter was already checked and ready.

"Brad, can you hear me?" Hunter's voice came through the headphones.

"Yes Sir, I copy."

"The name is Walt."

"Walt, I copy," Lehman replied, speaking through the pressure-demand oxygen mask on his face.

"Okay, now we will taxi this bird out here to the end of the runway. I'll perform some last checks and we will be up for takeoff."

"Copy." Lehman heard Hunter's radio conversations with the tower as the T-33 rolled easily into position. Cleared for takeoff, Hunter released the brakes and added power. The small silver jet gained speed rapidly and was airborne, climbing into a clear spring sky. Off the right wing loomed Mount Rainier, mantled with fresh new snow. Captain Hunter banked in that direction.

"Hey, Brad, I have never seen Camp Muir. Take me over there, what do you say?"

"Be happy to, Sir."

"Call me Walt."

"Yes Sir, Walt, sorry."

"I'll hold the altitude here at eight," Hunter said. Go ahead and take the control stick lightly in your right hand. The T-33 responds to light inputs. Got the stick?"

"Yes."

"Okay, it's yours. I have let go of the stick. Fly me over there. Keep your eyes on the horizon. I'll look for traffic."

"Copy. Can I make some turns?"

"Sure!"

Lehman felt completely relaxed. He gently turned the T-33 first to the right, then left, then to the right again in a circle. "Man, this is incredibly responsive!"

"See that road down there below us?"

"Yes, It's Meridian Road," Bradford said.

"Affirmative. Level it out along the straightaway there, and perform a figure-eight turn over it." Lehman smoothly complied.

"Good job, Brad. Where did you learn to coordinate turns? You kept the plane dead on center with no slip, and didn't change altitude at all. You're a natural at this."

"Well, not quite. I have flown occasionally with Jimmy Beech up at Rainier. He is the bush pilot who flies a Cessna 185 out of Ashford, and does all the resupply for the Rainier Guide Service up at Muir. He let me fly to and from the drops. After the AFROTC pilot's ground school you taught this winter, and were gracious enough to allow me to attend, I obtained my private pilot's license on my own nickel. But this jet is so much quieter than the Cessna."

"Outstanding! You got your wings on your own initiative. Now take me to Camp Muir. When we get close I will take the stick."

Lehman flew the straight-winged silver jet south to Eatonville, and then banked east toward Ashford and Paradise. As he did so,

Bradford gave Hunter a running commentary on the surrounding towns, rivers, and lakes, leading into Mount Rainier National Park. He flew the nimble jet up over Paradise. Looking down, Lehman saw the Inn, its roof almost buried by the winter snows.

"See that broad ascending snowfield on the right, Walt?"

"Affirmative."

"Camp Muir is in the middle of the rock saddle there at the top, at just over ten."

"Copy, Brad. We're getting close. I'll take the stick." Hunter added power and climbed with the rapidly rising ground. "I see it, yes, the rock huts there!" Hunter exclaimed. He flipped the T-33 up on its left side. Hunter and Lehman looked straight down at Camp Muir's huts, no more than one hundred feet below. They too were mostly buried in snow. Then Hunter snapped the bird into a climbing right turn, skimmed around the southeast side of Rainier, and took up an easterly heading toward Fairchild Air Force Base, Spokane. The T-33 landed there in less than an hour.

Captain Hunter taxied over next to a HH-43 Huskie sitting on the tarmac, and shut down the engine. As the crew chief unhooked Lehman, and gave him a pat on the shoulder to indicate that the ejection seat had been made safe, Bradford unbuckled from his seat harness and climbed down the ladder. Captain Hunter followed. Lehman took his helmet off and shook hands with familiar colleagues: Special Agent Rubayat Castellano, Otto Palmrich, John Ring, and Captain Rick Champion, the Huskie's command pilot.

"Well, Brad, how did you like the ride out here?" Rube said, sporting a wide toothy grin.

"It was superb! Incredible!"

"Great. Now you get to fly in a *real* bird," Castellano said, pointing to the helicopter.

"We jet jockeys caress the air, and you helicopter pilots beat it into submission," Hunter kidded. With all the backslapping going on, it became apparent to Bradford that the spook business was a small, close, community.

Otto Palmrich spoke up: "Hey, Rube, can you take these two conscripts up to Mica peak? I'd like to stay a bit and knock back a few with 'The Hunter' over at the Officer's Club."

"You know, Walt, you can't fly that jet back to McChord today if you're soused," Champion quipped.

"I am *sure* --" Hunter nodded to the crew chief, "that the good Sergeant Sims, here, can find enough wrong with the bird to keep me here overnight." Sims nodded back with a smile.

*   *   *

At Mica Peak the next morning, Castellano and Palmrich escorted Ring and Lehman to a newly constructed portable building. An Air Police sentry nodded them through the front entrance. The same plush leather recliner chairs were there from last year, with one added to accommodate Ring. Fresh coffee and donuts were ready on a side table by the window, which was covered with an opaque shade.

Rube began: "Good to see you boys again, welcome back. Our analysts have been busy over the past few months. We will not reveal sources of information unless it is obvious, like recon photos, etc. Our purpose is to give you two enough information to conduct further counter-threat operations on the mountain, when the season opens this summer. We have already briefed you on the SR-71 Blackbird. You know it flew regular missions over Mount Rainier on days you both were up there -- and on some days you were not. We are still mulling over introducing an FBI agent discreetly into the RGS, or as a seasonal Park Ranger, to assist your efforts. There is a short-list of agents for this. If it materializes, and it remains a big *if*, the key is that whomever we select must be brought up to speed quickly, so he doesn't function more as a liability to you two than a help, which is what he will be, if we don't get it right. FBI Agents are trained to lead, and it makes finding the right personality -- someone who will listen, learn, and follow -- a challenge."

"Thanks Rube, it warms the cockles of my heart to finally witness a Bureau agent taking a mere support role," Palmrich interjected.

"Your cockles have been warm and getting you in trouble since I have known you, Palmrich," Rube rejoined. Castellano continued: "Here's what we have developed as 'best guesses' on why the GRU has chosen Rainier. Kudos to you, Lehman -- you guessed most of them in our last meeting here at Mica Peak. The Russians harbor an underlying lack of confidence in the ability of their weapon systems to penetrate the defenses of the United States. Mount Rainier is almost fifteen thousand feet high, and located near major urban areas and critical West Coast civilian, and military infrastructure – including B-52 bombers here at Fairchild, and nuclear submarines, stationed at Bangor Naval Base on the Olympic Peninsula. A portable "Backpack" nuke, detonated high on Rainier, would raise definite hell here in the CONUS. It may not be a knockout blow, but it could be enough of a hit to create doubt in the minds of the President and his generals, causing the United States to cease military engagement and negotiate, before Mother Russia is completely wiped out. The GRU's view is that Russia can bleed – it bled profusely in the Great Patriotic War -- World War II – and survived. America, on the other hand, has never bled in modern times at the hands of a foreign foe. Thus it follows, that the United States does not have the moral fiber to sustain itself in such bleeding and devastation, and will quit."

"Do the KGB and GRU compete against each other? Do they get along?" Ring asked.

"No, John, they dislike and distrust each other," Lehman answered. "In 1919 Lenin infiltrated NKVD agents, the forerunner to the KGB, into the GRU. There has been no love lost between them since."

"Excellent Brad," Palmrich said. "This is correct. It is roughly akin to the inherent rivalry between the FBI and CIA."

"Only much more pronounced," Castellano added. "You see for yourselves, that I get along with these mopes pretty well, here on the 'street.' We have operational missions that overlap, even though the CIA is chartered to be outward looking, beyond U.S. borders, and the FBI inward looking, focusing on federal criminal violations, and counterintelligence operations, within our borders. It is the 'Empty Suits,' at middle and upper management, and at the SOG, where rivalries are fiercest. But the KGB and GRU have a genuinely deep distrust for each other. And you might be surprised to know that the GRU actually has more agents in the United States than the KGB. But you rarely hear of them. The KGB is the more public face of Soviet Intelligence. The GRU is the private face. In fact, the GRU is so private, that even the Secretary of the Communist Party of the Soviet Union, cannot walk into GRU headquarters without submitting to a security screening."

The briefings spawned spirited discussions on Cold War tensions and politics, that lasted through the rest of the morning's training. Lehman found the information sobering. He was astute at history and current events, but it was the bitter global scale, and intricacies of the conflict, expertly and succinctly summed up by Castellano and Palmrich, that etched itself into Bradford's mind. *Most Americans don't have the slightest clue of the brinksmanship and peril that the*

Soviet Union and the United States have engaged in. Hell, Lehman,
the Cold War really isn't cold at all.

Following lunch, Castellano and Palmrich completed their briefings to Lehman and Ring on the workings and general activities of the KGB and GRU, and discussed their roles in Soviet projection of power around the world. The group took a coffee break, and then Lehman and Ring were ushered into another large room. It was bare, except for four folding chairs positioned with their backs against the wall. Palmrich walked over to a large roll of thick paper. The ends of the roll left only two feet of free space on each side of the room. Otto took off his shoes and donned a pair of soft cloth booties.

Rube did the same, and tossed booties to Ring and Lehman. "Put these on," he said, and then flicked the light switch. The room lit up brightly. Palmrich unrolled the paper, the far end of which was tacked down to keep the paper from rolling itself back up. John and Bradford could not believe their eyes. Appearing before them on the floor, the size of the fifteen-by-twenty-foot room, was the summit crater of Mount Rainier.

"This is unbelievable. Look at the incredible detail!" Lehman said. John whistled.

"Go ahead. You can walk out on it," Rube said, as he and Palmrich secured the far end of the photograph.

"Hey, that's me!" Bradford exclaimed. He walked over, and bent to look closely at his own image. "And that is Don McPherson sitting right next to me. I've got something up to my face. Crap! You caught me photographing panoramic shots of the crater."

"Son-of-a-bitch!" John said, adding another whistle. "Look at the detail!"

A COLD PARADISE

"The image at your feet was taken by our SR-71 Blackbird, out of Beale Air Force Base," Palmrich said, "flying at more than Mach three and above seventy thousand feet."

"Jeez," Rube said, "The guy next to you Lehman -- is he a hippie or something? He needs a haircut."

"No, Rube he is not a hippie, at least in the derogatory sense of the word. He's merely a grizzled old rock climber and RGS guide who is accustomed to living out of his car and eating beans and peanut butter. But you know what's funny? When this photograph was taken I was just telling him to get a haircut!"

"Good," Castellano said, nodding approvingly.

"Let's walk the crater," Palmrich said. He and Rubayat grabbed pointers and waved Ring and Lehman to follow. "See this large steam vent over here next to this big black rock on the crater's southwest side?"

"192 degrees on the compass if you are standing in the middle of the snow of the crater facing north," Rube added.

"Magnetic?" Lehman asked.

"No, true," Rube said. "We will issue you compasses tuned to true north at this precise location, and to this image. As both you and John know, Rainier is big enough to produce its own magnetic variation on a compass, but for most climbers it's not enough to matter."

"Your Eveready Battery sensors have picked up elevated radiation levels here." Palmrich plopped his pointer down on the mouth of the big steam vent. "Now, let's turn completely around, and walk to this vent over here, at 18 degrees. You can see it is not quite as large a vent, but substantial, compared to the rest of them dispersed around the crater rim. There is no obvious landmark there except for this shaded area above it, and slightly left, looking north. That is actually a yellowish-orange sulfur patch. The advantage you have is that it is eighteen degrees off north, so it will be easy to pinpoint."

"Crap," Lehman said.

"What's the matter kid?" Rube asked.

"On a climb over the Fourth of July, last summer, I was up on the summit with Gary Olin. I was trying to observe, but nodded off. People were crawling around everywhere like ants -- typical for that weekend. When I woke up, I asked Olin if he had seen anything unusual, and he said 'No, not really, except for two clowns flashing each other with mirrors from opposite sides of the crater.' Olin thought it was part of a Fourth of July celebration, and I assumed so too. Earlier, on a climb with Teo up on Pinnacle Peak in the Tatoosh, I also saw several mirror flashes from near the southwest rim of the crater. But they made no sense. It was not an SOS or anything. And climbers use mirrors up on the hill frequently. Sorry I didn't report it."

Rube pondered a few seconds. "That's okay, kid. Shit always slides through. We try to catch everything but we don't. Hell, we don't even come *near* to catching it all. It even happens on surveillances where the target is being observed and followed by ten guys. Remember though, assumptions are often wrong -- and sometimes fatal."

"Brad," Palmrich said, "your little tidbits here actually buttress our data, and suspicions that the Russians may have planted a nuclear device on the crater."

The phrase hit Ring and Lehman like a hammer. They now could fathom the full nature of the threat. They were standing on it.

* * *

"The firing range is hot!" Rube's voice boomed through Lehman's ear protectors. "When I blow the whistle, draw your weapons on your way to the prone position, like we demonstrated. Your packs are on, to force you both to draw and fire under normal climbing conditions. Keep your fingers out of the trigger until you acquire the target. We have spared you the blizzards, snow, and ice, here at the range today."

The whistle blew. Lehman and Ring hit the quick release buckles on the hip straps on their packs, slipped out of one shoulder strap as they went to their knees, allowing the packs to slide sideways off their backs, and drew their pistols as they went prone, facing the target. They then fired three rounds at the target ten yards away.

"The last round was fired at five seconds," Rube said. "All your rounds were center of mass. That's good -- but not good enough. Stand up, and do it again. I want it done in three seconds." The draw-and-fire drills went on for two more hours. Finally, Rube blew his whistle ending the exercise.

"Under three seconds. Good job guys. Clean your weapons, and let's grab a beer."

During the break, as Castellano, Palmrich, Ring and Lehman drank cold beer at the range, John and Rube entered into a lengthy discussion on calibers of pistol ammunition. Ring had used the .45 caliber, Colt 1911 pistol in Vietnam. He loved its knockdown power, but conceded that it was not practical for dragging up and down Mount Rainier. It was too heavy and bulky, and not easily concealable.

"I hear you Ring," Rube said. "Ideally I'd carry a twelve-gauge shotgun if I could. It's hard to miss with that, and it travels nicely through bulky clothing. But it is not practical for your operations. The .32-caliber pistol that you and Lehman carry may not penetrate thick clothing, and the body under it, to deliver a fatal wound. It might on a nice summer's day, if the target is wearing a wool shirt over long underwear, and a nylon windbreaker over that. But not in cold or bad conditions."

"Then how would you handle a threat with it up there?" Bradford asked.

"We have trained intensively with shots to the center of mass and to the head," Rube said. "The head is the place to go with that Walther -- right in the 'mask area' around the eyes and nose -- especially if you see bulky clothing. The best shot is always the well-placed shot. It is not the size or caliber of the bullet. One careful shot, where you see your front sight, beats pulling the trigger until you go empty, no matter how big the gun. Beats it all to hell. *Always.*"

The rest of the training week at Mica Peak went quickly. The last instruction block analyzed, and attempted to predict, the GRU operations on Rainier.

"HumInt and SigInt analysis on this issue paints a bit of a confusing picture," Palmrich advised. "On the one hand there is sustained, intense interest in the upper reaches of the mountain, as you have personally experienced. There is every indication that this interest will continue. On the other hand, we have no hard evidence that a nuclear device has actually been positioned, or is being maintained, by the Russians up there – yet. I say *maintained*, because even if they position it, the device needs a continuous power source to remain operational."

Castellano continued the presentation. "From the Bureau's perspective, we believe these bastards are playing hardball in our park, and are continuing to do so, because the Russian's conventional offensive delivery capabilities – bombers, submarines, and missile systems -- have been significantly over-estimated by our press and military. This is partly due to the Soviet's own active measures program, which rattles the Soviet saber -- puffery; and to our military chiefs, who benefit from bigger budgets and arsenals. Self-serving bureaucracy at its finest may be seen on both sides in the Cold War."

"Is Bob still behind this operation?" Lehman asked.

"As you and John know," Rube said, "McNamara resigned as Secretary of Defense a couple of months ago. Clark Clifford succeeded him. The dust hasn't settled yet on where Clifford stands. He has been briefed, but he's still getting up to speed with the Vietnam War. I suspect he supports it, though."

"You may be wondering what your specific mission is for the upcoming climbing season," Palmrich said. Ring and Lehman nodded. "Your primary mission is to scout and locate any device or devices, and to pinpoint their locations, if found. Your secondary mission may be to lead specialists to the locations to make them safe, recover a device or devices, and if necessary, neutralize GRU presence on Rainier. The goal of intelligence work is mainly to observe and exploit the enemy. But as Rube eloquently expressed, those boys are playing hardball here. What does that mean to you, Bradford?"

"It means, Otto, that they will defend anything they have cached or put in place on the mountain -- to the death, if necessary. It means they may see Ring and me, and any others who get in their way, as direct threats, and will try to eliminate them. In fact, if paranoia is a big motivator for these GRU agents, and an agent has already died on the hill, who knows how that is being sold to their bosses back in Moscow?"

"Lehman you have read my mind again," Rube said. "Georgi Kulikov, AKA, George Coleman, from our information, may have been promoted and put in charge of the GRU operation on Rainier. This would mean that he has sold Moscow Center on his story of what transpired up on Mount Rainier with his esteemed -- and now deceased -- colleague, Boris Velantin. Would he report to the Center that he cut the rope on his buddy? That is not a career-builder in the GRU. What would get him promoted? Reporting to Moscow Center that Boris Velantin simply disappeared in the middle of the operation. That would fuel the GRU's built-in paranoia, and up the ante -- get him extra resources, like bringing in trained assassins, to protect placement of the device, or defend it after it's in place."

"But why would the Russians risk that? Bradford asked. "Wouldn't this go public, and be perceived as an act of war on U.S. soil?"

"Because shit like this has been covered up by both sides, in other times and places in Cold War history," Rube said. Ring and Lehman were silent. "Seems incredible doesn't it?"

Lehman and Ring nodded.

"But it isn't really," Rube continued. "Put yourselves in the shoes of the President. Would you want to hold a press conference and admit that the Russians have successfully placed a nuclear device on American soil, and on your watch? First of all, that is a political shit-sandwich. Secondly, consider the 'panic factor' in our population -- the hysteria it could foster, if it became known. It is better to let Americans go to work, eat their cheeseburgers, feel secure, and to handle this whole thing covertly. And that is where you guys come in."

There was a long silence. It was the sound of Cold War realities setting in.

"Rube," Lehman finally responded, "if that's what is going to happen – if this is going to be played out with a mountain guide and a climbing ranger, we are way the hell outgunned if they're sending in their hit men. We need more backup."

"Hell, that's the understatement of the day," Ring added.

Castellano and Palmrich nodded.

"Yes you do need backup," Rube said. "I have decided. We will be inserting an FBI agent into this operation with you. He will in turn have more direct backup by our agencies."

"Why only one?" John asked.

"Because, until we get tangible confirmation that a device is on the mountain, the operation will have to remain small to keep it unobtrusive. So, gentlemen, our first order of business, when the RGS season opens in the next couple of months, will be to search the caves in the summit crater, starting with the steam vents we have identified as possible radiation hits. Any questions? No questions? Good. So now let me give you the six phases of a typical FBI and CIA operation: enthusiasm; disillusionment; panic; search for the guilty; punishment of the innocent; and praise and honors for the non-participants."

"Thanks, Rube. That gives Ring and me a hell of a lot of confidence," Lehman said, with a half-hearted smile.

"You're most welcome, kid!" Rube grinned. He laughed and grabbed Lehman's shoulder. "I thought that would perk you up! Ring has worked for the government. He already knows the culture well. You will learn it. Don't worry. The Bureau and the Agency get shit done in spite of themselves. We'll nail these Russian bastards. Come on, let's go get a beer and a steak."

* * *

Bradford Lehman flew back to McChord Air Force Base, from Mica Peak Air Station, at the end of the week. Spring break was over.

"Brad, take the stick and fly this thing," Captain Hunter offered, through the intercom.

"That's okay, Walt, you fly. My mind isn't on it today."

Hunter understood. The flight went quietly. There was only the faint whine of the silver T-33's engine as it traversed the high blue sky, and the sound of Bradford's own breathing in his oxygen mask.

18

MAY 1968: FIRST EVIDENCE

Teo noticed a change in Bradford Lehman when he returned from his second training evolution at Mica Peak. Her love for him was growing apace with their time together. But his love for her had grown exponentially -- as had his passion. She loved it, and responded in kind. He drew out passion in her that she hadn't known existed.

"You are my guide. Lead me," she told him.

It was her favorite phrase, and Bradford redefined the experience for her every time they were together. He loved with fire, but she also noticed that he now brooded with intensity. It didn't last long. Sometimes he would fall silent after they made love, and were in each other's arms. When it happened, Teo wisely understood that Lehman, in those moments was a universe away, focusing. She knew by now that his "flash-focusing" was a substitute for fear: that it was survival. He was working out a threat in his mind, perhaps with a client or condition on the mountain. More likely however, she reasoned rightly, it related to his covert operation with the FBI -- because that involved the Russians, the Cold War, and all the anticipated horrors she fathomed that might stem from that mission.

But Teo was also a climber, tough and wise beyond her years -- as agent Castellano observed. It was so difficult to wait, and not to know. She now better understood the words that Rube spoke to Bradford and her the previous fall – "There is nothing more difficult than to have to be on the outside, in the dark, waiting. *Nothing tougher.*"

Teo could only hang on to her man. She was not letting go.

In early May, a month after the Mica Peak training, Special Agent Castellano met with Lehman for lunch near the University of Puget Sound campus.

"Brad, how are your studies coming along? Are you ready for final exams?"

"Yes, Rube, they are in two weeks but I'm more than prepared."

"Good, because I've arranged through Dean Thomas, and Professor Prins, for you to take them two days from now."

"Wait! How did you do that?" Lehman asked, surprised.

"With my silver-tongued wit and schmoozing," Rube replied, with a toothy grin.   "Say, that Thomas, your Dean of the Faculty, is a hell of a good man. We had coffee. Talked for almost three hours. He's a brilliant fellow, highly perceptive. He has his feet squarely on the ground -- unlike so many other college professors these days -- screaming against the Vietnam War, and all. Actually I don't mind the screaming. They have their First Amendment right to do that. Hell, I scream myself all the time. I just don't like them spitting on our servicemen. But they have a point about the war. We can't win it."

"Why not?" Again Lehman was surprised.

"Because the war is too remote from the psyche of the normal U.S. citizen and voter. It is costing too much blood and money. And the last, and best reason is -- the enemy *lives* there -- and we *don't.* That's what I told Bob before he hung it up as Secretary of Defense.

He finally saw the writing on the wall. The math for him didn't work out for any kind of a win for the United States in a war of attrition. President Johnson and the Joint Chiefs, on the other hand, were pushing for higher troop levels. So Bob stepped aside, and went over to the World Bank. Bullshit job, if you ask me, but that's where he went. We still keep in touch."

"Next time you see him, say hello for me," Lehman said.

"Will do, kid. Every time I see him he asks about you. Why in the world he would is beyond me!" Rube's words rolled out over a grin. "But back to business. You will take your finals in two days, so study your ass off and nail them. Hell, I don't need to tell you that."

"Why did you meet with Doctor Prins? He teaches my *English Legal History* course."

"It had nothing to do with this operation, Brad, but he can put two and two together. He was a colleague and counterpart of mine overseas, during World War II. Prins was a major player in the Dutch underground, fighting the Nazi occupation of Holland. He and I met and worked briefly together on a joint OSS-Dutch operation before I moved on. We've been friends ever since. Lehman, did you know that he actually fought with the White Russians against the Bolsheviks in the Russian Revolution, way back in 1917?"

"Yes, Rube. Doctor Prins is an amazing gentleman."

Castellano waved for another refill on his coffee. "Okay, so here's the deal. You and John Ring are going to break early, get your fannies up to Rainier the week before the RGS season opens, and search the crater caves."

"Sounds like a plan,"

"And there's one more thing. I've selected a young gung-ho agent to operate undercover with you two."

"What's his name?"

"He is Special Agent J. Ronald Makinson. He grew up in New Jersey, played basketball for the University of Tampa, and was in Vietnam as an artillery commander."

"Okay, Rube, so let me get this straight," Lehman summarized: "This agent came from New Jersey, lots of big mountains there, went to school in Florida, lots of big mountains there, and was an artillery officer -- which means that he prefers to ride instead of walk. Man, Rube, you made a hell of a choice."

"But it gets better kid," Castellano smiled. "He's going to be a new RGS guide up on the hill with you this summer. And you and Ring are going to train him. Really Brad, it'll be easy. He is in great shape. Plays basketball half the day on Bureau time, and still investigates rings around his fellow agents. He screws with the sign-in sheets, 'bangs the books,' as we agents say, with the best of them. Hell, he even outdoes *me!*"

"Rube, what the hell are you thinking? There are only nine fulltime RGS guides. They are, except for me, the cream of the big mountain climbing crop in America. You know that many of the Everest climbers on the American expedition in 1963, were RGS guides, including the first to summit, Jim Whittaker. And you want to put a New Jersey guy with *no climbing experience* on the RGS staff? That's laughable, Rube. Herb Magill will never agree to that."

"Oh, but he already has, Brad." Rube raised one hand, rubbed his thumb along his fingers, and leaned forward. "Money talks with old Herb! God I love those CIA boys. Should have stayed with them. Lots of money -- and no vouchers, Number-One Registers, or Three-Cards."

Lehman did not ask what Rube's administrative Bureau-speak meant. He was worried about the new anchor around his neck – Special

Agent J. Ronald Makinson. Castellano paid the bill, and the two men headed to their cars.

Rube, sensing Lehman's concern, stopped outside the restaurant. "Really, Brad, Makinson will be a breeze to work with. Don't sweat it. He even loves the outdoors. Hell, he goes out fly-fishing every chance he gets – sometimes even on Bureau time. Gets away with it. He's brilliant!"

*   *   *

Climbing Ranger John Ring and Bradford Lehman met Castellano, and the new RGS "guide," in the Paradise Inn parking lot. It was the last week of May, 1968.

"John Ring, meet Ron Makinson, Ron meet John, Brad meet Ron, and Ron meet Brad. It looks like you boys have all of your shit ready. Makinson brought some special gear with him for ya'll. See you boys in a few days. Take lots of pictures to show to our families. Give me a call when you get back." Rube waved, quickly got into his Chevy Caprice, and drove away.

J. Ronald Makinson was six feet tall, sported a lean build, long arms, and wide shoulders, topped with a thin smiling face, and short black hair. Lehman judged him to be in his late twenties.

"How ya doin' guys, we climbing that today?" Makinson said. He pointed to the mountain.

"Not today, Ron," Lehman said.

"We hike up to high camp at Muir today, train and acclimatize for a day, and climb the next," Ring said. "Why do you have your crampons on in the parking lot?"

"Just thought I needed to be ready. What?" Makinson noticed Ring and Lehman staring at him.

"Nothing," Lehman said. "Let's get started. It's going to be a long day."

There was a solid wind crust on the snow as the three men climbed up over Panorama Point and took their first break at Pebble Creek. Makinson, affable and chatty, was asking questions nonstop about the points of interest. The day was cool, but sunny. John and Bradford taught Ron the rest-step, so he wouldn't scramble and wear himself out. They taught him how to carry his ice axe properly, how to use his crampons to climb a steep snow slope, and how to switch hands with his ice axe when traversing. They were impressed with his overall enthusiasm, willingness to learn, and stamina.

John approached Lehman out of earshot. "You know, so far Brad, Ron here seems like a quick study. He's strong as an ox too. Jeez, he must be carrying eighty pounds in that big frame pack he's got."

"Yeah, he does appear to be a fast learner," Lehman conceded. "Do you think we should tell him that he's got his gaiters on backwards?"

"No, when he feels the snow melt through the zippers and down into the heels of his boots he'll figure it out," Ring said with a grin.

Up near Anvil Rock, John Ring broke out a goldline climbing rope from his pack. He and Bradford proceeded to teach Makinson how to self-arrest on the hard snow crust. They practiced with him separately, and then roped up as a team. They rehearsed arresting to both strong and weak sides, falling head down on the belly, and sliding head down on the back, which entailed rotating and flipping the hips from a half-sit-up position, to get the chest onto the axe's shaft for leverage. Then they trained in team self-arrests, first with one man yelling out "Falling!" as he slid, then with two team members sliding, and finally with all three. Lastly, Lehman and Ring stood up and ran straight downhill, jerking Makinson off his feet and into a self-arrest.

They continued to pull him, as he dug furrows in the snow with the pick of his axe, to see if he would quit. He didn't.

The team stayed in the Guide Hut at Camp Muir that night. The next morning, they headed back down to Anvil Rock on the Muir Snowfield where Ring and Lehman taught Makinson rappelling, knot tying, and belaying techniques. They then roped up and traversed northeast around the base of Anvil onto the Cowlitz Glacier, where the young FBI agent-come-guide was taught glacier travel and team rope handling.

On the loop back to Muir, Lehman found a big crevasse and took Makinson through a rescue drill. He learned how to climb up the rope with prusik slings and Jumar ascenders, and how to get out of a crevasse using the bulgari technique. It was late in the afternoon when the three finally made it back to the Guide Hut.

"How are you feeling Ron?" Ring asked, as he opened a can of beef stew for dinner. Makinson sat on the bottom bunk, lancing the blisters on the backs of his heels. Lehman was outside, laying out the climbing rope for an early start on the next day's summit climb.

"Pretty good, John, all considered. But what I can't understand is why water is running down into the backs of my boots and giving me these damned blisters."

"I think I have the answer, Ron. Turn your nylon gaiters around so the zippers are on the front. That should work better." Makinson smiled sheepishly and laughed.

Lehman returned to the hut and he and Ring discussed the next day's climb over dinner. "Got your silver and gold Eveready batteries taped together for your headlamp and sensor Ron?" Bradford asked.

"Yup, all done."

"We've got excellent weather forecast for the next two days," Lehman said. "The goal, as we've been briefed, is to summit, enter two major steam caves, and follow them down to any source of radiation. We've all got flash-equipped cameras, and will photograph the hell out of the place, and try to map the cave system under the crater for reference. Ring and I will carry extra food, a stove, and utensils. We will all carry sleeping bags and foam pads. Ron, you carry the 'special gear' Rube gave you, like the gas masks for all of us, and the issued compasses."

Makinson gave a thumbs-up.

Lehman glanced at his watch. "It's 1830 now. We will sack out until 2300, and leave at midnight after breakfast. Ring, anything to add?"

"No. Sounds good."

"Ron?"

"Nope, anything sounds good to me!" he grinned.

"Now, I know you're a Special Agent and all," Lehman continued, "But in spite of that, Ring and I will ride your ass if we catch you screwing up. Just the mountaineering part of this mission is plenty dangerous. Like we've discussed, bad things always happen when you lose vigilance or concentration. The mountain will lull you to sleep. Climbing this thing is ninety-nine percent boredom -- putting one foot in front of the other -- and one percent 'oh shit.'"

"That beats the hell out of one hundred percent boredom," Makinson said.

"What do you mean, Ron?" Lehman asked.

"Like, 'watching the doors' down in Elbe." That's one hundred percent freaking boredom!"

"Time to eat," Ring announced.

The team was out the door of the Guide Hut at midnight. The night was crisp. Gusts of wind snapped parka hoods, as they quickly roped up and headed out across the Cowlitz Glacier toward Cathedral Gap. There were no previous tracks to follow. Lehman led, followed by Makinson in the middle, and Ring on the end. John placed wands to mark the trail. At the top of Cathedral Gap, they took a break.

"How are you doing Ron?" Lehman asked.

"Good. I'm feeling much better with the altitude."

"It is amazing how an extra twenty-four hours at Muir can get you acclimatized," Ring said. "Still, you may get a headache."

"I'm used to it now. Man, look at all the stars out. It's amazing how much light there is, with the little moon we have."

"Yes, and this early in the climbing season," Lehman said. "The snow is not yet dirty from blowing dust and dirt, so it reflects more light."

Ring and Lehman could see that Makinson was thrilled to be on the mountain, and not cowed by its extreme environment.

"Let's keep our headlamps off as much as possible," Ring said. "There's no sense in advertising our presence up here more than we need to."

The team climbed out onto the Ingraham Glacier, traversed next to Cathedral Rocks in the moon's shadow, and then emerged abruptly into moonlight at Cadaver Gap, at the base of Gibraltar Rock. More than a thousand feet below they could see the tiny dark huts of Camp Muir. Lehman decided to stay off of Disappointment Cleaver to save time, and to climb the Ingraham Headwall instead. As they skirted under the north side of Gibraltar, small chunks of rock and ice, spit out somewhere high above among the black looming cliffs, whirred down and splashed the snow near the team.

Lehman noticed Makinson's headlamp switching on and off, nervously scanning the cliffs above. "Ron, you're doing well. Don't worry about the small stuff. Technically it can kill you, but the odds are slim. It's the big rocks and ice falls that kill. Relax, and move steadily through this section. Make sure you breathe deeply. We'll be out of this bowling alley in another rope length."

"Bowling alley. That's a good one!" Makinson laughed.

Presently the team reached the base of the Ingraham Headwall.

"John, why don't you lead from here on up?" Lehman said. "Give me your wands and I'll mark the route." Ring nodded, and the rope reversed itself with Makinson remaining the middleman. It was 0400, and the first faint glow of sunrise was showing.

John front-pointed up the headwall, taking short relaxed steps.

"Ron, see how John is moving?" Lehman said. "Watch, and copy him. Take short steps up and keep the slack out of the rope, like you were trained."

Makinson nodded. He was concentrating and listening. All business.

"You're doing great, Ron. We are more than halfway up this thing. You are trusting your feet and equipment like a pro," Lehman said.

At the top of the headwall where the slope eased off, Special Agent Makinson became ebullient. "Wow, this is something!"

"Beats hell out of sitting in the office huh, Ron?" Ring said.

"Damn right, any day!"

"Ron, we are now at twelve thousand three hundred feet, and can view the long flat top of Gibraltar. Camp Comfort sits in there," Lehman said, pointing southeast. Then he pointed along the slope running uphill toward the summit. "You can see that big crevasse up there -- it marks the beginning of the summit ice cap. That big crevasse is called a bergschrund."

"Yeah, I see it. It looks close," Ron said.

"Well, it isn't," Bradford said. "But note the glacial terrain in front of us. Right here, a few hundred feet above the top of Gibraltar, you can see a faint seam where Gib splits the summit ice cap into separate glaciers, the Ingraham that we're on, and over to the west, the Nisqually glacier."

"I see it," Ron said.

"What specifically do you see?" Lehman asked.

"It looks like right on that seam the crevasses we can see begin to skew uphill."

"Exactly. Good observation. The crevasses we have crossed so far have run at right angles to the fall line of the hill. But now as the glaciers are split, as they flow past Gibraltar, we get 'vertical' crevasses. These are especially dangerous because, if hidden, a whole rope team can fall into one of them at once. This happened right in this area ten years ago. An RGS guide and two clients fell. They broke through a hidden vertical crevasse."

"What happened?"

"One of the clients broke his neck and died before he could be hauled off the hill." Makinson put his head down and shook his head soberly. *Lehman, Ron's getting perspective on this business. He is respecting the mountain.*

The party made good time as it zigzagged upward among huge crevasses, and in three hours they un-roped at the crater rim. The red morning sun finally rose fully above the eastern horizon.

Agent Makinson was breathless, but euphoric, as the three climbers sat down at the summit register. "Wow, fantastic! The views are unbelievable!" Bradford and Ring shook Ron's mittened hand and slapped him on the back.

"Congratulations Makinson. You are now one small but significant step closer to becoming a RGS guide," Lehman said. "How do you feel?"

"Great! Better than I thought I would."

"Okay," Ring said, "I'll break out the stove and make some hot tea. Let's have a bite to eat, sack out for two or three hours, and then we will check out the caves."

Lehman pulled out a compact pair of Leica binoculars Rube had issued to him, and slowly scanned the crater rim. He located the two steam vents targeted on the reconnaissance imagery, mentally noted them, and laid down for a nap.

* * *

"Wake up Bradford." John Ring's hand gently shook Lehman's shoulder. Startled, Lehman began to reach for his pistol. Ring smiled. It reminded him of his Green Beret days in Vietnam.

"Don't shoot, friendlies coming in!" Ring said. Ron laughed. He knew that Ring was a Green Beret, but hadn't talked to him about it yet. Makinson had been a U.S. Army battery commander of 105mm howitzers at LZ Action, a firebase near the Mang Yang Pass, twenty-three kilometers west of AnKe, Vietnam. Ring and Makinson broke into animated conversation about their tours over there. Lehman went back to sleep. Fifteen minutes later John shook him back awake. "Tea's ready." It was 1100 hours.

"Okay, you trained killers," Lehman said, "'here's the drill,' as Rube would say. We are all going to stick together. First, we will walk the entire crater rim looking for any clues or signs of activity by the

Russians. Obviously, if we see any, we will photograph them in place, and then decide whether to pick them up or leave them. That will take an hour, until about 1230. We can skip using the special compasses, though we'll carry them in case we lose our visibility. I scanned the rim when we got here and have pinpointed the target vents. So after we check the rim, we will go to those and begin exploring -- again staying together."

"Sounds like a plan," Ring said. Ron nodded, smiling.

"You really enjoy this don't you Makinson?" Lehman said.

"Hell yes!" Ron said. "Look at where we are. No paperwork, no supervisors, no bullshit."

"Jeez, you're just like Castellano. Are all you G-Men that way?"

"No, only the smart ones."

"In other words, not many," Ring rejoined.

The walk around the crater rim was uneventful, except for Makinson's excitement about the scenery. He talked nonstop.

"Man, Makinson, could you take a breath once in awhile? The air's thin up here, you know," Bradford said.

Ron laughed, and kept talking. Finally, they stopped at the entrance to a cave next to a large patch of mustard-colored pumice.

"This is the cave shown on the SR-71 photo, sitting at eighteen degrees off of true north," Ring said. He checked his compass and nodded. They all dropped their packs.

Makinson pulled out three gas masks, a small Geiger Counter, and surgical gloves. He handed out the masks and gloves. "Put the gloves on. The idea, according to Rube and the Atomic Energy Commission guys, is to put on our light hooded windbreakers, and tape the cuffs to the gloves, and then cinch the hoods down tight around our masks. That provides some protection in case there is any radiation that might be in any dust we kick up. I am carrying this small Geiger Counter here that will not only record, like our Gold Eveready batteries, but will also beep if radiation thresholds begin to creep too high. Any questions? No? Let's gear up." The three men checked each other over one last time.

"Everyone got their guns where they can get to them?" Lehman asked. Ring nodded.

"Locked and Loaded!" Ron's muffled voice wafted out of his gas mask.

"I think your mask is faulty," Lehman said.

With a look of concern, Makinson, took his gas mask off, put it back on, and cinched it more tightly against his face. "The seal feels good."

"It can't be good. I can still hear you talking," Lehman said. Makinson gave Lehman a shove. Lehman turned and ducked into the vent. The men had to hunch down as they descended a moderate twenty-five-degree slope of volcanic pumice, rocks, and scree.

"This is eerie as shit in here," Makinson exclaimed. "But it's amazing. Can anyone smell any rotten eggs – sulphur gas?"

"No," Lehman replied. Ring shook his head.

"Okay, the masks are sealed and working, then. By the way, I have a gas meter with me, and so far there are no dangerous readings on it."

"Ron, you should have tested it out when you ate your beef stew the other night," Ring said.

"I did. It worked."

The ice and snow tunnels, caught in the beams of three powerful headlamps, shimmered in glazes of white, green, and blue. This, combined with rising steam and the contrasting black scree, made the scene otherworldly. The ice above comprised decades of snowfall that filled in the crater's bowl. The snow fell and layered, year after year, out of the high wet Northwest skies. Four hundred feet down the tunnel the team came to a large snow cavern, and were able to stand upright. There was a small pool of clear water where the wall of ice met the warm volcanic rock at the cavern's floor. It was the size of a living room with a ceiling eighteen feet high.

"The faceplate on my mask is fogging up badly," Lehman complained.

"Mine is too," Ring said.

"Ron, I can barely see your face, you're all fogged up too," Lehman said.

"Check your sensors. Maybe it's safe to take them off."

Makinson checked his meters. "Low readings on radiation showing here – all normal. And the gas meter hardly even registers."

"I'm taking my mask off," Lehman said. "I can't accomplish anything here with it on." He slid the mask off his face. Ring and Makinson watched him intently. Bradford began wobbling and his legs buckled. Ring and Makinson grabbed him under the arms. Lehman stood up with a grin. "Just kidding."

"Lehman, you scared the shit out of us!" Makinson exclaimed.

"That was the point. But seriously, it only smells a little like rotten eggs like you'd get at a hot spring."

Ring and Makinson took off their masks and stowed them in their packs.

"That's a hell of a lot better," Makinson said.

"Not even as strong-smelling as the hot springs down at Longmire," Ring observed.

"Holy crap, this is beautiful down here," Makinson said, scanning the chamber.

"Ron, you have waxed as poetic as I've ever heard a G-Man talk," Lehman said.

The team walked to the end of the cave, bent down, and slithered through a small passageway running east. That in turn opened up to a smaller snow chamber where the men could stand.

"We've looked at what, maybe a half mile of this section so far?" Bradford said.

"I'd say so," John said, looking at his watch. "It's almost 1500. There's nothing of note in here, mission-wise. Agreed?" Lehman and Makinson nodded. "So I suggest we retrace our steps, grab a bite to eat, and try the second vent on the southwest rim." They all agreed. Lehman felt the fatigue and lack of sleep eroding his concentration.

Back at Register Rock, the three men finished their lunches and discussed options. Though the weather remained clear, the wind was picking up, and all were tired.

"My watch shows 1700," Lehman said. "It's getting colder. If we explore this next vent, we'll be out of there by the time it is almost dark out here. Then we will freeze our asses off trying to sleep. Why don't we sleep now while we have sunlight, get some dinner, and then do the next cave?

"Sounds like a great plan," Makinson said. "I'm beat."

"Let's hit the rack," Ring said.

The team slept fitfully for the next six hours, got up, had dinner, and drank hot tea. Then they shouldered their packs and walked to Columbia Crest. They stood there for a few minutes admiring the view. It was 2330 hours.

"Man this is incredible," Makinson whistled. "Look at the lights of Seattle and Tacoma. It's so clear up here I can see the traffic lights change color. How far away is that?"

"Forty to sixty miles as the crow flies," Ring replied, as he turned left and started plodding. The team walked the crater rim counter-clockwise for a few hundred yards. Ring stopped next to a big black rock at the entrance to a cave. He pulled out his compass. "This is it -- one-ninety-two degrees off true."

At the cave's entrance they switched on their headlamps.

"John, you do the honors and go first this time," Lehman said. "I'll bring up the rear." Ring nodded and bent low past the entrance lip of the cave, followed by Makinson and Bradford. The angle of slope was not as steep as at the first vent, and as they descended the passage it quickly opened up, allowing the men to walk hunched over, and then upright. There was even less of a sulfur smell in this cave. They came to a side passage that forked to the left. It had an ice wall that extended up waist-high at its entrance.

"Which one do we take?" Ring asked. "Shall we flip a coin?"

"No, Ring, I don't trust your coins anymore," Lehman said. They laughed.

"What?" Ron asked quizzically.

"It's an inside joke, Ron -- in this case -- literally," Lehman said. As he spoke, he searched the ground with his headlamp. "Hey guys, look at that." The beam of Bradford's light caught a small symmetrical shape in the dirt, next to the left passageway.

"Damn, that's a footprint," John said. He bent down and photographed it. "None of you stepped over there yet, did you?"

"Nope," Ron replied. Bradford shook his head.

"Well, the left passage it is then," Lehman said. "After you, Ring."

John put his hands on the snow wall and swung his body over it, followed by Makinson and Lehman. No one talked. Bradford felt the hair rising on the back of his neck as they moved. Thirty feet along the passage it narrowed down to the width of a phone booth, and then opened wide into a huge chamber, the size of a ballroom. A clear pool of water lay placidly, reflecting sparkling light off of the cupped ice ceiling thirty feet above. The three stood in awe, taking photographs. At the far end of the chamber, there was a steady hissing sound.

"Steam vent," Lehman said. "A good sized one." They shined their lights toward it.

"Shit, did you see that?" Makinson said.

"What?" Ring asked.

"It's something silver-colored right next to where the steam is escaping."

The men approached the object slowly. Lehman took pictures.

"There are a ton of boot prints around it," Ring said. His voice grew tense.

"What the hell is it? It's too small to be a nuke," Ron said. The men eased up around the rectangular metal object. All of them were taking pictures. It was about the size of a silver aluminum mailbox, and domed at the top like one. Out of the base of the box ran a thick black wire that split into red and green wires about five feet away, where there was a leveled rectangular four-by-six-foot dirt platform. The curved wall of the ice cave had been carved out to make it vertical on two sides up to chest high.

Makinson carefully knelt down and lifted one end of the box. "Damn, it's heavier than it looks – thirty pounds, at least."

"I have an idea what this is," Lehman said in a quiet voice. "Remember when Palmrich said that portable nukes needed maintenance and a power source? Look at the connectors at the end of the wire. They are common car battery connectors. This silver thing must be a turbine generator. They position it over the steam vent, the generator spins, it charges a car battery, which in turn keeps the nuke powered up."

"But the nuke and the car battery aren't here," Makinson said.

"Yeah," Ring said, probing around the big chamber with his light, "so either they've had it here and took it out, or they are preparing to bring it in."

"They may indeed be preparing the site," Lehman said. "From what Castellano and Palmrich told us about the mentality of GRU agents, it would take pulling teeth, even under orders by their own government, to make them pack a nuke out of here once it has been deployed. What we have found is a hidden site for a portable nuke, with a clever means of generating electricity utilizing geothermal steam to spin this turbine and recharge a battery. We know from our briefings that a car battery is more than ample as a power source to keep the weapon operational indefinitely. The dimensions of the level platform easily match those of a Backpack bomb with a yield as large as ten kilotons, like we've been briefed. At one hundred pounds, it is a load that a couple of motivated GRU agents could pack up here."

The impact of Lehman's words left the great ice cavern quiet, except for the sound of hissing steam. The faces of the men reflected both seriousness and anger. They all knew in that moment -- in what they witnessed before them -- that in all probability the Russians were attempting something so brazen and deadly, that is was almost beyond comprehension to consider. Yet here was the chilling evidence: a custom-built steam generator sitting next to an active steam vent, and ready to be placed over it. There it would turn, and produce a constant flow of electricity. Wires leading out of the generator were ready to hook up to a battery. And next to where the wires ended, stood a carefully prepared level platform, where a Backpack nuclear weapon would neatly fit.

This was all done with loving care, Bradford. Lehman felt his face flush.

"The Geiger-Counter reads normal, and I haven't heard any beeps to indicate that we have passed any hot spots on the way in," Makinson said. His voice sounded solemn.

"So what do we do?" Ring asked.

"We have to leave this site pristine," Lehman said. "We do not want the Russians to know that we've found it. If we take the box, they will know the site is compromised, and we will be obliged to start all over trying to find and disable the bomb."

"I absolutely agree, Brad," Makinson said. "We cannot disturb this site. We've got to get this new information back down the hill for analysis, and to figure out our next steps. But first, let's carefully turn this box over and get photos of the underside."

On their climb back out toward the surface, the team reconnoitered the right-hand passage, thinking that the Backpack could have been cached somewhere in it. But the passage dead-ended in only thirty feet. There was nothing there. They carefully swept away their tracks on the climb out of the cave, and were back at Register Rock by 0400. Lehman, Ring, and Makinson tried to sleep -- but they could not. The implications of their discovery kept them awake. They sat, talked quietly, drank hot tea, and stamped the cold out of their feet. Dawn rose slowly.

19

De-briefings, Setting up a Cover, and Needles in Haystacks

Bradford Lehman, John Ring, and Special Agent J. Ronald Makinson sat around a big table in the Glacier Room Bar at the Paradise Inn. They were drinking strong black coffee to stay awake. It was 1400 hours on the day the team slogged down from the top of Mount Rainier – the same long day that included locating the silver "Mailbox," and the prepared platform in the crater cave. CIA and FBI agents sat by the locked entrance door, and scattered themselves around other tables in the room. Otto Palmrich and Rubayat Castellano looked into the tired faces of the men at their table. There was none of the preliminary banter that normally colored their previous gatherings.

Palmrich spoke first. "We are sorry that you guys have not had a chance to clean up and get some sleep before our meeting. But we are also glad that you got off the hill in good order. Our communications worked flawlessly for a change. Ron, we received the three squelch breaks on your walkie-talkie at 0415, loud and clear."

"I heard your one 'click' back loud and clear too," Makinson said, "followed by two more -- so we knew we would be meeting you here at two o'clock. Amazing how fourteen thousand feet of altitude can improve radio communications. They are usually the first thing to crap out in an operation."

Rube nodded knowingly, and pulled out a notebook and pen. "First, let's get the film you shot," he said. The men slid over their thirty-five millimeter film canisters to Otto Palmrich, who dropped them into his knapsack. "I see Makinson here got worked over pretty good on this jaunt, and can't keep his eyes open," Rube continued. "Lehman and Ring, tell me what happened."

The debriefing lasted two hours.

Castellano looked at Ron. "I see Makinson is asleep at the switch, so I guess it's time to shove off, and get this information out to the SOG. It is going to ring some bells back there."

"I heard you Rube," Ron said, "I just nodded off a little."

"The hill kicked your ass, didn't it agent Makinson?" Rube said.

"It sure as hell did. But it was an amazing climb, thanks to my two buddies. Worth every step."

"I have arranged for you three to be quartered at the old Guide House across from the Inn here," Rube said. "It is a lot closer to our meeting place. You will each have separate adjoining rooms on the top floor."

"What about the other RGS guides?" Lehman asked.

"They will still remain down at the Henry Jackson Visitor Center, or DUB, as you call it," Rube said. He tapped the table, finished the rest of his beer, and stood up. "I'm out of here. We will be back up tomorrow, when the Inn opens officially for the Memorial Day weekend. I will update all of you then. Meanwhile, get some sleep."

He started to walk out, stopped, and turned. "Outstanding job, you three."

* * *

Bradford Lehman had no idea how long he had slept. Slowly, first in a sublime dream, then materializing into breathtaking reality, his eyes opened. Teo Maloney was lying next to him. She was up on one elbow, her head cocked in her hand, looking quietly at him. Her soft red lips held a faint smile, and her raven black hair spilled onto her shoulder. Bradford tiredly reached his arm around her, and slowly brought her head and lips against his. He kissed her for long moments -- he had no idea how long -- but he let his half-waking body fold warmly in against hers, reveling in her softness and scent.

"I love your perfume, girl."

"Essence of Bear Grass," Teo said with a chuckle, rubbing Bradford's nose with hers, and kissing him again.

"Teo, how long have you been here with me?"

"Since eleven o'clock last evening, when Mister Castellano drove me up."

"Rube's here?" Lehman started to get up, but Teo placed her hand on his chest and gently pushed him back down.

"Yes," she said softly. "He and others are in rooms down stairs. They are sleeping. It's okay, Bradford. There is no rush at all for you to get up. John is still sleeping. But that new guide -- Ron Makinson – he has been up for awhile already. He's out asking the rangers where the best places are to fish. He is all stiff, and bent-over from the climb. He's a character!"

"That he is, love. Good man though. Tough." Lehman felt himself drifting back to sleep.

"God you're handsome, Bradford. You are even more handsome when you are asleep."

"I know. My dad used to tell me I was the best kid when I was asleep," Lehman mumbled. Teo snorted, and put her hands to her mouth to stifle a laugh. It didn't wake him. Bradford Lehman was dead out.

When he finally got up at 1300, Lehman dressed in jeans, slipped his Walther pistol into its waistband, buttoned on a green Pendleton wool shirt over his long underwear top, and followed his nose downstairs to the smell of coffee and bacon. Teo, in jeans and a light blue cashmere sweater, had an apron on, and was standing at the stove.

"Good morning, Rip Van Winkle!" Rubayat Castellano greeted Lehman in his usual booming voice. "Have a seat. You know Brad, this girlfriend of yours is a most amazing cook. I've already had six pancakes."

"-- And four eggs, and eight pieces of bacon," Teo interrupted, as she plopped a full plate in front of Bradford and kissed him on the cheek.

"Damn, kid, marry her right now! She is smart as hell, she's gorgeous, and she cooks. Crap, what the hell am I saying -- don't marry her yet – shit!" Rube grinned and patted his tight stomach. "When you are finished eating, Brad, come on over to the bar. Ring is already there, getting a head start on the beer. Makinson will be along in a bit. Jeez, he is all stiff and bent over!"

"What did Makinson do, Rube -- drop the soap?"

Agent Castellano, in the middle of taking a swallow of coffee, spit it out. He let out a booming laugh and slapped the table. "Teo, this kid is a keeper!"

Rube got up and walked out the door, still laughing. Teo sat down next to Bradford, watching him wolf down his breakfast. "Goodness Brad, you are an amazingly passionate eater, too!"

"It is my second-favorite activity."

Teo blushed crimson and squeezed Lehman on the shoulder. "You sure are a ribald young man today," she said.

"It's simply my pathetic way of compensating, pretty lady."

"Hey, Brad!" Nancy Olszewski was standing outside the Dining Room. She motioned Lehman aside as he was headed around the corner to the Glacier Room. "Who is that man who just walked past me into the bar?"

"That's Ron Makinson. He is the new RGS guide."

"Really? He looked at me and said 'hello!'"

"I look at you and say 'hello' too, Nancy."

She elbowed Lehman. "He's handsome! Yes, I know Brad, you are too -- but you're taken. Where is he from?"

"New Jersey originally. And he loves to fly fish. Lives for it."

"Can you introduce me to him? Maybe tonight, over by the fireplace, around eight o'clock?"

"Sure, Nancy, I would be honored to introduce you two. You are two peas in a pod."

"Really?"

"Yes. You are a big city girl. He is a big city boy. It doesn't get any better than that."

Nancy's eyes brightened. "I'll be there at eight!"

Rubayat Castellano brought the meeting to order with a toast: "To Special Agent and RGS Guide J. Ronald Makinson, who has completed his first climb of Mount Rainier!"

"To J. Ronald Makinson!" Voices in the bar rang out. Beer mugs clanked.

"Sergeant at Arms, by the door there, is the bar secure?" Rube asked. The agent nodded. "All right folks, the purpose of this get-together is to formulate a plan on how to 'Run the Bear out of the Park,' as Mister Palmrich has so eloquently characterized this operation. Otto, you got the images developed in record time. Let's see them."

Palmrich pulled out a thick sheaf of eight-by-ten color photographic prints and distributed them around the table.

"Wow," Makinson said, letting out a whistle. "These are beautiful."

"Yes, and you all did an admirable job shooting under those conditions," Palmrich said. "I wish I could have been there. These caves are truly spectacular. But that aside, take a look at the boot print by the side chamber's entrance to the Ballroom. We have assigned that name to the site prepared for the weapon. Speaking of that, initial cursory analysis indicates that the prepared platform is precisely fitted for a Soviet RA-115 portable nuclear Backpack bomb, with appropriate space allowed around it for servicing. The weapon weighs somewhere in the neighborhood of one hundred pounds. Its estimated explosive yield is up to ten kilotons of TNT. By comparison, the Hiroshima bomb that helped America end World War II, had an effective yield of fifteen kilotons. At first blush, the Backpack is extremely small by comparison to the Hiroshima bomb. But it packs a hell of a wallop. The devil of this thing is that the Russians are apparently banking on using Rainier's volcanic crater as a force multiplier. How ultimately effective such a nuclear detonation be, our analysts are trying to work out. However, if the Backpack can trigger a volcanic eruption, or lahar, we are looking at a true mega-disaster for the Pacific Northwest – and points far beyond."

"Like what?" Makinson asked.

"Like the combined effect of over twenty hydrogen bombs – likely more," Palmrich said. His words sounded palpably final. "If the Russians are able to trigger a volcanic eruption, like what occurred on Rainier five thousand six hundred years ago, there would be an initial explosion of ash and super-heated rock, followed by a lahar, or mudflow, followed by many hours of continued eruption. A wall of debris over one hundred feet high would slice through all surrounding communities to the north and west of the mountain. The lahar would wipe out Tacoma on its way into Puget Sound, cutting highways and electrical grids. The ash would be deep enough to collapse roofs of houses and buildings in Seattle, and incapacitate all vehicles and transportation systems. The eruption would mushroom fifteen miles high into the stratosphere, be picked up by the jet stream, and then be dispersed hundreds of miles in all directions. It would not only carry millions of cubic tons of ash, but that fallout would now be radioactive from the initiating nuclear detonation. This would cause further deaths along with the devastation -- and the poisoning of water supplies."

"I think that sufficiently answers my question," Ron said quietly. A long silence followed.

Palmrich continued: "Now take a look at the silver-colored 'Mailbox' here in the photo. This is an ingenious piece of equipment. It is custom-built out of a solid block of stainless steel. Ron, this would explain its heavy weight for its size. The photo you took here of its underside shows a stainless steel screen covering. We have enhanced and enlarged the photograph --" Palmrich handed out enlargements, "-- and have determined that this unit is a low-revolution steam turbine. You can barely make out the turbine blades on the spindle there, beneath the screen. We have our people building a replica of this to test its electrical output. But that is academic. Our experts concede that such a turbine placed over an active steam vent, like the one beside it in the Ballroom, would easily charge a twelve-volt car battery, and thereby supply a limitless source of power for the Backpack to keep it on-line and active. And of course, that is what we see on these photos of the ends of the wires extending out from the Mailbox – car battery connectors. Any questions?"

There were none.

"All right, moving along…" Castellano said. "What are the next steps? We do not want to tip the GRU off that we know the placement location of their Backpack. We want to maintain as discreet a presence on the mountain as possible. But in light of the urgency that has arisen in the wake of what we have now proven, there must be an increase of manpower and resources."

"How are you going to do that, Rube?" Lehman asked.

"By creating a cover operation that masks our covert mission, which is now to locate the Backpack and neutralize the GRU agents who guard it, *before* they are able to get it operational or, god forbid, set it off. Our agencies will rent the whole Guide House, where you, Ring, and Makinson are now quartered. We will bring in a mix of FBI and CIA folks, who will pose as a United States Geological Survey research team, up on Mount Rainier for the summer conducting a "lahar study." It fits plausibly with what we are going to do, and where we have to go. We have fifteen support specialists and agents slated to live and work out of the Guide House under that cover. More are available if necessary -- but more is not necessarily better for this kind of neutralization mission. We also have priority over air and rescue assets at McChord Air Force Base, and over Army combat troops at Fort Lewis, should circumstances necessitate employing them."

Castellano took a deep breath and continued. "Lehman, Ring, and Makinson, as of now you are assigned to the USGS Lahar Research Team, AKA, the LRT. Ring, you are a Park Climbing Ranger on temporary assignment to the LRT. Lehman, your services are exclusively 'rented' from the RGS for the summer to assist the LRT. And Makinson, you are also a 'rented' RGS guide working for the LRT. I have worked things out with Herb McGill. He will backfill your regular guiding positions at the RGS. We have also paid him enough to give all his guides raises. That should help still the waters of any speculation from them. Lehman, you are the logical choice to be detailed to the LRT. You are the youngest guide at the Guide Service, and therefore 'drew the short straw' -- along with Makinson, the RGS's newest hireling -- for work on the survey. Any questions?"

There were none.

"Okay, Palmrich and I are going down the hill for a few days to get things organized. Meanwhile, you three intrepid climbers have the next four days off unless something comes up. Get out, move around, and keep your eyes open. By the way, we have arranged to have all your meals paid for at the Inn Dining Room, or at the Cafeteria down at the Visitors Center, or at Longmire, or Sunrise, or anywhere else in the Park that sells food. Just tell the cashier to charge it to the LRT. Also, if you need climbing equipment of any kind, Otto Palmrich will get it for you. Meeting adjourned."

As Bradford got up to leave the bar, Rube called him over to the corner. "Brad, I have good news for you. Teo has been hired as a 'Research and Climbing Assistant.' She is on the LRT payroll now. So she won't be working as a waitress for the Rainier National Park

Company this summer. She is now fully briefed into the operation, and will be rooming with you."

*　*　*

"Bradford," Teo took Lehman's face in her hands. "I knew you were under tremendous pressure in your work against the Russians. But I had no idea how big the threat was to you, and all of us. Now I know. I am very proud of you, my man. I want to tell you again how much I love you..." Her voice broke, and tears welled up. She hugged him. For long seconds she would not let go.

Lehman kissed her. There were tears in his eyes. "I love you, Teo. We are in this together. I am so relieved that you have been given all the information. But I also worry that what we are going through will hurt you. Anyone on this operation against the GRU is at risk. I am armed. You are not. That worries me." She smiled, her dark eyes looking deeply into his:

"Don't worry about me, Brad. Please. I am a strong girl."

"I know you are strong." He stroked her hair. "It is not about strength. It is about life and death. We need to get you armed and trained."

It was a busy night at the Paradise Inn. Guests crowded around the dance floor in the main hall to watch the talent show. At eight o'clock Teo, Bradford, and Ron, strolled into the Inn. Bradford promised to buy Ron a beer, which immediately lured him out of the Guide House.

"Hi Bradford and Teo!" Nancy Olszewski, dressed in a tight fitting royal blue sweater and jeans, was standing by the fireplace. They walked over and she gave them a hug.

"Nancy, meet Ron Makinson. He's a new RGS guide. Ron, meet Nancy Olszewski. She is the Manager of the Dining Room." They shook hands. Bradford noted Makinson's approving eyes quickly scanning the face and body of the woman in front of him.

"Very nice to meet you, Nancy," Ron said with a wide smile. "I saw you this morning when I ate here in the Dining Room, so it's good to know your name now."

"Ron, my name is on my lapel." Nancy smiled impishly.

"Oh yeah, that's right." He blushed. "Hey, we are headed to the Glacier Room, Nancy. Care to join us?"

"I'd love to!" Olszewski said smiling, casually bumping up against Makinson's arm.

"Man, I have never seen Ron so animated," Bradford whispered to Teo at the table.

"Well, look at Nancy. She's a knockout," Teo whispered back. "No. Don't look at her!" She smiled and squeezed Lehman's knee.

"Ron, will you take me fly fishing sometime?" Nancy asked. "John Ring says you are a pro at it. I have never done it before and it looks like fun. I have a day off tomorrow. Will you teach me?" As she spoke, Nancy leaned over and looked steadily into Ron's eyes.

"Sure! I've got my gear all packed up. Go grab a knapsack and some of your own gear, and meet me back at the front of the Inn in twenty minutes. We'll hike over to Fan Lake."

"Leave now?"

"Yeah! It's only eight-thirty. With the alpenglow up here there will be residual light for another hour, and then after that there is a full moon. Plenty of light, plus I will bring a headlamp. C'mon, it'll be fun. We will get out there and be ready early when the fish start to feed. I will cook up what we catch. What do you say?"

"Twenty minutes!" Nancy squeezed Ron's shoulder and walked out of the bar. Makinson hurriedly finished his beer and left.

Bradford and Teo looked at each other. "Damn, that was quick," Bradford said. Teo smiled. Love was in the air.

Bradford and Teo climbed together over the next three days, out on the lower Nisqually Glacier. There, Lehman honed Teo's skills in crevasse rescue and ice climbing. Teo was a strong climber, athletic, and a keen learner. Lehman was impressed, and proud of Teo's progress. The two cherished their time together on the mountain. They quickly became a durable bond, not only as friends and lovers, but now too as a honed mountaineering team.

One evening they drove down to a theater in Eatonville, and laughed through the movie *The Pink Panther,* starring Peter Sellers, as Inspector Clouseau. From then on, Bradford never failed to crack Teo up by mimicking the bumbling, ego-centered Inspector.

* * *

Special Agent Rubayat Castellano and Otto Palmrich called another meeting in Rube's favorite watering hole. Otto Palmrich, now worked under light cover as "Otto P. Rich," Director of the USGS Lahar Research Team, headquartered for the summer of 1968 in the Guide House at Paradise, Mount Rainier. He introduced several new technical members of the LRT. He did not indicate whether they were FBI or CIA agents. Lehman had no particular interest in knowing their derivations. *As long as they have our backs out there,* he thought. *Just back us up, and don't screw up. That's all I ask of myself -- and all I ask of you – don't screw up.*

Palmrich also provided succinct intelligence updates on the information retrieved from the Ballroom under the crater of Mount Rainier's summit. "Further analysis has confirmed the following:

- That the package meant to be positioned in the Ballroom fits the dimensions of a RA-115 Backpack nuclear weapon;
- That the Backpack has been in the Soviet arsenal for at least the past five years;
- That the Spetsnaz and GRU are the custodians of the RA-115;
- That the unit is highly stable, and requires minimal maintenance;
- That the bomb must have a steady low-current electrical source to remain 'online' and operational;
- That the weapon has a redundant safety system built in, requiring correct sequencing of switches to arm it;
- That if any step in the arming sequence is performed out of order, the Backpack will automatically "safe" itself within thirty seconds, rendering it inoperable;
- That regarding the Mailbox -- it is a custom-built slow-speed steam turbine;
- That it will trickle charge, and indefinitely maintain the charge of a twelve-volt car battery, with as little as three pounds-per-square-inch (PSI) delivered to the turbine blades. This is well within the estimated continuous output of five to ten PSI by the steam vent depicted in the photos."

Rube asked if the experts knew how long the Backpack could go without some form of power and remain operable.

"We do not yet know the answer to that question," Palmrich said. "But likely not long. Perhaps an hour or two."

"How is the bomb triggered once it is armed?" Makinson asked.

"By a low-frequency radio signal transmitted from a safe distance away -- or by hand."

"So by an act of suicide?"

"Correct," Otto said flatly. "Since your debriefing revealed that none of you saw any wire leading from the Ballroom out to the crater rim, we must presume for now that the GRU is contemplating the latter option." A hush fell over the room.

Teo looked at Bradford, who sat with his head down. She suddenly felt vulnerable – terribly vulnerable. Fear knotted her stomach and rose like an iron hand tightening around her throat. She knew that Bradford must feel the same way. Again she wondered why Bradford, John, and now she, were selected for this operation. Based on what was at stake, and the implacable foe they were up against, why were the three of them here?

Castellano walked to the front of the group and spoke:

"Most of you are probably asking yourselves 'why am I here? Why me?' Well, folks, we live in a most imperfect world. There is rarely a perfect fit for any situation. But let me say that Otto and I have been on many operations in our professional lives. You people are as good a team -- as perfect a fit -- as I have ever seen. Why? Because all of you were selected for your discreet expertise, solid reliability, and judgment."

Rube nodded to Bradford. "Lehman, you are young, but as good or better on this hill than any of the RGS guides. You have the most recent and comprehensive knowledge of Rainier of anyone -- from all sides -- top to bottom. You are not an Everest climber. That functions in our favor because you do not attract attention. The Whittaker brothers would."

Rube looked at Ron. "Makinson, you are new to the hill, but are strong and you will listen to Lehman and Ring -- and they will listen to you when tactical situations arise. You also don't have the build of a knuckle-dragging military commando. You have the look and actions of an outdoorsman, and with a little more experience, a guide on the hill. You are unobtrusive -- unmilitary."

Rube looked at John. "Ring, despite your Green Beret combat experience, you too are not one to catch a GRU agent's eye as an operator – again, unobtrusive."

Rube then turned his gaze to Teo. "Teo, you are beautiful and therefore anything but unobtrusive." There was a ripple of laughter in the room. She blushed. "However, as a female you will not attract attention of the GRU as an operator on the mountain. It is unthinkable for the Russians -- with their traditional male-centered philosophy -- that a female could *possibly* be an operator in such an extreme environment on the upper reaches of Mount Rainier."

"Note moreover," Castellano continued, "that having a female on the LRT also strongly reinforces the cover of Makinson, Ring, and Lehman. In the minds of the GRU, if these men are climbing with a woman, they also cannot possibly be operators. Researchers and scientists? Yes. Operators? No. So you see, our team here is well chosen -- and so are all you good souls acting in support – handpicked, in fact." Rube nodded to the faces around the room. "The bottom line is, that the LRT Team looks and functions normally, like any mixed party of climbers on Rainier."

Castellano cleared his throat. "Now a word about our enemies. We have SIGINT indicating elevated movement and activity by Spetsnaz and the GRU corresponding with the events here on the hill. You have witnessed how serious these boys are. They are willing to take losses to accomplish their mission. They are willing to kill, and summarily dispose of, anyone who gets in their way. This is a big mountain with lots of crevasses. That works in their favor, but only in a limited way. By contrast, because of your collective local expertise and skills, Mount Rainier works much more in our favor than theirs. Much more."

"So what's next?" Makinson asked.

"We have sensors to deploy," Palmrich said. We have more SR-71 missions to fly. We must conduct a discreet surveillance of the Ballroom. That is the site they have prepared for the weapon, so that is where we keep watch. But the first item on our agenda is to explore the rest of the cave system. The Backpack may be stored somewhere else in the caves."

"I agree, Otto," Lehman said. "We definitely need to survey and explore all the caves under the crater for sure. But I believe the weapon is not yet on the mountain. If it is, it is not anywhere near the crater caves."

"Why do you think that, Brad?" Rube asked.

"Because when we climbed the route it was pristine. We were almost certainly the first party up the Headwall, or any other route from this side of Rainier. There were no tracks, or wands, or fixed ropes, or any other evidence that anyone has been on the mountain since the season ended last summer. That likely means that the GRU simply prepared the site in the Ballroom for the nuke – but that the nuke itself is not on the mountain – yet. It is probably being stored somewhere in a less harsh environment."

"You mean its plugged into a wall outlet somewhere down in Tacoma?" Makinson asked with a half-smile.

Rube and Otto looked at each other. "Lehman," Rube said, "that is a damned good observation. Ron, it may not be 'plugged into a wall outlet' as you characterize it, but the weapon may indeed be sitting in a storage locker somewhere in a surrounding city, waiting to be deployed. A needle in a haystack." There was a moment of contemplation as Rube and Otto considered Lehman's words…

"Let's survey the caves and deploy our sensors up in the crater," Palmrich said. "That is our best shot. The site up there is prepared. It is ready. Eventually the needle must come to the haystack. Agreed?"

"I agree," Castellano said. Everyone else in the room nodded.

20

Early June 1968: Summit Caves Survey, and Other Recon

One portion of the agreement reached between FBI Special Agent Rubayat Castellano, and Owner Herb McGill of the Rainier Guide Service, was that the "USGS," AKA the FBI/CIA, would pay for resupply of all provisions at Camp Muir. RGS guides ordinarily carried sixty to eighty pounds of food and other perishables to Camp Muir during the first day of summit climbs, to restock the Guide Hut. Now all provisions, under Rube's shrewd logistical planning, including the heavy propane fuel canisters used for cooking, would be air-dropped at the high camp under contract with bush pilot Jimmy Beech, flying out of Ashford.

The RGS guides loved having their loads lightened on the days before their summit climbs, and McGill loved the fact that all supplies were purchased and delivered on the LRT's nickel. Castellano, ever mindful of reducing jealousies and curiosity about what their two "rented" RGS guides were actually doing at the LRT, let it be known that Lehman had suggested that the USGS make this gesture to relieve the toils of the guides. In exchange, the RGS would allow the LRT to use the Guide Hut when it was not occupied by the guides.

"Damn, Lehman, brilliant idea. Thanks!" Gary Olin said, slapping Bradford on the back before they sat down to breakfast at the Paradise Inn Dining Room.

"Which brilliant idea?" Bradford asked, hiding his bewilderment.

"Your idea to share resources and to resupply Camp Muir for us by air. Hell, that takes a huge load off our backs, and we won't be dragging our asses so badly on summit day."

"Oh, *that* brilliant idea. Gary, it is the least we can do for you over there. The LRT is remarkably well-funded. In fact, I can even buy your breakfast."

Olin, a senior RGS guide, had just returned from scouting a route up the mountain. The season officially started the next day.

"I saw your wanded route up the Ingraham Headwall, Brad. Damn, it is really straightforward. And unlike last summer, the glacier is not nearly as broken up. I would love to run our clients up that route. I hate the Disappointment Cleaver. It is more dangerous and exposed, in my opinion."

"Be our guest, Gary," Bradford said. "Consider our route as yours. It is now the 'RGS Route.' We have stashed five-foot aluminum pickets, snow flukes, ice screws, and other LRT gear up at Cadaver Gap, along with six hundred feet of extra goldline, and a thousand feet of spooled half-inch nylon line for fixed ropes, if you need them. The LRT will be up and down the hill all summer using your route -- so I encourage you to use our gear. But you guys are going to be on the route constantly, compared to us, so what about this setup Gary -- the LRT supplies the gear, and in exchange the RGS uses it to keep the route open and maintained. That goldline will work nicely as a fixed rope on the Headwall, for starters."

Gary wiped his lips with his linen napkin and stuck out his hand. "Deal, Lehman, thanks! Man, this season is starting off exceptionally well. We even got raises from McGill – gratuitously, out of thin air -- and without anyone even asking. I wonder if Herb is feeling well." They laughed.

The following day Lehman, Ring, Makinson, and Teo Maloney, shouldered their climbing packs and headed up the hill toward Camp Muir. It was 0500. The dawn's light glowed faintly through the fog and cold gusting wind as the LRT team, making good time, pushed over Panorama Point and past Pebble Creek onto the Muir Snowfield.

The Snowfield was actually a glacier. It contained crevasses that opened up later in the summer. This always baffled Bradford: *Why do they name some snowfields up here 'glaciers' and some glaciers 'snowfields? Odd...* Lehman thoughts wandered as he plodded along, following the bamboo wands they had placed a week before.

The five-mile, five-thousand-vertical-foot trek to Camp Muir from Paradise was dangerously deceptive. Many hikers and climbers had lost their lives on its slopes, especially in this weather, with limited visibility. Two years before Lehman had lost a friend, Elmer Portis, on the Snowfield. Portis had become disoriented in a storm with his young son and nephew while trying to hike to Muir late in the summer. Elmer bivouacked in a crevasse with the kids to shelter for the night. He and his son froze to death in their sleep. Only the nephew survived. Bradford was on that rescue, and helped recover Portis' body. He remembered talking to the corpse. It was strapped crossways in a litter against Lehman's chest, as it was pulled out of the cold blue crevasse:

"Elmer, why did you let yourself go to sleep? You were my client, and we shared a tent together for a week on a seminar. We talked about bivouacking. I taught you about the need to stay awake if you had no sleeping bag, and were underequipped, and cold. What a damned shame." Lehman had wiped the snow away from his friend's chalky frozen face. *"Why did you and your young son go to sleep?"* The corpse was mute. Corpses and big mountains never talked.

The fog on the Snowfield cleared, and the party hiked on in bright sunshine.

"Brad, you have been quiet now for a while. What are you thinking?" Teo asked gently.

"Nothing much really," Lehman lied. "I was concentrating on seeing the next wand when we were in the fog." Lehman turned, smiled at Teo, and looked past her. He needed to change the subject in his mind.

"How are you doing, Makinson?" Lehman shouted. "You must be fine. I haven't heard you stop talking since we left Pebble Creek."

"Ring and I are regaling each other about our time in Vietnam. Turns out my artillery base, LZ Action, delivered several fire missions for old John here, to help him and his tribesmen get their asses out of Viet Cong and North Vietnamese Army ambushes."

"That's right," John said. "This character here bailed me out of trouble several times. Small world, huh?"

"Yeah," Lehman grinned. "Sometimes, Makinson, it is a little too small. Don't sunburn the roof of your mouth."

*   *   *

Two rope teams -- Lehman and Maloney, and Ring and Makinson -- departed Camp Muir for the summit of Mount Rainier at 2230. They climbed under a waxing gibbous moon. It was windy, with intermittent clouds and fog. Only when fog curled tightly in around them, did they switch on their headlamps. They topped the Ingraham Headwall at 0230, and arrived at Rainier's summit at 0450. The gear they carried, including packs, was marked "USGS-LRT," in bold stenciled letters, in keeping with their cover mission.

"Congratulations girl!" Lehman gave Teo a big hug up at Columbia Crest as the party stood there, buffeted by the wind. "Congratulations to you too Ron -- but I'm not hugging you. This is the second ascent of Mount Rainier for you both. Great job! We made excellent time up the hill." Bradford detected pride in their hood-wrapped faces. They saw it in his.

Taking cover back under Register Rock on the west rim, the party decided to split up. Each two-man team would search steam caves from opposite sides of the Crater, and at ninety degrees to the vents explored the week before. This would greatly speed up their exploration.

"Okay, Lehman and Teo," Ring said, "you two start across there on the east side and Makinson and I will search from here on the west. We will meet back by our ropes and other gear no later than 0930. Leave a wand at the entrance point when you go in. That way, if we have to come and find you, we can. And when we come back out, we photograph our sites from the outside before we pull the wands, like we were briefed, okay?" Lehman gave a thumbs-up and he and Teo walked over to the east rim.

"Oh Brad, this is incredible in here! I thought the photos were fantastic, but they don't do it justice."

"It definitely is, babe." Lehman grabbed Teo's mittened hand and gave it a squeeze. They slowly worked their way along an undulating passage, taking photos as they went, as the cave angled left and down. Except for the occasional soft hissing of steam and the sounds of their boots on the rocks and scree, it was quiet. They bent down and rounded a corner. The passage opened up into a cavern. It was perhaps a third smaller than the Ballroom. A clear pool of water glistened from its floor. Out of it rose a giant column of ice, six feet in diameter, tapering to three feet at the cave's ceiling thirty feet above.

"Brad, this is stunning!" Teo's headlamp reflected coruscating greens and blues. Lehman scanned the rest of the chamber. There was no sign that anyone had ever been there.

"Well, Teo, you are the first to discover this. What do you want to name it?"

"The Arcade," Teo said, breathlessly.

"Great name, girl." Bradford reached a gloved hand around Teo's shoulder and kissed her. "Great name."

The two teams met back at Register Rock at 0930. No one had yet found signs of the GRU, or any other human presence in the rest of the cave system. The wind calmed, and the bright morning sun suddenly reminded the team that they had been climbing for two days with little sleep.

"Gary Olin's guided party will be along in the next few hours," Lehman said, checking his watch. "Let's take a nap, and when he gets here we can boil up some tea for the guides and clients. They will only stay an hour or so, and then head back down the hill. We can sleep again after that for six or eight hours. Then we will hit the caves again after we have dinner and things quiet down."

"We have acoustic sensors to set up too, so remind me to get them out of my pack…" Makinson's words faded. He drifted off to sleep.

"It would be good if he did that more frequently," Lehman said quietly, as he and Teo nestled together in their down parkas. She elbowed him in the ribs.

"Friendlies coming in." Ring's words woke the team. John had already melted snow and boiled up tea in the large aluminum pot he had wedged solidly between two big rocks. The gas stove burned furiously under it. Olin and his group arrived at the east rim, unroped, and dribbled across to Register Rock in small clusters.

"Man, talk about service," Gary Olin said, as he took a steaming cup of hot tea from Ring's outstretched hand.

Olin turned to his clients: "Step up folks, you are lucky today. You get tea service on the summit. We only do this for clients a couple times a summer. Step on up!" The clients, many wobbly-legged, and all parched, queued up. Their expressions were tired and grateful. They reminded Lehman of pictures taken of people in soup kitchen lines during the Great Depression. Olin looked over his steaming cup.

"Damned good route you kicked in for us, Lehman and…"

"Makinson – Ron Makinson," Ron said, half awake.

"Makinson, yes. Where did you get your experience, Ron? Himalayas? Cascades? South America?" Olin asked, as he took a drink of hot tea.

"I didn't," Makinson answered.

Olin coughed out his tea. "What do you mean you didn't?"

"That's right," Ron smiled, "I am learning as I go. Lehman and Ring here are teaching me."

"Then why the hell were you hired?" Olin asked incredulously.

"My uncle is a very rich stock broker on Wall Street. I am apparently the black sheep in my family, and my dear old dad – and uncle -- won't let me back into it until I 'prove myself,' or some shit like that," Makinson said, yawning. "Why the hell else do you think you and the other guides got a raise? It wasn't McGill's money. It was my dear old uncle's." Makinson leaned back, hands behind his head, and went to sleep.

Olin's mouth dropped open. He stared unbelievingly at Ron for a long moment, and then shook his head. Makinson began snoring.

"Ron is beautiful when he's sleeping isn't he Gary?" Lehman said, smiling.

Turning to walk away, Gary spoke into Lehman's ear. "Damn, Brad, I'm sure glad the LRT has him and not us. Can you imagine what he would do with the clients?"

"Oh yes, Gary, I can very well imagine what he would do with them. You just give the nod anytime and we will send him back over to the RGS."

"No, you keep him. Jeez!"

"Gary, you know the old story about the goose and the golden egg, right?"

"Yeah."

"Well, Makinson here is the goose." Lehman stuck his thumb back toward Ron. "I would keep this revelation between us. There is no reason to kill the golden goose. No goose, no eggs." Olin stared long at Lehman, then nodded slightly and shook his head again. *He is not going to talk. Olin knows there's nothing to be gained by stirring things up with the other guides. He understands – no goose, no eggs.*

The RGS party departed the crater rim at 1245, heading back down the hill with their weary clients. The LRT went to sleep. It stirred awake at 2000 hours, ate dinner under a brilliant canopy of stars, and prepared to set off to complete their survey of the caves.

"Jeez, Makinson, you sure laid a load of crap on Gary Olin," Bradford said. Ron let out a loud laugh and shook Lehman's hand.

"I got two birds with one stone with that one," Makinson grinned.

"How so?" Ring asked.

"I handily handled Mister Olin's snooping around. That's one bird," Ron said.

"What's the other bird?" Teo asked.

"A brand new yellow Porsche Targa convertible," Makinson said, his face rippling into a wide grin. "Rube's gotta rent me one now to maintain my cover story – a rich spoiled black sheep – yes!" Ron pumped his arm.

"Bullshit. Rube will never do that," Ring said.

"No bullshit, John, he'll get me the Porsche. He has to!" There was a long pause as Bradford, Teo, and John took turns shaking their heads in disbelief.

Makinson looked at them. "What? I'll let you all *ride* in it. And if you're really good, I might even let you *drive* it!"

* * *

Bradford and Teo finished their cave survey and were back at Register Rock by midnight, before Ring and Makinson. They lit the stove and began melting snow for hot tea. Then they walked a short way north along the crater rim, holding hands. They sat down on a foam ground pad to watch the traffic lights change in Tacoma. The massive white summit of Liberty Cap slept serenely in the moonlight to the west.

"Brad," Teo said, hugging his arm, "I can't think of a more beautiful scene. It is like an amazing dream – being here with you, on this big mountain. Never in my wildest dreams would I have imagined my life coming together here, with you, my handsome guide. I am so happy and proud, all at once!"

"And a little scared?"

"Yes, Brad. A lot scared. I would be untruthful if I said I wasn't. But it is worth it, every bit, to be with you."

Lehman looked at Teo. The coyote fur that trimmed the hood of her down parka flicked softly across her pale face, mixed with the wisps of her fine dark hair, and danced together like spindrift in the wind. He concentrated on the picture of that lovely face, nested so serenely next to his. He made it indelible.

"Behold, thou art fair, my love; behold, thou art fair; thou hast doves' eyes within thy locks."

"That is beautiful, Brad. Where did you get that quote?"

"Song of Solomon. The Bible."

Teo pressed her lips against his. His face felt the caress of the fur and her silky hair. The breathless ancient passage from the Bible became now. Cold was kissed away.

"I have decided."

"What Brad?" Teo's question was more exhaled than spoken.

"You never would have dated me in high school. 'Thou art too fair.' But here we are now, thank God. Timing is everything isn't it girl?" A flicker of light came from the direction of Register Rock. Makinson and Ring had returned. "And speaking of timing..." Teo laughed.

The team sat on the summit of Mount Rainier, waiting out the night to return to Paradise. Their exploration of the crater caves was complete. There was no Backpack nuclear bomb in them. There was nothing imminently ready to be detonated. That was some consolation. Agent Makinson had discreetly placed the acoustic sensor, the weight, shape, and color of which identically matched a crater rock, near the entrance of the passage down to the Ballroom. He decided not to place any other sensors on the rim, deeming that to do so would "heat up" the area and spook the GRU into moving the Backpack site somewhere else.

Agents Castellano and Palmrich later concurred with Makinson's decision. And to the utter astonishment of Lehman, Maloney, and Ring, Agent Makinson got his yellow 1968 Porsche Targa. Rube was fine with it, since Palmrich convinced the CIA to spend the money for it to maintain Makinson's "rich-kid" cover. The caveat was that Makinson had to keep the Porsche parked down by the Visitor's Center, away from the Guide House. "Let that god-damned 'sore thumb' stick out down there," Castellano told Ron. "Damn, Makinson, you've got a hell of a knack. Yellow Porsche – shit!"

"Rube, look at it this way. When an agent puts his life on the line for his country, don't you think it is only proper to give that agent all the tools necessary to fulfill his mission and to keep him comfortable? Hell, it only costs twice as much to fly first class. And I *do* have a rich uncle."

"Bullshit, Makinson, who?" Rube asked.

"Good old Uncle Sam!"

Such were the odd contrasts and delicate vagaries of the world of counterintelligence, the Cold War, and the ghastly looming potential for thermonuclear annihilation. Young Lehman was beginning to understand these vagaries and it bothered him. It was not the presence of the threat, or the mission, or the experience, or the agents in the operation, or even the expense that bothered him. It was his emerging understanding of the *process* of it all that did. *The gestalt of it --* Lehman pondered -- *so serene on the outside, so sullen and vicious on the inside. Bizarre.*

*   *   *

In mid-June the Lahar Research Team gained a new member in the person of Jack Rose of the CIA. Jack was nondescript – five feet nine inches tall, with a thin build, ruddy complexion, close-cut salt and pepper hair, and a round face. Lehman reckoned him to be in his early forties. His distinguishing feature was his dark-rimmed glasses. The lenses were so thick that they magnified his perennially inquisitive hazel eyes.

Jack Rose and Rubayat Castellano acted as though they had known each other for years. They had. Both fought together in the OSS in World War II. Rose was studious and imperturbable. Agent Castellano was brash and animated. Castellano and Rose so complemented each other's abilities that their operations, and co-operation, became legendary. As they advanced in their respective agencies, Castellano and Rose -- "C-R" as they were known in tandem -- became valued back-channel advisors throughout the U.S. intelligence community, Congress, and successive U.S. Presidents. They were smart, discreet, direct, levelheaded, and utterly reliable. When the mission required, "C-R" could deftly walk the tightrope between politics and operational requirements. In the present operation, both Otto Palmrich and Rubayat Castellano lobbied superiors to bring Jack Rose onto the team. When the nod was given, Rose was summarily pulled out of a clandestine operation along the Ho Chi Minh Trail in Laos, and flown back to the CONUS. Jack was now happily ensconced with the Lahar Research Team on Mount Rainier. Wherever he was, Rose was simply happy to be.

* * *

Otto, Rube, and now Jack Rose, took stock of the intelligence -- or lack thereof -- that had been gathered from the LRT's survey of Mount Rainier's summit cave system. They had a large acetate-covered map of the caves drawn up, with an inset showing an enlargement of the Ballroom. Lehman was impressed. It appeared to be drawn to scale.

There was also a big bar-locked map cabinet in the basement of the Guide House where SR-71 imagery, and all the photographs taken by Lehman and other LRT members were stored. The auditorium door was always locked, and the room guarded from the inside by armed plain-clothed agents. To Rube's chagrin, the LRT began conducting operational meetings in the auditorium, rather than commandeering the Glacier Room during off-hours.

Whenever he could, Lehman assisted Jimmy Beech in his air resupply missions to Camp Muir. Teo often went along. The old bush pilot gradually let Lehman fly closer to Rainier, as Bradford gained the "feel" of close-in flying on the big mountain. Bradford noted carefully when and where Jimmy made his turns, added and reduced power, and went into side-slips, teasing the Cessna around rocks and over glaciers -- riding the familiar folds of bumpy air made by a big mountain lifting its bulk toward the jet stream.

"Many aircraft, big and small, have tried to move this mountain over the years," Jimmy said, "and none has ever succeeded."

Lehman and Teo were always looking for any climbers, or signs of them, out of the ordinary. Beech was a bush pilot, so he didn't mind flying anywhere, especially around Mount Rainier. The LRT was paying him well for his services. But as hard as Lehman and Maloney scouted all the routes, on every side of the mountain, nothing stood out -- except on one occasion.

Jimmy had made a drop of supplies at Camp Muir, and was banking the Cessna 185 south, skimming the surface of the Nisqually Glacier, when Bradford caught a bright flash out of the corner of his eye. It came from the left, somewhere around the nine-thousand-foot level between the Nisqually Glacier and the Muir Snowfield. Lehman asked Jimmy to fly the same pattern again. He did, but there were no flashes – nothing. And there was no sign of climbers. Only ice, snow, and rock cliffs. Lehman noticed that Jimmy had a silver watchband on his left wrist. *That must have been what reflected in the sun and caught my attention,* Lehman thought. He dismissed the event.

June ended with the LRT still waiting, "surveying," and watching. Jack and Rube had decided to set up a "discreet perimeter" on the big mountain. Acoustic sensors, built to look like surrounding rocks at each location, were placed at all the high camps on Rainier, and were continually monitored. They were even placed in the Paradise Ice Caves. Except for the single sensor near the entranceway to the Ballroom, nothing was positioned on the summit or crater rim. Jack and Rube agreed that the target area should remain as pristine as possible -- for the present.

21

MID-JULY 1968: DEATH AND NEAR-DEATH

The LRT's climbing team of Lehman, Ring, Makinson, and Maloney, made two more ascents of Rainier during and after the first week of July. One was up the Emmons Glacier, via Camp Schurman. The other was up the Kautz Glacier, via Camp Hazard. Otto Palmrich accompanied the team on the Kautz trip. He had never been up that route. These climbs were to service and replace sensors as necessary, and to eliminate the possibility that the GRU may be utilizing those routes to access the summit caves. Indications were that it had not. Maloney and Makinson both honed their mountaineering skills expeditiously on these climbs. The trip up the Emmons was done in a whiteout and blizzard. It was on this exercise that Ron Makinson slipped, and was slow to go into a self arrest. He was stopped by his rope-mate, John Ring.

"What slowed you down, Ron?" Bradford shouted back over the wind. There was concern in his voice.

"Crap, I thought I was standing upright and I just fell over. I was so surprised I was falling that I didn't react fast enough."

"Spatial disorientation," Lehman said. "It can happen in whiteouts where the snow and sky are blended and there is no sense of slope or horizon. Now that you know the sensation, Ron, get into your self arrest posthaste." Makinson gave a thumbs up, and the trek continued uneventfully thereafter.

All climbs were Spartan, with bivouacs -- without tents or hot food – "Frank Lehman style," as Lehman referred to it. "*Eat cold, drink hot,*" Lehman's father would say. "*Get up, eat quick, and get the hell out of high camp.*"

This was sage operational advice and it enabled the team to move swiftly up and down the routes. As for conditions, the RGS Route was a night-and-day-contrast to the 1967 season. The Cowlitz and Ingraham Glaciers were much less broken up and easier to navigate. Down deep, Lehman sensed that the GRU would stay on the RGS Route. *George Coleman and company are under pressure to complete their mission. They will stick with what little they know about Rainier. And that means they will use our route.*

John Ring and Ron Makinson were well on their way to becoming fast friends. Both liked to fly fish. Makinson had somehow talked Jimmy Beech into taking him on aerial fish re-stocking runs for the Park Service, thus revealing some of the good backcountry lakes near Paradise. He even co-opted Jimmy into dropping some fish into Fan Lake, which had become Makinson's favorite hike and camping spot on his days off. "Spillage," Ron called it. Makinson was now taking Nancy Olszewski out on his fishing trips in place of Ring. Nancy also thoroughly enjoyed being driven around the Park in Makinson's yellow Porsche Targa.

"Nancy has caught on to fly fishing real fast," Ron said with a grin.

"I haven't the slightest doubt that she has, Ron," Lehman said. "She has spent many hours -- and nights -- with you learning the fine points of the sport."

"And *sports cars* too," Makinson laughed.

Teo and Bradford were growing steadily in love and affection for each other. Often, rather than walk the few feet over to the Inn to watch the nightly talent shows, they stayed in their room together and read history – sometimes to each other. One quote Bradford discovered was by his hero, Winston Churchill. It lodged in his mind:

"Play the game for more than you can afford to loose. Only then will you learn the game."

* * *

Maybe it was the operational pressure. Lehman didn't think so. Or maybe it was his worries about the pending divorce of his father and mother. Frank Lehman had called a few days before, cryptically informing Bradford that he was filing. Lehman knew it was coming, as surely as winter follows fall. It was the timing of it that bothered Bradford, and purely for his own selfish reasons, he understood.

Couldn't dad have waited a few more months? Why did he have to file now, while I'm on the hill trying to keep my ass, and others, from getting chewed up? Well, Lehman he loves you and so does your mom – but they are wrapped around their own axles. Their world has closed in on them too.

The world of divorces, unhappy lives, and the petty family mind games of trying to persuade Bradford toward favoring one side or the other – all seemed so far away now.

Why don't they shut up, settle their own crap, and leave me out of it? Hell, I'm not in the house anymore. Give me a break.

Lehman was painfully aware, however, that such is so often the course and the curse of families where parents constantly fight. Kids are pawns. They get wrung out and dragged into the fray. *Hell, that's the objective of it. That is what they want. Selfish bastards.*

Lehman was surprised at his mind's blunt reaction. But he had a mountain to contend with, along with a desperate sliver of the Cold War to fight there. That was enough. His plate was full. But he did have Teo. She was aware of the Lehman family's travails, and of the impending divorce. She did what she could to be there for Bradford. Mainly, Teo just listened.

Thus, as June turned tensely toward July with no discernable movement shown by the GRU, Lehman took to early morning hikes. He loved to see the sunrise at Paradise -- and it was his best time to think. Most of the time Teo got up and hiked with him. But on this particular day, as she lay next to him sleeping peacefully, he decided not to wake her. It was just as well. Today he needed to think through his family problems – or better yet, walk them off. Lehman quietly pulled on his climbing knickers, holstered his pistol, donned a wool shirt with a light windbreaker over it, and carefully closed the door. It was 0450.

On his way out of the Guide House, and almost without thinking, he grabbed his Kelty frame pack and shouldered it while he walked. There was little weight in it: a sweater, sunglasses, gloves, sunscreen, a twenty-foot length of nylon web-sling, and his Rollei 35T camera. Since he didn't feel the weight, he did not think to buckle the Kelty's waistband around his hips. He left his Grivel ice axe behind. Wind, fog, and snow lashed at Bradford, but he took no notice. They were his old, cold friends – familiar elements in his climbing world.

The snow was melted out along the sides of the Alta Vista Trail, but as he hiked further uphill the dirt trail became one of dirty snow, then gradually whitened into the solid snow track that took hikers toward Panorama Point, and on up the mountain toward Camp Muir. Fingers of blowing fog alternately wrapped him tightly, and then broke to reveal straight dark forms of alpine firs shaping the meadows and dotting the hillsides. When gusts of wind struck them, they spoke their soft hissing white noise into Bradford's ear. It was as though they were listening, embracing, comforting. Lehman breathed in the chill of the rushing wet air. He felt his stress abating.

At the first big switchback turn that would have taken him up to the top Panorama, Bradford chose instead to hike straight ahead paralleling the eastern edge of the Nisqually Glacier and the broad ridgeline of the Muir Snowfield. Fog again swirled close around him. Flakes of snow stung his lips. The farther he hiked the fewer tracks could be seen until, after walking half a mile, he was following only a single set of tracks. Lehman took deep breaths. The muscles of his legs relaxed into the brisk pace he set for them. He was in rhythm with the mountain.

Bradford had just realized that the tracks he was following were fresh, and had abruptly turned to the right, when he heard a muffled *pop*. He felt a sharp sting in his neck that spun him sideways. Bradford Lehman knew instantly that he had been shot. All of his training and instincts took over. And as time slowed his movements down in his mind, he drew his Walther PPK pistol as he was turning, slipped out of his pack's left shoulder strap, and sprawled prone on the snow facing the origin of the shot. Bradford Lehman did not fear – he focused. It was 0520…

*   *   *

"Beautiful lady, I have been shot." Lehman spoke his words softly, directly, and without emotion. Teo had just dressed. She turned around when Lehman opened the door to their room. He was holding his red scarf against the left side of his neck.

"Oh my god, Bradford. Come with me!" Teo's mountain medicine and first aid training now kicked in. She grabbed Lehman's hand, took him downstairs to the Guide House Kitchen, and sat him down. No one else was there.

"Have you lost much blood?"

"No."

"Keep your hand propped against the wound. Keep pressure on it," Teo commanded. She grabbed a medical kit from the storeroom and opened it. She pulled out a field dressing, the kind being used in combat in Vietnam to cover sucking chest wounds. She did not know yet what she would see. Bradford watched as she worked -- calmly, efficiently. He smiled. *This girl is squared away, Lehman.*

"Okay, Bradford, I am going to pull your hand and scarf away. It may bleed. But stay with me."

"I'd never leave a gorgeous woman like you. I'm staying."

Teo ignored his banter. She was focused. She lifted the scarf away. Some of the congealed blood came with it. The wound began bleeding again, but not profusely.

"You have a furrow-like wound about a quarter of an inch deep, extending horizontally about five inches along your neck." Teo's clinical words began to soften. "You may need stitches. Let me clean it up and butterfly it. How are you doing, my lover and handsome guide?" Teo bent down and put her face right in front of him, her large dark eyes looking intently into his.

"Fine, love, but I'm tired."

"You may be in shock." She cleaned the wound with iodine solution, applied antibiotic ointment, and closed the wound with butterfly bandages. The bandages were filling up with blood, so she wrapped several layers of gauze around his neck over the top of them. She watched and noted that no blood was oozing through. This was a good sign. Bradford's blood was clotting.

Finished, Teo again bent down. She took Lehman's head in her hands and looked deeply into his eyes, trying to determine if he was in shock. Bradford focused on Teo's face – her dark fine hair falling around it, and the keen bright eyes looking into his.

"I'm not in shock, woman. Just in love," Lehman said. "Same thing, though, I guess. God, you are beautiful."

"Yes, I know," Teo said. They both laughed. It released the tension in Lehman's gut. He relaxed. But it was not enough to deaden the pain of his wound.

"Hey beautiful," Lehman said, "can you scare up some aspirin? This damned thing is really hurting." Teo gave him two pills and a glass of water. Then she brought him a plastic bag filled with ice so he could hold it on the wound.

The emergency now resolved, Teo's eyes misted up with relief. She kissed Bradford over and over on his lips, and then on his nose and forehead.

Lehman put the ice pack down, and reached up and placed his hands over hers. He Leaned forward. Tears began running down his face. Then he whispered softly in her ear. "I killed the son-of-a-bitch, Teo…"

22

TWO HOURS LATER: DEBRIEFINGS OF ARMED ENGAGEMENT

Lehman, Castellano, Palmrich, Makinson, Maloney, and Rose, were present, along with several FBI and CIA agents providing security.

"Tell us what happened," Rube said, as he pulled the pen from his shirt pocket and opened his notebook.

Lehman methodically told the story of his shootout with the GRU agent. He flatly stated the time, place, and conditions of the ambush. He spoke of the "pop" of a silenced gun coming somewhere out of the fog from his two o'clock direction. He related the scene with his eyes closed, as though replaying a movie in his mind. He spoke of the shots he took at his assailant looming out of the fog. The first one fired at the left shin, at the "viewable" target of the dark-colored gaiters above the assailant's white climbing boots; and then at the "mask" of the figure's face, the area of the eyes, as he became acutely aware of the killer's gun. It was big, and deadly. It rose slowly up in the man's hand, pointing at Bradford, like a giant black finger – pointing. But he forced himself to ignore the gun. It was the man behind it that would kill him. Bradford concentrated on the mask.

Lehman began to sweat profusely. He spoke of seeing the front sight on his Walther PPK pistol -- of seeing it with such clarity that he could distinguish the steps, or serrations, cut into its front metal ramp. He spoke of why he took each action, or found himself automatically taking each. Breathing more easily now, Lehman opened his eyes, but kept them focused on a picture on the far wall. It was a photo taken in the 1920s of RGS clients, sitting in a long line, stacked together, preparing to slide down a snowy hillside. Everyone was smiling at the camera. He looked at the guides on each end of the line. Maybe one was his father. But his father was not in the picture.

Bradford continued. He noted that he recalled Rube's conversation with Ring at the training up at Mica Peak last spring -- about the limitations of the Walther's light .32 caliber round, and how that influenced his decisions on where to place his shots. He talked of waiting until the killer stopped writhing and became a quiet corpse. He told of reloading his Walther pistol, standing up, binding his own neck wound with his red scarf stuffed with snow, and walking up to the body. He spoke of his decision to photograph the corpse, first as it lay, then spread-eagled, with all pockets turned out and the contents from them lying on the snow. He furnished a detailed physical description of the body -- its black close-cropped hair, pockmarked round face, dark dilated eyes, the weight and height of the body -- and the thick, powerful, calloused hands.

"I already gave you his pistol so you have that," Lehman said.

Rube nodded.

Lehman then described how he disposed of the assailant's body in the adjacent crevasse on the Nisqually Glacier. Of how he tied the corpse's feet together with a length of nylon web-sling, and dragged the body over to the lip of the crevasse; how the web-sling became slippery with the blood he got on his hands when he tended his own wound; how the body moved more easily than he thought; how he untied the web-sling from the feet, and rolled the corpse into the crevasse; and finally, how he heard the sounds of its falling fade away the further and deeper it fell...

Lehman finished by telling how he carefully kicked snow over the bloody slide track made by the body, from the edge of the crevasse all the way back to the where the GRU agent died; and how he carefully covered the dark pool of blood where the head had been, and then covered over his own blood, spilled a few yards away. He told of how the blowing snow erased all tracks – how the mountain had helped him keep his secret. Softly, he spoke of his walk back to the Guide House, of passing early hikers who nodded and smiled at him, and how he had nodded and smiled back. Lehman stopped and took a deep breath. He put his head down. He was finished. The room was dead silent.

Bradford was unaware that Teo placed her hand on his arm and was squeezing it, supporting him. Lehman was aware of only one thing. He had to get every last detail out. Right then. Right there. He knew his mind and understood that this was what he must do.

Despite the experience of killing another man being new to him, the act felt old to Lehman. To him, in fact, it was as ancient as mankind. It was as old as Kane and Abel -- history itself -- as old as life and death. Bradford also intuitively knew that to live in the shadow of its effects without being forever scarred, if that were possible, he must rationalize. To rationalize was to heal. Healing would be easier in this case because the rationalization was as blatant and obvious as the bullet wound in his neck. *You had no choice Lehman. It was self-defense. Kill, or be killed.*

The clicking of Special Agent Castellano's ballpoint pen brought Bradford back to the room, the table, his friends, and his lover. The movie was over.

Castellano broke the silence with his deep powerful voice: "Son-of-a-bitch, kid. *Son-of-a-bitch!*" Rube reached across the table and shook Lehman's hand. His grip, normally crushing, was firm but gentle. Makinson and Ring both breathed out audibly and followed Rube to shake Bradford's hand. Palmrich, smiling, nodded and gave a "thumbs-up."

Teo was sitting next to Bradford, but he didn't want to look at her. *What will she think of me now? What will she do now that this operation has escalated into killing?* He felt her hand on his cheek. It turned his face toward hers. She kissed him softly on the lips.

"Magnificent!" Jack Rose exclaimed. His declaration sounded as though he was pronouncing them married. Indeed, to Rose, they *were* now married – to the mission.

A wave of relief flooded over Lehman as he looked into Teo's approving eyes. He reached up and ran a hand through her hair. He returned to himself.

Lehman reached into the front pocket of his jeans. He pulled out a metal film canister and moved it, as though taking a turn on a chessboard, across the varnished wooden table to Castellano. Rube picked up the canister and handed it to Jack.

"You can process this faster, and will likely have a better handle on who the perpetrator was." Jack nodded with a studious smile.

"Care to guess who's in the can?" Lehman asked. He raised his hand for another round of beers. Jack instinctively looked around before answering.

"Don't worry Jack," Palmrich said, "you know we booked the whole bar, the bartender is an agent, and the room is secure." Jack glanced at the others in the room, and smiled at them.

"None of them are drinking," Lehman said.

"Yeah, and it pisses my guys off," Rube responded. "But they can drink a little later when the bar re-opens to the public."

Jack Rose began speaking. His words were quiet, contemplating.

"Brad, you asked me if I could guess who attacked you. Rube and I discussed the possibilities extensively in the car driving up here, since you phoned us this morning and provided an initial description of the body."

"You ride in cars together?" Lehman needled. He wanted to cut the stress down in the room, and in himself. "Do Hoover, and Helms actually authorize that?"

"Nope," Rube replied for Jack. "They'd both shit bricks if they heard about it. You know, the usual jealous rivalry. But what they don't know won't hurt 'em."

Jack nodded, smiling. Jack Rose, if that was his real name, always smiled. He seemed serene -- a perpetual muse. Lehman found Jack's demeanor calming. Rube took a swallow of beer. Jack patiently started over.

"You asked me, Brad, if we could guess who attacked you. Rube and I both reached the same conclusion." Jack looked at Rube.

"Go ahead, tell Lehman," Rube said. "He's wired in, and this morning he has definitely paid his dues."

"We predict that your shooter was one of the Karin brothers," Jack said. "They are Armenians, and work as assassins for the GRU. They belong to a sub-group under Spetsnaz. There are four brothers, and..." Jack paused as though pondering a philosophical point, "... and if they are now down to three, they will not be happy about it."

Rube, in the middle of a swallow of beer, choked. "That is a fuc--" he glanced at Teo -- "That's a hell of an understatement! Jack, you perennially amaze me." Though like Jack, Rube was articulate, he never let that attribute get in the way of gritty observations. He was, at bottom, an FBI agent.

Jack, outwardly oblivious to his animated colleague, continued: "My guess is Brad, based upon your excellent description, that it is Ivan Karin. But of course, we will have to see what the film develops."

Bradford Lehman pondered in the moment. Here he was, sitting incongruously in the Glacier Room at Mount Rainier, an under-age drinker, in the presence of the "Feds," and "Spooks."

Rubayat and John sat, quietly sipping their beers, letting him ponder. Never would Bradford have envisioned being in such a strange situation – up on a beautiful mountain, in a gorgeous national park, working a lucrative summer job at the Rainier Guide Service, training and goading clients, dodging rock and icefall -- and now bullets. *What the hell have I gotten myself into?*

Rube finally spoke: "You are probably thinking 'What in the hell have I gotten myself into?'" Lehman looked up. Both Rube and Jack were eying him intently with fatherly looks. Pride was in their eyes, especially in Jack's, as his were magnified by his glasses. Lehman stifled a grin.

Jack leaned over and clasped Lehman's shoulder. "Rube and Otto briefed you on this and talked of this possibility extensively Brad, in your training last spring at Mica Peak. But let me tell you -- you are an equal or the better of any agent I've worked with, regardless of age. You handled your attacker like a pro. You only gave him one chance. He missed and you made him pay."

"And dumping his sorry ass into the crevasse was brilliant! No body, no paperwork, no problems!" Castellano added, giving Lehman an A-Okay sign with his thumb and forefinger. "Brilliant!"

"But if this guy had killed me," Lehman said firmly, "that same crevasse would have had my name on it instead of his. In fact, this GRU agent may have planned it that way -- kill me, drag me over to the crevasse, and dump me there. Then you and your agencies would be left with a missing man in an operation, wondering what the hell happened."

Jack Rose leaned toward Lehman, his large eyes deep with compassion. "Bradford, are you okay? Your experience today, especially being the first one, can be traumatic."

"I am fine, Jack. I drag bodies off the hill on recoveries all the time. Some in pieces. We've had a ton of search and recovery missions already this summer. It's been a bitch. I've been on four of them. I'm fine with the bodies," Bradford nodded at Ring, who nodded back. "But this bastard tried to kill me."

The summer of 1968 on Mount Rainier had been a good 'route year,' for climbing the upper mountain. Yet, the Park Service Rangers and RGS guides dealt with an abnormal number of search and rescue missions. There had been nine all together. Four were lost climbers and hikers who were located and brought in alive. One was a recovery of a body where a woman fell from a cliff. One climber was found dead of hypothermia. But three hikers simply disappeared. None of the three had been on summit climbs. Two of the three had signed the register at the Paradise Ranger Station, indicating their destinations were Camp Muir. The third hadn't signed the register, but family and friends disclosed that the hiker told them that he was going to Muir.

"Brad, it's no different than when you and Ring trained me," Makinson said, smiling. "You both claimed I was trying to kill you." Lehman and the group laughed. Teo slapped Makinson on the shoulder. It broke the tension in the room.

"Bradford, I see how this relates to your experience," Jack said. He appeared to be thinking, as if trying to solve a delightful puzzle. "Yes, it *is* a slightly different set of circumstances for you. But look at this as sort of..." Jack paused, feeling for the right words, "...as sort of a *reverse* recovery exercise. Instead of rescuing someone and bringing them *in*, you put someone *away*."

"Ha! That's one of your better ones Jack," Rube chuckled. "The kid dumped the body in the crevasse. That Russian son-of-a-bitch won't be spit out of the end of the glacier for a hundred years. Perfect!"

"Yes, this is so," Rose reflected. He looked up toward the ceiling. "And in the broader scheme of life, Bradford, think of it this way: *everybody has to be somewhere. He is there, and you are here.*"

Castellano cocked his head and looked at Jack: "That is fuc--" Rube glanced apologetically at Teo, then rephrased his words. "That's helpful, Rose."

Rube then pulled another Walther pistol out of the knapsack by his chair and slid it over to Lehman. "Swap your weapon for this one."

"Why Rube? I love my Walther. It saved my life."

"I know, Brad, but this one is tuned exactly like yours. The boys back at our FBI Firearms Unit added a tritium front sight to this one, and put on a bigger trigger guard to make it easier shooting with gloves on." There was a touch of pride in Rube's voice.

"What is a tritium sight?"

"It glows in the dark so you can acquire your front sight in the dark."

"Will it set off the radiation detector you gave me?"

Castellano and Rose looked at each other. Rose nodded.

"Forget it," Rube said. He reached over, grabbed the new Walther, and put it back in his knapsack. "The other one saved your life. Keep it."

Jack Rose's face spawned a Cheshire grin.

Rube cleared his throat. "And since you gave us your Kelty frame pack with all the goodies inside --" Rube picked up a brand new Kelty from next to his chair and handed it to Lehman "--You now have this. It's got a few more goodies in it for you."

"I see it's a lot bigger," Lehman smiled. "I suppose you guys now expect me to drag my rear end around with more weight on my back."

"Pack it up however you want kid," Rube said, adding, "I said 'kid,' but from now on I am no longer calling you kid. You have been blooded in this business and have earned the right to be treated as an equal in this operation. And you don't need to say 'rear end.' You can say 'ass.' 'Ass' records better in our depraved brains."

"To put an additional appropriate point on this matter," Jack said, "We are doubling your pay, back-dated to the beginning of the month."

"Which month? To last January?" Lehman jibed.

"This month, July, smart ass," Rube shot back, with a smile and a pat on Lehman's back. With that they got up and walked out of the Glacier Room. It was beer call time for the other agents.

*   *   *

Lehman was checked over the day of the attack by the medic assigned to the LRT. A Green Beret, who had recently rotated back to the CONUS from Vietnam at the end of his second combat tour, it was in his knowing hands that Lehman had his gunshot wound tended to, and monitored.

"There's going to be a scar there, but we won't stitch it up," the medic said. "Better to butterfly it, keep it clean, and let it drain. I will get you lined up with a course of antibiotics to be on the safe side. You were less than an inch away from the bullet severing your left jugular, which would have been lights-out fatal for you. The wound's contact with the snow kept the bleeding minimal. Miss Maloney did a superb job of rendering first aid. If I were you I'd celebrate tonight – with her – she's amazing. What a knockout."

He's right, Lehman thought. *Like Jack Rose said, "Everybody has to be somewhere. Be with her."*

Everyone on the LRT shook Lehman's hand when they saw him. So too did all the security and surveillance agents in the bar who sat in the Glacier Room. He couldn't buy a beer. John Ring and Ron Makinson, who had bonded as only two who have seen war can, now treated Lehman as a combat veteran. He had been "blooded." Bradford owned that in one sense he had earned it. But in another, he knew he hadn't. No one had -- because nothing regarding the ultimate threat had changed. The Backpack nuke was still somewhere on or near Mount Rainier.

Lehman began having nightmares.

Two days later the LRT held a meeting in the basement auditorium of the Guide House instead of in the bar, to Rube's chagrin, to further debrief Lehman's engagement with the GRU agent. The climbing team and other support agents of the LRT were present.

Jack Rose handed out the developed photographs from Lehman's Rollei camera. Bradford could hear Teo catch her breath when she looked at them.

Makinson whistled. "Remind me not to get on your bad side, Brad," he grinned.

Jack Rose began. "First Bradford, let me complement you on your excellent photographic skills--"

"--And shooting skills," Rube interjected.

Jack continued: "The images in front of us confirm that this is the body of GRU-Spetsnaz assassin Ivan Karin, age approximately thirty-five, height five feet eleven inches, weight approximately two hundred pounds. His rank is unknown, but he is likely a senior noncommissioned officer. He was trained with special Spetsnaz brigades in the late 1950s to operate beyond Soviet reconnaissance forces in Europe, to counter nuclear threats posed to them by our deployment of tactical nuclear missiles. He was therefore trained to handle a weapon such as a Backpack nuke. He is also a sniper and assassin. We believe Ivan here was involved in several assassinations of anti-Soviet dissident leaders within the USSR; and of a couple of foreign dignitaries in the Middle East. We also suspect that he went by the code name "Castor," because that name has been used in communications with Moscow Center, and SIGINT has revealed a spike in use of the name in the past forty-eight hours."

"Castor has just had his sorry ass *cast* into a crevasse!" Rube said, with a toothy grin directed at Lehman. Teo put her hand on Bradford's knee. She was beginning to understand that the way agents adapted to their chronic immersion in the Cold War business was through a morbid sense of humor.

"That means," Rose continued, "That they are baffled as to his whereabouts. And this is a good thing for us. The more we force them out of their plan the more mistakes they will make. We are also getting hints that the KGB may be opposed to the GRU's operation on Rainier. But they are merely hints."

Rose handed around other photos showing the wound to Karin's shin. "Here we see a clean accurate shot that struck the shin bone, or tibia, dead center, passed on through the fibula, and broke the leg. The .32 caliber ammunition fired by Lehman from his Walther PPK pistol was a seventy-three grain copper-coated 'ball,' solid lead bullet. It was not a hollow-point. So it deformed slightly when it hit bone, but did not fragment. It then passed through the calf muscle of the lower leg. You can see here in this next photograph that there is a little blood under the left calf, so the round likely exited there." Jack and Rube handed out more photos showing the body spread-eagled.

"Snow Angels! God, I loved doing those as a kid!" Makinson said. Rube guffawed.

Jack, ever smiling, placed a ruler along the outside of the left leg. "If you look closely, you will observe a deformation of the lower leg, confirming our supposition that it was indeed broken with Lehman's first shot. This confirms Bradford's recollection that Ivan let out a scream and immediately collapsed into a ball. The shot from the Walther literally snapped Karin's leg out from under him. And now addressing the second shot, the one to Karin's head..." Jack handed around more photos. "The entry wound here is almost dead center between the eyes, a hair below the brow-line, and slightly -- maybe a centimeter -- toward the left eye socket. Again this was a ball-ammo round. It did not fragment, but continued on through the brain, and actually exited the posterior side of the skull. We know this by all the blood pooling in the snow behind the head, there." Bradford stole a glance at Teo. She was engrossed in the briefing and photos, but her face looked white. *Good girl, you're hanging in there.*

"So we see by these photos that the Walther PPK and its ammunition performed very well," Rose said. "And so, obviously, did the shooter Mister Lehman here. Brad, you took the head shot, from what we can ascertain, at between seven and ten yards. Accuracy at that distance, and with the short sight radius on a diminutive weapon like the Walther, requires strong focus, concentration, and dead-still hands. Add the element of surprise, the combat threat, and a shootout into the mix, and seasoned agents in that scenario will lose fifty percent of their shooting accuracy."

"In other words Lehman," Rube added, "You maintained your concentration. You kept your head, focused on your targets, watched your front site, controlled your breathing, and squeezed the trigger smoothly -- just like you were taught at Mica Peak. You then changed magazines to make sure you were topped-off. My hat is off to you." Rube smiled. Lehman became embarrassed.

"I only did what I had to do to save my own ass. Nothing more."

"Well, Brad," Castellano replied, "you did do more -- *a hell of a lot more.* You continued with the mission. You were wounded at the outset of the fight. Notwithstanding, you systematically neutralized a professional assassin. After that you could have bailed out and run back to the Guide House, but you didn't. You made the perfect decision to dispose of Ivan in the crevasse -- but only after you photographed him, gathered the evidence, and 'sanitized' the scene. You did it all discreetly and efficiently. Now those Russian sons-of-bitches have no idea what happened to him. Like you succinctly said, Brad, they are the ones who now have the mysterious 'missing man.' What are their options?"

"Very few," Lehman replied. His voice was calm, clinical. "They must continue their mission short-handed. If they are on a schedule, they cannot take much time to look for Ivan. They can only wonder."

"Yes, exactly, Bradford," Rose said. "And a wondering adversary is a confused adversary. A confused adversary is a weakened adversary. And here is where it gets interesting --" Jack's eyes looked gleeful -- "A weakened Russian feels cornered. And the cornered Russian Bear is ferocious." His smile broadened.

Damn, Rose loves these operations. I would not want to be up against him -- or Castellano either. Trench-fighters. They savor their work.

"Now we will see the Bear's ferocity work against itself," Rose continued. "It will push harder, make more mistakes -- lash out, even. Why will it lash out? Because the Bear is paranoid. It is wired into the Russian Bear's genes."

"So Jack," Makinson asked, "If I hear you right, the Russians have two possible conclusions as to why Ivan Karin is missing: that Ivan walked into a crevasse in the fog -- a natural accident; or that Ivan was knocked off by one of us. You are saying that the Russians will reach the latter conclusion?"

"Precisely," Jack said. "Especially the GRU. The KGB would seriously consider the first possibility, and may indeed conclude that an accident occurred. They would back off of the operation and reassess their options and manpower. The GRU will not back off."

"That is consistent with what we experienced with the GRU advisors to the North Vietnamese in Vietnam," Ring said. "They are die-hard tough."

Rube spoke up. "I would suggest that the LRT Team always be armed and always operate in groups of two or more. No more solo hikes. No more morning strolls," he looked at Lehman, "and no more solo fly fishing trips." He looked at Makinson.

"That's okay, Rube, John and I will just go fly fishing together!" Makinson said. Rube shook his head and smiled. "Teo, you're going down the hill with Lehman and me to a local rock quarry for firearms training."

"Okay, Rube, thanks," Teo said solemnly. She looked at the pictures of Ivan Karin on the table. "I am ready."

Jack Rose pulled out Ivan Karin's pistol and laid it on the table. "This is a handsome exemplar of a tried-and-true Soviet Cold War pistol: The Tokarev 7.62X25. The capacity of this model is nine rounds, eight in the magazine, with one round in the chamber. The suppressor, or silencer, on it is extremely well made and impressively quiet, as you experienced, Bradford."

Lehman nodded.

"Remember that you said you heard one 'pop' and then you engaged the target? Jack asked.

"Yes," Bradford said.

"And you recall that after you neutralized him, you grabbed Ivan's dead hand, with his finger in the trigger, fired once, and then six more times before the slide locked back?"

"Yes."

"That leaves one round unaccounted for, based on your recollection, Brad. We have accounted for it." Rose nodded to Castellano.

Rube reached below the table and picked up Lehman's old Kelty frame pack. He held it up with one finger. The finger was sticking through a neatly drilled hole in the green rip-stop nylon fabric near the upper support strut on the back of the pack.

"There's Ivan's second round, Brad," Rube said. "He fired at you more than once. Probably his second shot was taken as you were spinning, and you didn't even hear it. That is normal. When you go into self-defense mode you get tunnel vision and your hearing shuts down too. Did you hear your Walther go off?"

"Come to think of it, no. I only felt the recoil of the gun," Lehman said.

"There you go," Rube nodded, confirming the assumption. He slapped a meaty hand on the table. "Ivan, our big, tough, finely-trained and skilled Spetsnaz GRU assassin -- choked. And you, Lehman, didn't!" Rubayat Castellano beamed. Jack Rose smiled.

Bradford Lehman, now a "blooded" combatant in the Cold War, took a deep breath. "Well Rube, do you want to know why I *really* killed him -- what *really* motivated me?"

"What motivated you, Brad?" Castellano asked.

"Yes Bradford, tell us." Jack Rose said. He leaned forward, listening intently, his eyes large and intense.

"Because Ivan Karin was a pain in the neck."

* * *

The next day Rubayat Castellano took not only Teo Maloney and Lehman to the firing range, but Ring and Makinson as well. Maloney proved to be an expert marksman, and was issued a Walther PPK.

"Damn, Hoover should make women eligible to become FBI Agents. I've been telling him that for years, but the old man's back is bowed," Castellano said, as he graded Teo's target.

The range was a rock quarry in a deep forest located fifteen miles outside Mount Rainier National Park. Agents guarded the entrance to the quarry as the LRT set up targets, and Rube ran the firing line. The team executed the same drills that had been conducted at Mica Peak -- drawing weapons, unslinging packs, and firing prone. But they also ran standard courses of fire from the kneeling, standing, and barricade positions, which encompassed both strong and weak-hand shooting.

During the first break Rube brought the team back to the trunk of his Chevy and pulled out a large black weapon case. "I have brought along several Colt .38 Supers. They are heavier than the Walther but are a much better match against the Tokarevs. They are tuned to a tee, have smooth triggers, and are damned sweet-shooters. They have a ten round capacity. The Tokarev carries nine. So you beat the Russians by one round before you need to reload -- and one more round than your opponent in a shootout may make the difference. I also have suppressors already built for two of them."

"Rube, at our training up at Mica Peak this spring you indicated that accuracy beats caliber every time. Are you changing your mind on that?" Ring asked.

"Good question, John. The answer is 'no.' I haven't changed my mind at all. But I have been giving the situation a lot of thought since Lehman's scrap with Ivan Karin. The Russians are on the hill carrying the Tokarev. These GRU goons are thoroughly professional, elite fighters. As a rule, they beat us in that category, though Brad here just proved the rule through his spectacular exception to it. We beat the goons on our knowledge of the mountain and with our superior climbing abilities. My concern is that we must match the Tokarev's performance and ballistics or the GRU will have an advantage over us at longer ranges. When we engage these bastards we must do it either by outperforming them at distance or through the element of surprise. Surprise trumps everything. Surprise 'em and we win. But if we lose the element of surprise, we must take them out at distance. If you get in close with the Russian Bear he will gut you out, and leave your clothes folded."

Bradford looked at Teo. She met his eyes and nodded grimly.

Castellano continued: "These Colt Supers have been in the FBI Firearms Unit's 'back room' inventory since the 1930s, and the outlaw days of John Dillinger. The .38 Super is a hot, flat-shooting round, much on the order of the Tokarev's 7.62X25. Our boys used them to penetrate car doors and thick clothing in the Chicago winters. So let's rearm and up-gun."

"This Colt Super is a hell of a nice pistol," Makinson said, after completing several courses of fire. "It has very little kick. Comfortable."

"I'm in with this weapon," Ring said. "It is a lot closer to the punch of a .45, but higher capacity and quite thin – concealable."

Teo opted to stay with the Walther. It fit her smaller hand.

"Brad, your scores were even higher with the Super with it than with the Walther," Rube said.

"I loved it. It is more accurate at distance."

"The Colt's longer sight radius enhances its accuracy. I want you to carry it instead of the Walther. Was the shoulder holster you were using comfortable?"

"Yes, very."

Castellano could see that Lehman was torn. "I know the Walther has saved your life, Brad. It is only natural thereafter to have an affinity for it. But it is underpowered for penetrating thick clothing. You knew that when you took your shots at Ivan and had the presence of mind to compensate. You won't need to with this weapon."

"Give me the Colt, Rube," Bradford said. Then he handed his silver Walther PPK to Teo. "Is it all right if Teo takes it?"

"Absolutely, Brad. I couldn't think of a better – or prettier -- person to issue it to."

*   *   *

The LRT kept close to the Guide House in the immediate days that followed. The team climbed out on the lower Nisqually Glacier and practiced rappelling and crevasse rescue, and made a couple of trips to Camp Muir, to service and replace sensors. The device placed on Rainier's crater near the entranceway to the Ballroom was quiet. It picked up sounds every week or so of climbers walking past as they circled the crater's rim.

Afternoons during these days were primarily spent in analysis and planning, sometimes in the Glacier Room, but mostly in the Guide House auditorium.

Inevitably word seeped out to the RGS and Park employees that Lehman had done something important. No one knew what, and they didn't ask. But they saw the edges of the bandage that Bradford wore under his turtleneck sweater and assumed it had something to do with the mysterious event. Some said that Lehman had stopped his falling rope team and was injured. That was the rumor that eventually stuck – with the help of Otto and Rube. The adulation made Lehman uncomfortable. But he tried to understand and to overcome his shyness. *These good folks back you one hundred percent, Lehman. They are simply trying to express that.*

Teo's love for Bradford deepened, and his for her. They laughed and had fun, as lovers and friends do when time blossoms good relationships.

When Lehman returned from a reconnaissance or training exercise without Teo, she would invariably ask him in a sexy, breathy voice as they lay in bed: "Bradford, was it hard on the mountain?"

"Not nearly as hard as the mountain is now, my darling," Lehman would coo back, in his best Inspector Clouseau accent. Teo would crack up and snort.

* * *

"Why don't we see these GRU humps carrying any packs?" Rube threw the question out to the climbing team, and to Jack Rose, as they drank beer brought in from the Glacier Room Bar. They were sitting in the Guide House auditorium, secured by agents in climbing clothes and jeans.

"Simple, Rube," Makinson said. "Just like going into battle. They stash their gear somewhere, and only take what is absolutely necessary into the fight."

"I agree," Ring said. "They are caching their crap somewhere. The Backpack nuke is probably stored with it."

"Yes, this makes sense," Jack said. "But if they are, the caches are further away than what we would expect to see. We are not picking anything up on the acoustic or radiation sensors at the normal high camps on the mountain, or up at the Ballroom on the summit."

"If these GRU Spetsnaz guys are as tough as you say," Lehman said, "and if they are accustomed to operate out beyond the regular reconnaissance units of the Soviet Army, then long-range caching of supplies would be in their comfort zone. They probably can go several days on very light rations and water. But the Backpack nuke is a different matter. It would take a two-man team, switching off carrying the load, to muscle it to the top of Rainier -- and shouldering a heavy car battery with it to boot. They might make it in a day, but probably not. They would have to bivouac somewhere. It would have to be somewhere that climbers seldom go, but near the regular RGS Route." Bradford stood up and walked over to the photomontage of Rainier's south side, which covered the entire front wall of the auditorium. The rest of the LRT members followed.

"What place fits that premise?" Lehman asked. "Teo, where would you hide in relatively plain sight? Put on your RGS guide hat." Bradford smiled at her. He and the rest of the team watched as she slowly traced the route with her finger: past Camp Muir, and behind Cathedral Rocks. Her finger moved up and stopped at Cadaver Gap.

"There," Teo said. Then she continued tracing the route up the Ingraham Headwall. "And there." Her finger stopped to the south of the route, on the top of Gibraltar Rock – at Camp Comfort.

"Excellent, young lady!" Lehman kissed her on the cheek. Teo blushed.

23

LATE JULY 1968: TAKING THE HILL

"How does the route look up the Headwall? Is it holding up?" Lehman asked Gary Olin, over a beer in the Glacier Room. Gary had just returned hours before from a successful summit climb.

"Yes, it is holding for now. Some snow bridges have fallen out on the approach to Cadaver Gap, but we re-routed over others. It's a hell of a lot better than last year. Man, that gear the LRT has provided has been a godsend on the Headwall. The fixed rope up there cuts down on a lot of the stress for the clients in that section. Of course, the giant crevasses above it are continuing to open up more. It is getting tricky there, but that section is still climbable."

"So when do you anticipate having to bag the Headwall altogether and re-route onto Disappointment Cleaver?"

"In another week. Two at the most." Olin scowled as he spoke the words, as though he did not want to face that eventuality. He changed the subject. "Say, Lehman, how is 'Black Sheep' Makinson doing? I see you've got him teamed up with Ring, and you are with Teo. Good call. Teo is a great climber, and damned good looking to boot!" Olin raised his beer mug and they toasted her. "Wish she was over guiding with us."

"I'll bet you do, Gary. "And I'll bet no one is asking to get me back at the RGS."

"True!" Olin said. They both laughed. "No one is asking for you Brad, because Makinson is your ball-and-chain. They figure if you come back, you're bringing Makinson with you."

"You know, Gary, Ron has been a fast learner. He's as strong as an ox, altitude doesn't bother him, and when you get him on the hill he exhibits good judgment. I was skeptical at first, to say the least. But he and Ring have Vietnam combat experience in common, and Ring has used that connection to bring the fellow along nicely."

"That is great to hear, Lehman. But you keep him." Gary finished the last of his beer, stood up, and brushed back his unruly blond hair. They walked out of the bar.

* * *

"Our GRU goons have a week and a half -- at the most -- to make their move toward the Ballroom with the nuke," Lehman announced.

"Why, Brad?" Rube asked. He and Rose were sipping coffee in the kitchen of the Guide House when Lehman walked in.

"I spoke with Gary Olin, who came off the hill this afternoon. The Headwall route is deteriorating. It will become unusable in that time. Likely sooner. The RGS will then shift the route over to Disappointment Cleaver – which means that both Cadaver Gap and Camp Comfort will become untenable for caching the Backpack."

"Maloney, Makinson, and Ring, come in here please," Castellano called through the doorway to the next room. Jack locked the kitchen door.

"It is interesting you say that Bradford," Rose replied. "We got sensor data back today from the last two SR-71 missions over the mountain. Elevated radiation readings were recorded near Cadaver Gap. They could be false ones. As you all are well aware, we've recorded those frequently. But the engineers are tweaking the receiver on the bird to filter out false-positive readings. At least it corroborates, however thinly, Teo's reckoning about the probable location of the Backpack being cached near Cadaver Gap or Camp Comfort."

"We were considering placing sensors in those spots," Rube said. The room fell quiet as members of the group thought through the implications of an impending change in the RGS summit route.

Makinson broke the silence. "As of today, screwing around with sensors may be out of the question if we are facing that much of a shrinking window with the Headwall route. Rube and Jack, I suggest we come up with a direct action plan, forthwith. The sensors are helpful but they are not perfect. With Lehman's new information here on route conditions, it is my humble and inexperienced opinion that we need to get our asses in gear. We either need to be up on the summit when the GRU agents get there, or be positioned to shadow them to the top. Either way there is going to be a gunfight. That writing is already on the wall – as Lehman's recent nasty skirmish with the GRU demonstrates. So folks, we might as well dust off the old play book and get moving." Makinson, usually jovial, spoke with forceful seriousness.

"I concur," Ring said.

"I concur as well." Rose spoke with a smile of anticipation.

"Teo, what say you?"

"Go. It must get done, Rube." Her voice was firm.

"Lehman?

"Go."

"Good." Rube glanced at the calendar on the wall. "Tomorrow is Wednesday. I will notify the RGS and the Park Service that the Ice Caves will be off limits for the day while the USGS Lahar Research Team 'gathers samples' in there. We will practice tactically clearing the big cave that runs five hundred feet east of the main entrance. Be out there by 0630."

"For purposes of the actual operation," Jack Rose said, "I will work with the Park Service to contact the media, and disseminate a notice everywhere inside the park, that Mount Rainier will be closed to all climbers for twenty-four hours, effective this Friday, due to 'LRT research requirements – removing rock samples, instrumentation and calibration,' or something of that sort. We will make sure that this gets broadcast through all the local television and radio stations. The Russians are monitoring weather broadcasts, so we will get our 'closure' information for Rainier out on both ends of them. As part of the broadcasts we will also announce that the standard climbing route will be changed over to Disappointment Cleaver following the twenty-four-hour closure. This should light a fire under our GRU friends."

"Yeah, Jack, it'll be 'shit or get off the pot' time for them." Rube said.

* * *

Teo and Bradford went to their room early. They had eaten dinner with Makinson and Ring at the Dining Room an hour before, and then walked hand-in-hand back to the Guide House where they organized their packs. Makinson had hung around the Dining Room to chat with Nancy Olszewski.

"How are you doing my handsome guide?" Teo said quietly.

"Whenever I'm with you, girl, I couldn't be better."

"You love this, don't you?" Teo had a quizzical smile.

"Being with you? Damned straight, beautiful woman!"

"No Bradford, I mean this whole operation. You love the danger. I am amazed at your coolness under pressure. You know, after seeing those pictures of the attack on you, I realize that I can't even come close to fathoming what you went through. Brad, you are a real hero. You're not just *my* hero – you are a genuine *American* hero. I love you."

"You know, girl, F. Scott Fitzgerald wrote cryptically about both words."

"Which words?"

"'Hero,' and 'love."

"What did he write?"

"'Show me a hero, and I will write you a tragedy.'"

"Oh my, that's dark."

"Yes, but it's a most enlightened darkness."

Teo kissed Bradford. "And what about 'love?' What did he have to say about that?"

"He wrote that 'All life is just a progression toward, and then a recession from, one phrase — *I love you*.'" Bradford kissed Teo and pulled her head into his shoulder. "I love you, Teo. We are progressing wonderfully toward it. May it never recede."

"God no," Teo said. "God in heaven, no." She kissed Bradford's ear as she whispered her words into it.

"But seriously girl, I don't see myself as any kind of a hero. To the contrary, I got myself into a scrape. Like Rube said, I should not have been out hiking alone. I stumbled upon Ivan. Or more accurately, he sensed I was following him. He circled around to kill me and missed. Simple as that. For those few minutes he held all the cards.

I stupidly walked into an ambush. I was incredibly lucky, Teo. That is not heroism."

"Yes it is," she smiled.

"No it isn't."

"Yes it is!" Teo pulled Bradford down on the bed and rolled on top of him. She kissed him sensuously. He felt the fullness of her soft breasts on his chest, and the strength of her hips and thighs, as she pressed hard against him.

"Yes, it is," Bradford spoke softly. "You are wonderfully right, my beautiful woman. It is whatever you say it is. I surrender."

Lehman sensed that Teo also loved the danger. Danger was a stimulant to them both. That night their passions reveled in it.

* * *

The LRT spent the next day firing at paper targets inside the Ice Caves, and practiced moving and shooting as two, three, and four-man teams. FBI agents stationed back in other parts of the cave system fired Tokarev pistols, so that the team could distinguish between the Russian's weapons and their own.

Makinson, Ring, and Lehman each put five hundred rounds through their Colt .38 Supers. Maloney fired a like number through the Walther she inherited from Bradford. The weapons performed flawlessly, even though the team also practiced malfunction drills with them, along with endless reloading, and magazine changes. As the training progressed, and the team fired and moved, confidence grew apace. "You are attaining fluidity of movement," Rube said.

Rose and Palmrich produced a full-scale cardboard replica of the Soviet RA-115 Backpack nuke. They advised that shooting at the weapon would disable it -- but would also risk unsafe leakage of radiation.

"The Backpack radiates, but it is shielded to keep the bomb at safe handling levels," Otto Palmrich said. "So be informed that breaching the shield will create a hazard."

"That's a fuc—," Rube glanced at Teo. "That is the understatement of the day Palmrich!"

At the end of its training, the team was issued small dosimeters to record the amount of radiation each member would receive. The devices were merely squares of radiological film, the size of postage stamps, enclosed in plastic with a belt clip on them. The LRT gathered around the main entrance to the Ice Caves as agents picked up all the expended shell casings, and the last shreds of target paper from the interior.

"The plan is to move the team up the mountain starting tomorrow," Rube said. "You will stage at Camp Muir in the Guide Hut. The weather is forecast to be stable and clear. We will go by the usual coded squelch breaks on the radios. If we lose all communications, we will launch a special operations team out of Fort Lewis and land a couple of helicopters up in the crater to execute Plan B -- which is to find and disable the nuke, and kill anything that moves along the way. Of course, that could mean *you*, if any of you are still moving around in the dark. You all did very well today. You worked as a team like you have all summer on the hill. That is why you are 'Plan A.' Now let's head back to Paradise, clean our weapons, grab a beer, and get our shit together."

* * *

"The Russians have already been through here, I'll wager. They are ahead of us," Lehman said. He had just set his pack down on the steps of the Guide Hut.

"Why do you say that, Brad?" Teo asked.

"I'm afraid to tell you guys because you'll think I'm nuts."

"It won't make any difference to us, Brad," Makinson said, smiling. "Ring and I already think you're nuts."

"The big raven is not here at Camp Muir this afternoon. The weather is perfect. It is stable. He only leaves for two reasons – when bad weather is coming…"

"And what's the second reason, Brad?" Ring asked.

"…And when he doesn't like someone."

"Who among our elite team would he not like?" Makinson quipped.

"It's not us. It's the Russians. He doesn't like the Russians. Maybe he distinguishes their different smell, but I'm sure he left today because they came through here."

"Jeez, Daniel Boone, when did you come up with that theory?" Makinson asked.

"Last year; and just now. The raven left Camp Muir when Boris Velantin and Georgi Kulikov stayed in the Public Hut last summer."

"How do you know the raven left Muir then, too, Brad?" Ring asked.

"I remember it clearly, because it was great weather, and I saw him leave. I wondered why. He stays put here in good weather."

Ring shrugged his shoulders, and Makinson smiled.

"You feeling okay, Brad? Any recent headaches or anything?" Ron asked with a grin.

"Feeling great, Ron. That big raven knows the difference between Americans and Russians. I'm sure of it. He must have seen or smelled them, and took off. They've been here already."

"All right Mister Boone," Makinson said, still grinning. "Hell, if you're right, I'll take all the clues and help I can get – even from a bird. In Vietnam we listened to the birds at night in the jungle. When they went silent we knew that the NVA were there, snooping around out beyond the wire. So maybe there's something to it."

The Guide Hut at Camp Muir was comfortable for Bradford, Teo, John, and Ron – the "LRT Assault Team." Jimmy Beech's aerial supply runs had kept the RGS amply stocked. The Park Service had closed the mountain to all climbers, including the RGS. The Public Hut at Muir was empty, as was Camp Schurman on the Emmons Glacier. Ring had confirmed this by radio with other rangers who were watching those high camps.

Coincidentally, a rock section the size of a basketball court had crashed down from the north wall of Little Tahoma onto the Emmons Glacier four days before. This raised concerns about another impending major collapse like that which occurred in December 1963, when a half-cubic mile of rock and snow peeled off of Little Tahoma's crumbling rock face, and careened several miles down the Emmons Glacier. It nearly wiped out the White River Campground and the road to Sunrise. To Lehman it was a good omen. *It is as if the big mountain is tensing up for this fight. At least it gives Rube and Jack a great cover story to the outside world. We are the 'USGS Lahar Research Team,' after all.*

The LRT carried with them a special small radio receiver that scanned the planted acoustic sensors at Camp Muir's Public Hut and up at the Ballroom's entrance on the crater. All was quiet.

"The chicken noodle casserole is ready," Ring announced, pulling his fingers out of the hot pot and licking them. As they ate, Makinson kept up his usual banter. Lehman liked it for a change. It mimicked normalcy. Teo rolled her eyes and smiled. Ring enjoyed talking fishing – and extolling the driving pleasures of Makinson's yellow Porsche. Makinson let John drive it frequently. Ninety percent of

Makinson's life surrounded fishing and the yellow Porsche. No one wanted to know what the other ten percent was about, or wanted to bring it up. Lehman guessed that Nancy Olszewski was finding that out – repeatedly -- if her radiant smile around Ron was any indication. Makinson, on the other hand, rarely talked about his duties as a FBI Special Agent. Clearly for Ron, the sun did not rise and set on Mister J. Edgar Hoover. Lehman suspected that this was one of the main reasons Castellano chose Makinson for this operation.

After dinner the team stepped outside, remaining carefully in the shadow of the Guide Hut, to watch darkness fall softly on the mountain. Everyone looked up toward Cadaver Gap. The Gap, from the vantage point of Muir, sat one thousand three hundred vertical feet above, nestled between the eastern base of Gibraltar and Cathedral Ridge. Below the Gap ran a steep snow gully that was part of the Cowlitz Glacier. The gully was rarely climbed or descended, because it was a catch basin for frequent rock and icefall from the crumbling cliffs of Gibraltar. Cadaver Gap earned its grizzly name in 1929 when RGS guides and rangers dragged the bodies of two climbers through it during a recovery operation. Bradford's father had been one of the guides on that recovery.

"Shit! Did you see that?" Ron exclaimed. "It was only the quickest flicker of light." Everyone strained to see.

"No," Ring said.

"Yes, there it is!" Teo pointed toward the bottom end of the Gap, where it connected with Cathedral Ridge.

"Damn it's faint." Lehman said, straining to see. "Whoever is using that light is moving back and forth behind the rocks of Cathedral. They are definitely avoiding shining it down here."

"Well kids," Makinson said, "these bastards most certainly got the word that Jack Rose put out about closing the mountain and moving the route over to Disappointment Cleaver. They beat us up here. Score one for Brad and his raven! Looks like we will have to shadow them."

"No sweat. It's just as well we are following these goons," Bradford said. He glanced at his watch. "Time to saddle up." He felt his body relaxing as he moved. *Rube, you are right. It is always tougher to wait.*

It was 2140 hours.

The two-man teams roped up and coiled in together in the shadow of the Guide Hut until the thin wisp of light at Cadaver Gap faded out of sight around the north side of Gibraltar. Then Bradford and Teo, followed by John and Ron, swiftly traversed the Cowlitz Glacier and crested the broad saddle of Cathedral Gap. They were screened from Cadaver Gap, three hundred vertical feet above, by the intervening hulk of Cathedral Ridge. There was no moon, but stars were resplendent, providing plenty of light for climbing without headlamps.

"Ron, you have the Starlight Scope," Lehman said. "Why don't you sneak around the corner with John and fix the enemy's position on the route?"

"'The enemy.' Damned well-said, Brad. Let's see what these squirrely bastards are up to." He rummaged in his pack. The Scope, a passive image intensifier for low light battlefield use, was familiar to Makinson. He had employed it frequently at LZ Action in Vietnam to keep the enemy away from "the wire," the firebase's barbed wire perimeter. Ring took along his bulky light-gathering binoculars and disappeared with Makinson around the corner onto the Ingraham Glacier.

Lehman and Teo sat together on the rocks, in the light wind of the cool night.

"How are you doing girl?"

"I'm fine Brad, but scared," Teo said, as she nestled in against Lehman's body. He kissed her cheek.

"It's natural, Teo. You know, I am so proud of you. You are one hell of a shot – out-scored all of us at the range and in the Ice Caves. I saw your shots. Ours were mostly to the target's torsos. Yours were to the head. Clean, tight groups right in the 'mask' area. Rube was impressed. Rube has always been impressed with you. It's your ability, beauty, and brains!"

Teo let out a quiet snort through her gloved hand and gave Lehman a nudge.

"Teo, you and I know this is going to get nasty up on top. You talk about me being cool. Crap, I don't hold a candle to you, girl!"

"I like holding your candle."

Bradford put his gloves to his face and laughed. It was his turn to snort.

Ring and Makinson returned a few minutes later. "There are three climbers," Ring said. "They have topped the Headwall, and have turned back toward Camp Comfort."

"Teo, you called it," Bradford said. "Let's move on up to Cadaver Gap."

Ring nodded, took out his radio, and keyed the talk button once, signifying that the GRU had been sighted again. He had done the same thing at Camp Muir when the headlamps had been spotted up at the Gap. He waited a couple of seconds and keyed the "brick" twice more, signifying that the target was at Camp Comfort. One squelch break came back in reply, acknowledging receipt of the transmission by Jack or Rube.

Ring and Makinson entered Cadaver Gap with their guns drawn. They spent some minutes clearing the small notch. Then they waved Lehman and Teo in. No one turned on headlamps.

"Drag marks here on the scree," Makinson said, kneeling down in the dark. "They fit the dimensions of the Backpack. You can see where it was dragged a little way out here on the snow, and then it stops. The boot prints gather around there and then move out single file up the hill."

"It must be where they helped one of them shoulder the Backpack," Lehman said. "The guy carrying it probably kneeled down and the others hoisted it onto his shoulders and helped him stand up."

"So the Backpack was here, and not up at Camp Comfort," Ring said.

"It appears so," Makinson said. "Then why did they turn back toward Camp Comfort if the nuke wasn't up there?"

"Great question," Lehman said. Maybe other gear was stashed there -- like the car battery. But we won't be able to check it out. Camp Comfort is a couple of hundred yards off the route on the flat top of Gibraltar. If we try to walk over there on our way up behind these guys, we will risk being seen from above. We will have to stay on the route and well back, so that we remain out of their sight in the curve of the glacier's fall line, like we planned."

The team grabbed a quick bite to eat and a drink of water. It was 2330 hours. Lehman decided that Makinson would lead up to the bottom of the fixed ropes at the Ingraham Headwall, tracking the GRU agents occasionally with his Starlight Scope, until they climbed upward out of sight on the summit ice cap. Then Lehman would lead. He could reckon best how fast to climb and remain hidden from the view of the climbers above them.

The team inched along under the shadow of Gibraltar Rock. Every few minutes rocks or ice plummeted down from somewhere high on the Gib's ledges. With every clatter of falling rock or ice, the party froze in its tracks, and eyes strained to pick up splashes in the snow a few yards uphill to the left. If they discerned something falling near, they hunkered down and turned their packs toward the sound, and prayed no one would be hit. No one was -- but moving slowly through one of the most exposed parts of the route jangled nerves.

"How are you doing girl?" Bradford called to Teo, sixty feet back.

I'm hanging in there, Brad," she replied. Her voice was calm. He gave her a thumbs-up.

Makinson reached the bottom of the Headwall. "Shit, they cut the fixed rope." It lay in a heap at his feet.

"This simply confirms that these guys are our targets," Lehman said. "I expected they might cut the rope."

"Yeah, they like their knives," Ring said.

"So Makinson, you're *sure* we are following only three people?" Lehman asked.

"Positive."

"Great. We've got the bastards heavily outnumbered."

"The Starlight Scope clearly sees only one rope team of three," Makinson continued, with a chuckle. "They are mostly climbing without headlamps like we are – but the lead man switches his on and off frequently."

"Makes sense," Lehman said. "He is using his headlamp to locate the next wand on the route, and then switching off."

Lehman led up the Headwall. In spite of his focus on the mission, the guide in Bradford could not help keeping watch on his team.

Damn, Teo and Ron are front-pointing up this thing magnificently. I'm proud of them.

The higher he climbed the more relaxed Lehman felt, despite the tension of the unfolding operation. He recalled one of his father's favorite sayings: *"You can plan all you want, but there comes a time when the damned thing's going to happen on its own, and you just have to go with it."*

Bradford cautiously climbed over the top of the Ingraham Headwall. He strained to see any movement or climbers above him, but could not. Satisfied that the GRU agents were out of sight, Lehman belayed Teo up and waited for Ring and Makinson.

"Ron, scope this for me."

"All clear."

The team plodded on. It was 0137 hours.

At thirteen thousand two hundred feet, below the bergschrund, Lehman broke left off of the RGS route, and began looking for another snow bridge over the big crevasse. Six rope-lengths to the west he found one. He gingerly probed his way over it with his ice axe while Teo belayed him. Then Lehman took the team circuitously along the summit ice cap toward the west. He planned to approach the entrance to the Ballroom from a different direction – the southwest – where climbers seldom access the crater. If lucky, the team would see the GRU agent guarding the entrance to the cave before he saw them. Bradford checked his altimeter. It read fourteen thousand, one hundred and fifty feet. The angle of the slope eased off. Lehman kneeled down and motioned the team to coil up to him.

"Ron, if you rise up slowly with your scope you will see the rocks of the crater rim. If I am correct on the approach here, you should see someone sitting or standing at the entrance to the Ballroom." Ron broke out his scope, slowly straightened up, and came back down.

"Yup, there's a man sitting on a rock right at our one o'clock, about three hundred feet out, dressed all in black. He is looking off in the opposite direction."

"Perfect, just what I had hoped," Bradford said. "He is watching the rim where the RGS Route enters it off to the east. We are also downwind of him. All right, Makinson and Ring, I place the rest of this operation in your capable hands. It is solid snow here, and only a gentle slope with no crevasses between the target and us. Let's un-rope and take off our crampons."

"Yes," Ring said, "We need to de-noise ourselves as much as possible."

"I agree," Makinson said, as he unbuckled his crampons and left them in the snow.

"Let's leave our ice axes here as well," Lehman said. "There is too much risk, with them hanging off our wrists, that the damned things will bang into rocks as we approach this guy with our guns out."

Ring and Makinson pulled out their pistols from their shoulder holsters and screwed silencers onto the ends of the barrels. Bradford and Teo re-checked their own un-silenced weapons, and placed extra magazines into their outer pockets. Lehman looked at Teo's hands. They were steady. The team members pulled carabiners, ice screws, and all other hardware, off of themselves that could make noise. Then they cinched up the waistbands on their packs, donned their headlamps, kept them switched off, and checked each other again, making sure nothing on them would rattle or clank. Lehman took his Gerber Shorty knife off of his belt and slid it, in its leather sheath, into the strong-side cargo pocket of his climbing pants. He put on the thin leather shooting gloves he'd trained with at the firing range. His fingers felt supple -- warmer than he had anticipated.

Lehman, you're ready. Focus. He took two deep breaths and relaxed.

Makinson called a huddle. "Okay, we look good to go," Ron whispered. "Everyone have a round in the chamber of their weapons, safeties off, and fingers out of the trigger?" All nodded. "Great. Once again, here is the plan: I will walk point, with Ring, then Lehman, and Maloney at the end. Stay bunched up. I mean tightly bunched, like we practiced in the Ice Caves. I want you to be able to *feel* the person moving in front of you. We will take our time closing this last three hundred feet. I will watch my feet and the target. The rest of you watch your feet, like we practiced, so we don't make noise by kicking rocks loose. If I stop and get down, you do the same. If I get up, you get up." Everyone nodded. "Ring and I have the silencers. I will get as close as I can to make the shot. It will be to the head if I am within seven yards, and several to the body if farther away. Once I fire we may be in a dynamic engagement. But if we can eliminate the goon cleanly at the entrance, we will stage again there. If not, we will continue down into the cave and clear it, as we trained. If I miss the goon and he retreats, we have to be on his heels quick. Maloney, you will take up position at the entrance and provide rear-guard, in case some other goon we don't know about wanders in. Also, while we advance on this first target, keep an eye peeled behind us, especially on the crater rim toward the west." Teo nodded forcefully. "Okay Ring, give Rube the clicks."

John Ring keyed his radio five times, indicating the assault was beginning. He got one squelch break back in his earpiece. Then he turned off the radio and slipped it into his jacket. He nodded to Makinson. It was 0320 hours.

"Follow me," Makinson whispered.

*   *   *

The team slowly approached the dark figure at the cave's entrance. With each step, it got larger and clearer. The head was focused in the opposite direction. Every few seconds the head would drop and then pull itself back up.

This tough bastard is going to sleep. Altitude and fatigue affect him too. He's not so tough.

Once, the head began to turn toward them, and the team froze. But the head stopped halfway and then lazily turned back, looking eastward.

His hood is over his head. He's got no peripheral vision.

Twenty yards. Ten. Bradford could see Makinson's Colt .38 Super, with its long silencer -- pointing -- glued on the figure. Makinson was taking tiny soft steps, first placing his heal down, and then slowly rocking his boot forward. Step and rock. Step and rock. Ring's pistol was angled off to the left, trained on the entrance to the cave.

Jeez, Makinson, shoot the son-of-a-bitch. You're almost on top of him! Shit Lehman, relax. You're getting wound up. Breathe. Breathe. Good.

Ron Raised his weak hand in a fist signaling the rest of the team to stop. He took four more short soft crouching steps. His silencer was almost touching the hood on the figure's head. He squeezed the trigger of the Colt. The figure lurched forward.

Damn, that was quiet. No way anyone is going to hear it from the cave.

Springing with the swiftness of a cat, Makinson grabbed the back of the dead man's parka and straddled him, forcing the twitching body to the ground. He kept his weight on it until it became quiet.

He motioned Teo to take up her guard position next to the entrance to the cave, released his weight off of the body, and kneeled next to it, covering the interior of the cave. Lehman and Ring moved in next to Makinson.

"I'm going to scope the entrance with the Starlight, and then move down with it into the cave as far as it will work. It is four hundred feet down to the split that breaks into the left-hand passageway. That is where I would put another goon, so they may have it guarded. Let's try to slither our way down there without lights. Do not use your lights unless you are engaging a target. Hang onto the guy in front. Let's go."

The three men stepped down past Teo into the cave's entrance. Bradford squeezed her arm as he went by. She squeezed his. Then she raised her Walther again and began scanning the outside perimeter.

*   *   *

Time. It took so much time. Makinson holstered his pistol, so as to have both hands on the Starlight Scope. He swept the cave with it before he took each step. Ring extended his shooting arm and rested it on Makinson's left shoulder, covering the threat area to Ron's front. Lehman shuffled behind, concentrating on keeping his finger out of the trigger, and the muzzle of his Colt pointed down and away from the backs of his teammates. He was in the dark.

You are completely blind, Lehman. You might as well have a blanket over your head. Concentrate on breathing. Relax, trust your teammates. There was only the hissing of steam to be heard off to his left and right. *Dante's Inferno. Shit, this is spooky as hell without headlamps. Breathe.* Bradford recalled his conversation about these caves with Robert McNamara on their walk around the crater two years before, when he told the Secretary: *"It would be fun to explore them someday." Well, here you are, young Lehman – you're exploring the hell out of them now. Are you having fun? Yeah right.*

Makinson stopped and whispered back: "Ring, get out one of your light wool gloves. Stretch it over your headlamp so the weave opens up on it a little. Then turn on your headlamp. I'm running out of light down here. Maybe your muffled headlamp can give me a little visual acuity."

John Ring slipped a glove over his headlamp and switched it on. The light shining through the glove was just enough for Bradford to see the faintest outlines of his teammates and surrounding features. Makinson put the Starlight Scope to his eye, gave a thumbs-up, and continued moving forward.

In fifteen long minutes, Makinson, Ring, and Lehman stealthily crept the four hundred feet down the cave's main passage. They were nearing the split where the left-hand fork led to the Ballroom.

Suddenly Makinson stopped. Again he whispered back: "Headlamp, and it is right by the fork to the Ballroom. I will keep the scope on it. In twenty feet we will make the turn and be right on this guy. Ring, when I go around the corner you will feel me reach up to get ready to switch on my headlamp. I will give you a countdown with my left hand starting with three fingers. Then I will switch on my headlamp and step around the corner. Keep your ass glued to mine. Take careful aim, Ring, and drop him. And don't forget to take the glove off you headlamp. From there on in we will be dynamic – so the faster we can move to get to the Ballroom, the better."

Ring Squeezed Makinson's shoulder, signaling his "Okay." Then he turned and whispered the plan to Lehman. Bradford squeezed Ring's shoulder.

Slowly they edged forward. Lehman took a deep breath. He was well aware of the importance at this altitude not to hold his breath and "gray-out," when acquiring a target. As he breathed he felt the tension easing in his body. *I breathe, therefore I am.* The thought traced a faint grim smile on his lips. He could now see stabs of light playing off the sides of the cave from the Russian's headlamp. Makinson held up a fist and stopped. He slipped his Starlight Scope into the cargo pocket of his climbing pants and drew his silenced Colt Super out of its shoulder holster inside his jacket. Makinson took a small silent step forward and stopped. Ring did the same, followed by Bradford. No one stepped simultaneously. Boots were placed ripple-fashion, like a caterpillar walking in stop-motion. It took a full eight minutes to move the last twenty feet. Lehman, from his position as the last man, noted that the light of the headlamp around the corner was not bobbing around as much.

You're getting sleepy, you son-of-a-bitch. He willed the Russian to sleep.

Makinson held up his left hand. Lehman could now see them clearly, with the benefit of the Russian's headlamp, which had now stopped bouncing around. Three fingers, two, one – Ron stepped around the corner and switched on his headlamp. Hearing the crunch of a boot, the Russian's face jerked up. It had a stark look of confusion and terror as it was caught in the dazzling beams of the team's headlamps. *Pop, pop.* Two quick shots from Ring's silenced Colt spun the big Russian off his feet, and he sank heavily down to a sitting position. His face was frozen in surprise and fear. *Pop.* The big Russian's head whipped back and bounced off the ice wall of the cave, where it left a large spatter of blood, before the body toppled lifeless onto its side. A Tokarev pistol fell out of its hand.

Instantly, Makinson, Ring, and Lehman sprang over the snow wall of the left-hand passage and entered it. Knowing it was thirty feet to where the passage opened up into the Ballroom, the team hunched down and broke into a jog on the leveling ground. It was a long thirty feet.

Lehman became peripherally aware of sprays of ice particles hitting him in the face. They were in the Ballroom, and all hell was breaking loose. Bradford saw Makinson spin to his left, grab his leg, and go down. Fifteen feet ahead, Ring had gone into a kneeling position, his pistol spitting fire. Across the Ballroom a Russian with blond hair was firing on Ring, and then at Lehman. The Russian was hiding behind a barrel-sized dark green object – the Backpack. The distance was at least sixty feet. The Russian was popping out from the side of the device, firing two or three shots and ducking back behind it. Ring was returning fire. Lehman heard firing from a silenced Colt Super behind him, and knew Makinson was still in the fight. It was evident from the snow and ice spraying above and around the Backpack that Ring and Makinson were diverting their fire slightly away from it. They were trying to flush the blond Russian out.

Lehman moved to his right, stepping calf-deep into the pool of water. Orange and purple colors from muzzle flashes merged with the light from headlamps, and the shimmering ice reflected it from the irregular crystal surface of the cave. Lehman had a fleeting impression of the deadly scene's dark beauty. A round kicked up a tall splash at Bradford's feet. The spray was cold on his face. *He sees me trying to flank him. He's going to kill you, Lehman. The next time he sticks his head out from behind that bomb, he is going to kill you. You must shoot now. Kill or be killed.*

Bradford looked down the sights of his Colt .38 Super. They shone brightly in the beam of his headlamp. *Breathe in Lehman. Let your breath out slowly. Concentrate on the front sight. Keep the light even on both sides of it with your back sight. Slowly take up slack in your trigger. And when he sticks his head out again…*

The report of Bradford's un-silenced Colt crashed and echoed. The head, sticking out from behind the Backpack didn't move.

Shit, Lehman you missed!

The blond-headed Russian stood straight up. His face had a look of panic. Blood was spurting in a steaming red arc from his neck onto the ice wall next to where he stood. Bradford breathed again, exhaled slowly, and added pressure to the trigger. Lehman's round caught the blond Russian in the top of his forehead, snapped his head back, and dropped him straight down. Suddenly the crashing noise stopped. Smoke from all the weapons being discharged in the Ballroom curled down from the ceiling of the cave, and swirled around the beam of Lehman's headlamp. There was a strong smell of gunpowder. Mixed with it was the taste of atomized metallic iron. Blood was in the air.

"Ring, you okay?" Lehman asked.

"Yeah."

"Makinson?"

"I guess, shit, my leg."

"Can you get up?"

"I think so." Ring stepped over and helped Makinson stand. He could barely put weight on his left leg.

"Bleeding?" Ring asked.

"I don't think so," Makinson said. He pulled up his left pant leg.

"I can't see any blood Ron," Ring said.

"Okay, Let's go make this damned thing safe," Lehman said. The three men moved forward. "Ron, you were trained on the switches to this. Run your hands over it."

Makinson, grimacing, hobbled up to the Backpack, and looked it over front and back. The silver steam turbine was spinning with a low whine, furnishing electricity to the car battery next to the bomb.

"Shit, would you believe it?" Makinson said. "The idiots bought a low-end Pay N' Pak car battery. Cheap bastards!" He unsheathed his Ka-Bar knife and levered off the positive connection to the battery's terminal. "Step one complete," he said, wincing back to his feet and putting his hands on the Backpack. He unsnapped a heavy canvas door on its front. Inside was a long series of colored switches embedded in an outer metal panel on the bomb. "Let's see, was it green first, then red, then blue… No. It was red first, then green… Jeez, I can't remember."

"Makinson, you son-of-a-bitch! You'd better remember!" Ring's voice rang out, echoing around the Ballroom. Ron looked up into his teammate's headlamps. Despite the pain, he had an evil grin on his face. "Actually, Ring, it doesn't matter. There is at least a million-to-one chance that I will flip the correct switches to detonate this bastard."

Without waiting for feedback, Makinson quickly flipped six of the switches at random, and then looked at his watch's sweeping second hand. Thirty seconds later a soft "click" was heard inside the mechanism.

"Bingo!" Makinson said. "You can take your fingers out of your ears now, John."

The bomb had tripped its own safety. This Soviet RA-115 Backpack nuclear weapon, with a yield of ten kilotons, sitting quietly in the corner of the Ballroom Cave in the summit crater of Mount Rainier, now became just another heavy object among billions of other heavy objects placidly reposing on the big mountain. It was 0427 hours.

*   *   *

Ring sat Makinson down and checked his leg again.

"Ron, you are incredibly lucky. A round from "Blondie's" Tokarev hit your Starlight Scope. It deflected the round, but you will have a wonderful bruise there for a few days."

"Okay, John, thanks," Makinson said.

"Ring, you go outside and radio Rube and Jack that the world has been made safe for democracy," Lehman said. "I will stay here with Ron, take some photos, and then we'll hobble our asses out of here." John nodded and disappeared out of the Ballroom.

Ring emerged from the entrance of the cave at the crater rim, and gave Teo the thumbs up. They hugged.

"God, it seemed like you were down there forever," Teo said. "I didn't hear anything from up here. Is everything okay John?" Her words voiced plaintive concern.

"Yes, Teo, everything is okay. Ron only got a bruise on his leg. Everyone is okay. You're clear to go down and help. I'll make the radio report to Rube and Jack from here."

Teo let out a long sigh of relief and squeezed Ring's shoulder. She holstered her Walther pistol, switched on her headlamp, and scrambled down to the Ballroom. At the left-hand fork, she glimpsed the second dead Russian GRU agent, lying on his side in a fetal position. It was the second time she had seen a dead body, other than in pictures. The first one she saw was at the mouth of the cave. She saw the congealed blood at the entry wound on the corpse's head, and the large dark pool of blood next to it. It could have shocked her, but it didn't. Teo knew full well what that corpse was sworn to do when it lived, and of its deadly mission of hate and destruction. Shrugging off the bloody scene without further thought, Teo climbed over the snow wall and joined Makinson and Lehman in the Ballroom.

"Hey, pretty lady!" Ron said.

"Quit hitting on my girlfriend, Makinson. Teo and I are going to get on either side of you and help you out of here. Put your arms around each of our shoulders. But I'm going to be watching your arm around Teo – and your hands."

Makinson let out a laugh and immediately winced in pain. "Deal, Brad. Get my ass out of here, and I'll keep my hands where you can see 'em."

"And can I drive your Porsche whenever I want?"

Grinning, Makinson reached into his pocket, pulled out the keys, and held them up. "Brad, you can even drive it now if you want."

Smiling and shaking her head, Teo helped Bradford support Makinson. They slowly walked him out of the Ballroom and up to the crater rim. Lehman noticed that they were all now breathing hard with the altitude. The threat of a nuclear weapon had been neutralized – but the big mountain's presence remained. It immutably remained.

"Six Pedros out of McChord will be landing in the Crater in an hour," John Ring said. "Pedro" was the U.S. Air Force's universal call sign for the HH-43 Huskie. "I'm beat. Let's drag our asses over to Register Rock, crank up the stove, and brew up some tea."

"Great idea John," Teo replied. The team helped Makinson over there and quickly melted snow in the big aluminum pot they retrieved from a nearby steam cave. On a previous climb they had cached the pot, a stove, fuel, cups, utensils, and tea there. They drank and talked. The team was dog-tired, but sleep was out of the question.

"How are you doing, girl?" Bradford asked the question, nestled against her. They had both put on their bulky Thaw down parkas. They were international orange, with large "USGS Lahar Research Team" letters sewn in black thread on the left breast.

Teo smiled. "Okay, Brad." Her voice was pensive. She rolled toward Lehman, gave him a long kiss, and caressed his face with the soft thick wool of her mittened hand. "I was so worried about you and Ron and John down there in the Ballroom. It was completely dead quiet up at the entrance. It took so long. It seemed like forever, and I knew there was going to be a fight..." Her voice trailed off.

"But you knew we were going to win it."

"Yes. I didn't have the slightest doubt. But the longer I waited the more worried I became that one of you may be badly hurt or wounded. I had visions of you guys trying to climb out of there and I couldn't help."

"You did your job and watched our backs and stayed in position. The whole thing seemed like an eternity to me too. But you had to wait for us, completely out of touch. It's like Rube said – there's nothing harder than to have to wait and worry."

Bradford kissed Teo and hugged her closer.

"We aren't kids anymore are we Bradford?"

Lehman smiled and kissed her again. "No, Teo, we aren't. But our childhood wasn't lost today. Not today. Today we were adults. But we had been for a while, beautiful lady. Today we did an adult job, and lived to walk away from it. Today we completed a mission that damned few adults have done, or ever could do."

Teo took a deep breath and sighed, looking into Lehman's blue-gray eyes. They were soft now. "When did we become adults then, Bradford?"

"When you hiked up to Camp Muir last summer, and we made love all night together – and found love. Love brought us to adulthood, Teo, not this mission. Not the killing. Anyone can kill. I can't even see those dead Russians over there in the caves as adults. They are just bad children who grew up. No matter how old they are, or highly trained, those Russians we defeated today are merely brain-washed children who grew up mean."

Teo smiled, pressed her face into the folds of Bradford's parka, and dosed.

*   *   *

Sounds of rotor blades broke the stillness of the dawn. It was 0630. Six Kaman Huskies, flying in echelon trail formation, hammered their way in from the west across the top of the Tahoma Glacier and over the broad saddle between Liberty Cap and Columbia Crest. Three were painted in camouflage jungle green, and three were the normal gunmetal gray. The kerosene smell of their exhausts met Lehman's nostrils as they circled the crater at fifty feet, and one by one, engines whining to maintain lift in the high thin air, the Pedros flared for landings on the crater's inner flat snowfield. Lehman snapped a photo of the impressive sight and walked out with Teo and John to meet the occupants. Makinson, his leg sore and stiffened up, remained to tend the stove.

Special Agent Rubayat Castellano, wearing an oxygen mask, and carrying a small portable oxygen bottle, jumped out of the first bird and hugged Teo, lifting her off the ground. Then he set her down, wheezing. "Damn the air is thin up here, even *with* the oxygen. I forgot!"

Jack Rose and Otto Palmrich slogged over to the team from other helicopters. Everyone shook hands and slapped each other on the back. Captain Rick Champion, the commander of the flight of Huskies, hiked over with his obligatory mask and bottle, and everyone backslapped and shook hands again.

"Come on over to our kitchen for a cup of tea," Teo said, motioning the group to follow.

"Let me take a peek in the Ballroom first," Jack replied, out of breath. "I've got my people in there pulling out the Backpack." He waved and walked slowly off toward the group of CIA and FBI agents who were milling around the entrance to the cave, next to the corpse of the GRU agent.

"I've seen enough dead bodies," Rube said, breathing heavily. "The nuke would be cool to see, but I will have plenty of time for that." He had unhooked one side of his oxygen mask from his flight helmet so he could be better heard, but when he stopped speaking he clamped it back, holding it on his face with a gloved hand.

"You said 'cool' Rube," Lehman said. "Is that in the FBI's lexicon?"

"Oh, hell no. Hoover would censor my ass for using 'subversive slang.' But let him come up here and do it!"

The team and Castellano sat around the stove by Register Rock. Captain Champion slogged back to the crater snowfield to mind his flock of birds. It was cold, but the sun was up and finally warming bodies from the outside. Hot tea warmed them from the inside.

"Damn, I have never liked tea – until now," Rube said, as he took a gulp of the hot liquid. Castellano always gulped. "Okay troops, give me a quick overview of how the operation went down." As he spoke he pulled a small tape recorder out from the inside of his orange LRT parka and turned it on. Only one of the reels turned. "Shit, this always happens. I hate these damned things."

"Here, Rube, let me fix it." Lehman took the recorder, threaded the tape back onto the second reel, turned the machine on, and handed it back to Castellano.

"Thanks Brad. Now tell me what happened."

"As for the assault phase I will defer to Agent Makinson, and Ranger Ring." Makinson nodded, and he and Ring told a stark, succinct account of the action. Neither Lehman nor Maloney added to the commentary.

Rube shut off the recorder. "At least I can do that." He slipped the machine into his knapsack. "Everyone, from the President on down, is dying to know the details on this – even Bob McNamara." Rube smiled at Lehman. "As you all know, I generally write this all down, but with all the pressure for information, I will fly this tape back to McChord Air Force Base. We have a transcription stenographer there who can whip this out, and we can send an Immediate Teletype. But for now the bastards can wait." Rube waved his hand dismissively. "But all that bullshit aside, let me tell you guys -- and you pretty lady -- how proud I am of what you have done. You are the best bunch of irregulars I have ever coached or worked with."

"Thanks Rube," Makinson said.

"Yes, Ron, you are a most 'irregular' FBI Agent," Rube said, grinning. Castellano slowly scanned each of the team member's faces. "This operation ran as smoothly as anyone could have imagined. You have neutralized a *huge* threat here, and very possibly thwarted a nuclear exchange."

"So we *did* make the world safe for Democracy Rube?" Lehman asked with a grin. Makinson grinned along with him.

"Smart-asses!" Rube shook his head and looked down at his steaming tin cup. "Damned good tea. Maybe I'll substitute it for beer. The wife says I should. What do you say about that Miss Maloney?"

"Stick with the beer, Rube. It becomes you." Teo put her hand on Castellano's big shoulder.

"Now there is a woman who understands me! If I were twenty years younger, I'd…" Rube reached over and gave Teo a hug. "Marry her Brad, right now! No, don't marry her now -- what the hell am I saying? She's too good an agent!"

"Brad, what's wrong with your boot?" John Ring asked. The group looked down at Lehman's feet. Embedded in the chrome-tanned leather outer shell of his right Nanga Parbat expedition boot was a bullet. The back end of it stuck out a quarter of an inch.

"Shit, Brad, that's a round from a Tokarev 7.62X25," Rube said.

"It must have come from Blondie in the Ballroom. My boot was under water when we were firing at each other."

"Damn, you were lucky," Rube said. "Take off your boot."

Bradford sat down, unlaced his outer boot, slipped it off, and slid his hand in up to its toe. "Yup, I can feel the nose of the bullet. It's sticking through in there about a quarter of an inch." He slid off his leather inner lining and the inner felt bootie for Rube's inspection.

"I can see a slight mark there on the leather toe of the inner boot, but it didn't penetrate." Lehman held up his foot and wiggled his toes through his wool climbing socks.

"So you didn't feel anything Brad?" Makinson asked, shaking his head.

"No, not a thing. But come to think of it, this foot did feel a little heavier. I thought it was just because it was wet." The men laughed. Teo did not. Bradford gave her a consoling hug. "We walked away from it, girl. That's what counts."

"Thank god we were not playing horseshoes," she said, looking at Bradford's boot and letting out a sigh.

There was the thunder of a jet engine. The startled party looked up to see a silver T-33 cross above their heads, seventy-five feet above the crater, and waggle its wings.

"Lehman, that's our buddy Walt Hunter. He is flying 'Cap' for our birds," Rube said. "We did not want anyone interfering with our work up here from the ground -- or air. He got the 'All Green' transmission with the rest of us, and knows the operation is a success."

The T-33 circled. Sunlight caught the silver on its wings and flashed brilliantly. It made another climbing pass and did a victory roll over Mount Rainier's summit. The team waved. The sight of the sleek silver jet streaking overhead, against the backdrop of the helicopters in the crater, swelled the hearts of the team with pride.

We have reclaimed this mountain. It is American. It is ours. Teo put her arm around Bradford and hugged him close.

As the sound of the jet died away, the team looked across to the workers on the crater rim. Gasping agents had manhandled the Backpack out of the cave on a litter, dragged it across the crater, and strapped it into the nearest bird. They collapsed to rest, and took turns breathing pure oxygen from portable masks. Other struggling agents carried three body bags down the rocks of the rim and across the crater snowfield. They deposited each in separate helicopters under directions from crew chiefs. Jack Rose slogged over, sat down, and gratefully accepted hot tea.

"Hi Jack, where is Otto Palmrich?" Bradford asked, after lacing his boot back on.

"He is supervising the rest of the recovery," Jack said, with a breathless smile. "Rube, you should see what this team did. It dropped those men one after another. There were at least a dozen bullet holes around the Backpack, but they didn't so much as scratch it. The radiation readings are well in the normal range for the bomb.

I cannot say enough about how magnificently you guys -- and you young lady -- performed on this mission. That Russian nuke will be a goldmine for our weapons analysts. What you all did was simply incredible!" Jack was not normally effusive, but he was now. His words led to another round of handshakes and hugs. Teo was just hugged.

"I am getting the thumbs-up from my lead agent," Rube said. "Look at him sucking on that oxygen!" Castellano chuckled. "Our tagging, bagging, and dragging gig is finished. It's time to blow this cave. Team, go out and grab all your shit, and let's go." He strapped the mask back on his face and began re-oxygenating his bloodstream in preparation for co-piloting the flight out.

Lehman and Ring hustled over and picked up the climbing gear the team had discarded before beginning the assault, and then jogged back to the helicopters. Four of the Pedros had already left. They had slipped away again toward the west to avoid being viewed by curious eyes down at Paradise. Rube waved Bradford and John over to Champion's helicopter. They strapped in and lifted off. Lehman looked over at Teo's enthralled face. It was her first helicopter ride.

24

INITIAL DEBRIEFINGS AND A SPECIAL PHONE CALL

The LRT climbing team was ushered into the pilot's briefing room at the 318th Fighter Interceptor Squadron's headquarters at McChord Air Force Base. The 318th "Green Dragons" flew Convair F-106 Delta Dart fighters, under direction of the U.S. Air Force's Aerospace Defense Command, and the joint American-Canadian North American Air Defense Command. Thirty minutes after leaving Mount Rainier's high crater, four of the Pedros that extracted the team and the Russian RA-115 Backpack nuclear bomb from the summit were parked neatly in a row on the 318th FIS tarmac. The other two Huskies carrying the three GRU bodies landed at Madigan Hospital, at the adjacent Fort Lewis.

"The President wants to talk to you." Rubayat Castellano, standing at the red secure phone in the pilot's briefing room, handed the phone to John Ring.

"Yes, Mister President. Thank you. You are most kind, thank you. I was just doing my job. Yes, Mister President, I will put her on." Ring waived Teo over.

"Johnson likes the chicks," Rube winked at Lehman.

"Yes, Mister President. Thank you. You are most kind, thank you. I was just doing my job. Yes, it was stressful. No, Mister President, I did not shoot anyone. Yes, Mister President, I did carry a gun. No, Mister President, I am not married." She smiled at Bradford. "Okay, thank you, Mister President. Yes, I will put him on." She waved Lehman over.

"I'm sorry, who am I speaking with again?" Bradford asked. Teo snorted and put her hands to her face. Fighter and helicopter pilots, crowded tightly into the briefing room, erupted in raucous laughter.

"Wise ass!" Rube mouthed with a smile, shaking his head. Makinson, sporting an impish grin, gave Lehman a thumb's up. Ring shook his head.

The debriefing lasted the rest of the day. There was a two-hour break at 1430, to allow the team members to sleep. They had been awake for forty-eight hours, and now not even strong coffee was keeping them awake. When they got up they showered and were issued flight suits to wear.

Due to Jack and Rube's prowess at covert operations, the press had not gotten wind of the LRT's true mission. It never would. Helicopters were noted flying around the summit of Mount Rainier, but no one knew how many. It became a back-story about collecting rock samples and placing sensors for the USGS Lahar Research Team.

When the debriefing was completed the LRT members repaired to the McChord Officer's Club. They were served Beef Wellington, as many helpings as they wanted, with all the trimmings. Then they adjourned to the bar. Rube brought Lehman's boot with the bullet lodged in it, and it was passed around. It graphically bespoke the mission just completed. After the first mugs of beer, Bradford and Teo sat down on a brown leather couch in the back corner and fell asleep on each other's shoulders. Thumbs pointed back toward them periodically by the drinkers at the bar. There was no ribald mocking – only respect and pride in the happy voices. Among them, unbeknownst to Bradford, was Major Walt Hunter, who arrived late. He flew two other missions that day. His T-33 was used as a "target" for several of the 318th's fighters. Their mission was to intercept him, but he was wily, and even maneuvered himself onto the tail of one of the interceptors and scored his own "kill." The Hunter had recently been promoted to Major.

The following day Lehman, Teo, Ring, and Makinson, accompanied by Rube, who again flew as copilot next to Captain Champion, were airlifted back up to the Paradise Ice Caves. When he awoke that morning, Bradford saw that there was a brand new set of Nanga Parbat expedition boots at his bedside, along with a new pair of Converse sneakers.

Before they left McChord, the assault team swapped out their firearms for new ones. FBI ballistics experts flown in from the FBI Laboratory in Washington D.C., needed the team's weapons -- and Bradford's boot -- to determine who shot whom, and with what. Otto Palmrich and Jack Rose remained behind to attend the autopsies on the three dead GRU agents and write up reports.

On the flight back up to Mount Rainier, Rube talked to the team over the intercom: "The Army was mad as hell that they were not allowed to run this operation. I told the General that the Army was in the process of fucking up one war, and I wasn't going to give it the opportunity to fuck up another one. He wanted to go commando and all that shit, but we over-ruled him. Posse Comitatus Act, baby! Of course, they still demanded to come along, but we fixed them."

"What is Posse Comitatus, Rube?" Teo asked.

"It is a federal law that prohibits the U.S. Army from conducting any law enforcement action within the United States. And this, pretty lady, was a law enforcement action carried out here in the good old U.S. of A. So that put 'em up shit creek. But this General still demanded to go."

"So why didn't he?" Ring asked.

"Well, there were seven birds scheduled to fly to the crater. The General and one of his assault teams were on board the seventh, when we spooled up the Pedros. I was afraid that they would jump in and take over the operation. So I arranged to have their Huskie develop 'engine problems.' Warming up the bird, their Air Force command pilot radioed that he had to abort – low hydraulic pressure. The rest of us lifted off and waved to the bird as we left. The pilot gave me a thumbs-up. Man, was the General pissed!" Rube glanced back into the cabin with a toothy grin.

"Sort of like telling the ASAC from Seattle to 'watch the doors,' right Rube?" Lehman said.

"Yeah, Brad, it was a definite variation on that theme. By the way, the Seattle ASAC, Charlie Anderson, has now been variously nicknamed 'Charlie The Doors,' 'Charlie Two-Doors,' or just 'Doors,' by the guys in the office. Agents will walk by his office whistling 'Come on Baby Light My Fire,' by the Doors. Drives him bat-shit!" Castellano clapped his gloved hands.

"I can't believe that the ASAC is completely worthless."

"God no, Lehman, he's not completely worthless. He does a masterful job of being a bad example. Anyway, back to the General.

Our birds carrying the GRU bodies requested to land at Madigan Hospital, and he told them he would not let them into Fort Lewis for the autopsies. He told them, 'This is my god-damned base and you sons-of-bitches ain't coming in here.' So I radioed the Command Post, got patched into the Pentagon, and bingo -- I got the green light to take the bodies into Madigan."

"What happened to the General's order?" Makinson asked.

"Oh, it got rescinded. And so did he. Yesterday afternoon he was fired and retired. So, along with the other stats for this operation, I bagged a two-star general. I wish there was a stat I could claim for that asshole."

"Rube?"

"Yeah, Makinson?"

"Remind me not to get on your bad side, okay?"

As the helicopter gracefully flared and landed at the Ice Caves, Rube gave a thumbs-up. "I will be back up at Paradise in a day or two with Palmrich, to continue debriefings and provide autopsy results. Meanwhile I have a shit-load of paper to write up. Get some well-earned rest, gang!"

The LRT grabbed its climbing gear, shouldered packs, and stepped off the helicopter.

The Park Service had re-opened the mountain for the RGS and private climbing parties, and Lehman passed several Ice Caves tour groups led by RGS guides. Each had greeted him warmly, but Bradford detected consuming curiosity in their eyes.

"Hey, Brad, hi Teo, good to see you!" Jay Olin said. He was not normally warm toward Lehman. "How did it go on the hill? There was a lot of activity up there a day or two ago."

"It went great, Jay," Lehman said. "The LRT surveyed several sites and came out with a ton of rock samples. It was very productive. We bagged a few in the Ice Caves here."

"Why?"

"For comparison to those pulled out of the Crater."

"Why didn't the geologists grab any old rocks around here? Why from the Caves?" Jay asked.

"Because the rocks are not as 'weathered' there, so the geologists tell us," Lehman said.

"Oh, yeah. I can see that," Jay said, nodding. "Man, it looked like you had several helicopters up there at the top."

"Yeah, a couple. There were lots of heavy samples. We decided that it would be better to shut the mountain down for a day or so, and get them all flown out at once, rather than disrupt the RGS and private climbers over several days. Besides, McGill has been driving you guys hard. You could use a little extra rest."

"For sure, Brad. When we go back up, starting today, we will be relocating the route from the headwall over to Disappointment Cleaver. We sent McPherson up to Cadaver Gap to grab the fixed rope and other LRT gear, to use it on the access ramp off the Ingraham to the Cleaver."

"Great, Jay, perfect plan," Lehman said. "We anticipated you would be moving the route, so we undid the fixed rope on the Headwall. McPherson should find it somewhere at the bottom of it. It will save him some time and effort. Hey, I gotta go Jay, see ya!" Lehman waved, and continued down the trail with Teo. *Nice try, big guy.*

Teo took his hand. "'The rocks aren't as weathered in the Caves?' Brad, that was brilliant!"

"Ah yes, my darling," Lehman responded, in his best Inspector Clouseau voice, "When one is on the case, one must have the sharp wits to keep up the facades, you know." Teo laughed and slapped Bradford's shoulder.

The morning sun warmed their backs. An airy sound of distant tumbling waterfalls met their ears, and they smelled the rich fragrance of the meadow's wild flowers. Teo stopped Bradford when there was a break in the crowds. They kissed. Passion's song returned. They were back in Paradise. They were home. They were together. They were alive.

25

Early August 1968: Running the Bear out of the Park

The basement auditorium of the Guide House was crammed to standing-room-only capacity. John Townsley, the Superintendent of Rainier National Park, attended, along with all of the FBI and CIA surveillance agents who had supported the operation – including the SAC from the FBI's Seattle Office, J. Earl Mills, and his ASAC Charles Anderson, AKA, Charlie Two Doors. They looked uncomfortable and out of place in new blue jeans, and matching flannel shirts.

Lehman leaned over to Rube: "Why are they here?"

"You can't keep the empty suits out forever. There comes a time when you gotta let 'em in, Lehman," Rube whispered over a toothy grin. "But only *after* they can't do any damage. They would have taken over and screwed this operation up royally, just like the Army."

"I don't see the new Commanding General from Fort Lewis here. Did you invite him?"

"Yeah, but he's hiding, after what happened to his predecessor. He sent his aide instead. He is in civvies sitting over there."

"He looks a lot like Charlie Two Doors," Lehman observed. "And he has a red flannel shirt on, too."

"Ha!" Rube slapped Lehman on the back. "Brad, you are cannily perceptive for your youth!"

Confirming that the room was secure, and that all present had appropriate Top Secret clearances, and the "need to know," Otto Palmrich passed around photos of the RA-115 Backpack in the Ballroom, of the scenes of the shootouts, and of the bodies of the GRU agents as they were found *in situ.* Palmrich, normally professorial and laconic, was all smiles.

"Rube and Jack will brief you on the operation and autopsy results," Otto said. "My purpose here today is to provide you with an overview of technical findings. You will not be privy to anything in-depth," he nodded. The audience nodded back. "Suffice it to say that the Backpack is a treasure trove. It has already been flown out to New Mexico where it is undergoing a thorough 'physical' there, as you might imagine." He beamed as though a long-lost child had finally come home.

Palmrich continued: "Initial impressions are that the Backpack does not have as big a bang as we had predicted. Its yield is likely somewhere slightly south of ten kilotons. Yet it is quite enough, if detonated in the Ballroom, to trigger an eruption, a lahar, or both. Detonating the device in the crater of an active volcano with an ice plug on top of it, as we describe the crater's snowfield, would channel a substantial amount of the force and shock wave of the blast downward into the magma chamber of the mountain. Our volcanologists and geologists are trying to map that out, but the process of doing so, and predicting precisely what would have happened, is presently more of an art than a science. Mount Rainier is a fickle beast!"

Man, Palmrich, you can say that again. Lehman nodded.

"The beauty of it, and again I must commend our climbing and assault team here," Otto said, "is that we obtained an intact device without any compromise to its shielding or systems. It is evident, in how the assault team returned fire from the last GRU agent 'Blondie,' as he has been nicknamed pending identification, that great care was taken not to hit the Backpack. Speaking of shielding, the device emitted less radiation than a SR-71 pilot would receive on a normal mission flying above seventy thousand feet. The dosimeters of team members have all been checked, and all are well within normal readings. The doses they received were less than one one-thousandth of what they would receive in one chest X-ray."

Bradford leaned over and whispered to Teo, "Well, girl, I can still have kids. Looks like you will have to stay on the pill." She blushed and squeezed his knee.

Palmrich continued: "It appears that the Russians took special care in shielding the RA-115 – much more than we have observed on their nuclear submarines. That suggests, not so much that they wanted their handlers to be safe, but that they desired the weapon to be as stealthy and undetectable as possible when placed at a target location. This is at least one reason why our radiation sensors and recorders were spotty in their results. Now, with respect to the switches on the device and so forth, I am not at liberty to say much. I can only say that when the assault team engaged Blondie -- the deceased GRU agent you see lying here by the Backpack in the photograph -- he already had the back canvas hatch cover off and was beginning to attach a thin antenna wire to connectors -- there. His body was found with a spool of thin wire in his parka. The wire was more than long enough to reach beyond the entrance to the cave and onto the crater rim. Also found was a very simple, but functional, antenna that could be set up unobtrusively to look like a scientific sensor. In fact, the antenna had a canvas sign, 'Property of USGS Do Not Remove' printed on its base. Note that the Russians dropped the 'the' preceding 'USGS' in the signage, as is their lingual habit, when translating Russian into English. So they were certainly aware of the 'Lahar Research Team Study,' and fortunately were fooled by it. But to their credit, they also shrewdly used it here to their advantage as a means of protecting the antenna. The antenna was designed to receive a signal which could be delivered, do to the antenna's altitude, from many miles away – certainly at a safe distance from ground zero. I now turn you over to Special Agent Rubayat Castellano and John Rose."

Agent Castellano took the stage while Jack Rose handed out autopsy photos of the three GRU bodies. "The Assault Team, composed of Ron Makinson, John Ring, Brad Lehman, and Teo Maloney, staged at Camp Muir," Rube began. "It detected a faint light source at Cadaver Gap and began shadowing the targets, keeping out of sight. The team then moved up the hill along the standard guided route to Cadaver Gap. There, drag marks were discovered in the snow, matching the dimensions of the Backpack. As the team shadowed the targets discreetly, Bradford Lehman, the climbing leader, took the Team off the route to the west, to a point below the target cave where an assault could be launched from the southwest – an unexpected direction. Lehman then relinquished command of the team to Special Agent Makinson to lead the tactical approach and assault." Rube nodded toward Ron.

"At this point, I will let our acoustic sensor at the cave entrance tell you what happens." Castellano punched the "Play" button on a large reel-to-reel tape recorder, hooked to a set of equally large speakers. The recording played what sounded like clanking and scraping, followed by Russian voices spoken clearly: "Der'mo eto tyazhelaya. Polegche! Okay." Rube stopped the recording. "They said, 'Shit this is heavy. Take it easy! Okay."

Laughter rippled the auditorium.

"The time of this first conversation is 0210." Rube pushed "Play" again: "Vy okhranyayut vkhod. Ne spat'!" "You guard the entrance. Don't go to sleep!" Rube translated. The recorder continued playing. There were dragging sounds that faded and became quiet. "The two GRU agents muscled the Backpack down to the Ballroom. The time was 0220, exactly one hour before our assault team arrived." Rube fast-forwarded to another point on the tape. "And now to the assault. It is 0320, and we have been given the squelch breaks over the radio that it is commencing." He pushed the "Play" button, and the reels on the recorder turned. There was a cough. "That's the guard coughing," Rube said. Five seconds later there was a sharp sound -- like a balloon popping. Some in the audience jumped. This was followed by scrabbling of boots on rocks and a low gurgling sound. "Quiet, you rat bastard!" The words were muttered, breathless, but utterly clear.

Rube shut down the recorder. There was shocked silence in the auditorium. "Folks," he said, "That's the sound of Makinson's suppressed Colt Super taking out the guard, followed by Makinson's words of encouragement for him to die. If I may be permitted to editorialize..." He slowly scanned the room. "These are the sounds that sum up the Cold War. They are the still small sounds of a long, bloody, and desperate conflict. For some of us, this damned thing seems to have gone on forever. But with these Russian rogues running around locked and cocked, and carrying nukes, there's not a god-damned thing we can do about it but ferret out every last one of the little bastards and eliminate them. They're not the type of sons-of-bitches that will come to the table to talk. They will only come to kill you." Rube's face turned red.

Rube, you are a trench-fighter. Bradford detected a hint of tiredness in Castellano's indignant words. *But you are an old trench-fighter. You are looking over an audience of young CIA and FBI agents, and the rest of us that compose our team. You know that you, and Jack Rose, and others of your generation, will not see this through. You are looking to us to do it. We have. We will.*

A pin-drop quiet enveloped the auditorium as Castellano walked slowly back to the podium. Teo glanced at Bradford and nodded. Her normal sprightly and gentle demeanor now had a look of grim solemnity. *She understands this business. She understands the gestalt of it.* Lehman felt a touch of pride for her – and sadness.

Rube continued: "As you heard for yourselves from our acoustic sensor recording, Agent Makinson, followed by Climbing Ranger John Ring, Brad Lehman, and Teo Maloney, were able to achieve complete surprise over the GRU agent guarding the cave entrance. You can also see by the photos of the scene, that the shot taken by Makinson with a suppressed Colt .38 Super semiautomatic pistol, was a near-contact shot to the back of the GRU agent's head. The autopsy photo here shows gunpowder stippling and feathers embedded in the entrance wound. The feathers are from the down insulation of the GRU agent's parka. This man did not know what hit him. Agent Makinson advised that the GRU guard appeared to be dozing. If so, this round from the suppressed Colt put him permanently to sleep. LRT member Teo Maloney was thereafter posted as an armed guard at the outer entrance of the cave, to protect the rear of the assault team. Makinson, Ring, and Lehman proceeded carefully down into the cave. They elected to retain the element of surprise for as long as possible by utilizing the Starlight Scope carried by Makinson. This allowed them to keep their headlamps switched off. As the team crept slowly down in almost total darkness, the headlamp from GRU agent number two, stationed at the left-hand entrance fork leading to the Ballroom, provided enough light to the Starlight scope's sensor to afford an effective approach for the Team. Only when Makinson stepped around the corner and switched on his headlamp, did the second GRU agent realize he was compromised. At this moment Ranger Ring fired two rounds from his suppressed Colt .38 Super at a range of twenty feet. Both rounds struck the second Russian agent in the chest. Makinson, advancing, fired one round from a range of ten feet, hitting agent number two slightly below the right eye, and taking him out of the fight. Now folks, please go to your handout photographs of the Ballroom."

There was a flurry of shuffling papers.

Castellano continued: "At this point, Makinson, Ring, and Lehman, aware that their presence was likely now known by GRU agent number three, AKA Blondie, kept their headlamps switched on and moved together quickly toward the Ballroom, and the Backpack RA-115, positioned at its far end. They immediately came under fire from Blondie, who took cover behind the Backpack. Makinson was struck in the left pant cargo pocket of his climbing pants by a 7.62X25 ball round from Blondie's suppressed Tokarev semiautomatic pistol. Fortunately, the round struck the Starlight Scope and was deflected away from Makinson's leg, though it did knock him down." Rube passed around the damaged Scope.

"I suppose the U.S. Army Quartermaster who issued this to us will now expect the FBI to pay for the damned thing." There was another ripple of laughter. Rube continued. "Notwithstanding taking the round, Agent Makinson regained his feet and continued the assault. Blondie fired a total of thirteen rounds. When his weapon was recovered it had five rounds left in it. One empty magazine was recovered behind the Backpack, and four extra full eight-round magazines were in his pockets. Blondie would pop out from the side of the Backpack, fire, and go back behind cover. While Makinson and Ring continued to engage Blondie, effectively providing suppressive fire, and taking care not to strike the Backpack, Lehman moved to his right into that large pool of water – the one you see in your photographs -- attempting to flank Blondie." Rube held up his photo of the Ballroom and pointed to the glistening pool of water. "Blondie fired at least three rounds at Lehman. Two rounds struck the wall of the Ballroom behind Lehman's head; and one round was fired low into the water at Lehman's feet – literally."

Rube picked up Lehman's Nanga Parbat outer boot, with the Tokarev bullet lodged in it, and handed it to someone in the first row. "Pass it around. It was a bitch smuggling that thing out of our Laboratory Division, but I wanted you all to get a 'hands on' perspective of how this operation transpired in the caves."

Rube continued: "As Blondie popped out again to fire on Lehman, Lehman took a calculated shot at Blondie's head with his un-silenced Colt .38 Super. The round struck Blondie in the neck, severing his left carotid artery, whereupon Blondie stood up. Lehman then took a second shot that struck Blondie in the middle of his upper forehead. Lehman's fatal shots were delivered from a distance of thirty-five feet."

Low murmurs came from the agents in the room. Teo squeezed Bradford's knee.

Rube cleared his throat. "You can see these wounds on the photos we have handed around. That ended the fight. Thereafter, Special Agent Makinson accessed the panel of switches on the Backpack and initiated a sequence that instructed the Backpack to 'safe' itself.

Makinson also detached the positive connector from the steam turbine here -- running to the car battery – here." He held up a photo and pointed to the items. "That eliminated the Backpack's continuous power source. This act alone, in 'unplugging' the Backpack, would have caused the nuke to gradually lose power. Ultimately this would have induced the RA-115 to 'safe' itself some hours later, even if Agent Makinson's shutdown sequence failed to work."

There was a ripple of laughter in the room as the audience noticed the cheap Pay N' Pak car battery in the photo.

"Yeah, you're right," Castellano said with a grin, "These GRU agents were cheap bastards." I now turn you over to Jack Rose. He will close this briefing with the recovery and transport of the RA-115, and the ingress and egress of all personnel and equipment."

Jack Rose took the stage. He talked in his accustomed clinical, smiling, unruffled style: "We launched the six Pedros, that's the call sign for the HH-43 Huskies, from McChord Air Force Base five minutes after receiving Ranger Ring's 'All Green' voice transmission, repeated three times – signifying that the GRU threat was neutralized, that the Backpack was secure and shut down, and that the team had taken no casualties. We at the Command Post acknowledged with one squelch break, or 'click' by keying our radio. The Assault Team then knew that we were on our way and would arrive within an hour. We then went out with our recovery and evidence teams of combined FBI and CIA personnel, boarded the helicopters, and lifted off en route to Rainier. I will note here as a point of interest, that Castellano and I had attempted to acclimatize these team members to working on the fourteen thousand four-hundred-foot summit of the mountain by having them spend time in the hypobaric, or 'Altitude Chamber' at McChord Air Force Base. The jury is out on whether this helped them much." As Rose spoke, he scanned his eyes around the audience, looking at the recovery team. "Ah, I see most are shaking their heads 'no.'"

Jack smiled, and continued: "We landed the six Pedros on the snowfield within Mount Rainier's summit crater. I cannot say enough about the consummate skill of Flight Commander Captain Rick Champion, and his pilots and crews, for their safe handling of such a large formation of birds at that altitude, and in such a confined space. I believe this has never been accomplished before." Jack saluted Champion, who sat in civilian clothes in the front row. Champion nodded and saluted back. "Our teams deployed efficiently, the scenes were photographed and processed quickly, and the RA-115 nuclear weapon was safely removed, and placed on a helicopter without any glitches. Bodies of the GRU agents were bagged and placed on helicopters, and all personnel, including the LRT assault team, were airborne and en-route back to McChord within an hour and a half from the time the birds touched down in the crater. That concludes this briefing."

There was a long pause. Then the auditorium erupted in a standing ovation. Agents and team members whistled and cheered. Bradford and Teo hugged each other. People were slapping their backs. Lehman looked at Teo. Tears were streaming down her cheeks. Tears welled up in Bradford's eyes. They kissed.

The celebration sprang from a heady mixture of the sweet relief felt in the neutralization of a dire national threat; and from a sense of victory – a clean, clear, direct victory over an implacable foe – the Russian Bear.

* * *

Seattle SAC J. Earl Mills, a thin man of slight build, and sharp dark penetrating eyes menacingly framed in heavy black-rimmed glasses, was all smiles. He stepped up and shook each team member's hand, including Miss Teo Maloney's. "Incredible, I have to say!" he said.

Rube talked into Bradford's ear: "True, he *has* to say it. He knows Hoover's signature is all over this operation. Begrudging bastard."

"Where is Charlie Two Doors?" Lehman asked.

"He left. He is probably out warming up the Bureau car for his boss so they can get the hell out of here."

Lehman shook hands with Makinson. "Well, Ron, you are now not simply a trained and blooded Special Agent of the FBI, but you are also a full-fledged qualified RGS guide. I saw that your Seattle boss, Mister Mills, congratulated you when he shook your hand."

Makinson laughed. "He's not my boss, Brad. I work out of the Chicago FBI Office. I'm only temporarily assigned to the Seattle Office for purposes of this operation. He did congratulate me, though -- but then he told me that I was three expense vouchers behind, and that he wanted them submitted by COB today."

"What does COB mean?"

"That's FBI-speak for Close of Business."

"Well, Makinson, you'd better get on those vouchers – now," Lehman said.

"Yeah, I'll jump right on that, Lehman," Makinson said, sporting a mischievous grin. "Let me give you some advice in working with bureaucracies: don't respond until they ask for it the third time. If they don't ask for it three times they don't really want it."

The meeting adjourned and the members of the USGS Lahar Research Team repaired to the Glacier Room, which was reserved and secured. There were many toasts that followed. But the one made repeatedly was: "Here's to running the Bear out of the Park!" It was a noisy, joyous, and thoroughly proud-to-be-an-American, celebration.

Bradford and Teo left the festivities early. The two lovers and friends ate a leisurely dinner in the Dining Room, doted over by Nancy Olszewski, and then went for a walk together. Distant sounds of merrymaking confirmed that the party was still going strong in the Glacier Room. As they walked out the Inn's front door, and passed by the kitchen at the back of the building, Harry Pappajohn came flying out the back door banging two pan lids together. The bear pillaging the garbage ran away. "Run the bear out of the Park, Harry! Run the bear out of the Park!" they shouted. Pappajohn swore in Greek and slammed the door.

26

Mid-August 1968: The Bear's Reprise

Over the next few days Bradford and Teo slept, made passionate love, reveled in relaxation with each other, and ate. They also took long hikes together. All of the LRT climbing team carried their weapons and moved around outside of the Paradise Inn parking lot in pairs. This was done on Castellano's orders: "Too many operations I have been on have suffered casualties after the pressure was off. The pressure is never completely 'off ' in this business, especially while still in proximity to a combat area. And as pretty as Paradise and Mount Rainier are, it *is* a combat zone. Rose and I need to fly out to the SOG for a few days. Keep your tits out of the ringer until we get back," Castellano said.

"C-R" flew off to Washington D.C. to present more detailed briefings to the President, select members of Congress, Hoover at the FBI, Helms at the CIA, and the heads of the other participating agencies. They were slated to be gone a week.

Bradford and Teo discussed going on another summit climb again, but neither relished climbing Disappointment Cleaver. They decided to stick close to Paradise. They did more short climbs in the Tatoosh Range, and went on a day-hike to the top of Pyramid Peak. One clear sunny morning after breakfast, Bradford and Teo decided to climb to Camp Muir via the Nisqually Glacier. Though normally thoroughly broken up by August, this season the Nisqually still remained passable. So it seemed. It was one of B.F. Lehman's favorite trips, and Bradford had climbed it with his father and the Shelton climbing crew many times.

They donned their gear, hiked out past Glacier Vista, roped up near the crevasse that now sheathed the body of GRU assassin Ivan Karin, and stepped onto the Nisqually. The glacier was badly broken up in the middle, but remained negotiable on its right side, as it skirted the walls of the Muir Snowfield's precipitous western edge.

"Hey girl," Lehman said, "you lead and route-find through this section. I'll follow. I love watching your gorgeous rear end!"

"Okay, Brad!" Teo smiled and gave Lehman a hug. Her teeth, bleached whiter by the high altitude ultraviolet sunlight from a summer spent on Rainier, made her beautiful face even more stunning. She now sported a few freckles, but the rigorous application of sunscreen had saved her from the perennial pain and damage of sunburn, the former hallmark of high-mountain life. It had saved Lehman's face as well. He put his mouth close to hers. He could see his own reflection in her dark glasses. *It has the look of a man in love, Lehman.* They kissed softly.

For an hour they climbed. They plodded and breathed, skirted crevasses, and belayed each other over snow bridges. The route forced them inexorably east, closer to the right-hand cliffs of the Muir Snowfield's ridgeline. Teo began probing her way with her ice axe across a long large snow bridge, on belay from Lehman. Far to the right, out of the corner of his eye, Bradford noticed a lone figure at the edge of the glacier. It just stood there. Lehman nodded to it. The figure did not acknowledge him. Then it started moving. *Why the hell is this guy climbing solo out onto the glacier like that? Does he need help? He's not acting like he does.* Then it dawned on him. *Shit!*

A little geyser of snow sprouted next to Teo's feet. Bradford grabbed the climbing rope and yanked her backwards. She let out a yell of surprise, and fell to her right into the crevasse. Flying snow splashed Lehman. He heard the now familiar suppressed *pop* of a Tokarev pistol. He was helpless in his belay stance. With all his strength, Bradford yanked his ice axe up out of the boot-axe belay, and the weight of Teo's falling body quickly took up the coiled slack in the goldline as she fell. *You have no choice Bradford. Jump!* Lehman leaped over the edge of the crevasse on the left-hand side of the snow bridge. *Come on baby, hold!* The goldline sawed into the ice on the bridge, and jerked him to a stop.

"Brad! What the hell?" Teo cried out. Her voice carried a mix of fear and anger. She was hanging in thin air thirty feet below him, spinning in her seat harness.

"Teo, we are both being shot at. A round barely missed you. There is a man climbing toward us. This was all I could do -- pull you down into the crevasse -- and then jump in myself." Lehman's voice was firm. Teo fell quiet. Lehman's mind raced. Then the name came to him: *Coleman. He is the sole GRU agent not accounted for. Rube and Jack thought he'd left the mountain. Obviously they were wrong.* With that revelation, and with the certainty that his conclusion was right, Lehman felt himself relaxing. *Focus.*

Taking a deep breath, he carefully drew his Colt Super from his waistband and looked down. Teo had her Walther out.

"Good girl. In a minute or two he is going to make his way up to our crevasse and look over. He will not cut the rope on us right away.

He is gloating that he has us where he wants us. But he is curious. He will look over. He is out in bright sunlight. When he looks down trying to see, and before his eyes adjust to the darkness, he will not notice that we have weapons. That is our time to shoot. Got it?"

"Yes, Brad," Teo said evenly. There was tenacity in her voice -- *"A fixity of purpose," as Winston Churchill termed it.* Lehman smiled. Teo was backing him up. Lehman's pride in her poise and strength relaxed him further.

It seemed an eternity. But Lehman was calm, patient. He could hear Teo below him, as she took in deep controlled breaths and let them out. *That a girl, breathe, focus.* A shadow approached the lip of the crevasse, followed by a head and torso looking over the edge.

"Hello Coleman," Bradford shouted up.

"Ah! You know my name! I thought it was you who gave me the ticket last year. I watched you through my field glasses. I decided I would return the favor." Coleman held a big knife out for Lehman to see.

"Coleman, you are in violation of Park rules. Again you are climbing solo on a glacier. That is another three hundred dollar fine, you know."

"Ha!" Coleman tossed his head back and laughed. "You are a man with spirit! What is your name young man?" *Revenge. My name is revenge.*

"My name is Bradford Washburn Lehman. And did you know, George Coleman, that there is a federal warrant out for your arrest?" As he finished his words, Lehman leaned back in his climbing harness, lifted his feet above his head, and dug the front points of his crampons into the icy underside of the snow bridge, to gain more stability, and to stop the swing of the rope. He took a deep breath, let it out slowly, and brought his Colt Super smoothly up toward the dark figure's head. Coleman's head and torso was framed starkly in the light of the opening of the big crevasse. Lehman held the pistol with both hands at arms-length -- pulling back with the weak hand, and pushing forward with the strong hand -- to lock the weapon into a solid isometric triangle, as he was taught by Rube. *"A good stable shooting platform from any position."* Rube's words calmed Bradford, and brought the trace of a smile. *Rube, if you could only see me in this position now. I'm almost upside down.* Lehman concentrated on the front sight. He had a good site picture.

"No, Mister Bradford Washburn Lehman, I did not know that. So, *big man* down there, are you going to arrest--." Coleman had raised his sunglasses and was leering down speaking his words, when Lehman felt the recoil of his pistol. He was oblivious to its sound. The dark glasses exploded off of the top of Coleman's head, and were replaced with a halo of bloody spray. The Russian's body, a rag doll now, toppled forward into the crevasse. It glanced off of Lehman's pack and spun him violently. Then the corpse careened into the blackness. The thumping noises that it made as it bounced off the walls of the crevasse grew swiftly faint.

"No, Coleman, I am not going to waste my time arresting you." Lehman angrily spat the words out as he looked down into the void of the cold crevasse that now held the body of GRU Captain Georgi Kulikov – AKA, George Coleman.

"Teo, are you okay?"

"Yes, Brad." Her voice came back thin, but steady.

"Wonderful, girl," Lehman said. "I'm fine too. Not a scratch." There followed a few seconds of silence as Bradford and Teo swung gently in their harnesses, letting the violent reality of what had happened wash over them. Lehman concentrated on controlling his breathing. He felt his heart rate begin to normalize. "Well, girl, we *were* going to Camp Muir -- but what do you say we do a little crevasse rescue practice instead?"

"You're the guide. Lead me." He saw a smile on her face.

"God you are beautiful, woman, even down here!"

"Oh, you like getting your women in the dark, don't you?" she said in a scolding voice.

"Ha!" Lehman laughed. It felt good to laugh. "So here's the drill, Teo. Get your Jumars out and come on up next to me." Teo nodded. Lehman re-holstered his Colt .38 Super. He watched approvingly as Teo clicked the ascenders into her rope, and efficiently pulled herself up.

In a few minutes she was hanging even with Lehman, three feet away, on the other side of the snow bridge. He reached over and they touched hands.

"The rope has been lodged in this bridge for at least fifteen minutes now," Bradford said. "It has probably frozen itself in place. I'm looking at twenty feet here on my side to reach the lip of the crevasse next to the bridge. I will Jumar up as close as I can on our rope. The bridge looks thick and stable enough from underneath, but I do not want to kick around on it more than I need to. Let me get up there."

Lehman carefully ascended the goldline on his side of the snow bridge. Assessing the situation, he unclipped an ice screw from his harness, reached out at arm's length, and screwed it into the wall of the bridge. Then he snapped one of his ascenders into it with a carabiner. Slowly, carefully, he placed his boot into the stirrup of the Jumar's sling and transferred his weight to it. It held. The climbing rope, now un-weighted from his side of the snow bridge, but still holding Teo on the other, did not slip – yet. Bradford swiftly tied a double overhand knot in the slack of the goldline, next to where the rope disappeared into the snow bridge. *If the friction doesn't hold the rope to Teo, maybe this knot will.* Lehman took a deep breath and relaxed.

"Okay girl, looking good. But be very still. Only the surface area of the frozen rope is holding you now. I put in a double overhand knot on my side, so if the rope does slip, the knot should jam and stop you." Teo nodded, and looked down into the black hole. At that instant her body dropped another foot.

"Oh!" Teo exclaimed quietly. She looked up at Bradford and gave him a thumbs-up as she swayed in her seat harness. The knot Bradford tied had jammed into the bridge and was holding.

"The knot just seated here in the snow, Teo. It's good. Sorry it gave you a start. Hang in there, girl."

"That's all I can do, Brad. I am – literally!"

Lehman reached back and unhooked the second Jumar from the goldline. He grabbed another ice screw from his harness, placed it another arm's length away next to the lip of the crevasse, and stepped gingerly into its stirrup. He then took his ice axe, cut away some of the lip on the top of the crevasse, and swung the pick of the axe down on the top of the snow. Gaining a firm hold, he pulled himself up with it, front-pointing with his crampons, and wriggled out of the crevasse into the sunlight. He stood up and glanced back down at Teo.

"Hey beautiful, how are you doing down there?"

"Okay, Bradford, but I am more than ready to get out of this thing."

"A man can't ask for anything more that a woman who is more than ready."

Lehman set in an ice screw near the crevasse's lip on Teo's side of the snow bridge, and snapped a carabiner into it with two nylon rope slings tied end-to-end. He tossed the line down to Teo. "All right pretty lady, Jumar up this." When Teo's arms came up over the lip, Bradford grabbed them and gently lifted her out. The two collapsed together, catching their breath.

The Nisqually was peaceful, quiet. It willingly stored yet another Cold War secret. It had nearly stored Lehman and Maloney. Bradford thought of Jack Ring's philosophy of life: *Everybody has to be somewhere.* This time he smiled.

*　　*　　*

"Damn, Lehman, every time I issue you one of our Bureau guns, you go around killing people with it." Rube sat in the Glacier Room swilling his beer. He smiled a toothy grin. Jack Rose sat next to Castellano. Palmrich, Lehman, Maloney, Ring, and Makinson were there. The room was secure. "Jeez, we were only back at the SOG for a couple of days, and then had to fly right back. My ass is lagged out with all the time changes," Rube complained. He opened his notebook and pulled the pen from his pocket.

"Okay, Lehman and Maloney, tell me what happened."

When Bradford and Teo finished an hour later, both Rose and Castellano shook their heads.

"No question this was George Coleman," Rube said.

"No question," Jack said. "He answered to the name." His voice then turned apologetic. "I am sorry, Brad and Teo, that we missed the boat on Coleman. We had indications that he was likely out of the country."

"No sweat, Jack," Lehman said. "Like Rube said, assumptions can be wrong, and when they are they can be deadly. The whole intelligence analysis process, viewed from my humble experience as a neophyte in this business, is more of an art than a science. You and

Rube both told us to stay vigilant. I suppose Teo and I were, given the circumstances. But our route-finding problem up the glacier definitely divided out concentration."

"Luckily it was not divided enough to get you two killed, at least," Rose said. "How did you make the decision to jump into the crevasse on the opposite side of the snow bridge? That was amazing."

"Not really. Depending on the exposure situation, when I knew that I couldn't self-arrest a client -- on a steep traverse between two close crevasses for instance – I have bailed into the uphill one to stop a client from falling into the lower one. It is definitely counter-intuitive; but if it is thought through before hand, it's not so bad. And it's quick."

Otto Palmrich gave Bradford an understanding smile. As a mountaineer himself, he knew the value of checking off the "what if's" in the course of a climb. It was all part of staying vigilant – and alive.

"So, Brad, you are really racking these GRU agents up!" Rube's deep resonant voice was almost booming. "Shit, they are already calling you 'Head Shot Lehman' back at FBI Headquarters. Now you've bagged another one!"

"I only responded to threats and took what was presented to me."

Rube slapped him on the back and squeezed his shoulder. "I know, Brad, and I am immensely proud of you, and you Miss Maloney, and all of you here on this team. You all have excelled in your training and used your best judgment in neutralizing these threats, and bringing success to this operation." He waved for more beers all around.

"We have preliminary identities on the GRU agents you all eliminated in the crater," Jack said.

"Two more Karin brothers were taken care of – Dmitri, and Alexei. Ron killed Dimitri on the crater rim, at the outside entrance to the cave, and John and Ron killed Alexei at the second entrance to the passageway to the Ballroom. That leaves one left -- Valery Karin, the oldest brother. Valery has dark hair and a heavy build like his brothers. Our intelligence indicates that he is not in the United States, but is on GRU-run operations somewhere in Africa, possibly in the Congo. And again, we may assume he is going to be quite angry about losing his brothers when he hears of their demise."

"That's a fuc--. That is an incredible understatement Jack," Castellano said. He looked apologetically at Teo.

"We are still trying to identify 'Blondie,'" Jack continued, "the one you eliminated, Bradford. We believe he hails from the technical side of the GRU – probably a specialist in handling and deploying these small nuclear weapons."Castellano changed the subject back to Coleman: "Jack, regarding cleanup of this operation -- there's no need to go back and dig out Georgi Kulikov, AKA, George Coleman, is there?"

Rose sat forward, his large eyes pondering, hands slowly rotating his beer mug back and forth on the table. "I think not. We can trust Brad and Teo that Kulikov took a fatal round and fall. We have blood and brain matter on Brad's cap and sweater. That attests sufficiently to the event. There are also new signs from SigInt that Moscow Center is wondering why he has not checked in."

"Well," Lehman said, "Teo and I walked up to Glacier Vista this morning before you got up here, and put the binoculars on the crevasse. The snow bridge over it has collapsed. So Coleman is not only over four hundred feet down at the bottom of the Nisqually, he now has tons of snow on top of him. That son-of-a-bitch isn't checking in with Moscow anytime soon."

Rube lifted his mug in a toast. "That's what I like to hear, Lehman -- no autopsies, no reports, no receipts, no bulky evidence, no paper. Perfect! Brilliant, Lehman and Maloney! And no checking in with Moscow Center, because Coleman's checked out. Radio silence, baby. Here's to checking the bastard out!" The team drank to it.

"Brad," Teo spoke up. "I just remembered. You called up to Coleman when we were down in the crevasse. You told him there was a warrant out for his arrest. Why did you say that?"

"To distract him and buy time," Lehman said.

"But was that true?" Teo asked.

"Yes."

"Yes, Teo, it is true!" Ring seconded Bradford. "George Coleman had a bench warrant out on him ordered by the federal magistrate in Seattle."

"But why?"

"Because the asshole never showed up in court to answer the summons on the citation I wrote on him last year -- when Bradford and I caught him climbing solo after he cut the rope on his buddy, below Camp Misery."

"'There's a warrant out for your arrest.' *Priceless!*" Makinson slapped the table, put his hand out, and shook Bradford's hand. "Lehman, you stuck it to him. I love it!"

Jack Rose stood up and directed the team to reconvene in the basement of the Guide house. When they were seated and settled there, Jack spoke: "There is another matter regarding 'cleanup,' here. We do not yet know where the GRU agents located their base camp for their forays up the hill." He walked over to the wall photograph of the south side of Mount Rainier and picked up the pointer.

"Brad, you were shot about here by Ivan Karin, right?" Jack pointed to the right of the big crevasse on the Nisqually Glacier beyond Panorama Point.

"Yes that's the spot, Jack."

"And three days ago you and Teo were shot at by Coleman here?" Jack moved the pointer a mile farther up the glacier near its right edge.

"Yes, that is where it happened," Teo said.

"So then, if you extend the lines of direction – first for Ivan, who was initially walking north next to the glacier, and then back from Coleman, who was seen entering the glacier from the same side of the Nisqually, but at right angles, the lines actually intersect. You see this rock buttress here to the east, two hundred yards away? It is part of the Muir Snowfield's western ridge complex."

"Yes, I see it," Lehman said, stepping up to the map to get a closer look. "There is a small platform in there at the base of that cliff. It would be a perfect spot for a base camp. No one ever goes over there, and yet it would be easy to hump supplies into it from Paradise. No need to even rope up under normal conditions. And the lines you describe intersect there. Jack, I think you've nailed it!"

"Yes," Rube said, "And it also explains why Ivan circled back and ambushed you, Brad. Ivan thought you were following him, and you were walking toward his camp."

"It also explains something else," Lehman said. "On an air resupply drop for Camp Muir with Jimmy Beech some days ago, my eye caught a mirror flash from that general area. We made another pass to confirm, but saw nothing. Remember, Teo, when we climbed Pinnacle Peak last season and I told you about mirror flashes from the south rim of the crater?"

"Yes, I remember," she said.

"It could well be that there was some kind of signal mirror communication set up by the GRU between the summit and its base camp."

"That would explain why we never heard them on any radios," Rube said. "Simple, discreet -- and it blended into the habits of other climbers up on the hill."

*　　*　　*

The next day the LRT performed its last mission on the mountain. As Jack had predicted, there was indeed a base camp and cache of supplies at the bottom of the cliff adjoining the middle of the Muir Snowfield. Large snow caves were dug into the side of the slope where the GRU agents slept and ate, and organized their equipment. The entire camp cleverly covered and concealed with white nylon camouflage tarps. Lehman and the rest of the team, along with Rube and Jack, snapped photographs, and then pulled all the items out of the site and dragged them to a landing zone, for Captain Champion to airlift out. Among the gear was a short wave radio transceiver, GRU codebooks, and an operations manual on the RA-115 nuclear bomb. "Ah, more stats for me!" Castellano grinned.

The operation was begun at 0430 hours and was completed at 0750.

"Do you good folks want a lift back to the Paradise parking lot?" Captain Champion asked Rube, who was in the cargo bay of the HH-43, helping the crew chief secure the Russian equipment.

"No, Rick, you go on ahead. Jack and I will be down there in a day or so to help sort this crap out. Our agents are at McChord now, waiting to pick this gear up at that end."

Champion gave a thumbs-up, and Rube stepped off the bird. The Huskie lifted off gracefully, skimmed across the jumbled blue-green crevasse fields of the Nisqually Glacier, and disappeared southwest over the fire-red Indian Paintbrush blanketing the meadows of Van Trump Park. The group meandered casually back toward the trails to Paradise. Bradford and Teo walked hand in hand behind the others. There was no bravado, no loud excited chatter – only quiet conversations among friends and colleagues, who had been through a long harrowing operation, and were finally seeing it end.

Lehman sensed an odd sadness in its closure. *Why do I feel this way? I should be lighthearted, celebratory. Maybe Rube was right. Maybe I am cut out for this business.*

Bradford Lehman, who just a few weeks before had had his moral equilibrium tested, was no longer disturbed with the obscure, grotesque process of fighting the Cold War. *It is what it is,* he concluded. He still had occasional nightmares, but now he understood. It was part of the effects of sublimating stress. He had survived, and he was with Teo. Together they had "defended the hill," a place they both loved, and where they had both found love.

Will we be able to continue to grow together when we are off the hill? As the question begged his thoughts, Bradford's memory retrieved Agent Castellano's words spoken to Teo and him the summer before --*"But the crux of it is: 'Will we grow together?' I predict that, based on your solid steady characters, you will. It's going to take patience, and believe me a lot of humor, for you to make it in life. I'm not trying to marry you now, or tell you to go do it. Indeed... I'd counsel against it... All I'm saying to the two of you is -- live. Let life take you to where friendship and love is."*

Teo and Bradford turned their heads to a sound coming from behind them. It was the *cawing* of a crow or raven.

"It's my old raven buddy from Camp Muir, Teo." As they watched, the big bird swooped past the old Russian base camp, circled once, and winged effortlessly toward them. He came so close that Teo started to duck.

"It's okay Teo, he's just happy this is over. He hates Russians."

As the jet black bird shot past them head-high with the swiftness of an arrow, Bradford could hear its pinion feathers hissing in the wind.

"Just you and us now, big guy...." Lehman squeezed Teo's hand. "And no more Russians."

The rest of the group walked and talked a hundred feet in front of Lehman and Maloney. Their discussion centered on what they'd discovered at the GRU agent's base camp.

"You all saw the blue JanSport frame pack we recovered, from under one of the sleeping cots," Rube said. Rose, Ring, and Makinson nodded. "Jack and I looked in it. The wallets and driver's licenses of three missing hikers were in there. Jack and I suspect that they will match those who went missing on their trips to Camp Muir this summer. They are all males, ranging in age from nineteen to twenty-four. If they got close enough to this site, the GRU would definitely see them as threats."

"Shit. The bastard's killed them and dumped their bodies in crevasses," Ring concluded.

"It certainly appears so," Jack said.

"Are you going to notify their next of kin?" Ring asked.

"Unfortunately we cannot do that," Rube said. There was genuine sadness in his voice. "To do so would tip off the operation, which as we all know, is highly classified. I know, Ring, it is your ranger's duty to close these loose ends for families. This hangs heavily on all of us. But we can't compromise the operation." There was a long pause, as the three men plodded along.

"So they will go down as forever lost on the mountain," Ring said. His voice sounded resigned.

"I'm afraid so John," Jack said. "The civil court process will eventually declare them dead. I am sorry we cannot give the victims' families better closure."

"Rube, are you going to tell Bradford and Teo?" Makinson asked.

"What do you all think?"

"I wouldn't tell them," Castellano said. "Brad and Teo have been through enough in adapting to this nasty business of Cold War operations. We don't need to heap that information on them. Besides, Lehman is still having nightmares from his experiences. Telling him that he was the sole survivor among four hikers who crossed the GRU will only aggravate what he's already dealing with."

"I agree as well," Ring said.

Rose nodded. He was not smiling.

27

It Concludes

Lehman reached over and took Teo gently in his arms, bringing her back to here, to now, to safety, to love -- to him. She was having nightmares the same as he. She made gasping noises, cried out, and kicked at the covers on the bed. He knew that she was again spinning helplessly in the dark crevasse, with a menacing figure bending over her, smirking, holding a knife ready to sever the last gossamer thread that separated life from death. She was suffering as he suffered -- reliving the infinite possibilities of the past.

"You shot George Coleman too, didn't you girl?" Bradford spoke the words softly in Teo's ear after her nightmare had passed, and her breathing quieted. It was pitch dark in their Guide House room. Lehman had been wrestling in his mind whether to bring it up to Teo. But he knew now that what she did could not be held in – not and still preserve the loving inner beauty that defined her as a woman.

"Yes," Teo said. She began sobbing against Bradford's shoulder. Lehman sensed that she was terrified. She had killed a man. It did not matter that he was going to kill her. From Bradford's perspective as a man he could relate. He thought of how he had rationalized killing Ivan Karin. *All that helped, yet the memory is still there – like those of the others you killed on your mountain. It will always be there, like the scar on your neck that has hardened. Only time will mellow it. You are not stone inside, Bradford. And neither is she.*

Lehman switched on the light next to the bed, and embraced Teo as she continued to cry, her tears running down his bare chest. He held her more tightly, rocking gently. Minutes passed. Teo's sobs gradually abated. Lehman didn't talk. He knew that in this moment all words failed.

"I'm getting you all wet, Brad," she finally said, sniffing.

"You don't need to cry to do that."

Teo chuckled through her sniffles and laid her head down on his chest. "Bradford, I don't know how you cope with all this."

"I cope because you are here with me, young lady."

Teo kissed him softly on the lips. "That can't be the whole reason."

"No it isn't the entire reason. But from now on it's going to be a bigger one." He stroked her fine silky hair.

"What do you mean, Bradford?"

"Because you and I, closest of friends and lovers, are even closer. Now we can face these things together. We have lived through them – together. We no longer need to struggle to imagine what the other is experiencing. We have both experienced it."

Teo sniffed again and nodded.

"When I fired at Coleman," Bradford continued, "I was concentrating on his nose and eyes. But as my pistol went off I saw a hole appear in his forehead. That was your shot, wasn't it?"

"Yes," Teo said softly, looking up into Bradford's eyes. "But I don't want anyone to know that I fired." Her eyes began to tear up.

"No one will know, Teo. Coleman is at the bottom of the Nisqually. He has taken our places there. The mountain keeps its secrets. But we must not keep them from each other. We must talk. To talk, to cry, to love -- is to heal."

"But I worry about you Brad. You don't cry. You have nightmares. They are getting better, but you don't cry." Teo was calm now.

Bradford put his face close to hers and bobbed his eyebrows: "Guides who climb the beeg mountains do not cry, my darling," Lehman whispered back in his Inspector Clouseau voice. "Are you ready to stop crying and to climb the beeg mountain?"

Teo laughed, and rolled on top of him. Her breasts wiped away the tears on his chest. "Oh, yes, my darling!" She cooed. "I am *sooo* ready to climb the beeg mountain!"

Love heals. So does laughter.

28

AFTERWORD

Such were the strange and guarded machinations of the Cold War, as it was fought out relentlessly by our military and intelligence agencies, both abroad and at home. For a brief moment, in the summers of 1967 and 1968, Paradise was "Cold."

President Johnson, soon to leave office, used the operation as leverage to bring the Russian Bear to heal. He picked up the Red Phone to Moscow, even before he talked with Lehman and the rest of the team at McChord Air Force Base. He informed Soviet Premier Leonid Ilyich Brezhnev of the fate of his GRU agents. He communicated bluntly: "This action by your country is an outright provocation, and an act of precipitation of war." The President followed up the conversation by sending Brezhnev photographs of his agent's corpses, and of the Soviet RA-115 Backpack nuclear bomb, now in U.S. possession. Brezhnev got the message. All GRU activities surrounding their "Bomb Placement Program," as Jack Rose smilingly characterized it, ceased. And though the Backpack nuke never was detonated, there was plenty of fallout. Back at Moscow Center nearly the entire GRU hierarchy was sacked and replaced.

Special Agent Rubayat Castellano and Jack Rose had predicted the outcome. "Never embarrass the Bureau," was Rube's mantra. "Never embarrass Moscow Center," was the logical corollary. He predicted that internal consequences by the Russians following their failed mission would be swift. They were. And Lehman was certain that Rube would claim "Stats" for each GRU head that rolled. Days later, over lunch with Lehman and Maloney down in Tacoma, Bradford's supposition was confirmed.

"You are damned right, Lehman," Rube said with a toothy grin, "I claimed every one of those bastards. And Hoover approved them!"

Other Backpack devices -- if there were others -- were withdrawn. That is what Brezhnev assured the thirty-seventh President of the United States, Richard Nixon, who was sworn into office in January of 1969. Nixon and his intelligence agencies continued to remain doubtful that all such weapons on U.S. soil were retrieved.

In 1992, following the collapse of the Soviet Union, a high-ranking Russian GRU agent defected to the United States. His assertions that the GRU actively pursued "nuclear sabotage" operations in the United States and other western countries, briefly rekindled old Cold War apprehensions about backpack nuclear bombs being secretly stored in America. Congress launched an investigation. Venues where nuclear weapons were allegedly sequestered were searched. Nothing was found. Mount Rainier's crater caves were not on the list of suspect locations. Following the shootout there in 1968, both the GRU and KGB gave the big mountain a wide berth. Even the traditional dead drop sites around Paradise, Longmire, Sunrise and other locations in the Park, were never re-activated.

FBI Special Agent Rubayat Castellano, and CIA Agent Jack Rose, used their significant reputations to lobby President Johnson to bestow the Medal of Freedom on Bradford Lehman, John Ring, J. Ronald Makinson, and Teo Maloney, "For making especially meritorious contributions to the security and national interests of the United States." It didn't take much lobbying. Late in the fall of 1968, the team flew out to Washington D.C., where the President, *in camera,* pinned the medals on them all. Neither families nor friends were allowed to attend the secret ceremony. Robert S. McNamara did attend, however. A photograph taken after the presentation showed Bradford Lehman being embraced by him. There was pride showing on the former Secretary's face. Throughout subsequent years they remained in touch.

Climbing Ranger John Ring continued in that seasonal capacity for Rainier National Park for another summer, until he obtained his Masters in Business Administration at the University of Washington, and became a manager at a recreational equipment company in Seattle.

CIA Agent Jack Rose submerged back into the murky depths of global intelligence operations. He resurfaced occasionally to contact Bradford, Teo, and other members of the old "Lahar Research Team."

* * *

In 1975, a high level KGB agent defected to the West. Jack Rose and Rube conducted portions of the agent's debriefing. The agent well knew of the GRU operation on Mount Rainier. He described Georgi Kulikov, AKA, George Coleman, as part of a "rogue faction" of the GRU. He shook his head grimly and added: "We came so close to nuclear war because of them. They were rabid. You will not believe, but the whole Mount Rainier mission by GRU started as a bet. One drunken general bet another that U.S.A. is so soft, that he could detonate a portable bomb in the crater of Rainier, and America would not retaliate."

"Not retaliate, why?" Rose asked, disguising his shock at the statement. Rube's face turned red.

"Because, Jack, the general reasoned that exploding the bomb in crater of Mount Rainier would cause eruption."

"That's bullshit," Rube said angrily, "we would know immediately, because of the radiation fallout, mixed with the airborne volcanic ash and lahar mudflows, that a nuclear bomb started it."

"Yes, Mister Castellano, you, Mister Rose, and all of your intelligence agencies -- and the President – you would all know. But still knowing, they would not broadcast this knowledge to American public. They would keep it secret. They would say something like…" The old KGB agent ran his thumbs over the tips of his cupped fingers… "Like, eruption caused major radiation leak at nearby nuclear reservation. Hanford, is it? This was essence of the drunken bet – that America is corrupt and will quickly cover up – like snows of a Russian winter."

"That is utter bullshit," Rube said. But back in a corner of his long-jaded Cold War mind, Castellano had to acknowledge that, bizarre as it was, it could be a possibility. It was just bizarre enough to be credible. He shook his head. Jack Rose said nothing.

"So you see gentlemen, I am most glad that your country eliminated these rabid GRU dogs. They were grave threats to both United States and Soviet Union. We in the KGB wished to give medals to those who killed them."

"Who was the GRU official that wagered that the U.S. would cover this up?" Rose asked.

The defector leaned close over the table and smiled. "It is none other than General Vasyli Kulikov, hero in Great Patriotic War – and father of Georgi Kulikov -- 'AKA,' as you say agent Castellano, George Coleman."

*   *   *

FBI Special Agent Rubayat Castellano continued his counterintelligence work in the FBI, and remained, along with Rose, a confidant of high officials in Washington D.C., at the "Seat of Government."

FBI Director J. Edgar Hoover wrote letters of commendation to each of the team members. However, the one he wrote to Teo Maloney was clipped and terse. Teo was not offended, but Bradford was. He rejected the letter sent to him by Hoover. In his rejection he wrote back on the original letter: *"Dear Director Hoover: While I am deeply honored by your letter of commendation, I am apprised that your letters to my team members in this operation were not commensurate. The letter you sent to Miss Teo Maloney evidently sets her below the other members of the team, both in your estimation, and appreciation. This is unacceptable, as Maloney placed herself in harms way, and performed her duties with the same merit and diligence as the other team members. I am therefore respectfully returning this letter. Sincerely, Bradford Washburn Lehman."* He requested that Special Agent Rubayat Castellano deliver the letter, and its appended message, directly back to Director Hoover. Castellano did -- with relish.

J. Edgar Hoover was not happy. He wrote in blue ink at the bottom of the page: *"This man is not worthy of consideration for future hiring."* It went into Lehman's FBI file. When Hoover died in 1972, the letter, with the comments appended, disappeared from Bradford's file and was replaced with a "new original" -- without any comments. This effectively reinstated Lehman's good standing with the Bureau. Agent Rubayat Castellano had no idea how that could have happened.

Special Agent J. Ronald Makinson went back to the Chicago FBI Office where he was permanently assigned. His undercover duties completed, Makinson turned in the Yellow Porsche Targa – but not until he and Ring took it for one last happy spin around the myriad hairpin turns of Rainier National Park. "Let's turn it in with as much dirt and mileage on it as possible, Ring," Ron said. Makinson left the Porsche at the Sea-Tac Airport in a designated parking slot, for pickup by the CIA. He then boarded his flight to Chicago.

To Dining Room Manager Nancy Olszewski's amazement and joy, she eventually learned that Ron was a Special Agent of the FBI, and that he was assigned to her own Windy City. Makinson continued dating Nancy Olszewski back in Chicago and soon married her. She never went fly-fishing with him again.

Upon being awarded the Medal of Freedom, Special Agent Makinson was given his choice of FBI offices for transfer. His time on Mount Rainier hooked him on the beauty of the Northwest. He selected the Portland Oregon Office, partly because Oregon had excellent fly-fishing, and partly because ASAC Charlie "Two Doors" Anderson was in Seattle. However, by the time Makinson completed his transfer back out to the Northwest, with new wife Nancy in hand, Anderson was moved down to the Portland FBI Office as the ASAC there. "I can put up with Charlie," Makinson shrugged, philosophically, "as long as I'm near the good fishing." He was happy. So was Nancy Makinson, née, Nancy Olszewski.

For the rest of the month of August, 1968, Bradford Lehman and Teo Maloney finished their season at Paradise by hiking together. They hung up their climbing gear. Both needed a break from the high cold ice and rock of the big mountain. They trekked over sections of the Wonderland Trail. They reveled in the colors of the trees and flowers, and in their time together. Teo, with Rubayat Castellano's help, successfully transferred all her credits from Pacific Lutheran University over to the University of Puget Sound. She broke the news to Bradford as they lay together in a tent up at Indian Henry's Hunting Ground. It was cause for loving celebration.

Though Bradford and Teo were honored to receive the Medal of Freedom, they were simply happy that they had made it through together with their lives, friends, friendship, and love intact. They rented an apartment together off campus at the University of Puget Sound and took the same classes. They got good grades. Sometime down the road they contemplated marriage. They understood that they were young. For the present they were content to live in the now, and to reflect with satisfaction, that they had helped to run the Russian Bear out of the Park.

*   *   *

Bradford Washburn Lehman had served his brief time as a Cold War warrior. His career as a guide on Mount Rainier was over. But his time as a warrior was not. Upon graduation from the University of Puget Sound in 1970, he was commissioned as a Second Lieutenant in the U.S. Air Force. Teo proudly pinned the gold bars on Bradford's blue Class A uniform at his swearing-in ceremony, as Major Walter Hunter approvingly observed, along with Lehman's mother, Ruth. Bradford and Teo were thankful that she attended. She was now divorced from Bradford's father. Notably absent was B.F. Lehman. Bradford had asked him to attend the graduation and commissioning, but he declined because Ruth was there. Bradford could only ask himself why. *It is his way of stewing. He is rejecting you Bradford, and because he is, he will need to be left to himself for now. Timing is everything -- and with dad, this is bad timing. He will have to find his own way to heal.* As much as he loved and respected his father, what Bradford had recently experienced up at Paradise provided new perspective on B.F. Lehman. It would become the catalyst for Bradford's own healing – and of going his own way in the world. *My father has not put himself in my shoes. I will not put myself in his. Let him go – for now.* But healing was painful. It often is.

Lehman went on to serve overseas in the Vietnam War, as an intelligence officer in the Strategic Air Command, targeting B-52 bombing strikes. He wore his Medal of Freedom ribbon, with others on his uniform, as authorized. His superiors were invariably perplexed, and awed by his "MOF," because the award simply appeared in his record without any accompanying citation. It was just there. Like the continuous clandestine struggles of the Cold War, and the bright looming majesty of a big mountain –

It was just there.

Mount Rainier stands today much the same as it did in the 1960s. Extensive lahar and volcanology research has been conducted in the decades since. The Paradise Ice Caves have disappeared, but Rainier's summit crater caves remain. They were explored and mapped in 1972, and again in recent years they have gleaned further interest from scientists. Someday perhaps, one of these researchers may stumble upon strange items: an innocuous gray wool glove — the one Climbing Ranger John Ring pulled off of his headlamp an instant before he engaged the second GRU agent down near the ballroom. In the melee it was dropped and forgotten. Or even more incongruously, they may find shell casings from a Russian Tokarev or Colt .38 Super. Such little jewels, caught perchance, as a sparkle in the light of a headlamp, will testify to the deadly mission that quietly ended a desperate Cold War struggle. It was a struggle that threatened nuclear devastation, and possible volcanic eruption. The scientists will be astounded. So many questions will be asked.

But the big mountain will not answer. It never does.